WRECKLEAF

JD STEINER

This is a work of fiction. Names, characters, places, and incidents are products of the author's imagination or are used fictitiously and are not to be construed as real. Any resemblance to actual events, locales, organizations, or persons, living or dead, is entirely coincidental.

Cover Design by Dark Unicorn Designs

Cover Art by Wit & Whimsy Cover Design

Edited by Kathrin Hutson at KLH CreateWorks

ISBN: 978-0-692-10452-1

For my gang,
without whom I wouldn't exist—nor would Nerissa.

Always keep reading,
never stop dreaming—
Enjoy!
JD Steiner

ACKNOWLEDGEMENTS

A huge thank you:

To Matthew, my tether and sounding board, for your unending support, reassurance, and patience—I can't imagine taking this journey with anyone else by my side. To my kids, Quintin and Sage, two lights that always lead the way, who love without boundaries and have taught me more about life than anyone. To my father, Walter, who has inspired me in more ways than he'll ever realize. To Ansley Blackstock, for helping me bring Wreckleaf to life, out of my dreams and into reality. To all the members, past and present, of the "Breakfast Club"—you are my inspiration as well as my aspiration. To Kathrin Hutson, Bridgette O'Hare, Brian Hayden, and Marina Papadatos, for your creative and technical talents, guidance and T.L.C. To all my teachers in all their forms. To all my friends and family, near and far, who cheered me on, believed in my dream, and stuck with me through the long haul—I couldn't have done this without you. A special thanks to Blue Ventures marine conservation, (www.blueventures.org) for their important and expansive work. And finally, thank you, Universe—we are one.

Caulerpa Periculosis Abscondita/C. Periculosis Abscondita: (kaw-ler-pa periku-lo-sis abs-kon-di-ta)

Commonly known as Wreckleaf—of the seaweed family Caulerpaceae (among the green algae)—a fast growing, attractive but deceptively hazardous sea plant. Grows on runners with root-like holdfasts. To date, unable to propagate in simulated environments, and considered extremely rare.

Dolhuphemale: Dolphin-Human-Female
(doll-hue-fe-male)

A novelty species created for recreational use, with a focus on appearance, demeanor and ease of care; consisting of a precise combination of: Species Homo sapiens, Family delphinidae, Family Acanthuridae, Species Pterois volitans, Species Pterapogon kauderni. Endemic to the Panacea Island trio, the species is generally thought to be extinct.

References:

-Organismic and Applied Topics in Phytochemistry, August James Educational Series.

-Dr. Robert Q. Matthews, "Breaking the Source Barriers: Advancements in Genetic Modification", the International Encyclopedia of Theoretical and Applied Genetics and Biotechnology, (IETAGB).

CONTENTS

PREFACE

I was born a novelty, a disposable toy left to fend for myself. I'm not even supposed to exist, yet I do. And now the whole world can see who I am. No more disguises, no more lies. No one will tell me who I am, ever again.

Everything is about to change. And no matter what the outcome, I will have unchained myself—from my past, from my present, and from a future I didn't choose. Freedom will be mine.

I'm the lone pebble thrown into glassy water...

1 – ANASTASIA

SATURDAY, AUGUST 6TH

So the rumors are true!

I was fourteen years old that summer. Anastasia was sixteen. Everything about her drew me in—her cool demeanor, her magenta hair, the way she flaunted herself. She carried herself with pride and confidence, insisted I do the same, and pushed me to explore the world outside our own.

"We are creations of this Universe, Nerissa, not just a product of mankind. We're exactly as we're intended to be. Celebrate yourself." She slid her hands along her waist, down to the curve of her hips, and smiled at me. "Trust me, it feels good to step into your own power."

It was Saturday, deep in the summer tourist Season, and stories of scouting and acquisition—of-age family members seeking out suitable mates—were plentiful. Anastasia convinced me to swim to Panacea Island with her to do a little scouting trip of our own. *Fun practice* she called it, so we'd really be prepared when it was our time. But underage trips alone from our island home of Albatross to Panacea were forbidden.

I was hesitant at first. But I eventually accepted her offer, along with her foolish naiveté, and as we swam past the halfway point, my nerves turned to excitement. Breaking the rules suddenly became seductive and undeniable.

We spent the day exploring the island, relaxing in the happy summer vibe. Panacea, the ultimate playground for the ultra-wealthy—considered a veritable fountain of youth because of its rare natural resources and incomparable beauty. As the island was incredibly difficult to get to, only the rich could afford Panacea's exclusive offerings, and because of that, they were pampered like spoiled children. Thanks to Anastasia's charm and confidence, we fit right in with the pure-humans, no one ever suspecting us of not belonging.

"See, Nerissa? Playing human is fun. And why shouldn't we experience this lifestyle? They're no better than us."

"I could get used to this."

"And so you shall..." she promised.

Day turned to evening, and we found ourselves outside of Wave, the island's busiest club. The energy pouring from the building was contagious, only a glimpse of what lie within. But we were underage—they'd never let us enter.

Anastasia and I were about to leave, when we were approached by a group of men.

"Good evening, Beauties."

"Good evening, gentlemen," Anastasia purred. "Mmm... somebody smells good."

"Would you care to join us inside?"

Anastasia giggled and slid her fingers through her hair. "We'd love to join you, but we're a tiny bit too young to—"

"Come on, you're with us," said a sun-burned blond guy in expensive-looking clothes.

We were whisked into the pulsating club with these strangers, abandoning every caution as their money led the way.

The booming music entered my feet and spread itself inside of me. Lights of every color danced above and below. Musky sweat and leather, citrus, flowers, and the smell of alcohol filled my nose. Walking through the hypnotizing crowd of gyrating people—a spectacle of new sensations in a world I never knew existed—triggered unknown parts of myself—an unfamiliar, primal yearning. And I wanted more.

We found ourselves on the dance floor, fusing into the energy of the crowd. We passed a strong concoction that, despite being disguised in sweet coconut, burned my throat. It didn't stop me from drinking more—a lot more. Soon the world was spinning and consisted of only what was in front of me, the edges all blurred. I laughed a lot, wondering why it had taken me so long to allow myself this pleasure.

The seven men with whom we had entered this sparkling, fragrant rainbow-explosion had whittled down to four, two dancing with me, two with Anastasia. I didn't know any of their names, and I didn't care. Hands were all over me—on my hips, the small of my back, my neck. Then lips and breath. I didn't mind. The drinks continued, the laughter, the spinning.

A long stretch of dancing in my own small world ended with a song too slow and sweet. I looked up and scanned the crowded floor for Ana but didn't see her. I focused harder, sure I would eventually spot her. But she had vanished. Her two dance partners were missing as well.

A slight detached panic began to whisper. I ignored it, intoxicated not only by the drinks but by my power over these strangers. Anastasia would pop up any second. But she never did. And I began to grow irritated by my dance team.

"Excuse me for a minute!" I yelled over the music.

"Where are you going?" somebody yelled back.

"I'm going to look for my friend."

"No, don't leave. We're just getting started!"

"I have to go..."

"That's okay," the tomato-faced blond hollered; he'd appeared out of nowhere. "We'll help you find her."

I didn't want their company anymore. Our night needed to come to an end. But I accepted their offer to help.

After scouring the club, we exited through a back door leading out onto a terrace and down to a marina.

"I think your friend is out here with my buddy. What's her name again?"

"It's Anastasia."

"Nice name. I'm sorry, darling, your name?"

"It's Nerissa. And yours?"

"Unusual. Suits you well. You're kind of special, aren't you, Nerissa?"

Regret was swallowing me. He wasn't interested in helping me find Anastasia. And he seemed to be getting off on knowing that I realized it.

"I come here every summer. So do my buddies, and we've never seen you before. Didn't you say you live here?"

I didn't talk to anybody about myself, or where I lived. I tried to protest, but he wasn't done.

"How old did you say you are?"

"I didn't. Are you going to help me? If not, I'll go. Thank you for the fun night." I turned to leave.

"You're a Water Doll, aren't you?"

Frozen, my heart in my throat, I was unable to respond. I hadn't heard anybody use that term in a long, long time.

"Ah-ha! I knew it. A pretty little Water Doll." He seemed to have amazed himself, as though he made some scientific world discovery.

I turned to face him and his two drunk friends. "What do you want from me?" I was calm, neither confirming nor denying his claim.

"That fiery little friend of yours has a big mouth. She couldn't stop bragging about her custom design and superhuman abilities. If we liked how she moved on the dance floor, we'd be blown away by her abilities in the water. She made my buddy some promises with her body language that no warm-blooded man could ever ignore." His sloppy exaggerations were disgusting. "I guess the drinks got to her. Or is it the boredom of living without any men?"

"Go to hell."

"So the rumors are true! Only in our wildest dreams did anyone imagine Water Dolls still existed, until now. And tonight, you're mine."

"I am not a Water Doll!" I detested the nickname. "I'm a Dolhuphemale. And I don't belong to anyone, ever."

He looked like a kid who just saw a unicorn. "Hot damn, I knew it. Doll, you *are* mine. Period."

"I'm only fourteen. Let me leave, please."

"Fourteen? No way." He barely stopped to consider. "Well, that may be, but you're more woman than I've ever known. And I don't think anyone would miss an illegal hybrid posing as a human. Tonight is our night. You play nice, and I'll make things go okay for you."

I turned and tried to run. Between my awkward feet and my intoxicated state, I wasn't fast enough.

The sweaty, drunken stranger locked against my back, one arm around my waist, the other at my chest.

"Tom's got a girlfriend!" one of his drunk posse yelled.

"Show her what it's like to have a real man, then we'll show her, too," the other fool slurred.

"We know exactly who you are now, little Doll," Tom whispered. "Or should I say, *what* you are. You can thank Anastasia for that."

"Where is she?"

"She's fine, Beauty. My buddy is taking good care of her, just like I'll take care of you."

These monsters, these *real men*, thought they knew who I was. They knew nothing. It wasn't the way this night was supposed to end, but it was him or me.

"You're right. Let's have some fun."

"Yes, it's our night. Now, how about some of that magical weed? What's it called? Wreckleaf? If you're real, it must be, too."

"Sorry, I don't have any."

He spun me around, tightening his grip, his sun-bleached brow furled into a deep, angry crease. "That's too bad." He blew out an exaggerated sigh, and I could taste his sticky, rum-scented breath. "Okay, maybe on our next date. You and I have a real future together, don't you think?" Sickening laughter contorted his face while his two inebriated cheerleaders stumbled over one another in hysterics.

"Let me sing you a song instead." I began to hum.

Tom misunderstood my palpable resolve. "That's my girl," he oozed, glazing over with a lust so twisted, my mouth watered with nausea. "God, you're beautiful." I held his eyes as Tom spoke what he didn't realize were his last words. "Kiss me."

And so I obliged. I pressed my lips against his. He responded aggressively, his sloppy, vile mouth covering mine. I fought back the urge to vomit, and instead delivered the kiss of a lifetime. We lingered, and Tom swayed. When our lips parted, his manicured fingertips dug into my flesh, his unfocused eyes searching mine. He tried in vain to form words as confusion spread across his face. For a second—just one second—I felt sorry for him.

"Still think you know me? Guess you didn't know everything."

He hit the pier hard, his color draining quickly, his eyes glossing over. Not shocked by their friend's collapse, the other two howled with laughter.

"What an idiot! Tom can't handle his liquor or his women. It's my turn, Doll," the one in the pink shorts declared.

"Me first," grunted the other stooge.

They had yet to realize their pal was dead. And the last thing they'd want was a turn kissing me. I needed to leave, or they'd have to be next.

My eyes darted from Tom to his friends, then back again. I turned to go, but sudden dizziness made the pier spin. Everything blurred, and in an instant, the air grew thick and heavy.

Breathe, Nerissa, just breathe... you're okay.

But I couldn't take a normal breath or control my galloping heart. Darkness shrouded everything, my shock pushing down on me, squeezing harder and harder. Searching for relief, I shut my eyes tight.

From somewhere inside my head, I heard a ticking clock, then my mother's voice reminding me to trust no one. The faintest familiar melody pulled at me.

I succumbed to the slowing of time. "I'm sorry," I whispered.

"You have nothing to be sorry for. I'm the one who's sorry. Can you swim?" The dreamlike question made me giggle, which seemed so out of place.

"Yes, of course I can swim." *Did I say that out loud?*

A sudden, powerful shove launched me off the pier, and I slapped the water hard. My body didn't respond, and I sank. From behind closed eyes, I observed myself as the world faded away and my poison mouth was cleansed by sharp salt. I was sure it was the end, and all I could wonder was if my mother would be ashamed of me.

I woke up on Albatross the next day with my head in my mother's lap. I thought I was dead—or dreaming, at least. She was so tender, so kind, stroking my face and hair, singing a lullaby from my childhood.

"Mom?"

"Yes, I'm here."

"Am I dead?"

"Of course not."

Tom's face flashed in my mind.

"Is it over?"

"No, Nerissa. It's just the beginning."

A week after the incident at Wave, Anastasia was still missing, presumably turned over to the island's governing officials. The Dolhuphemale breed was forced out of hiding—ordered off Albatross Island to be integrated back onto Panacea, our breed's place of origin. The Matriarchs considered refusing to cooperate but knew it would result in total elimination. They would leave no survivors this time. Instead, the Cooperative—the documented act that has enslaved us to pose as pure-humans and serve them in their hedonistic and gluttonous world—was formed between the Panacea Island branch of the First World Government and us.

Three days after the Cooperative was signed and government officials reported her daughter's unexplained death, Anastasia's mother, Marja, took her own life.

2 – PANACEA

WEDNESDAY, MAY 29TH—Three years later.

This island never ceases to impress me ... a terrible Beauty.

"What are you thinking about?" Kendra's voice pulls me back to the present.

"My feet." I lie to my best friend so I don't have to tell her what I'm really thinking about ... again.

"What about them?"

"How ugly they are."

"I love our feet. They're perfect."

"I guess I'm not as evolved as you."

"That's right, my Beauty." She settles back on the warm sand and closes her eyes. I envy her peace of mind.

I could blame the hot sun for my sweaty upper lip, for my too-fast heartbeat or fists full of sand. But my mother thinks I suffer from post-traumatic stress disorder. Maybe she's right. If I can't find peace here, with Kendra, on such a perfect day ... will I ever?

"Nerissa, you probably would have been killed. Or worse." My mother likes to remind me.

"But I wasn't. I'm okay."

"How can you possibly be okay? You murdered someone."

"It's not like you haven't."

"You shouldn't have been there in the first place. Your skills were not developed, and you weren't fully trained."

She doesn't care that I had to kill that human waste. What she's really trying to say is how disappointed she is that I left witnesses, that I let Anastasia get captured, and that I'm responsible for the discovery of our existence.

I stretch my fingers, and Kendra's soft, rhythmic breathing returns me to the beach; we call it Our Beach, because it's inaccessible except to our kind. My gaze gets trapped in her hair, so unlike the blazing copper calamity atop my head. Kendra is an anomaly. None of us are blonde. We're all born with a shade of red hair. That's how we were designed, along with the other obvious exaggerations. I'm a walking cliché.

Our beauty is a paradox. I'd give anything to be average. But even though I sometimes think they look frightening, I'll keep my eyes. My mother says they hold the winter sky, and I'm unique. I must look like my father, because I don't really resemble her. But I'll never know. She doesn't have much memory of him either. That's what one quick night of romance will do.

"I can feel you staring at me," Kendra grumbles.

"Go back to sleep."

Nothing is better than the freedom of lazing away a breezy afternoon on the privacy of Our Beach. We crashed on the cashmere sand hours ago, and I could stay forever. But this is the end of these days. The first of the summer tourists have started trickling in. When the rest arrive via zeppelin, the island will be crawling. Year after year, like herded sheep they flock, seeking their salvation in some magic potion or pill or concoction. And belittling those of us who attend to their needs apparently goes hand in hand with their desperate goal of perfection—as though they are the cream rising to the top of their own crystal chalice, their servants the sludge left at the bottom. But their money simply cannot buy the true healing powers of this island and its waters. And no amount will ever mask their entitlement and self-importance.

At work, a typical exchange with a tourist goes something like this:

'Welcome to Panacea. How may I be of service to you?'
'I have an itch on my back. Scratch it.'
'Yes, of course. My pleasure, Beauty.'
'Yes, it is your pleasure.'
'How else may I please you today?'
'You cannot please me. Go get me a salad.'
'Yes, Beauty. It is my honor.'
'Yes, it is. Don't forget that.'

"The tide is rolling in, Kendra. Nap time is over."

She groans. "Why are you so perky? Have a good nap?"

"Um, no."

"Oh, right. You don't sleep anymore."

"We need to go. Display time." I point my index finger, and a small holograph springs to life in front of us. It comes from my rose quartz CNI—crystal nail-bed implant—the biotechnology that replaced external devices many years ago.

"You know you don't have to speak your command out loud. It'll load whatever you want with just a thought command."

"I know. I just forget. It seems so unnatural."

"It is unnatural. But that's how it works," Kendra reminds me.

"I suppose if I grew up with a crystal shoved in my nail-bed like everyone else, it wouldn't bother me so much. I swear I feel it growing sometimes."

"It's possible the implant is still adjusting to your biology."

"It's been almost three years," I say.

"Maybe you're still growing."

"Great. Let's go. We're going to get our butts kicked if we're late."

"Bye-bye, O.B. See you soon!" Kendra's voice bounces off the back of the cove and silences the seabirds.

"Aren't you powerful?"

"That's nothing..." She hops up and runs toward the water. I follow her.

The ocean is warm and inviting and lends me the welcome sensation of coming home. Once we navigate the treacherous outcroppings of Our Beach and push past the currents, we turn into a narrow inlet flanking the cliffside. Rounding a bend into the mouth of another sheltered, rocky cove, we weave our way through an isolated turquoise reef. Running parallel to the reef, the sheer rock walls are dotted with dozens of small dark caves. This entire area is untouched and pristine, and it is my favorite part of our long swim.

"Nerissa!" Kendra is twenty yards ahead of me.

"What?"

"C'mon, no time for sightseeing, Doll. We're going to be late."

"Coming."

We reach the other end of the sheltered reef and push our way into the now deep, foreboding water. We swim fast, without pause, for quite a while before a quick rest. The swells here are incredibly large and move us a tremendous distance. If we stay here too long, the ocean could capture us and end our lovely day by slamming us into the cliff walls.

"Let's go."

Another mile, and I spot the entry point where the cliffs end and the land continues to the east. Neither of us need to stop. We could continue all the way around the island, but someone might see us coming from where swimming is dangerous, humanly-impossible, and against the law. We need to get out right here. But our trek isn't over.

"After you, Beauty..." I offer my most gracious and condescending island etiquette.

"Please, you first, Beauty. I insist." Kendra extends an arm. I accept her gesture, rise out of the water, and step onto the landing.

We gather our belongings from under a pine tree and dress. We have a hike and another long swim ahead of us. And we're running late.

We climb the steep path to the top of the ridge. I'm not disappointed by what I anticipate as we clear the last few yards. From our vantage point, hidden in the trees, almost the entire island is visible. We only have seconds to pause. My eyes dart to the left and begin the sweep of the incomparable panorama.

The mountain Apollo rises in the dark rocky west, standing sentinel over the restricted base of the Panacea Island Branch of the First World Government. Just below lie the sweeping hills of the luxury sector, where the wealthiest call home for the summer Season. The opulent resorts sprawl along the north coast and glimmer in the brilliant sunshine. I shudder as my eyes float past Concordia on the Bay, my place of employment.

To the east lies the marina, where a spectacle of yachts bob in the cobalt water. Most of them never leave their moorings for fear of joining the hundreds of shipwrecks off every coast. They're floating showpieces, or a place to throw an amazing party. Just past the marina, the island's only public beach, Playa Rosa, stretches out—a billion glittering diamonds glowing rosy-beige.

This island never ceases to impress me. As required, I'm well educated in human history, and I know that Panacea is one of the last of its kind. It juts out of the ocean like a jagged monolith with a softened edge. Harsh and unyielding, lush and fragile. This island is a case study in contradictions—a terrible Beauty.

South of the resort section and dotted throughout the hillsides lives the island's year-round population, some of us native, some transplants from elsewhere. The house my mother and I were assigned is beautiful but way too big for just the two of us. Half the rooms are never used. Kendra and I have lived in the Oval—four concentric streets wrapping around a main road—for almost three years. It still feels like we're just visiting sometimes.

We begin jogging, and as we fall into a comfortable and steady clip, I zone out. I enjoy running, despite my inept feet.

We pass through the last section of thick forest and begin a steep descent, where the dark soil transitions to sand and we're no longer hidden by the trees. The deep green hues of the forest turn into the lime-green pop of the cacti and other tropical and medicinal plants.

"Finally," Kendra huffs as we step onto the road.

"I like it in there." I scan both directions. All clear.

We walk down the road as though we're coming from the Oval and eventually make our way to Playa Rosa. The beach is set up for the Season—the sand clean and raked, umbrella and chair rental stations stocked and ready—but it's still uncrowded. We'll have to be extra careful.

"Usual spot?" Kendra points.

"Yep."

"Just another day at the beach."

"Do you see Gabriel anywhere?" I whisper.

She doesn't even look up. "Nope. The old man is probably off somewhere getting high."

"Keep your voice down."

"Oh, relax, Nerissa. Nobody's looking at us."

But the truth is, everybody is always looking at us. Especially when there's just a sprinkling of people. It's much easier to blend in and go unnoticed when the beach is crowded with rich, beautiful tourists. The richer they are, the more beautiful they can afford to be, and we don't stand out as much.

We park ourselves at the only remaining lifeguard stand. It was decided that the others block the view and cheapen the beach, so they were removed. This one will be manned, inconsistently, during the busiest part of the Season. For now, a small, red-lettered sign reads: NO LIFEGUARD ON DUTY—SWIM AT YOUR OWN RISK. There's nothing like luxuriating in a little inconvenient drowning every once in a while. Whatever. Let these idiots work it out.

No one is too close, and we can take off our shoes. It's magical. Our clothes are next, and now I feel the eyes on every inch of my body. I imagine the disgusting thoughts racing through lustful minds.

"Would you please relax? We've done this a million times."

"I know." I sigh. "But we're in a hurry, and I just don't want to be stupid."

"I don't see anyone staring. But I did spot Gabriel."

"Where?" I whip my head from side to side.

"Be cool. We'll hear him soon. He's seen us."

"Oh, I see him."

Just like clockwork, predictable and dependable, Gabriel, our breed's one true ally, has appeared up the beach.

"How old do you think Gabriel is?" Kendra asks. "About a hundred and fifty? I can see his wrinkles from here."

"Stop it. Poor guy." But Kendra is right. Even from here, his dark skin looks so weathered, his long curly hair grayer than ever. But although old and slight, he still stands straight and walks with strength. I'm so grateful for Gabriel. Without him, we'd be lost.

A random face catches my eye. He's perched at the edge of his chair fifteen feet ahead of Gabriel. Our eyes meet and lock, just for a second. He puts his head down and scribbles something in a small book, then looks at me again, still and expressionless.

"Ice-cold drinks, here!" Gabriel's voice breaks the warped moment. I wonder if he noticed my random exchange with this curious stranger. His timing is impeccable.

"That's our cue, Nerissa."

We ease into the water. There's a handful of people, two on floats, three teenagers playing a game of catch, and a family with two young kids. We've gone as unnoticed as possible.

Back at the chairs, Gabriel continues his reverie, his iconic voice known by everyone. "Ice-cold drinks, here, folks. I've got the temptations, the libations, the medications and creations for your ultimate vacation... ha-ha-ha!" He spills his contagious laughter into the air and infects the crowd. "I've got the antibiotic for your anti-chaotic. The formulations for your relaxation. Ha-ha-ha!"

He's got everyone's attention, the promise of a refreshing tropical drink in their immediate futures. They're hanging on his every nuance as he delivers the code phrase. "Have I got a deal for you, folks. Ha-ha-ha!"

We slip under the ropes, and just like that, we're gone.

3 – ALBATROSS

WEDNESDAY, MAY 29TH

The folly of rich men is cruel and runs deep.

By the time we need to come up for air, we're well out of sight. With only a second to breathe, we have to make up for lost time. The water is deceptive and dangerous. This is the place that separates us from the humans.

Access to both of Panacea's daughter islands, Albatross and Black Rock to the west, is restricted. And people comply. Most believe the islands to be nothing more than uninhabitable, dangerous shards of rock, where countless people have lost their lives to shipwrecks of one kind or another in the furious and unpredictable waters. For the most part, their fears are justified.

For us, entry onto Albatross from the south side is forbidden. The terrain is sharp and un-level, posing great risk of injury. It's also possible, however remote, to be spotted from Panacea with high-powered binoculars. We must swim around.

We round the final turn on the northeast side and come up for one last breath. It's possible to get out here, climb up, and walk the rest of the way, but it's not ideal. The terrain is still challenging, and no one is excused from being late to a ceremony. We'll enter the arena from below, through the underwater caves.

"What's the problem, old lady?" Kendra notices my labored breath.

"Just a little tired, aren't you?"

"Nope. Not at all." She's lying.

"First one with their feet on the ground wins. Loser gets to explain if we're late. Deal?"

"Be prepared to lose," she says.

We dive under. Kendra quickly reminds me why she can justify being such a smartass by putting a sizable distance between us. This is also where I'm reminded I need to stop complaining about our feet. The fusion between her toes—another original design element that helps us swim more efficiently—is more pronounced than most, and as a consequence, she's fast. I can't beat her.

We enter the dark, narrow in-tube, and the current works against us. We have to proceed one by one, which seals the fate of this race. Just when the tube becomes disorienting with its dizzying twists and turns, it opens into a dimly lit chamber called the Hub, where we can come up for air one last time. This is the intersection connecting all the legendary underwater caves of Albatross.

The caves are the birthplace of age-old myth, beautifully grim fairy tales, and old island lore. They are both feared and revered in the minds of opportunistic men. But the stories are old and for the most part unproven. Most believe the tales of the caves—giving otherwise impossible access to shipwrecks bearing untold treasures, specialized creatures, and a mysterious sea plant called Wreckleaf—to be complete fantasy. Between the dangers and the restrictions, the temptation to prove otherwise is minimal.

To our right lies the passageway we need, leading to the arena, where ceremonies are held. We each grab a breath before gliding into the wider surrounding. To my surprise, we're side by side. Kendra must have slowed for a second too long at the Hub. She notices and pushes harder. I can see the light through the water from here. Forty yards ... thirty, I pass her. Fifteen, five ... I reach the opening and launch myself. The moment slows, and I feel her body even with mine. Almost. I hit the ground hard,

Kendra landing on me. We roll in a tangled, breathless mess, and I force the words I never imagined I'd speak.

"I win!"

She groans.

"Triumph is mine, Doll," I yell in her face.

"You got lucky," she hisses.

She lifts her head and peers over me. Her eyes grow wide, and my stomach drops as I realize what she sees. My mother, the Matriarch Tatiana, has appeared at the front of the arena.

We're on our feet and running. The ground is rocky, uneven, and slick. Feet, don't fail me now. We flounder and slip into the arena, and everyone turns to see what the commotion is about. There's nowhere to hide as we both struggle for composure, bent over from exhaustion. My guilt and shame rise in a deep flush, disapproval burning into me.

"Thank you for joining us, Nerissa, Kendra. Please take your seats quickly." We have no choice but to sit in the front row. We settle on the stone bench without haste.

"Welcome everyone," my mother begins, and the arena goes silent. "We are, of course, here today to honor Lillian, who I am pleased to confirm is pregnant." The arena coos. She breathes it in, closes her eyes, and lifts her arms high and wide.

My mother is in her element. At her side is Kendra's mother, Matriarch Giovanni. Atop each of their heads is an ornate wreath of sea grass and coral—a crown of sorts—adorning their ginger and auburn hair, respectively.

She opens her eyes and sweeps the arena with a gaze that seems to collect a piece of each of us. She exhales hard. Like this, I see my mother as I imagine the others do.

"As you all know, ours is a breed that has lived through much pain and difficulty. Let us not forget where we have come from."

I hate this part.

"The folly of rich men is cruel and runs deep. Our ancestors were created by such men. And as the temporary playthings we were designed to be, most of our ancestors were disposed of when man was done with them. But with true Dolhuphemale determination and spirit, the strongest few survived."

Okay, Mother, we all know the story. Let's get on with it. But when I look around, I'm struck by everyone's emotions. Even Kendra's eyes threaten to spill over.

"The perfected techniques of scouting the best-suited mate, enchanting and subduing the Contributor, and the mating ritual of acquisition itself have become our greatest assets. Yet although we've evolved these adaptations over many generations, we still find ourselves limited by our original design. Even our singular ability to harvest our beloved Wreckleaf from the sea and utilize its medicinal properties to assist with enchantment is not enough. Until one of us produces male offspring, we will remain dependent on mankind."

"Therefore," Giovanni says, embellishing my mother's sentiment with her softer, cooler tone, "the continuation of our existence rests in the hands and the hearts of our youth."

"Mankind has proven he cannot be trusted," my mother continues. "We must all do our part to ensure our independence. So while we'll continue to live by their rules..."

Like we have a choice!

"...we will also follow in Lillian's footsteps, as she has followed in many others' before her."

Total silence, and everyone seems to hold their breath.

"We must not rely on the FWG to supply selected Contributors to us. We must continue to choose our own," Giovanni adds.

"Now, it is with great pleasure that we present Lillian, bearing the fruit of her young."

The arena explodes.

I play along, clap, and smile brightly. I accept an elder's warm pat on my back and hopeful glance for my own future. I join in this joyous celebration alongside my best friend, even while I feel the knot growing in my stomach, just like it always does after my mother's absurd, cosmetic speech. It's like none of us are worth anything unless we're producing offspring, or planning it, or dreaming of it. I'm like a prostitute. We all are. My only accepted payment is nothing less than life itself.

"Everyone, please..." My mother waits for us to quiet down. "Turn your attention to Lillian. Allow her to be your teacher, especially those of you coming of age. The Season is upon us." She retreats to the chair behind Lillian, folds her hands in her lap, and turns toward the honoree. "Lillian, the arena is yours."

"Here we go," Kendra whispers in my ear. I almost forgot she was there. "I cannot believe this suck-up is in the chair. She's going to lay it on thick."

The chair is the highest place of honor in which one can find herself. Confirmed pregnant, Lillian sits in the chair like an ethereal princess.

Every eye is fixed upon her as she brushes a cinnamon wisp from her face and adjusts the ceremonial crown. It's supposed to be a symbol of accomplishment and fulfilled purpose. But to me, it's more a crown of thorns.

Lilian parts her lips and hesitates, as though her next words hinge together our existence. "I am honored beyond words to be sitting in this sacred chair, speaking to all of you."

Not a sound.

"As taught by our wise and gifted Matriarchs and elders, I began scouting a year ago, just after my eighteenth birthday. I must admit," she giggles, "I was a little nervous."

Kendra lets out a tiny snort. I pinch her leg hard.

"So... in exchange for his help with finding me the most suitable Contributors to scout," Lillian continues, "it was time to bring my payment of Wreckleaf to Gabriel. As you know, he can be a bit difficult. I think he smokes a little too much dried Wreckleaf for his own good. But I was able to handle him without any problems."

"One moment, please, Lillian. If I may..." My mother stands and interrupts little Miss Perfect.

"Oh, of course," Lillian stutters, not expecting to be cut off.

"I am unaware of any difficulties with Gabriel." She looks directly at Lillian. "Let us remember that he has proven himself to be the greatest ally our breed has ever known. Without Gabriel, maintaining our practices undetected while honoring the Cooperative would be extremely difficult, if not impossible."

"Yes," agrees Giovanni. "Without his assistance, we would be at the complete mercy of the FWG."

He hates those bastards, too, Lillian. Give the man his stash and the time of day, and he'll purr like a kitten and do cartwheels for you.

"Do not be so quick to judge Gabriel. He, too, has endured a troubled past at the hands of the FWG. He's on our side, and when treated with the respect he deserves, will be nothing but helpful." She pauses for effect. "Lillian, you may continue."

As Lillian goes on with her tale of self-importance, my mind wanders.

I was a child the first time I met Gabriel. Our breed's survival was unconfirmed, but tall tales of our existence had been told for decades, since the Elimination Program brought nearly two dozen complex species to extinction once our novelty wore off and our creators were done with us. I always thought it should be called exactly what it was—the Horrific Mass Execution of the Innocent.

My mother had brought me to Panacea. The swim strengthened our skills early, and learning the art of blending in with the pure-humans was invaluable. When we arrived at the river, a lone man stood fishing off the slick green banks. He didn't seem to notice us. We went about our business, pretending to be tourists exploring the island and enjoying our day as we played in the warm water. I laughed while my mother tossed me up in the air, and I landed with a bigger splash each time. The last time she threw me, one water-shoe flew off. I surfaced, and my mother's face had changed. She came toward me, shoe in hand, and crammed it onto my exposed foot. She turned to gather our things. I looked at the fisherman. He met my eyes.

"Hi, little Doll."

My mother snapped her head in his direction, the fear on her face unlike anything I'd ever seen. "What did you say?"

"I just said hi."

"No, after that... What did you call her?"

"I called her a Doll. That's what she is, isn't it? It's what you both are."

Lillian's annoying banter pulls me back into the arena.

"He asked me if I had payment for his services. I held out the satchel and he snatched it right out of my hand, then proceeded to open it and smell it, like I was trying to trick him or something—"

"Lillian!" booms Tatiana. "If he wants to inspect your delivery, you welcome him to do so." She addresses everyone. "Gabriel is a rarity. We will respect him and continue to abundantly compensate him for his services!"

Gabriel is without a doubt a rarity on Panacea. One of a small number of remaining island-born locals, he chooses to live a simple life in the midst of severe wealth and hedonism. He's referred to as homeless. But Gabriel insists that the island in its entirety is his home, therefore, he is never without one. As the novelty he has become, Gabriel was hired as a freelance beach attendant by several of the luxury resorts and maintains a service rotation. It seems that even as his lifestyle is frowned upon by most, the tourists like him in small doses, and if that makes them happy, that makes more money, and that's all that matters.

"Lillian, please continue," instructs Giovanni. "And remember, you are now a leader by example."

Lillian sits up straight, clears her throat, and continues. She goes on to tell about her meetings with Gabriel, then finally arrives at the point of her impossibly long story.

"After I had chosen my Contributor, and the timing was right, the enchantment and acquisition was easy," she brags. "Human men are so weak. Even as the moonlight glinted off his wedding band, the Contributor followed me. He danced behind me as I sang to him, onto the beach and into a secluded nook in the rocks."

She has even my attention now.

"He responded as expected, like a hungry animal. The actual acquisition was very fast. It seemed like my catch hadn't been with a woman in a very long time, even though he was married."

"Ha!" Tatiana blurts. "You are not just a woman, Lillian. None of you are. Remember that. Remember who you are. We were designed for the pleasure of men *by* men. And even though the design was long ago and we have changed, men will never change. Our Contributors are not accustomed to being around the likes of our kind. They are coming face to face with their own fantasies, and as they would have it, they will never be able to resist us."

I hate the term "Contributor"—like they're some kind of business partner. Except in this venture, they know nothing of their significant role. They are ill-equipped, unsuspecting pawns in our game of conception. And we never know anything about them, sometimes not even their names. Just like I never knew anything about my father, neither will any of our future daughters know theirs.

"After he got dressed, he didn't know what to do with himself. He kept looking around, fidgeting, making sure nobody was watching. It was amusing. I wish I could have left him like that. I mean, he'd just cheated on his wife with a complete stranger on their vacation. What a pig."

Really, Lillian?

"Before he could launch into some ridiculous explanation about why he had to leave, or why we couldn't ever talk about this, or meet again, blah, blah, blah, I said, 'I've got to go. Give me a kiss goodbye, and don't worry about a thing.' He was so relieved to know our encounter meant nothing more to me than it did to him."

Nothing more than a future daughter.

"He leaned in for his goodbye kiss, happy to get one last taste. I counted, and when I got to six, I pulled away. At first, I didn't think anything happened. But then his eyes started to cross, and I knew I'd done it. I helped him down to the sand and was even able to prop him up against a rock. That was it. He was out and would wake up hours later with no memories, peaceful and oblivious. I erased any evidence of being there and left. Mission accomplished."

The arena breaks into applause. Lillian is a hero, a role model, a superstar. And she loves it.

"Bravo, Lillian." My mother's voice rises above the celebration. "Two things of great importance have been realized by Lillian's masterful acts of scouting, enchantment, and acquisition. First and most important, her confirmed pregnancy. Second, because of Lillian's careful application of our techniques, her Contributor was spared and allowed to walk away without effect. The FWG, although tolerant of us subsidizing our own Contributors within reason, did not anticipate our adaptations and does not support our techniques. So well done, Lillian. Does anyone have any questions?"

Numerous hands bolt into the air, the young and eager determined to become as honorable as Lillian.

"Lillian, how did you choose your Contributor?"

"It's a combination of things. I think the more attracted you are to your Contributor, the more believable you'll be. But most important is to choose someone with obvious physical and intellectual attributes. This person's DNA must contribute to the advancement of our breed in all ways."

"Excellent question and excellent point, Lillian," Giovanni agrees. "Please remember, maids, your choices benefit all of us, now and in the future."

"How long were you working with Gabriel before the enchantment took place?"

"Twice for scouting. Then once I chose him, Gabriel and I met one more time to go over the plan and that was it. Easy."

I surprise myself as my hand shoots into the air, like some invisible string pulled it from above.

"Yes, Nerissa?"

"What was your Contributor's name?"

Lillian's face contorts. Her eyebrows rise, one higher than the other. Then she somehow smiles and frowns at the same time, looking like she might throw up. "Who the hell cares?"

After the tiniest pause, an eruption of laughter and cheers. And the only question left to ask is ... Who are the pigs now?

4 – THE CAVES

WEDNESDAY, MAY 29TH

This place would be my muse.

Leaving the arena after a ceremony is always a challenge, especially tonight. Kendra and I have about an hour to harvest before the caves are black. It's not a deal-breaker, just a huge inconvenience.

"Come on, Dolls. Let's *moo-ve* it!"

"Kendra, shut up."

"We need to get out of here." She's looking for our mothers.

"Don't worry, they're both talking with Lillian. Anyway, it wasn't our fault we were late. The beach wasn't crowded enough."

"Is that your excuse?"

"You mean your excuse. I won our race, remember?"

"Barely."

"Don't worry, I'll talk us out of it. As usual." I recall the beach, and the guy with the pen and paper. I didn't exactly recognize him, but I feel like I know him from somewhere. "Hey, did you see that guy on the beach?"

She laughs. "You're kidding, right? That guy? You think you can be a little more specific?"

"Yeah, sorry. He was just ahead of Gabriel. He's our age, maybe a little older, light-brown skin, and kind of curly brown hair with blond ends. He was sitting, but I think he's tall because his legs looked really long. And his eyes are dark and super intense. He had a book he was writing in... that's all I can remember. Did you see him?"

She's staring at me, her mouth open, lips curled.

"What?"

"Wow, you really got a good look at him. And even his eyes, huh? From that far away?" Her eyebrows are raised. "I may have seen him, but so what if he was looking at us? Everybody does."

"He wasn't just looking at us, he was observing us. Stalking us."

"Hmm, I didn't notice, but I'll see what I can find out."

"You don't have to," I protest without conviction.

"Well, hello." My mother is suddenly behind us, a hand on each of our shoulders. I feel the weight of her disappointment. I don't turn around.

"Hi, Mom."

"Hello, Matriarch John."

"Would you please explain why you almost missed ceremony?" She's cool and hollow.

I stretch my eyes sideways without turning my head. Kendra's silence cues me. I take a deep breath and face my mother. Even before I've made it all the way around, I know to brace myself. She has the power to instantly crumble me. Her deep blue eyes tear through me like lasers, and my resolve to be righteous and unremorseful evaporates. I blow out an exhale filled with surrender and hang my head in shame.

"I'm so sorry. We fell asleep on Our Beach, and by the time we got to Playa Rosa, we were running late."

"And Rosa wasn't right," Kendra interjects with a fast, nervous clip. "Gabriel was late, and there was this guy that wouldn't stop staring at us and a family who wanted us to play catch with their kids! It wasn't our fault."

I'm amazed by how easily she rambles off the exaggerations. But as my mother turns to look at her with the same intended intensity, her face softens as she meets Kendra's pathetic expression and big, soft eyes. I literally feel the stiffness fall out of her. Just like that, it's over. I wish I had the same effect on her.

"I know it's sometimes difficult when conditions are not ideal. Perhaps you shouldn't have been so far away in the first place. Why didn't you just stay on Albatross? There's a wonderful beach here."

"It's not the same, Mom. Our Beach is special. It's totally private, and we can relax there without a care in the world."

"But you must care enough to not be late, Nerissa. Don't let this happen again, or I'll have to ban you from going to your beach. Do you understand?"

"Our Beach. And yes, I understand."

"Well, thank you for the correction. Kendra? Do you understand?"

"Yes, Matriarch John."

My mother sighs. "Please, call me Tatiana. There's no need for the formality between us. And I truly detest that last name. It's not who I am."

"It won't happen again."

"Okay. Now let me get you through this crowd. You need to get into the caves. It's getting late."

Like the master she is, my mother guides us through the electrified gathering. Smiling and nodding, she maintains her steady demeanor, accepting compliments for another inspiring ceremony. They're all in love with her. If this were a scene in a fairy tale, I swear everyone's eyes would twinkle with magic as she walked by.

Finally at the mouth of the western caves, my mother has a few last words for us. "Nerissa, Kendra, remember to exercise caution, both here and on your swim back to Panacea. The dangers increase after dark. The currents will have shifted, the winds and waves will be stronger... and the night creatures become active. Do not be lazy with your safety."

"We'll be safe, Mother."

"We will be gone from Albatross by the time you're finished. I'll see you at home after delivery." She catches herself. "I'll see you at the Oval." She turns and leaves.

Time to go to work.

We have to wade for a bit in the warm, shallow water, and I take the opportunity to admire the cave walls—painted by nature in cool greens and blues and littered generously with brilliant, sparkling crystals. I love this section of the caves. It's here that I imagine the first exiled members of the original Dolhuphemale breed, forced into hiding after their families were methodically executed in the Elimination Program. I imagine them trying to heal their broken souls, their shattered lives, while finding their way through these uncharted surroundings. I hope they found comfort in this oasis, even before finding Wreckleaf.

I don't remember how old I was when I was first told the story of Wreckleaf. I just know I've always known it. One of the original survivors, a maid named Marielle, discovered it. It was the behavior of the marine life that drew her attention to it.

After their escape from Panacea, the few survivors began searching for resources. But the hybrids were used to being kept, not unlike the way we are today. Hunting and foraging was quite foreign. Luckily, their designer DNA and complex respiratory structure afforded them built-in instincts and abilities. Albatross provided abundantly.

Nutritious sea plants became a large part of their diets. They foraged wild berries, tubers, leafy greens, herbs, cacti, and edible flowers. The mineral springs flowed with fresh water. Seabirds provided occasional eggs, and the rocky east shores provided generous yields of mollusks. Fish were a last resort. However far-fetched, it somehow seemed cannibalistic. It still does. Cetacean has never been used in any way.

Once the breed established themselves, assured they had escaped undetected, Marielle spent countless hours in the ship graveyard on the west side, learning to master the currents and observing the behavior of the fish that frequented the area. After grazing on the unusual plants growing on the wrecks—which later became known as Wreckleaf—the fish grew stimulated. They swam faster, were more social, and their colors appeared to brighten. Overall, they seemed healthier, more robust. A sense of calm would eventually take over, and they would simply float and hover for long stretches, appearing content and unconcerned about predators.

Marielle later identified and observed particular groups of fish and even began to recognize individuals. Some would leave after eating Wreckleaf, some would stay close by, but without fail, all would return to the plant, a little less active, a bit duller. After grazing again at the Wreckleaf, the cycle would repeat. She wondered why only certain species ate the plant while others completely avoided it.

"Nerissa? Hello?"

Kendra startles me. "Yeah, what is it?"

"Hey, what are you doing? Let's go under."

We're almost chin-deep. "Oh, sorry. I was just thinking about Marielle."

"Who?"

"Never mind." I take a deep breath and dive under.

We weave our way through the tunnels and arrive at the last breathing chamber before they lead to the wrecks.

"Who do you want? The FWG, or us and Gabriel?" I ask.

"Both bags need to be filled."

"I know, but I try to pick the best stuff for us and Gabriel."

"It's all the best stuff, Nerissa. Always has been, always will be."

"Yeah, it just feels different depending on who's getting it."

"Then go for it. You pick for us and Gabriel—the good guys."

We both take one last, enormous breath and glide through the tube. It pitches steeply downward, narrow and dark. I feel the temperature drop as it leads into the open ocean.

All at once, there it is, one of my very favorite places, the western ship graveyard and the flowing Wreckleaf fields—the only known place on Earth the sea plant grows. As usual, I'm humbled. I don't consider myself a romantic, a poet, or an artist in any way, but if I were ... this place would be my muse.

I call the color here silent blue. It's rich, quiet, and always restful, no matter what time of day. But the water here defines itself. Its complicated movement is always evident in the furiously slavish currents and the quick, cautious darting of fish from one wreck to the next. Even the rays of sunlight on the brightest days break and shatter as they pierce through this liquid world. Atop the hulls of nameless ruins, Wreckleaf dances in the muffled chaos like a tall carpet of fluid green comfort. It spreads out across the rusted skeletons of countless shipwrecks, as far as we can see.

Many innocent lives have ended here—some not so innocent, I'm sure. Even against impossibly dangerous conditions, the lure of Panacea and her surroundings is undeniable, like a siren song. Greed, stupidity, and perhaps desperation, can motivate men to take risks they normally wouldn't. Trying to land a ship from the open ocean onto any of these shores will guarantee a spot in the graveyard.

I've spent countless hours exploring this beautifully terrifying world, daydreaming and contemplating my very existence.

This is the place, three years ago, just after our integration onto Panacea, that I found the ring I now never take off my finger. I lied to my mother when she asked where I had gotten it. We're not allowed to take anything but

Wreckleaf from the ship graveyard, first out of respect for the many who lost their lives here, but mostly as a statement that we're not lured by the greed and lust of humankind. But when I spotted my ring on the sea floor at the back end of a small wreck, I couldn't resist. It was so well camouflaged, covered in unknown years of debris, that at first I had no idea what it was. But I could tell it had a beautiful stone on it; one I'd never seen before. I scooped it up, tucked it away, and didn't look at it until I got home. After hours locked in my room, meticulous cleaning revealed an earthy, turquoise-blue stone with an orange vein traveling diagonally through it. Atop the large oval sat a delicate silver symbol, like two letter Cs with the rounded ends back to back, attached to a chunky silver setting. It fit my middle finger perfectly, and I've never taken it from my right hand since. I told my mother I found it on the road while riding home from work one day. The only reason she agreed to let me keep it was because she thought it helped me blend in and appear more human.

I can tell by the bend in the light that we have about thirty minutes before the caves are black. The currents aren't at their worst today. We should be able to gather our harvest quickly.

Being the faster swimmer, Kendra bolts to the farther, deeper wrecks, and I harvest from the ones close to the lead-in. It's important to take the plant from a variety of areas. Picking it stimulates its growth, and we must always maintain a steady supply.

I gently pry up the soft, slippery leaves. I love the way the fronds glide through my fingers as my hand closes around a bunch at the root. I'd like to eat some right now. But I'll wait for Kendra. After a short while, my bag is almost full.

Sometimes, I imagine what it was like for Marielle when she first decided to eat the Wreckleaf to see what it would do.

She had just realized the fish that ate the plant were never concerned with predators because Wreckleaf must have been poisonous, which rendered them a toxic menu choice. She confirmed this by capturing a Wreckleaf-eater and offering it to the seabirds for lunch. The birds were dead within moments. But why could the fish eat it in the first place? And if they could, could anyone else? Maybe it would affect her the same way it did the special fish. She was, after all, a distant relative. But then again, maybe it wouldn't. After the tragic decimation of her family and what must have been little hope for the future, Marielle likely felt she had nothing to lose. That first bite must have been terrifying. But it was that first bite that changed life for our breed as we know it.

I see Kendra materializing in the distance. She's still moving fast but looks tired. I move aside as she zips up the lead, and I follow her into the chamber.

"That was fun." She holds up her stuffed collection bag, patting it proudly.

"Holy crap, Beauty! That's quite a load you've got there."

"Well, Beauty, nothing makes me happier than delivering the FWG a great, big load."

5 – COPPICE INTERNAL

THURSDAY, MAY 30TH

Toes edged to the circle.

Wrapped in a cocoon of white sheets, I wake to the smell of coffee and the cool fluttering of billowy sheers. Just outside my window, a million birds sing above the distant rhythm of the ocean.

It's my last day of *freedom* before another Season of serving the entitled. I know just how I want to spend it.

There's a soft knock on my door.

"Come in."

My mother is dressed in a crisp white linen suit. "Good morning. How'd you sleep? Any bad dreams?"

"No, not at all."

"Good. What are you doing today?"

"I think I'll walk down to the river."

"Ride your board. Don't walk," she insists.

"Why not? I like to walk."

"You know why, Nerissa. Nobody walks, not even the locals anymore. You'll look out of place."

"I know, I just hate those things."

"Give it another chance. You might enjoy it."

"You won't be saying that when they design one to go over water."

"It'll never happen, not over this water. I have to go to work. Be smart and safe today. Trust no one, and remember who you are—"

"And who you're not." I finish her sentence.

My mother was assigned to manage the concierge team at the Breakwater Beach Club. She's really good at it, which is no surprise. She says as long as we have to keep up appearances and follow the rules of the Cooperative, we may as well try to find a sense of purpose and belonging. But that's a bunch of crap.

"Good work last night. You and Kendra really made up for your misstep at ceremony."

What's this? A compliment from my mother? "No big deal."

"It is a big deal. It is *the* deal, on so many levels. You two gathered a beautiful harvest. I'm sure Gabriel was pleased with his share."

"Gabriel is easy to please."

"I'll deliver the FWG's quota on my way to the Breakwater. The Officer will be more than satisfied."

"Okay, see you later. Have tons of fun at work today."

Frustrated with my sarcasm, she looks down and leaves. A few minutes later, I hear the front door open, then close. I'm alone.

I sit up, swing my legs over the edge of the bed, and contemplate the two dangling feet in front of me as though they're not attached. I drift into my little fantasy, rich with detail, of my feet surgically altered to appear completely human. An impossibly insane, pointless delusion.

I need music. My eyes settle on my index finger. The CNI almost matches my ring ... and my room. Tatiana was so angry when, without asking, I painted my perfect white room in our perfect white house a rich, sultry turquoise to match my ring. But she never made me change it back, and we never talked about it again.

"Display." The holograph comes to life, and I make my requests.

The room fills with my favorite song, "Ripple", performed by a girl on her piano. It's old-school, the way music used to be a long time ago.

Singing along as loud as I can, spinning and gyrating—almost convulsing—I catch a glimpse of myself in the mirror. Is that really what I look like? It's beyond comical; it's borderline scary. My blue pajamas are crumpled and worn at every edge. My hair is a nest in which surely something could live. Of course, there are my feet staring back at me. At least the two toenails are polished in coral.

Laughing out loud, I cannot fathom what is so appealing about me. I conjure the most twisted, offensive expression I can muster and shake my head to the beat. The nest of hair dances along. The song crescendos, and I freeze, staring at my image, my hairbrush-microphone poised and ready...

"Don't you see? You're not just a drop in the ocean. You are the ocean in a drop, oh, oh yeah!" My voice cracks on "yeah," and I've made myself dizzy. I better not quit my day job. Like I could ever do that.

Twenty minutes later, I've pulled myself together. I think even my mother would approve. I cram on my shoes and leave the house, ready for a private, relaxing day.

With a swipe of my CNI, my board comes to life with a soft, humming glow. It knows and anticipates everything about me. As soon as I tell it where I'm going, it takes over, and I don't have to do a thing. But if I have to use it, I want to be in charge, so I always set it on manual. I'll never get one with a seat, like a lot of the lazy humans have. I'm sure that somewhere, there's a machine or a service that wipes their butts for them when they're finished doing their business—because if you can pay someone to do something for you, whatever that may be, I guess that makes you a better person. Anyway, I like standing while I'm driving.

Down the hillside, I turn off a sleepy back road and ride along a small trail I've notched out for myself over the years. A little farther in, I park my board against the base of a huge, beautiful, old red tree. Continuing on foot, I welcome the crunch of the forest floor beneath me.

I reach my spot near the riverbank a moment later. A small, makeshift hook on a massive fallen trunk is where I hang my shorts and t-shirt. I leave my shoes just below. No need to hide myself here.

I round the tree trunk, where a slippery grass ramp leads me to the river's edge. Flowing down from the island's interior, the water here is cool and fresh, mixing with the salt of the warm ocean that backs up into the river at high tide. The mix of dessert pine, cedar, and woodland flowers with ocean salt and river water is intoxicating. It is heaven. And it's all mine, for now.

As I watch the dappled sun dance off the soft shallow water, I'm transported back in time. Some of my early memories of being here with my mother are pleasant. And although he scared me at first, knowing this is the place we first met Gabriel is comforting.

I go under and open my eyes. Time belongs to me alone.

But before I have the chance to enjoy my private escape, I notice something out of place. It looks like paper. And what at first appeared to be a few crumpled sheets I now realize is a veritable book-full of waste. What kind of thoughtless idiot would do this? It's unacceptable.

I grab the first ball of paper and un-crumple it. It's filled with almost illegible handwriting, scratched through, erased here and there. It's been written in pencil, not ink, so the words haven't bled everywhere. I read the word "biopsy" and then "benign".

I gather as much as I can, then head upstream. Around a grassy bank, I'm floored by what greets me. Dozens more of the papers, stark white and ridiculously out of place, punctuate the peaceful river like a strobe light in a twilight garden.

I pile what I'm holding on the grassy curve, unfolding the balled-up pieces to make them easier to stack. One catches my eye—a full page with a giant red-inked X over the entire thing, making it look like smeared blood. I take a deep breath and go under to read the scribble.

Surrender control, requested by self;
Dismantled fortress handed over
For biopsy of soul,
Ripped slowly from old foundation;
Benign intervention.
Leap from maintained boundaries
A heroic, costly extraction.
Fearing life lost
To the void of unknown.
But pleasures abound past gates
'Round the castle.
Have courage to stand
Toes edged to the circle,
Eternal tugging strings
Tied to the heart.
First steps taken
By power external
Transcends to internal.
A mutual agreement strengthens
New formations.
A liberating transaction
In actualization.
Engineered mastery,
Deep humble satisfaction

I just stare at it, as if that will bring me understanding. This is haunting but really beautiful. I wonder who wrote it. And why is it X-ed out? Wait…

I burst up out of the water

"Who?" I say aloud to no one, frantically searching the riverbanks. It's quiet except for a lone songbird above.

The sun streaming through the trees plays with my eyes. The breeze rustling the leaves fools my ears. I turn back to the papers still floating toward me and follow their broken line, left, then right, farther and farther upstream.

There. Right there. I spot someone sitting very still on the back end of a tiny red dock. The trees beyond blur together as one. But that face. I know it—the guy from the beach—and with what appears to be recognition spreading across his face, I assume he remembers me as well. Unbelievable.

I disappear under the water and propel myself with lightning speed. I clear the distance between us in seconds and pop up right in front of him.

"How'd you do that?" His voice trembles.

"Never mind that. How about you explain yourself, you filthy, thoughtless litterer!"

He stands up, shifting from one foot to the other.

"You can hold your breath for a really long time."

"Explain yourself!" I shout. "How dare you throw your garbage into this water? This is not a place to poison with whatever this crap is." I gesture toward the papers I've collected.

"It's private, that's what it is." He inhales sharply and clenches his jaw. "And it's none of your business."

"You made it my business when you filled my river with it."

"Your river?"

I stare at him, unwavering, fire under my skin. He can't hold eye contact any longer. He bends over and picks up a small pouch, a leather-bound journal, and a pair of tattered notebooks—the obvious source of the litter. He turns around and disappears into the forest. Lucky for him.

I gather the rest of the papers, grab the pile I made, and make my way back downstream. I should just burn everything before I go, leave the ashes to the forest floor. But I have nothing with which to light a fire. I'll take them with me. So much for a relaxing day on my own. This fool littered more than the river.

Back at the fallen tree, I sit down to let the breeze and the sun dry me. I stretch out on the massive trunk and close my eyes, but not even the soft green silence can lull my distracted mind.

'Eternal tugging strings tied to the heart…'

Whose heart? His?

'Dismantled fortress handed over for biopsy of soul…'

Whose soul?

'Pleasures abound past gates 'round the castle…'

What kinds of pleasures?

My eyes pop open. I don't care.

I force them shut. But one minute later, I'm staring at the treetops, then reaching for the stack of soggy, wrinkled papers at my side. Flipping through them one by one, I'm disgusted by my own curiosity.

Some have only a few random words, some are completely blank—what a waste. There are other, shorter versions of the red X poem. And then, I find this:

Coppice Internal

Perfumed majesty, sweet and heavy
Invasive, inescapable.
Canopy of cool mint
From breaking light to blackest floor
Infused with nourishment, turning with life
A penetrating unfamiliar hush
Wraps around the open spaces…

The second half of the poem is blurred and ripped at the left corner, but at the very bottom right, I can make out *Devin* … something, with today's date.

Devin. A name for Mr. Trash Basket. How can such intriguing words come out of such a slob? Seems his looks are the only thing going for him.

I've had enough. Time to go home. Thanks for ruining my day, Devin.

6 – CONCORDIA ON THE BAY

FRIDAY, MAY 31ST

I'm not impressed.

They stand in a circle in the grand beach-side foyer where I wait for my day to begin. The three girls are giggling, leaning into each other, their high-pitched squeals piercing my brain. They're disgusting, these spoiled little brats with their wearable pets—the most self-ish indulgence available on Panacea.

"Oh, Beauty, it's so everything," a shiny bald girl panders. Back and forth her friend tilts one flawless tanned hand, manicured lavender nails catching the light. Her ring is alive. It's a tiny golden snake, wrapped around her middle finger in a paralyzed coil. Its crystal-dusted scales sparkle with every little movement.

"Can you believe how cute it is? I named her Treasure." She bats her ridiculous lashes as tears form in her eyes.

Please.

"Her?" asks the third girl.

"Her, him, whatever." They share a robotic laugh.

The little bauble they're so flippantly referring to is alive. Whether a she or a he, it has a beating heart, it can feel. And no matter how primitive and simple its own awareness may be, without a doubt, it knows instinctively it's trapped.

"Look, did you see that? Do it again, Treasure, do it again!" she yells at the creature, commanding it to flick its tongue. Coincidence obliges her.

"Oh, Beauty!" Baldy squeaks.

At the tiny tip of the enslaved Treasure's tongue, a perfect round ruby is the surgically implanted cherry on top of an already indulgent lunacy.

"I thought they outlawed that crap." Kendra is suddenly beside me.

"Not the little harmless ones. You've seen others."

"Yeah, I guess, but is the snake really harmless? I bet it could still sink its tiny fangs into little Beauty over there."

"Nope, no fangs. They remove them. Just like they did to that fox scarf last Season. You remember?"

"How could I forget that atrocity? That vain bitch actually had them implant foam replicas."

"I'd love to give those three a piece of my mind."

"Let it go, there's nothing we can do."

She's right, if I even come close to reprimanding or insulting those girls, I'll be fired. As a result, I'd be in direct breach of the Cooperative.

"Come on, it's time to put on our happy faces and get to work."

Today is training day at Concordia on the Bay. It's unnecessary in my opinion but required for all food and drink servers, equipment handlers, towel service, and sprayers like me and Kendra. The three-month Season officially begins tomorrow.

As the perfectly groomed staff assembles for our briefing, I catch a reflection of myself in a window. I look ridiculous, like a cross between a plastic doll, a lingerie model, and some kind of twisted fairy. This year, my uniform is a white string bikini with iridescent, glittering angel wings. A fabric shoe covers just enough of my feet and wraps a silk ribbon up my lower legs. My makeup is flawless, with real gold flakes sweeping up both sides of my cheeks and around my eyes. My hair is pulled back into a giant orange waterfall. I'm the definition of exaggerated perfection. We're here to please the eye, serve the tourists' every whim, and sell goods and services. People want whatever we've got.

Concordia got lucky when the FWG appointed four Dolhuphemales to work at their resort. If they want perfect physical specimens representing their establishment, they can do no better than us. Three of us work as beach attendants. Kendra and I are sprayers, and Cassidy is a server. Cassidy has enchanted and acquired Contributors on several occasions without success, unable to get pregnant for unknown reasons. Because of her failures to reproduce, as well as the time spent and wasted scouting with Gabriel—he could have been helping one of us who could actually get the job done—Cassidy has become a bit of an outcast.

The fourth Dolhuphemale Concordia acquired, though not exclusively, is Kendra's mother, Giovanni. Just after the signing of the Cooperative, Giovanni made a bold move. Our identity assignments would place us into jobs that did little to engage or advance our intelligence. So she requested training in the island's main technology systems. She already had a natural affinity for sound-frequency vibration and crystal energies. So she made a compelling case to the FWG that, to reinforce our authenticity as pure-humans, we needed to be placed in diverse jobs. No one would ever believe or even consider that an illegal, government-produced hybrid, especially one believed to be extinct, would be working as a tech specialist in the most exclusive place on Earth. She trained tirelessly and now freelances, mainly for the "Big Six"—the six major luxury resorts on the north coast.

"Gather round, gather round, everyone." A flamboyant, yellow-haired man with a gleaming white smile and a perfect tan calls out to us. Clown college is about to begin.

"Ladies and Gentlemen, welcome to Concordia on the Bay. As many of you already know, my name is Marcus, and I am your manager. You all look amazing."

He pauses for effect.

"Newbies, look to the returning staff for guidance. There's a reason they're here. Our standards are very high, and our expectations of you are even higher. Our service, among other things, is what sets us apart."

All the resorts, especially the Big Six, boast about being "The Best". The best service, the most amazing spa with the newest in anti-aging treatments, the best gourmet food, and accommodations to die for ... The truth is, they're all the same—over-the-top playgrounds for the ultra-wealthy.

"Now, my little Beauties," continues Marcus, "we must always remember why we are here. Someone please tell me." He waves his hand in our direction, inviting our eager response. To my surprise, Kendra jumps in.

"We are to selflessly serve the beloved tourists who are here to rest and re-energize after their long and cruel wintering on the mainland." She smiles and curtseys. I love that smartass.

"Correct, Ms. Lucas. Expound... you, Taren." He points at the male version of Kendra and I. Taren looks impeccable if not ridiculous in his white tuxedo swim briefs and skimpy gold bolero. "Why do these good people need us?" Marcus asks. "What are they so desperately seeking on Panacea that only we can help them find?"

Without a thought, Taren replies, "The tourists are here to reboot, to reclaim their health, and to have fun and relax."

"Yes, good. And why can Panacea deliver those things to them?" He points at a young newbie girl who will be working towel service.

"Because Panacea is a veritable fountain of youth?"

"Yes! And why can Concordia deliver unparalleled results in their quest for recapturing their youth, health, and vibrancy?" He's really worked up now, almost like he's delivering a sermon, his arms flailing. "How do we assure that they feel the splendor and freedom of their glory days and leave with a true sense of the clock rewinding ten or twenty years?" He points at me.

Of course he does.

"Because at Concordia on the Bay, we stop at nothing to serve our guest. Their wish is our command."

"Yes! Bravo!" Elated, Marcus claps and smiles so wide, his teeth are blinding. If even a little of this crap were true, it may actually be inspiring.

"All right, my Beauties... The guests understand that today is training day. However, I expect nothing less than perfection. And remember to cross-promote." Now reading from a card he pulls from his inside breast pocket, he adds, "The spa will be running a special on a mineral mud bath/herbal infusion with powerful healing potential. It's called the Island Goddess Detox. Let the ladies know it will take up to a full inch off in an hour! Isn't that incredible?"

Back to the cue card. "The main dining room is featuring upland river trout with a medley of roasted Panacean land and sea vegetables. Also, Concordia has secured first launch rights to an exclusive new product called Aqua Tonic. It is a lightly carbonated, island-made energy elixir that contains..." He makes sure he's reading the card correctly. "...a proprietary blend of metabolic-boosting ingredients in a base of sparkling spring water and desalinized sea vapor." He looks up from the card. "We get it for a full two weeks before anyone else. So really promote it. It's healthy and fabulous. I've tried it. Now it's your turn."

Two servers appear, pushing carts with small plates of food and pretty, blue-green bottles. I leave the fish and eat the vegetables—nothing I haven't had before, but it's delicious. I take a small sip of the bubbly drink. It tastes bitter and sweet and leaves a tight, sharp sensation in my mouth. I pick up a bottle to read its label. It says: "Aqua Tonic—The Elixir of Life. Bottled at the source by Bio-Genesis Wave Technologies." What a cliché. And why the heck is a biotechnology company churning out bubbly water for spoiled tourists? Hey, I guess where there's money to be made ... whatever. I'm not impressed.

I look up. Everyone works their way toward the beach pavilion, with Marcus at the lead, walking backward.

"The old local man, Gabriel, will be joining us for a brief time today. He'll be featuring the new energy drink, along with the usual favorites. Take notice, servers especially. He is a master at what he does. Watch and learn. Let him inspire you, but do not copy."

I lean in close to Kendra, our fairy wings at risk of entanglement. "How about that pumped-up sugar water? Pretty gross, huh?"

"I kind of liked it."

"Who are you?"

We're at the beach pavilion. The sand is pristine, raked into a flawless pattern, with not a stone or twig to blemish it. The lounge chairs and umbrellas stand waiting to embrace the yearly herd. The equipment booth is set up, and the towel station is stocked and ready.

Tropical flowers and cooking food waft through the air. And as if Marcus ordered it, even the soft breeze is perfect. It blows straight in off the water so as not to ruffle anyone's coif. The water inside the swimming boundaries is clear and perfect, the view outstanding.

"Remember, everyone, remind our guests—without scaring them, of course—to stay within the swimming boundaries. We will not lose another guest, not this Season. *Not* on my watch!"

Because of Concordia's location as the westernmost resort before the shoreline turns rugged and begins to climb, guests enjoy the best views on the north shore, including beautiful sunrises and partial sunsets. But no amount of money affords anyone on the island the luxury of a full sunset view. The only reputed place to see a true sunset is from the top of Black Rock, which I'm sure is neither considered of value nor deserved, as the only ones allowed access to Black Rock are select Officers of the FWG, along with the scientists and employees of Bio-Gen.

The sprayers retrieve our waist-packs. Attached to a sparkling white strap with a gem-encrusted buckle hang four bottles of magical potions, like vials of liquid gold. I swear, some people would actually drink the stuff. It's Concordia's own, another trade-secret blend, which they pay handsomely to produce. It's also one of the only beauty products on the island containing Wreckleaf, which speeds up tanning and cell rejuvenation. Topically, Wreckleaf is like a magical salve. These tourists have no idea how lucky they are.

They can purchase it for use on the island, and they buy it by the bucket, but it cannot be taken home with them. There are very strict laws. All bags go through mandatory inspection at departure. But even if they buy it, there is nothing quite as lavish as having a beach attendant apply your sunscreen for you. And our formulas are more potent than the consumer versions. So Kendra, Taren, and I are very popular and stay busy all day. Typically, the women prefer the spray, the men the lotion. No surprise there. We're expected to do whatever it takes to satisfy the guests, so anything goes, and by the time my shift is over, my dignity has been smeared through the sand and stepped on countless times. I hate them for it. But I get it. Why lift a finger when someone else will do it for you? Why inconvenience your preferred lifestyle when you've grown so accustomed to it?

I've met a few decent people—nice, even—who say please and thank you. Some ask me about myself—what's my name, do I live here, how old am I, do I like my job? Of course, I can't tell them much, at least not the truth. But I've rehearsed well. And I usually don't have to get too personal or detailed. Most people don't even pretend to care about an attendant's life. So I just smile and put on my nothing-makes-me-feel-more-honored-and-fulfilled-than-serving-you face. And I don't need it, but I'm paid well and tipped even better.

A delicate chime rings out. Atop each chair rests two dainty crystal bells. Each produces a different tone that travels across the beach to signal either a server or an attendant for required service. I am closest. So before Marcus has a chance to direct me, I whisk down the sand to service my first guest, arriving at her lounger like an angelic butterfly. She's alone.

"Good morning, Beauty. Welcome to Concordia on the Bay. How may I be of service to you?"

"A full body spray with level two, please."

She said please.

"It will be my pleasure. It is, however, recommended to start with level one. It provides a higher SPF. You wouldn't want to start your holiday by burning your beautiful skin."

"I tan easily. Level two."

"Of course."

She flips over and lies face down on the chaise, spreading her limbs so I don't miss an inch. I begin at her neck, shoulders, and arms, spraying generously, even between her fingers.

I admit, the smell is intoxicating—a small consolation. I move down the petite woman's back, diligently spraying all exposed skin. She wears a tiny black bikini which barely covers anything but which I'd bet costs more than a night or two stay in her luxury accommodations.

After a moment's drying time, I instruct her to flip over. I'm almost finished when I hear another bell close by.

"I'll be right with—" I freeze. The bell ringer is Mr. Litter Bug from the river. I will myself not to launch a long-distance verbal assault. I force my focus back to my current guest and finish spraying her lower legs, pretending I haven't stalled and created a small river of oil down her shin.

I look up and see Marcus prompting me like a demented mime. Oh, right. Cross-promote.

"Thank you for the pleasure of servicing you, Beauty. I hope you're pleased with your application. Can I ring a server for you? Concordia is featuring a delicious lunch and a new energy elixir called Aqua Tonic. It boosts your metabolism and would certainly compliment the dark tan you'll surely have in a short while."

"No, not now. You can go." She holds out a large bill without opening her eyes. "Come back later."

"Thank you for your generosity." I take the money from her oiled hand. "Ring me any time."

Litter Bug is watching me closely. As I walk toward him, he says, "I'd like some lunch, and one of those energy elixirs, Nerissa. You can ring a server for me."

"Looks like you've already had your share." He's got a stack of plates and two empty bottles at his feet in the sand. "And I'm sure you're not going to clean those up either, are you?"

"I'm sorry, what?"

"Those bottles. You're just going to leave them there, aren't you?"

"Well, it's not my job to pick them up, it's yours."

"Just like at the river," I mumble under my breath.

"What did you say?"

I see Marcus clamoring toward me.

"It would be my pleasure." I stoop down and quickly pick up his dishes and empty bottles as Marcus arrives at my side. "Allow me to ring a server for you, sir."

Marcus greets him with a bow. "Good morning, sir. Welcome to Concordia on the Bay. I trust that Nerissa is attending to your every need?"

Another bell rings.

"Nerissa is a lovely girl and has been very accommodating." He smiles and stares at me.

"Thank you, sir. If you'll excuse me, I have another guest to attend to." I try to turn away, but he's not done.

"I would like to have a level-two spray, some lunch, and an Aqua Tonic, please."

"I'll ring a server for you and be back shortly for your application." I don't wait for his answer or Marcus' disapproval. Instead, I turn and walk away, hearing Marcus call Kendra's name.

The remainder of training day goes without further uncomfortable incidence. I don't know when Mr. Litter Bug leaves, but it's not before I see Kendra working him over with lotion from head to toe, chatting away like they've been friends for years.

The remaining tourists know our shift is over. They're a little agitated with the possibility their needs may not be instantly met. Not until tomorrow. Just as things are coming to a close, we hear Gabriel's unmistakable charm. He has materialized like a good witch, here for his final rotation and to usher out the day.

"Good afternoon, my good people. Gabriel is here with the medicine you need, the libations and salutations to bring you salvation and emancipation!" He sees me watching and winks. Finally, something real.

7 – WHO IS DEVIN BANKS?

FRIDAY, MAY 31ST

Well that's just great ... another lie to maintain.

Kendra and I stop by the office to check in with her mother. Giovanni is her usual brilliant self. I'm mesmerized by her as she trains a new employee.

"The thinner the crystal blank, the higher the frequency."

Her apprentice nods in understanding. I'm glad she gets it.

"There are additional resonances at the third and fifth harmonic overtones, and so on, whose frequencies are approximate but not exact—"

"Hi, Mom," Kendra interrupts.

"Oh, hello, Beauties."

"Mom, really?"

"Sorry, force of habit. How was training day?"

"You know... stupid, unnecessary, and a huge waste of time. A Doll's dream."

If looks could kill, Kendra would be on the floor, but only her eyes land there. Her trainee is not one of us, and by the look on her face, we all ought to feel lucky she's just an apprentice.

"Ladies, what can I do for you? Allison and I have a lot to go over."

"I just wanted to let you know we're going to Our Beach. I'll be home for dinner."

"Our Beach? Where is that?" Allison asks.

"That's just an inside joke about Playa Rosa," I say.

"Oh, the public beach."

Is she talking down to us? I'd love to tell this wannabe where we're really going.

"Yep, it's the best beach on the island."

"So Allison, you look familiar." Kendra can't stop herself. "You live in the Oval, right?"

She clears her throat. "Umm, yes, that's right."

"Right. Us, too. We're neighbors. Isn't that great?"

"Okay, we're going to let you two get back to work. It was nice to meet you, Allison. Goodbye, Ms. Lucas."

"Bye, Mom."

"Goodbye, ladies."

On our way to the lobby, we pass a large window that looks into the childcare center. It's a chaotic carnival of miniature versions of the demanding, entitled adults we serve and entertain.

We pass through the sprawling, opulent lobby where two giant, carved wood doors sense our approach and open automatically. They swing outward into the dazzling late-afternoon sun. I turn my face up and take a deep breath. It's always good to be leaving. As we do, we each tap a door—a ritual countdown of the number of days left in the Season.

Tap.

Tap. "Ninety-two... damn."

We hop on our boards and head southeast side by side. Once we clear the resort property, I speak my mind. "Were you trying to piss off your mom? Or get our friend Allison to start asking questions? Or both?"

She thinks I'm amused. "I know! Phew." She laughs.

"Kendra, I'm not joking. That was stupid."

"Oh, lighten up. It was nothing."

"Not true. And she lives in the Oval."

"So what?"

"You don't think she might be curious and come snooping?"

"Nerissa, we're really not that interesting."

We ride the rest of the way in silence.

We arrive at the trailhead and start a brisk walk up the crest. The forest smells perfect, the sun baking the pine needles and black dirt. We reach the top of the ridge where the trail turns right and heads southwest. Instead of following it, we slip through the evergreens and onto our own discreet footpath that leads us on a steep descent. At the water's edge, we undress and place our belongings under a large pine tree.

We're both eager to talk about training day, so we make fast work of getting to Our Beach. The ocean cooperates, and we're there in no time, settled on the untouched sand.

"Okay, Taren... yes or no?"

"Yes or no for what?"

"I might enchant him just for fun."

My cheeks sting a tiny bit at the thought of doing that just for fun. I change the subject. "Good tips?" I ask.

"Since when do you care about tips?"

"I don't. It's just amazing what these people will pay for service."

"So..." A sly smile spreads across her face. "This guy tipped me more than I made all day to rub his ears with lotion for ten minutes."

"Ew! You did not."

"Oh, yes I did. That was easy money, honey."

"You're such a slut."

"Thank you, Beauty. But this slut sends all her money to Blue Ventures, the oldest marine conservation program on the planet."

"Very admirable, Beauty."

"So did you make any memorable tips today?"

"Yeah." I don't embellish.

"Do tell."

"Ugh. You know, it was your typical female tourist. Well-groomed, skinny, fake boobs, all the high-end crap."

"And?" she prompts.

"And nothing. She tipped me ridiculously well."

"Why?"

"Because I gave her amazing service."

"Bull, Nerissa. Spill it."

I take a deep breath and exhale hard. "She asked me who did all my work. My face, my boobs, my hair. So I told her."

Kendra laughs, waiting for me to expound.

"During her application, I told her I was really lucky to have great genes, but that the only way I maintain everything is by having weekly phytoplankton spa therapies and island clay hair treatments at the resort. I also said that I hang on an inversion table every morning, and do a hundred upside-down crunches, which not only keeps my abs ripped but also keeps my boobs lifted, which by the way I rub every morning with quartz crystals. I told her the only thing I ever eat and drink is Concordia's salad and Aqua Tonic. And that, of course, the side effects of being a sprayer are really positive, since I soak up a lot of the oils."

Kendra's eyes are wide, her mouth open.

"And she listened to every word like her life depended on it."

Kendra laughs again. "Excellent!"

"Then she proceeded to pull out a little notepad and write down the name of her medi-spa doc, folded it over a big wad of cash, and handed it to me. She said when the time comes for more assertive measures, she swears by this doctor."

Kendra is speechless, and that's rare.

"I thanked her, then ordered her a kale and sea-greens salad and Aqua Tonic. Then I introduced her to an equipment handler who agreed to set up an inversion table in her suite to be rented for the remainder of the Season. I swear she looked at me like I was a god."

"Oh, Beauty, you *are*!" She bows down to me.

"I'll give you my tips to donate to that conservation group."

"Thanks. Wow, I bet Marcus was happy."

"Yeah, I think I scored a few points with him."

Kendra stretches and lies back in the sand. I do the same, and there's a long, comfortable pause between us before our conversation takes a turn.

"Speaking of hot guys..."

"Were we?" I know exactly where this is going.

"What happened today with that guy Devin?"

"Nothing. Really, I don't want to talk about it."

"So, nothing really happened? Or you don't want to talk about what really happened?"

"What?" I contemplate her twisted interpretation of my words. "No. I mean there's nothing to talk about. Really."

"Really? That's funny, because he sure had a lot to say about you. But whatever." She jumps to her feet. "I need a swim." She's in the water before I can respond.

My blood is unexpectedly boiling. What could this guy have possibly said about me? And why do I even care? I don't. I stretch out and gaze at the sky, then turn my focus to my breath.

Just as I'm drifting off, Kendra stands over me, saltwater dripping from her hair.

"So, his name is Devin Banks. He's eighteen years old, the youngest son of two, of Officer and Mrs. William Banks. He's here for the Season. He's come here every summer except one since he was eleven. They live on Sage Way in the Royal Palms neighborhood."

I wipe the water off my face and say nothing. Kendra waits it out. She knows I'll break, but I do my best to seem uninterested. She resumes her position on the sand next to me and closes her eyes. I try to force my thoughts to other things, imagining myself in the fragrant forest and the river. I sit up and look out at the water, blue and tranquil, and count the seconds between the surf. Nothing can hold my attention. Nothing except Devin Banks.

I let five more minutes tick by. "Okay, you win."

She says nothing, doesn't flinch.

"Okay, Kendra. What did he say?"

Just as I decide she's fallen asleep, a tiny smile forms at the edges of her mouth. A second later, she's up, legs crossed in front of her, at full attention. "Well, first he asked if I knew you. Or, to be more exact, if I knew 'that other snotty sprayer named Nerissa'."

"What? He's so arrogant. What did you say?"

"I said I know you a little. And he said you're lucky to be so pretty, because your people skills suck. And that he could have you fired in a minute. In fact, he's surprised Concordia even hired you."

I'm outraged. "I really hope you stuck up for me."

"Of course I did. I explained that your parents just got a divorce, and your dad moved back to the mainland, and because you're going through so much he should cut you some slack."

I'm dumbstruck. "You actually said that? Are you insane?"

"I guess not, because once I did, he calmed down and got all quiet. I may have just saved you from getting fired, or worse. You're welcome."

"Well, that's just great. Another lie to maintain. I guess I'll have to avoid him."

"That'll be impossible. He wants to talk with you."

"Damn it, Kendra."

"Hey, don't swear at me. You started it with him."

"Why divorce, Kendra? My identity assignment says my father died when I was little. Why didn't you just tell him I was having a bad day? Or my cat died or something?"

She gawks at me with that look of hers. "Nerissa, in case you didn't hear me, I said that Devin is the son of an Officer. When he said he could have you fired in a minute, he wasn't exaggerating. And tourists don't care if their servants are having a bad day or if their precious kitty died. When their pets die, they order another, custom-made. You needed to be entrenched in a big, personal human drama for the son of an Officer to care at all about why you were a snotty bitch to him. And I was on the spot. I did the best I could."

"But don't you think the families of the Officers all know about us? I mean, c'mon, can they really keep everything a secret? Devin will know you're lying."

"No way. Our existence is only known by a handful of Officers. Not everyone in the FWG knows. And for sure the ones that do know don't share that information with anyone else, not even their families. Those people are sworn under oath."

"How do you know for sure?"

"All I know is what my mother told me. I trust she knows what she's talking about."

I try to think of another reason to protest but can't. "Okay, I'm sorry."

She waits a few seconds before accepting my apology. "No problem."

"So, he thinks I'm pretty?"

She laughs. "Everyone thinks you're pretty. And yes, so does Devin Banks."

"Banks. Why do I know that name?"

"His father is an Officer. We've probably heard it before."

"Right."

"So, I think Devin would be a great Contributor. What do you think?"

"No way! The guy is an arrogant A-hole."

"They all are. But after I told Devin about your parents' divorce, he was really sweet and polite. And a good tipper."

"I bet he was, after that ridiculous application you gave him."

"My Beauty, are you jealous?"

"Absolutely not."

"Good. Then if you're not interested in him as a future Contributor, I am."

"Kendra, it's really best to pick people we don't have any relationship with."

"I don't have a relationship with him. I attended to his request once. He's a hot guy and no doubt well-educated. He's the perfect candidate. Besides, I think it would be a fun little irony to "employ" the son of an Officer."

Yes, a dangerous irony. I won't let Kendra take that kind of risk. I'd never put her in harm's way. "You know what?" I tell her. "You're right. He's a good candidate, and he's obviously into me. So, yeah, I'll pursue him."

"Make up your mind, Doll. First you can't stand him, now you want to pursue him."

"I do. So please leave him alone."

Her crinkled brow suggests I've offended her. And confused her.

But I'm the one who's confused. Am I looking out for Kendra? Or has Devin Banks stirred up something else inside me?

8 – SEASON OPENER

SATURDAY, JUNE 1ST

Your wish is our command.

I'm fed up. Disgusted, really. Training day can never truly prepare us for the flurry—no ... the *infestation* of tourists. Overnight, the island is crawling with them.

I feel sorry for the newbies like Towel Girl. She seems overwhelmed, unable to keep up with their demands, fumbling with both her words and the towels. But what she doesn't realize is they're on their best behavior when they first arrive, so happy to be back at their Garden of Eden. But by the end of the first week, we're nothing but invisible servants.

I haven't seen Devin Banks today. Fine by me.

It's 10:00 a.m., and the decadent Concordia breakfast service is in full swing. And even though it's early, the cocktails are flowing. Keeping pace is the Aqua Tonic. By noon, there'll be two kinds of people to deal with—the drunk or the wired. Worse yet, a combination of the two.

As their hunger and thirst are satisfied, the bells ring for sprayers.

"Welcome to Concordia on the Bay. How may I serve you?"

"Number One lotion," the woman mutters through her last mouthful of breakfast.

"You mean spray? Most women prefer it. It provides a very even application."

She puts her finger up in a wait-a-moment gesture and swallows hard. "No. I want the lotion. It works better."

"I assure you, Beauty, both products are equally effective."

"Listen here, little girl, I've been coming to this island longer than you've been alive. I know how to get results, better than most. But especially better than you. You're new. I don't remember you."

"I'm a returning employee."

"Well, you must not have left much of an impression, and you certainly didn't learn enough. Number One lotion. Now."

"My pleasure."

The witch lies down on her back and puts her arms above her head. "Do you know who I am?"

"My apologies, Beauty. I do not." I squirt the luscious, oil-infused lotion into my palm. Whoever she is, she's not worth the ingredients in my hand.

"I am Alexandria Allerton Bigelow."

She waits for my lightning-bolt recognition of her name. I'm silent.

"Oh, my word, child. Do you know nothing? I'm the one who made Concordia on the Bay a reality, the investor who brought Concordia to life."

"It's an honor to make your acquaintance, Ms. Bigelow. Thank you for investing in the greater good of Panacea, and for the opportunity to be part of such a magnificent entity. We are all so fortunate." I'm going to vomit.

My flattery seems to appease her a bit.

"Start at my feet. And stay on them awhile. I don't like a rush job."

"My pleasure, Beauty."

Another bell rings in my tone. I don't dare turn my attention away from Baroness Concordia. I slowly look sideways, and I'm greeted by the only thing that could make this encounter seem charming and prompt me to take my time. Devin Banks sits on a lounger at the edge of the beach under a knotty old juniper. His hands are behind his head, legs crossed at the ankles, a tattered old journal resting on his lap. He's wearing an easy, comfortable grin. Once again, the bottles and dishes are strewn under his chair.

I turn my attention back to Ms. Bigelow. Her arms dangle lifelessly at her sides. She must have either fallen asleep or died. I pray for the latter.

Devin's bell rings a second time. His smile widens, and he raises his eyebrows. I gently shrug and gesture toward the dead meat on the chair under me. Devin starts to laugh out loud. I can hear him from here. It looks like he's told himself a private joke. Against my will, I crack a smile, happy someone else is aware of this spectacle of a woman.

Another bell rings out, and in response, Devin aggressively rings his again, gesturing toward the new ringer that he is next in line. Like magic, Marcus appears at Devin's side, fawning over him in an attempt to quell his impatience. Devin works him like the well-oiled tool Marcus is. He stands up, gets in Marcus' face, and throws his hands around in the air. I watch closely, paying only slight mind to Alexandria, who I've coaxed to flip over and who now snores with her face smashed into the lounger. Devin is aware of my audience and wants me to understand what he's saying, so both his voice and his body language grow louder. Marcus fans himself, his other hand at his chest. It's hysterical.

Devin makes a grand, sweeping motion with his arms, acknowledging the entire crowded beach. Then he throws his fist in the air, which makes Marcus flinch, and he thrusts one, two, and three fingers in Marcus' face. He repeats over and over, "Three! Three!"

I finish up Ms. Bigelow as fast as possible, and she doesn't notice when I leave. Kendra has just arrived on the scene to stand at Marcus' side. I'm twenty-five feet from them when Devin throws his arms up in further protest and turns in my direction. He points at me and says, "I want her!"

"Yes, sir, you can choose whomever pleases you. They are all available and at your service. In fact, you can have all three at the same time. I insist." Marcus shifts on his feet and smiles.

"Well, that is a tempting offer, but there are other people waiting, like I've had to do, since you only have *three* sprayers for the entire beach! You need more. I suggest you make that happen."

"Yes, sir, Mr. Banks. I'll get on that immediately. In the meantime, which of these Beauties do you prefer?"

"I already told you." He turns and looks me in the eyes. "I want Nerissa."

My stomach flips.

"Your wish is our command. Nerissa, please take excellent care of Mr. Banks. And take your time." His eyes bore into mine, pleading.

"Of course, Marcus. Mr. Banks is in good hands." My lack of enthusiasm can't be unnoticed.

As the scene dissolves and the gapers go back to their own business, bells ring out in every direction. Most are for the servers to bring drinks to the parched onlookers. Marcus shoots me one last look along with a hand gesture prompting me to slow things down. I turn to Devin and hold my serious and professional expression for as long as possible before I smile. He begins to laugh again but quickly controls himself and sits down.

"Okay, we better look serious. I want a Number Two." I snap into action and reach for my sprayer. He stops me. "No, no. I want the lotion."

"Are you serious?" I ask quietly. "Can you give me a break?"

"I'm dead serious, and I'm pretty sure I just gave you a huge break. I guarantee you'll have at least one or two more sprayers by morning."

"Well, I appreciate the consideration, but more sprayers means less tips, which we all rely on."

"I thought you'd be happy to have the help."

"I'm not afraid of hard work. I'm used to it."

"You don't seem to be afraid of much."

I stand in silence, never breaking eye contact with him.

"Since you're so fearless and accustomed to hard work, how about you start working on me right now?"

I knew his little act was nothing more than a way to impress me. Another thing I'm used to. Guys do it all the time. He rolls over on his stomach. I begin his application, fire under my skin.

"Your friend Kendra is much better at this than you."

"You had your choice. You should have picked her."

"I'm just saying that you could learn a few things from her."

"Like what? How to turn a guy on while he gets lubed up?"

"Woah, c'mon, now... That's not what I'm saying." Devin sits up and looks at me with creased eyes. I feel embarrassed by what so easily slipped out of my mouth. "Can we just start over? This is not how I imagined things going today. Hi, my name is Devin Banks. It's a pleasure to meet you." He holds out his hand, waiting. I don't offer mine.

"I know who you are. But back up... how you imagined things?"

He sighs. "Yes. Kendra let me in on a few personal things about you, and I just wanted the opportunity to let you know that I feel bad for you."

Some friend Kendra is. "Why? Are your parents divorced?"

"No, but things are complicated." A long, awkward pause. "Nerissa, I'm no monster. I just wanted to tell you I'm sorry for what you're going through, and if you ever need a friend to talk to, I'm here."

"A friend? Is that what we are?"

"Sure, we can be that. As a matter of fact, how about you let me take you to dinner... as friends."

I'm riding a rollercoaster. First, he's a jerk, then he's funny and down to earth, then he's demanding and rude, and now he's switched back to nice and empathetic. Now he wants to be friends, but if I'm not mistaken, he's just asked me out on a date. All in two days' time. I'm pretty sure that's not the kind of friend I want.

"Mr. Banks..."

"It's Devin."

"Devin. As generous as that offer is, I have to decline."

"It's just a dinner invitation between friends."

"I'm sorry, it's still no. But thank you."

"Okay, maybe another time."

"Shall we continue with your application before I get in trouble for standing around talking?"

"No. We're done."

"No really, it's my pleasure to serve you."

"Nerissa, we're done here. Don't worry, I'll give Marcus a sparkling review."

"Okay." I bend over to pick up the dishes and empty bottles under his chair, and he puts his hand in front of my face. Peeking out from between his fingers is an enormous tip. I suddenly feel like a jerk. "No..." I try to protest, but he doesn't move.

"You rely on your tips. Take it."

I slowly reach out. He holds fast to the bill until our hands are touching. When he finally lets go and places the cash in my palm, he closes his warm fingers over mine and stays there for a second too long. I stand up, fumbling with the dishes enclosed in one arm.

"Your ring... It's terrific."

"It's just a ring."

"Not really. That's a pretty special symbol. Do you know what it means?"

"Of course I do," I lie. "Thanks, friend."

I turn and march away. I don't stop until I'm clear across the beach pavilion, where I deposit his mess. I linger for a moment before I casually turn back around. Devin Banks is nowhere in sight. He's disappeared like a feather in the wind. I can finally breathe.

SUNDAY, JUNE 2ND

The next morning, it's still dark when I wake. I lie in bed, recalling a dream.

I'm back on the pier the night Anastasia went missing, the night I killed my would-be rapist. Everything is the same, except I can hear nothing. The dream world is on mute. As words are spoken, they flash above the speaker's head in an elegant, scripted font that fades away as the next word is formed.

I can't hear the lust and aggression in Tom's voice or the sickening laughter of his friends. I don't feel the usual terror, and the dream takes on a very different quality. Not quite peaceful, but more fluid, a bit poetic, even, like a tragic opera painfully intriguing to watch.

When I'm fully awake, I remember today is Sunday. Concordia on the Bay will have to get along without me until Tuesday. I wonder if Mr. Emotional Rollercoaster will be there. Oh, well. Let someone else deal with him. I'm going back to sleep.

TUESDAY, JUNE 4TH

I've overslept. I swipe my CNI over my board, and nothing happens. No, not today. Marcus will make it miserable for me if I'm late. I try two more times, but nothing happens. I start to run.

If I could swim to work, I'd arrive with time to spare. But on foot, I come galloping through the employee entrance twenty minutes late. The locker room is empty and quiet.

I struggle with my uniform. I swear, for something with so little fabric, you'd think it'd go on easier. But it's so convoluted and intricate, it takes another five minutes to get it right. No time for makeup and hair. I check myself in the mirror at the end of a row of white lockers and take a deep breath.

No one can take your power from you unless you allow them to. I sigh, wishing I could believe myself. My power was taken from me long ago.

I exit the locker room and walk down the long hallway connecting a web of service entrances. Halfway down the hall, something catches my eye. I stop at a large, framed portrait of a fish-faced woman with a forced, plastic expression. A small carved plaque underneath reads:

Alexandria Allerton Bigelow
Concordia on the Bay's Founder
Our champion, angel, and fairest Beauty

Has that always been here? How have I not noticed it before? I have to remember to accidentally slash it with a knife sometime soon.

I burst through the door onto the beach pavilion. My first instinct is to look toward the spot Devin was Saturday. I can't quite see past all the chairs and umbrellas but do spot someone sitting there. It looks like two girls.

From a table just past the towel gazebo, I grab my waist pack.

"Hi, Newbie," I call to the slight girl behind the counter passing out towels, but she doesn't hear me. "Good morning," I say a bit louder, and she turns her head. But all she can muster is a slight grin. She says nothing. First year is an eye-opener.

A bell rings. I work my way toward a man getting settled in with his wife and young son. I'm about ten yards from the family when a tall blonde in the exact uniform I'm wearing steps in my path and leans over, her less-than-contained chest at eye level with the bell-ringer.

"Good morning, sir. Welcome to Concordia on the Bay. It will be my absolute pleasure to serve you today. How may I do so?" Her voice is like slow, wet sugar, and the man can't pull his eyes from her chest. His wife is oblivious, adjusting their toddler's sunhat.

"Well, well... Good morning. What's your name, Beauty?"

"My name is Jade, sir. How may I please you today?"

Who is this tramp? Can't his wife see what's going on right in front of her? I stop and watch the seduction unfold. I can't move a muscle.

"Well, Jade, as many ways as I imagine you could please me, I'd like you to service my wife first. We'll get to me later."

"You see, Nerissa? That is how you treat our guests. Anything it takes." Marcus has slid up next to me and makes his proud declaration inches from my ear.

"Who is that, Marcus?"

"That is Jade. Isn't she wonderful? What a Beauty."

"I guess if you like a brown-nosed floozy with fake boobs, then yeah, she's great."

He looks at me with such genuine disappointment, I actually feel bad for a second. "Nerissa, you were late. Don't let it happen again. And you look awful. What have you done with your hair?"

I couldn't look awful if I tried, Marcus. "I'm sorry. It was my board."

"I don't care what it was. Neither do any of these guests. You simply must be here on time."

"Thank goodness Jade was here to cover me."

"Yes, not only Jade, but Rocky as well." He points in the opposite direction at a new male attendant in the middle of an application on an elderly woman.

A small giggle escapes me. His muscles are steroid-huge, his hair a shocking platinum. I think I can even see plumped-up lips from here. The old lady in the lounger may just go into cardiac arrest.

Rocky and Jade. I wonder where he found these two. Way to keep it classy, Marcus.

"I must thank Mr. Banks for his suggestion to employ more sprayers. The other guests seem as pleased as he is with the additions to our team."

"So Devin—I mean, Mr. Banks... has had their services already?"

"Yes, of course. He was Jade's first client on Sunday. He was quite pleased."

I'm sure he was.

"Is Mr. Banks here today?"

"Indeed, he is."

"Does Mr. Banks' family rent or own in Concordia?"

"The Banks family owns property up in the luxury sector."

"Oh, really? Then why is he here every day?"

"He simply loves it here, obviously." His face crinkles.

"I don't remember him from last year."

"He frequented Infinity Club last Season. He said he decided to try something new this year and much prefers us, of course."

"Umm... Marcus?" I point to the couple Jade is servicing. Things appear to have gotten a little out of control, and people are watching. Jade is clearly providing more than just standard application services.

"Oh! Dear Guests." Marcus snaps into action and addresses the threesome. "May I suggest a move to one of our private beach cabanas? They can be rented by the day or the hour. You will have complete privacy and Jade's total confidentiality."

They all follow Marcus to a cabana. “Nerissa, see that the child gets to the youth club at once.”

Their little boy is left playing in the sand, content. He must be used to fending for himself, but the beach is no place to leave a small child. No gold stars for these parents. I bend down and gather up the toddler’s toys and belongings. “Hi, I’m Nerissa. Come on, we’re going for a walk.”

“No.”

“We’re going someplace really fun. Mommy and Daddy asked me to take you there.”

“No.” He doesn’t look up, just continues with his creation in the sand, his blue-checked sunhat shielding his eyes.

“It’s okay, I’m a friend.”

“No.”

A shadow appears over me.

“There’s a lot of that going around, isn’t there? A friend wants to take another friend out and show them a good time, but they just say no... It’s so sad, that lack of trust, don’t you think?”

I turn around and look up to see Devin standing over me, his strong silhouette outlined in the morning sun. I look back down at the boy. “Well, he doesn’t know me at all and has no reason to trust me.”

“But there’s also no reason for him not to trust you.”

“Well, that’s debatable. In his world, people are unreliable and act selfishly. He has no reason to believe my intentions are pure.”

“But your intentions are pure, aren’t they?”

“Yes, of course.”

“Then even though you—I mean, he... feels unsure and perhaps vulnerable, he must throw caution to the wind.”

I sigh and turn to face him. “I get your point. Well played, but I’m sorry. It’s just not wise for me to mix business and pleasure. Marcus frowns upon it.”

"Hmm, apparently not. We all saw what happened a few minutes ago. But that's not the kind of thing we're talking about, anyway. And really, what business is it of Marcus' what you do with your private time?"

"I hear you," I say, "but right now, I have to figure out a way to get this kid to the youth center ASAP. I don't know when babysitting became part of my job, but I have to escort the Little Prince to his destination."

"Nerissa, relax. Let me help you."

"I don't need any help."

He ignores me and bends down. "Hi, buddy. What's your name?"

"Ben"

"Hi, Ben. My name's Devin."

"How'd you do that? He wouldn't tell me his name."

"You didn't ask him his name."

Devin works his way with Ben, and moments later, we're dropping him off at the youth center. To no surprise, Ben seems to know the place and jumps right into the action, disappearing behind a wall. We stroll through the lobby back toward the entrance to the beach pavilion.

"Thank you for your help."

"You're very welcome."

"I can't believe Ben's parents left him like that with total strangers for such a nasty, selfish reason."

"People here are used to others taking care of them in every way. They just knew someone would accommodate their needs."

"Yeah, in more ways than one. I don't know. If you don't want to take care of a kid, don't have one."

"I'm sure they love their child."

"They have a funny way of showing it."

"Like I said, people here have different expectations."

"Well, I live here, and that's not the way I am. What about you? Is that the way your parents brought you up?"

He pauses. "Kind of. But look... I'm okay." He smiles.

"We all have scars, Devin."

The door to the beach pavilion swings open in front of us, and two familiar-looking girls walk inside.

"Devin! There you are!" The girl with a big orange sunhat bats her eyes at him.

"Dalma, this is Nerissa," he says. Her eyes turn to stone. "And this is Nora." He gestures toward the other girl drowning in a long, flowing caftan.

"It's nice to meet you both."

"Pleasure," Dalma graces me, while Nora simply nods and offers me a condescending smile. They both make no qualms about eyeballing me up and down. It's nothing I'm not used to, it's just not usually so up close and blatant. These two have no shame or manners. And after they size me up in a matter of seconds, they're done with me.

"Devin, sweetie, don't forget about the party tonight. You're coming for sure, right?"

"Yes, Nora. I told you earlier I'll be there. You have my word."

"We'd just miss you if you weren't there. You're the life of the party."

"I'll be there. And I'd like to bring a friend."

"Of course, Boyfriend, especially if he's as tall and gorgeous as you."

"Oh, yes. My friend is definitely tall and gorgeous."

"Excellent. We'll see you at eight. Come hungry. The chef is world class."

"See you then."

"Ta..." The two girls walk away without any further acknowledgement of me. Dalma removes her giant hat, revealing a shiny, bald head, and I realize why I recognized them. Thank goodness neither were wearing any live jewelry or accessories. I wouldn't have been able to control myself.

"Your friends are charming."

"They're not so bad, just a little insecure."

"A little? Right. And if you think I'm coming with you to their party, think again."

"You caught that?"

"Yes, unlike those two dimwits."

"Well, I meant what I said. My friend is gorgeous."

"And tall?"

"That, too." He smiles.

"All right. Thanks again for your help, but I've got to get back to work."

"Wait, not yet. Let's have some coffee or something? How about an AQT?"

"A what?"

"An Aqua Tonic. Let me treat you to one."

"I hate that stuff. It tastes terrible."

"Oh, really? I love it."

"Bye, Devin. I have to go."

"Let me at least walk you back to the beach."

"No, that's okay. I'm going to go back through the employee doors. I just want to keep things professional." I try to ignore his sad-puppy face.

"All right. I'll see you out there. Hope your day goes well. Don't work too hard."

"Thanks, I'll try." I walk away, and I can feel his eyes all over me.

WEDNESDAY, JUNE 5TH

"How about lunch? Friends go to lunch all the time," he yells but never looks up from his journal. As usual, Devin has parked himself under the junipers at the edge of the sand. It's only ten in the morning, and already, the underside of his lounger is home to numerous empty bottles and a pile of breakfast dishes. I stroll toward him.

"Sir, allow me to clear your area."

He doesn't speak but waves a hand in agreement, once again never looking up from his writing. I bend down, get very close to him, and reach under his chair.

"How was the party last night?" I whisper.

He answers with a full voice, "Obnoxious, over the top, lame. Same old, same old."

"Sorry I missed it."

"Never again will I allow such a travesty!" he yells and swings his arms above his head, maintaining his unbreakable gaze on his journal, and he's got me. I try to control my giggling but fail. He lowers his voice to a near whisper as I start to rise. "You think that's funny, do you?"

"I do, but I think everyone else thinks you're crazy."

"That's the way I like it... Then they'll leave me alone." He snorts, and I have to walk away.

"But the lunch! What about the lunch?"

THURSDAY, JUNE 6TH

It's the first day I can ever remember looking forward to going to work, and I'm up early. My board is still under repair. I'll have to walk again. They can't seem to figure out what the problem is. Maybe my CNI sent a telekinetic message to the board's mainframe telling it how much I detest riding it. Now, *that* would be smart technology.

I arrive early and tackle my uniform, war paint, and hair in near solitude, then go out to the beach for some peace and quiet before the day gets crazy.

The view is pristine, waves rolling in softly, the water a perfect, muted cerulean. I would give anything to jump in, swim past the boundaries, and never look back. The smell of salt and everything below water rides the breeze and drifts by my face. It reminds me of simpler times and fills me with a vague sadness.

From the corner of my eye, I see someone approaching. Gabriel flashes his crooked, toothy grin. He's like a breath of fresh air, dressed in his standard—worn denim pants rolled at the ankle, no shoes, and an old cotton t-shirt. He saunters toward me, his arms spread wide.

"Nerissa, child. Give Gabriel some sugar."

I don't hesitate and melt into Gabriel's open arms. He smells of the ocean and sun, and his skin is dry and warm. I surprise both of us with unexpected tears. Instead of reacting or trying to fix things, he simply strokes my back, careful not to get tangled in the wings, and holds me. He is what I imagine a good father would be.

"I'm sorry, Gabriel." I pull away and wipe my face, unable to meet his eyes.

"Do not be sorry, dear one. You owe no one an apology for expressing your emotions. It is difficult sometimes to maintain a positive perspective when up against so many obstacles."

How anyone could think Gabriel is simple-minded or unevolved is ridiculous. No one understands things, or understands me, better than him.

"How do you do it?" I ask him.

"How do I do what?"

"The whole thing... I mean, I feel so trapped, so used, so fake. I don't know how long I can continue to put on this costume and this mask and pretend like it brings me joy. It's not who I am. How do you do it?"

"Well, for me, I never allow myself to behave in a way that goes against who I really am."

"But I don't have a choice. I'm bound by the Cooperative."

"Nerissa, you must define your life's purpose and reconcile with it. And know that you always have a choice."

"You're saying that I have to accept my circumstances as my life purpose?"

"No one can tell you your purpose except yourself."

I pause and look around. The beach is coming to life, and Gabriel and I have mere moments before I must snap into the role I so despise. "What's your life's purpose, Gabriel?"

"I believe my life has a number of purposes. But primarily, I am a leader and a teacher by example. But then, aren't we all?"

"Ha! I'm no leader. I'm a pawn in a game I didn't sign up for. And so are you."

"Nerissa, no one can tell us who we are. You are exactly who you expect and want to be."

"I sure don't want this. This place, these people... It's such a sham. I just want to be free, to be real and to not have to hide or lie just to be accepted. Or safe."

"We all want the same thing. Every last one of us." He puts his hands on my shoulders, leans toward me, and plants a gentle, dry, and ancient kiss on my forehead. "Know, dear one, with every fiber of your being, that you are exactly who you are supposed to be, in exactly the right time and place. Know that if you are unclear of it now, your life's purpose will reveal itself to you when it is time. And above all else, know that you are already free, because you always have that choice."

I accept his words with frustration and one last embrace, then change the subject. "You're here early. Morning shift must be difficult."

"You'd be surprised. I sell all day... Just started on this end of the Big Six today. The tourists like their beverages, even in the morning. Some more than others, apparently." He gestures down the beach. I'm not quite sure what he's pointing at. Then I spot what appears to be three people sleeping on lounge chairs all the way at the end of the sand.

"Looks like they've been there all night. And not a lot of clothes on. They didn't move when I walked by and said good morning. I don't suppose they'll be feeling too well today."

A small panic rolls in my stomach, and my heart speeds up. Gabriel notices.

"What's the matter?"

"I'm fine. I just better get going. I don't want Marcus on my butt again."

"Yep, I've got to fill up my caddy. This crowd likes rum and AQT with their breakfast."

"Yuck. I hate that stuff."

"Good, don't drink it. It's garbage, no matter what they tell you. Good day, child."

I offer him a smile before he walks away. Then I snap my focus back down the beach, and with a bad feeling brewing, I slowly move toward them.

Two of them are entwined on a lounger, their backs toward me. The third is half on, half off a chair near their feet. Scattered around them are at least a dozen bottles, garbage, a large potted plant spilling black dirt over its edges, and a few articles of clothing. As I get closer, I realize two of them are in their underwear.

I step up to the scene to find my racing heart warranted. There lies Devin, shirtless, in his usual chair, entangled in a sloppy heap with Nora, her hair a knotted mess, drool spilling from the corner of her mouth. One of them is snoring. Dalma lies in what appears to be her own vomit, her red lipstick smeared up to her hairless head. As the breeze kicks in, the rising smell confirms it is indeed what it appears to be. No wonder she wasn't invited into the love nest. Never in my life have I wished someone were dead more than I do now. She may wish the same thing when I wake them up.

My eyes go to the potted plant. I don't know why it's here, and I don't care. I flip it over, spilling the earth and green foliage smelling like lemons into the sand and fill the heavy pot with chilly ocean water.

"Rise and shine, bitches!" I heave the water and remnants of black dirt in Devin's and Nora's faces. I wait about three seconds to watch their shock and disorientation before running back to the water for pot number two. Without stopping to see how the lovebirds are doing, I dump this load in Dalma's face. She doesn't move. She may actually be dead. I laugh and drop the pot.

"What is your problem?" Nora screams at me, her voice cracking and hoarse. She drops to the sand to attend to Dalma.

I turn to Devin. "Good morning, Mr. Banks. It's a pleasure to see you again. I trust that your evening was lovely. Can I bring you an aspirin, or a vomit bag? Or a big plate of bullshit? Oh wait, I know, an STD-detection kit? And perhaps some fresh clothes and cash to pay your whores. You know, from one friend to the other."

"Nerissa... stop."

"Did you just call us whores? You little insignificant bitch!" Nora is wide awake now. I address her as she attends to Baldy.

"Good morning, Beauty." I look her up and down like they did me the other day and start to giggle. "Well, maybe not so much."

"How dare you? You'll be without a job by day's end. You're finished!"

"Aw, really? You mean I won't be able to wipe the asses of the rich and spoiled anymore? That's too bad. I'm going to miss it so much." I wipe away pretend tears.

"You're just jealous. You want to be us."

"Actually, Nora, you're the ones who are jealous and insecure. You're so uncomfortable in your own skin that you need to degrade everyone else just to feel good about yourself, just to feel entitled and better than. And you look for validation in the attention of boys. It's pathetic."

"Go drown yourself."

"Good one. Solid comeback." I turn my back to them and begin to stomp away, but then I decide to add one last thing. "If that insufferable bald bitch is dead, get her and her stench off the beach. Littering is strictly prohibited at Concordia on the Bay."

I run, and I'm headed straight toward Kendra and Gabriel, who are coming to see what the commotion is about. I charge past them, tears streaking my face. I'm going to be fired, probably exiled, and possibly sentenced to death. I may have compromised the entire breed—again. My sobs are uncontained as I crash through the doors. I rip off my uniform, including my shoes, before I even reach my locker.

The cold metal supports my shaking body. I'm wrecked, tired of fighting and pretending to be something I'm not. I pound my fists into the locker over and over. It's painfully satisfying.

A cool hand is on my shoulder. "Nerissa, stop. You're going to hurt yourself." I obey and slowly turn, expecting to see Kendra. Instead I'm met by a girl nearly a foot shorter than me with plain brown eyes and hair. I feel disoriented, but I know this girl. She must know me, too.

"Nerissa, it's me, Allison. We met the other day in the office."

I cock my head to one side like a dog trying to understand its owner.

She tries again. "I was training with Giovanni Lucas, in the office at the tech port on Friday."

"Oh, hi, Allison," I say flatly.

"Nerissa, are you okay?"

"Yes, of course. I'm fine."

She takes my hands and holds them up, examining my bloody knuckles, which are already forming bruises and swelling into balloons.

"Oh. No problem. They'll be back to normal in no time."

"Hmm, I don't know about that. Maybe. But this locker has seen its better days."

I survey my unfortunate and unwilling opponent. The white steel locker is riddled with deep dents and smeared with bright red blood. It will have to be replaced. I won this battle, I guess. Embarrassment creeps in, and I hang my head to avoid any more eye contact with Allison. But suddenly, I'm launched into a whole new panic as I stare down at my bare feet and remember I'm naked from head to toe.

Is it too late? Has she seen my feet? How will I explain my deformity? A horrible accident. No, a birth defect.

In a brief, fleeting, and insane second, I'm tempted to tell her everything. How liberating it would be to sit down, put up my feet and say, 'So Allison... me, Cassidy, Kendra, and your boss, Giovanni, we're all part of a hybrid program created by the FWG a long time ago. We're not entirely human. Actually, we're much better. But we're not supposed to exist—classified as too dangerous... and that was even *before* Wreckleaf! Yet here we are. And by the way, don't piss me off, because I can kill you in ten seconds. You won't even fight.'

Allison hands me a big white towel. "Here. Why don't you get dressed, and I'll help you get to wherever you're going."

"I'm going home."

"What about work?"

"I don't work here anymore."

"Then I'll help you get home."

I meet her eyes. "Allison, thank you for your kindness, but I'm fine. I'll get myself home."

Allison offers a tiny, warm smile, then turns and leaves the locker room. There is no way she didn't see my feet, but she said nothing. She seems so nice, but I don't trust her.

I get cleaned up, dressed, and wrap my aching hands in two luxurious white towels—a parting gift for my loyal service. Like an oversized urn, the tall white garbage can in the corner of the locker room becomes the final resting place for my uniform. I won't be needing this atrocity again. Relief spreads over me like a warm blanket as the burden of my position is lifted away. I'm going to go absorb what will undoubtedly be my last moments of so-called freedom.

I make fast work of weaving my way through the grand foyer, being careful not to draw any attention to myself. I've got to touch the doors one last time—my last time walking out as an employed slave.

As the doors part with my approach and the sun streams through the opulent entrance, an unfamiliar sentiment blazes inside me. Not in a million years would I have expected to feel anything but satisfaction as I left Concordia for the last time. Yet a bittersweet wave washes over me as I pass through the doors.

Tap. "Done."

The walk up the road helps. With every step farther away from the resort district, my body relaxes, and my mind slows. A little. I don't know how I'm going to handle what's to come or what I'll tell my mother. She'll be so disappointed, and not even her influence will save me. No one can fix this for me. But the FWG must understand that I acted alone. So only I should be punished, not the entire breed.

My best fate is to be exiled to some remote island where I must live and die alone. I may even welcome that, at least for a while.

I could be sentenced to death, made an extreme example to keep the rest of us compliant.

But worse would be imprisonment, where I never felt the ocean or the earth again or looked into the sky. How would I be treated? Would they experiment on me or abuse me in untold ways? There are worse things than death.

I approach a long stand of my favorite evergreens to the right. This stretch of road marks the halfway point between work and home. I breathe in the comforting scent of the grand cypress guardsmen and hold it deep inside so I'll always have it with me, wherever I may find myself.

The sound of a vehicle approaching from behind breaks my thoughts, and I move to the side. But I realize the rider has slowed down to pull over. I turn around and cannot believe what I'm seeing. Why on Earth would he have followed me? Maybe he's come to take me in, or better yet, put me out of my misery.

"What could you possibly want, Devin?" I yell as he comes to a stop in front of me.

"Would you like a ride home?"

"Are you crazy? Or wait, I know, I get on the board and you drive me to your father. He's an Officer, right?"

He ignores my question. “Come on, let me give you a ride.”

“Do you think I have no dignity whatsoever? Why would I get on that board with you?”

He takes off his helmet, and after spending the night on the beach, he looks the way he sounds—disheveled, sloppy, weak, and pathetic. Even still, his eyes engage me. “Because I’ve been an ass, and I’m trying to apologize. Please, let me give you a ride.”

I sure didn’t see that coming, *if* he’s telling the truth. I hold my ground. “First of all, I’m surprised you’re even able to stand up after the night you must have had. You look awful, and I wouldn’t trust you to drive ten feet in your state. And second, let me remind you, we’re not at the resort. I don’t have to play nice or pretend to like you anymore. You don’t have to pretend anymore, either.”

“If that was you playing nice, I’d hate to see not nice.”

“You have no idea.”

“No matter what front you put up, Nerissa, I know for a fact you do like me. You’re not that good an actress.”

“You know nothing. Besides, it’s over for me at Concordia. I walked out before I got kicked out... or escorted out... Threw that ridiculous uniform in the garbage. I should have burned it.”

“Oh, that’s too bad. I like that uniform.”

“I bet you do, just like all the other pigs at that place.”

“Ouch. Nerissa, get on. Let me take you home.”

“What don’t you get? This game is over. Everything is over, and everything is about to change. So just go away and leave me alone. I don’t need any more complications.”

“I’m just a complication to you?” he asks, clearly wounded by my word choice.

“Yes, that’s right, you and whatever you’re doing here is just another un-needed complication in an already overly complicated life!”

“Welcome to the club, Nerissa!”

"Oh, I should have known... You people have a club for that, too."

"Very funny."

"You have no idea. Look at yourself, you spoiled little rich boy, getting by on your looks and Mom and Dad's money. You really think you're some sort of victim? You take everything for granted and have no idea how good you've got it."

He pauses, apparently in deep thought. "Okay. I only have one thing left to say, and then I'll leave you alone."

"Please get on with it then..."

"Not that I owe you any explanation, but I'm very aware of and grateful for my circumstances. But things aren't always as they appear and not always as perfect as they may seem. More importantly, with all the finger-pointing you do, you ought to take a good long look in the mirror."

I look him square in the eyes. "That was more than one thing. Blah, blah, blah..." I pretend to yawn.

"You're such a bitch." He turns to leave. Finally.

Just before he goes, he looks back at me. "You don't deserve to know this, but I told Marcus and the management at Concordia that Nora and Dalma were drunk and harassing you when you tried to assist me this morning and that they threatened to hurt you if you didn't leave immediately. I explained how they fabricated an elaborate story against you to get you fired because they're jealous of how I feel for you and that I won't stand for such behavior. They were escorted off the property and banned from ever returning."

My mouth has fallen open, and I can't respond.

"I'm sure you're expected at work tomorrow morning as usual. You better dig that uniform out of the garbage." He puts on his helmet. "And just for the record, I wasn't pretending, either." He turns his board around and speeds away. I watch him go, unable to move, his words buzzing through me like an electrical current.

9 - GAME CHANGER

FRIDAY, JUNE 7TH

He better not be playing me.

The dream wakes me with a deep gasp for air. It's 6:45 a.m. I sit up and notice the soft light peeking through the window. I'm in my room, and I've never been happier to be waking up here. My bed is strewn with tangible memories—a hand-written diary I kept the first year after the Cooperative was formed; a bright green feather I found floating in the river; whiskers kept in a tiny wooden box, which had come from the old cat that lived with us on Albatross. No one ever figured out how the cat with different colored eyes we named Neptune came to the island in the first place. But we all became attached, and he was treated like a deity. When he died, I secretly pulled a few of his whiskers and have kept them like a magical relic ever since.

The events of yesterday were confusing, to say the least. As things unfolded, I wasn't sure I should believe what Devin said just before he sped away. I was on high alert the rest of the day, waiting for officials to knock on the door, or for my mother to come bursting into my room, demanding to know what happened and why she was confronted by the FWG. I imagined being hauled away, not having the chance to say goodbye to Kendra or Gabriel or the rest of the breed. I imagined never again smelling the forest where the desert plants meet the trees, or getting to swim in the river, or resting in the sand on Our Beach. I was tempted to go to one or the other or escape to Albatross. But in the end, I decided to wait it out in my turquoise room, surrounded by the only physical mementos beginning to represent who I am, and I found comfort in that decision.

The light faded into dusk, and when my mother arrived home, as she does every evening, I believed Devin had told me the truth. Later, with my mind a twisted web of dark images and harsh voices, sleep eventually came, and it came on strong. As I rise this morning, it doesn't appear I moved an inch during the night, everything exactly as I placed it around me.

I'm still here, and today is a blank canvas. I owe Devin Banks an apology and my gratitude. Dare I say I owe him my life?

When I arrive at work, no one asks where I went the day before. I'm sure Marcus instructed everyone to remain professional and keep things buttoned-up. He even issued me a new uniform, because the garbage in the locker room was long gone. He didn't ask any questions when I hinted it had been ruined in the altercation the day before.

Only Kendra wanted answers.

"What really happened? If Marcus thinks I'd believe a story of bullying and intimidation, he's pretty dim. Nobody could send you running like that, especially those two. When Gabriel and I got to those crazy bitches, one was screaming something about how you tried to kill them in their sleep."

I laughed and told Kendra I'd explain it all to her later but that we would be smart to shut up about it and pretend like nothing happened. I did want to know why she didn't come to my house or message me.

"Gabriel pulled me aside as those girls got carried out of here and said, 'You'll see Nerissa tomorrow.'"

I wish he would have let me know that.

Marcus flits past us in a hurry. I'll have to leave Kendra hanging. Devin has arrived and settles in his favorite spot. Marcus waves for us to follow him. Then he pours it on thick.

"Mr. Banks, it is so wonderful to see you this morning. I sincerely hope all is well and we can start fresh, sir."

Devin takes off his shirt before answering, causing Marcus to inhale sharply and sway ever so slightly. I'm embarrassed and look away.

"Marcus, my good man." Marcus stands a little taller in anticipation. "You have been nothing but wonderful and accommodating, and I am very grateful."

I think Marcus is about to cry.

"After the disreputable event that took place here yesterday, I needed to take a long, hard look at where and how I spend my holiday."

"Mr. Banks, I assure you those two women and their families will never step foot on Concordia property again. I can promise you that your privacy and comfort are our top priority."

"Thank you, Marcus. It was emotionally draining to have been part of such barbaric behavior. I must have a place that I can feel comfortable and unguarded. And you know I love your property, as does the entire Banks Family. And I would enjoy continuing my holiday here."

"Yes, of course, sir. Whatever you desire is my pleasure to provide. Please, let my attendants cater to your every need." Marcus is talking so fast I'm surprised Devin can understand him. "Kendra and Nerissa are at your disposal, and Jade will be here shortly. I will place an order for your breakfast... a grand feast of all our best dishes and beverages, on the house, of course. And I will order whatever spa treatments you desire for the beach cabana."

Devin nods in agreement. He's playing Marcus perfectly. And by the smile on his face, enjoying every second of it. "Yes, the food, the drinks... that all sounds perfect, but I don't require the spa treatments, and I desire only one last thing from you."

"Yes, anything you wish."

"I would like the exclusive company of one attendant for the week to come. That way, I'm happy, and the rest of your guests are accommodated as well."

Marcus gives a little shrug of acceptance before Devin is even finished with his request. "Of course, it is Concordia's pleasure to provide you with your own personal attendant for as long as you desire. Who would you like to choose?"

We all know the answer to that. Marcus is simply providing a formality to ensure Devin's comfort.

"I would like Nerissa to join me. I feel somewhat responsible for the traumatic situation she was put in yesterday. She will be working, but I want her to understand that she is greatly appreciated and deserves respect."

Well played, Devin Banks.

Marcus oozes adoration. He turns to me with steely eyes and speaks slow and deliberate, over-annunciating every word, as though I'm not bright enough to otherwise understand. His chin quivers as he speaks. "Nerissa, you have been chosen by one of our most valued and beloved guests. Treat him with the utmost care, detail, and respect. Whatever his wish... is your command. This is a huge opportunity for you. Do you understand?"

I simply give him the slightest bow and curtsy, which causes his eyes to flutter, then close. He inhales deeply and nods his head. He is done with me and gathers Kendra, who smiles so wide her cheeks must hurt, and the two leave.

I turn to Devin and am relieved to see he isn't grinning like some macho brat who just won an arm-wrestling contest and was awarded the keys to Daddy's yacht. On the contrary.

"Nerissa, I'm sorry."

"No, I'm the one who's sorry. I acted like a lunatic."

He doesn't disagree. "I also acted like a fool. Here I'm trying to get you to go out with me, and I show up drunk on the beach after an all-nighter with two girls you're not exactly fond of. That must have looked really bad."

"Yeah, it looked bad."

"I swear, nothing happened between me and those girls. They wanted it to, but nothing did. They mean nothing to me."

"Then why were you with them? You said they were lame and over the top and boring."

"Because I was feeling sorry for myself and wanted some attention."

"Or maybe you were trying to get *my* attention?"

"Maybe."

"Well you got it. But listen, you don't owe me an explanation. Or anything else, for that matter."

"Yes, I do," he says. "So, I apologize. And I promise to stop badgering you about going out with me." A few seconds tick by, then Devin juts out his hand. "My name is Devin Banks. It's a pleasure to meet you."

"What are you doing?"

"Starting over."

I put my hand in his. They look good together, our skin colors complementing each other. "It's a pleasure to meet you, Devin. My name is Nerissa."

"Nerissa what?"

"Nerissa John. So nice to make your acquaintance."

"The pleasure is all mine. Let the week commence."

SATURDAY, JUNE 15TH

This has been the best week I have ever spent at Concordia. Devin has been a total gentleman. He's treated me more like a guest than his personal attendant. Each morning, we begin with Devin's application, to keep up appearances. But by early afternoon, I'm lounging next to him, sharing lunch, the two of us laughing and talking like lifelong friends. Even Gabriel has been in on the fun during his daily visits. At Devin's prompting, Gabriel mixed me a virgin coconut daiquiri. Devin ordered the real thing and snuck me a few sips. I passed on his frequent offer to share his AQT.

"How can you not like this drink? It's so good."

"I don't know. It reminds me of something, but not in a good way. And it tastes bitter and fake to me. It's me, I know. Look around. Everyone else seems to love it."

"You don't know what you're missing."

Every day after lunch, Devin goes for a swim. He asked me to join him only once. I used the excuse of not wanting to mess with my uniform. When he returns, he writes in his journal, sometimes for hours. I never interrupt him. I feel the most uncomfortable during that time. He asks nothing of me, we don't even speak, and I'm not serving him in any way. Instead, I lounge next to him like a tourist. I feel so self-conscious, like I'm doing something wrong. Sometimes, I can sense the other attendants' eyes on me, perhaps wondering how this is considered work. Kendra silently taunts me every time she passes. But I never sway. I play the part Devin wants—a friend who's maybe more than just a friend. It's beginning to feel good and strangely natural. And I'm beginning to think I could get used to it.

As the second Saturday of the Season comes to an end and the tourists start to clear the beach for the evening, Devin doesn't budge. He writes feverishly, obsessed, lost in his own world, and he doesn't notice me watching him. He writes with an old lead pencil that's been chewed on and worn down to almost nothing. Every ten minutes or so, he pulls out a tiny metal sharpener and cranks the pencil inside just enough to make a skinny tip, allowing the shavings to float away in the breeze along the sand.

Marcus has come to check on us and without a word conveys I am to remain vigilant. I can actually see the relief and gratitude in his eyes. Thanks to my assignment to Devin, I have successfully secured one of the most treasured and valuable guests to Concordia. And that makes Marcus look good.

Somehow, another hour ticks by. The beach is empty but for us, and the sun begins its descent to our left. The air has cooled, and I breathe it in. My exaggerated exhale is what finally pulls Devin out of his hypnosis.

"I'm sorry, I didn't mean to interrupt you."

He looks around, as if coming out of a deep sleep, his eyes adjusting. "Nerissa, what time is it?"

"I'm not sure."

"Oh, it's so late. I'm sorry I've kept you so long."

"It's okay. I've enjoyed sitting here." I shiver absent-mindedly.

"You're cold. Here." He takes off his t-shirt and hands it to me. I don't protest. I unhook my wings and slide his light green shirt over me. It's warm and smells of fresh laundry and him.

He laughs softly. "Wow, I'm really sorry. I get lost when I write. Why didn't you say anything?"

"I didn't want to interrupt you. Besides, Marcus told me to stay."

"Okay, let's be clear about something. Marcus is not a part of this equation."

"But he's my manager, and this is my job... which you saved. Thank you again."

"That may be true, but I'm hoping it wasn't your job that kept you here this late."

"What are you writing?"

"Umm... it's complicated."

"Tell me about it. I want to know."

"I'll tell you this... writing is my escape. I spend more time in my made-up worlds than I do in my real life. And that's a conscious choice. It's the only thing that's truly mine. And I'm sorry, but I'm not sure I want to share that. We all have our scars, remember?"

"Yes, we do." I leave it at that. The silent blue of the Wreckleaf fields is suddenly in my mind—my only real escape and the one thing that feels like it's truly mine.

"Let's get out of here. I'm sure you've got to get home."

We gather our things and stroll toward the employee entrance. The darkening sky is streaked gray and orange with the last bits of sun visible off the cliffs just past the property line.

"Nice sunset, isn't it?" I try to fill the silence.

"It is nice, but that's no true sunset. It can't compare."

"How do you know? The only place you can see a true sunset is on Black Rock."

"Technically, I think it's visible from parts of Albatross as well. But no one can go out there."

"It's not." I catch myself. "I've heard that Black Rock blocks the sunset from Albatross also. Not that it matters," I add. "Like you said, no one can go there, but no one can go to Black Rock, either."

"That's not entirely accurate."

"What? C'mon, are you saying you've actually been on Black Rock?"

"I go there almost every Sunday to work odd jobs."

"Are you kidding me?"

"Nope. Officer Banks thinks it's good for me to be involved with the family business. Except I'm usually just his gopher when I'm there. Or I'm cleaning up the labs or production areas, which is pretty gross sometimes."

I've never known anyone who's been to Black Rock, and I'm intrigued. My face must show it, and Devin knows how to work me.

"Honestly, it's not that special out there, other than the amazing sunset views from the observation deck. I've had some pretty inspired writing sessions up there."

"Can you actually see the sun meet the water?"

"Yes. And when you're up there, the horizon looks like it goes on forever. It's crazy."

"You're so lucky. I wish I could see that."

He stops and faces me. The last traces of sunlight play off his check. I'm strangely aware of the cool ocean air blowing against my bare legs, and I shiver.

"Do you want to go with me?" he asks.

"What?"

"Would you like to go to Black Rock with me sometime to see the sunset?"

I can't respond right away for fear I misunderstood him and am about to make a fool of myself. "Are you serious? You can take me to Black Rock?"

"The one and only."

I still don't answer, and Devin knows this is the first time he's made me an offer I might not be able to refuse.

"Tell you what... let's both go change, and you think about it. I'll meet you out front, and you can let me know what you decide."

As I change, I realize things couldn't have been scripted finer. He'd better not be playing me. I want to trust him, but he's human. Yet this week has been really good. Maybe it should end on that note. I could just say no thanks, keep it professional, and walk away. I shove Devin's shirt at the top of my bag so I remember to give it back to him.

He's waiting for me at the front entrance. He doesn't see me coming right away, and I watch him pace back and forth, destroying his thumbnail with his teeth. When he notices me, his demeanor changes back to his cool, calm self. I tap the door. Seventy-six.

"So, Miss John, will you be accompanying me to Black Rock tomorrow?"

"Tomorrow? That soon? Oh, I'm sorry, I have a previous commitment tomorrow." I'm disappointed and relieved, my decision being made for me by my obligation to harvest.

"No problem. Another time."

"Promise?"

He smiles a sweet, genuine smile. "Absolutely. Okay, let me take you to your board."

"I walked here today."

"Why?"

"My board was in repair all week. I got it back the other day, but honestly, I prefer walking."

"Well, I guess that's your prerogative, but I'm going to take you home tonight. I've kept you here too late. Hop on."

I have no reason to protest, so I step up behind him. He swipes his CNI—a brilliant, lapis-blue quartz—and the board comes to life. "Hang on." I wrap my arms around his waist, and we're air-bound, floating through the parking lot and onto the open road.

The evening air is perfect. The ride is so smooth that I barely need to hold on, but I keep my arms wrapped around his waist. Between my fingers, I feel the soft cotton of a faded, red-striped shirt. At his waist, a brown leather belt, worn at the edges, holds up his jeans.

I give Devin directions to the Oval, and in what feels like a minute, we pull up to my house. It's lit up, and I can make out my mother's shape through the kitchen window.

"Thanks for the ride."

"Of course, any time." He pauses. "It was a really nice week with you. I would love to do it again if I can get Marcus to agree."

"Marcus is afraid of you, Devin. He'll agree to whatever you want."

"What do you want?" His eyes search mine.

"I also had a great week. I'd be happy to do it again. I just don't want to make anyone mad, you know?"

"I get it. But let's remember what Marcus always says... my wish is your command." He moves in close to me. "And I command you, Nerissa John, to join me again as my personal attendant for the upcoming week."

"Is that so?"

"Yes, but this time, I'm actually going to put you to work."

"Oh, really? Doing what? Rubbing your shoulders and fetching you lunch and AQT?"

"Yes, among other things."

"You know, I could provide you with endless writing material."

"I bet you could. I'd love to hear your story someday."

"You know what they say. Truth is stranger than fiction."

"Nerissa! You're late for dinner. Come inside." My mother cranes her head out the front door, staring us down. I'm left breathless on the heels of our flirtatious conversation.

"Uh-oh," Devin says. "Guess you better go."

"Yep." I pause for a second, my mind spinning. "What time are you going to Black Rock tomorrow?"

He tilts his head, eyes smiling. "Well, I don't have to work, so I was thinking late afternoon. In time to see the sunset."

"I've heard it's really dangerous to go to the Rock."

"It can be, but we do it all the time and have it down to a science. I thought you were busy."

"I'm going to send a couple messages. Some friends owe me some favors. I'd like to go, if you're still up for it."

He smiles wide, and I have my answer. "Shall I pick you up?"

"Umm... no, thanks. I need to get back to using my board. I'll meet you there. Where do I go?"

"Ride across the island through the luxury sector, then all the way down the back road as far as you can go. You'll run into a fence and won't be able to go any farther. That's where I'll meet you. Five-thirty sharp."

"I'll see you then."

"Excellent. Good night, Miss John."

"Good night, Mr. Banks."

As he rides away, I juggle excitement with regret, then caution with something else—some other unfamiliar feeling.

I'm brought back to reality when my mother greets me in the kitchen. "What do you think you're doing?"

"Sorry I'm late. Marcus had me stay afterhours with one of the guests."

"The one who brought you home?"

"Yes. His name is Devin Banks."

"Why did he need to bring you home? I thought your board was fixed."

"It's still not right. I had to walk to work today," I lie with ease. "Devin was just being nice."

"Be careful, Nerissa. Trust no one, particularly a human male. And especially the son of an Officer. You're toying with all of our safety."

"It was just a ride. Don't worry, I would never compromise the breed."

She looks at me and bites her tongue. Good thing she didn't find out about Nora and Dalma.

After dinner, I clean up the kitchen and kiss my mother before I lock myself in my room for the night. I'm glad she didn't remind me about my harvest duties tomorrow with Kendra.

When I clean out my bag, I realize I forgot to return Devin's shirt. I convince myself I'm uncomfortable in my own and change into his. It smells like him.

I send a couple messages, and within an hour, I have Cassidy covering for me tomorrow. I'm not going to tell Kendra ahead of time. Cassidy will just meet her, and I'll tell her about everything later. She'll understand.

A while later, I curl up under the covers, and sleep captures me. Images from the week float inside the darkness. It's like watching a movie, like everything that happened this week happened to someone else. Yet I can feel all the moments as they drift into view. I can hear them, smell them, and touch them... touch him.

Deeper and deeper, I fade...

'Trust no one, Nerissa... especially the son of an Officer.'

Wait... I sit up. I don't remember telling her he's the son of an Officer.

10 – PROMISE DELIVERED

SUNDAY, JUNE 16TH

He has entered where no one has ever been allowed.

Without the disruption of any bad dreams, I sleep through the night like a baby. I wake to an unseasonable storm.

My mother is out of the house early. I find her note on the kitchen counter.

Nerissa, breakfast is in the fridge.
Be careful at harvest today. The weather is bad.
I'll be home late. I'm meeting Giovanni for dinner.
Please message us when you and Kendra get home.

Mom

I crumple up the note. Oops, I didn't see that, Mother. Are you sure you left a note?

Stuck in the house, I fill my day reading, drawing, and pacing. I can't imagine how cranky the tourists are, their precious suntans fading by the hour. No golf, no beach, no boating? Pity.

I absentmindedly stuff my face with junk food. By afternoon, I feel sick and even more anxious about meeting

Devin. Despite the weather, he hasn't cancelled. I get myself ready and walk out the door on schedule.

With a slick orange poncho and shin-high rubber boots, I ride through the pouring rain. Today, I'm thankful for my board. The base is at the farthest western point of the island, and it would be a long and torturous walk.

I ride out of the Oval and turn left onto the main road. The view is sweeping and impressive. The waves past the marina are so big, I can see them from here, running diagonally in both directions. The absurd, theatrical yachts, which look like toys from here, will take a beating today. But they'll be back to new and sparkly-clean in no time.

Down the road through the local community, I cross a beautiful old bridge that marks the entrance into the opulence of the northwest side. The road to my right leads down to the resort district on the north shore and the boutiques, restaurants, galleries, and clubs.

Ahead, the palm-lined road opens into a maze of smaller streets and private drives—one massive and extravagant property after another. The gleaming white Panacean homes look like luxury hotels. Here, the wealthiest reside—a few year-round, but most just for the Season. It seems like an incredible waste of space and money to me. Whatever.

The cobblestone streets are empty. I'm the only idiot out today. But as I float past mansion after mansion, I can't help but feel like I'm being watched. Unless I'm here to give someone a massage or clean a house, a local person, even one like me, just doesn't belong. I'm happy to make one final turn and finish my tour of this gluttonous exhibition.

Out of the manicured neighborhoods and back onto the open road, the wind and rain smack me in the face. The peak of Apollo stretches up and out to my left, dark and formidable, guarding over the business of the FWG. I ride forever on this deserted, lonely road before I coast up one last hill, round a curve, and finally reach a gate connected to a tall, impenetrable fence. Bold red letters on a white metal sign confront me. The rain is blinding, pelting me sideways. But the sign is perfectly clear:

KEEP OUT!
NO TRESPASSING!
Violators will be prosecuted.
These premises under surveillance and guarded by security animal.

Security animal. Not guard dog. I wonder what kind of furry friend the FWG has designed to defend their temple. I hope I don't find out.

Devin pops up behind me.

"Hi! You made it."

"Oh! You scared me. I didn't hear you coming."

"Sorry, loud rain."

"Yeah, it's too bad about this weather. Guess we'll have to do it another time."

"No, we're going."

"Devin, it's dangerous enough on the water on a good day, but in a storm like this? Deadly. And we'll never even see the sunset."

"It's supposed to clear soon. Besides, we can navigate that channel rain or shine. It may not be ideal, but don't be scared. You'll be safe."

Yeah, I wasn't worried about myself.

Devin swipes his CNI and punches a code into a keypad at the gate. A loud buzz followed by a double click cues him to push down the handle. It swings open.

"Ladies first." He gestures forward.

"Umm... what about the security animal?" I make quotation marks with my fingers.

"Don't worry. They knew I was coming. It's gone."

"It?"

"Yeah, It."

Great. I shift my gaze past the gate and walk inside. "It's beautiful!" I yell above the rain. "Not at all what I expected."

"What were you expecting?"

"I'm not sure, but not this."

Past the gate stand a dozen red-roofed cottages along tidy, landscaped walkways. Everything is sheltered by giant, ancient trees.

"Where is everyone?" I ask.

"There's never many people here on the weekends. Come on." He reaches out, and I take his hand like we've been doing it forever. Our wet fingers slide together and fit perfectly against each other. Even in the cold rain, a warm wave rises inside me.

We walk along a gravel path to a large and halting limestone boulder. Devin guides me through a narrow corridor in the rock. Down hard-hewn and challenging steps, lower and lower we go. I should be watching where I'm going, but instead, I'm staring at his back—his sun-bleached curls popping out from under his hood; his tall, muscular body beneath his dark-green poncho. I feel safe holding his hand while he leads me on this descent into the unknown.

It seems the rough, slippery stairs will never end when we clear a sharp turn and reach the bottom. Across the channel in front of us, Black Rock rises out of the ocean, and I'm hit with its energy. Dark, heavy, and loud, it declares its impenetrable, age-old tyranny over everything in its presence.

Just before the water's edge stands a long, gray, windowless building. At one end, a huge steel pipe juts out over the water and disappears into a cover of fog.

"What's that?"

"That's the cargo tube. It's how we get things on and off the Rock."

"Well, can we just take the tube instead of a boat? It seems safer."

He smiles. "It's not. The tubes never survive from one Season to the next. It's too far across, the conditions too unstable. They're working on alternatives, but for now, the tube is just for stuff."

"What about a chopper?"

"Too dangerous."

At the front end of the building, a door opens, and a tall man dressed in uniform steps out. He seems disturbed by the sight of me, but as he confirms who I'm with, his face softens.

"Devin," he yells. "Get inside."

We clear the now level but rocky ground in front of us and make our way toward the unwelcoming building and its occupant. "Didn't you say they were expecting us?" I asked.

"I said they were expecting me. But don't worry, my father is Officer William Banks. I have privileges."

I stop walking.

"It's okay, I promise. C'mon, we've come so far, we can't turn back now. Trust me, you won't regret it."

I have a bad feeling, but I force myself to ignore it.

Inside, I expect to be greeted with cold, dark, and depressing, but instead, we find ourselves in a peaceful room with a green velvet couch and an antique mahogany desk. Soft piano music plays in the background, and a fireplace offers salvation. Devin takes off his poncho and drapes it over a chair in front of the fire. I do the same. Atop the mantle, and all around the room, are plants. A lot of them. I now see the solar tubes running up through the roof, which I couldn't see outside. On a twisted, knotty branch suspended from the ceiling perches a big, beautiful bird with electric-blue plumage. Just as I'm trying to decide whether or not the bird is real, it turns to us and says, "Welcome back, Devin. It's good to see you again."

My mouth drops open.

"Hi, Hermes. Good to see you again, too." Devin tips an invisible hat at the bird, who curtseys in response.

"Who's your friend?" asks Hermes with perfect annunciation.

"This is Nerissa."

"Nice to meet you." He takes a slice of mango from the uniformed man.

"That's remarkable!" I squeal.

"He's pretty special," the man agrees. "But most of what Hermes says is simple imitation."

"It's still amazing."

"I don't know," Devin adds. "I've heard Hermes say some pretty intelligent stuff before... definitely not imitation."

"I'm Emmanuelle." The man says, extending a hand toward me.

I offer a firm but friendly shake. "I'm Nerissa. Nice to meet you."

"So, we're taking a ride over to Black Rock today?"

"Only if it's safe. This weather is pretty bad."

"I assured her it's safe," Devin interjects, "and this weather is supposed to pass soon anyway."

"Yeah, we should wait it out a little while," Emmanuelle suggests.

"Just a bit. We're hoping to see the sunset. And we won't be too long after that. I don't want my father coming out here looking for me."

"Sorry, kid. He's already on the Rock." Devin sucks in a breath, then sighs. "And I have to be honest," Emmanuelle continues, "unless he knows about this little Beauty, which I didn't, thank you very much for the surprise... he's not going to be too happy you brought a visitor without prior clearance. This better not get me in trouble."

"Relax, Manny, my man. Everything will be fine."

We spend the next fifteen minutes talking with Hermes and feeding him mango. I learn that Hermes is a cross between a blue macaw and a once-believed extinct species of the elephant bird. He's highly intelligent, and I'm in awe.

Manny's collection of plants is just as impressive. He has healing and medicinal plants from across the island—herbs, succulents, wildflowers, and cacti. He even has some mosses, lichen, and predatory species. But the aquatic garden takes the prize, even without Wreckleaf; its growing conditions cannot be replicated, so it can't ever be manipulated or reproduced. I suppose if it could, I wouldn't be standing here. I wouldn't be needed, and if I'm being honest with myself... I wouldn't be alive.

As I explore, Manny and Devin talk and laugh, slapping each other on the back. They've known each other a long time, part of the FWG family.

Absorbed in the garden, settling on a scaly, lichen-covered rock in a damp terrarium, I feel someone standing behind me. I smile, glad to show Devin some of these valuable plants.

"Beautiful, isn't it?" a breathy voice whispers in my ear. I spin to find myself eye to eye with Emmanuelle, our faces inches apart.

"Yes, it is," I agree. He's backed me into the table.

"I've spent many, many hours caring for these creations, loving them, and tending to their every demand. I'm familiar with *all* the island's flora and fauna. But as you may know, some cannot be kept by artificial means. Not yet, anyway."

I clear my throat. "Well, wonderful job... they're all beautiful. Everything on the island is."

"Yes. All the island's bounty is beautiful." He stretches out the word 'beautiful' too long and stares at me with such intensity, he looks like he might explode or run out of air.

Before he pops, I force an awkward move and duck to the right. Devin looks up from Hermes as I walk toward him.

"Well, shall we give it a try? The clock is ticking."

"Yes, let's go."

"That's the spirit. We'll be fine."

Manny inspects the plants as though he's making sure I haven't damaged any of them. He's not exactly the light-hearted jokester I first made him out to be.

Devin collects our ponchos. Manny grabs a loaded key ring from his top desk drawer. He locks the front door we came in from the inside, pulling on it to double- then triple-check that it's locked tight.

"Aren't you forgetting something?" Devin asks him.

"All clear, Hermes?"

"All clear," the bird responds. "Time to amp it up."

Manny clears his throat. "Let's go."

"Nerissa, look..." Devin points to one of the solar tubes. It's lit up with sunlight. The storm is over.

We join Manny behind his desk. Among what must be hundreds, he reaches for one particular book high on a shelf. There, he presses something and triggers a low hum inside the wall. The shelf moves back and away from us, then to the right, disappearing behind the wall from which it separated.

Manny proceeds and disappears into the dark void. Devin flanks me and slides his hand into mine, lacing our fingers together again, and guides me into the darkness. As soon as we step over the threshold, the bookshelf slides back into place, sealing us into the black room with one last low hum and click.

Overhead, a blinding florescent light comes to life, revealing the tiny space we've come to occupy. This sealed room has no windows. There is no obvious door, other than the one we entered. My guess is there's at least one other, but I can't see where. The floor is a dull, hard concrete. The cold walls around us are some kind of metal, painted a matte black. I hear nothing but our breathing.

"Nerissa, repeat after me..." Manny breaks the silence with a flat voice.

"No, this is not necessary," Devin objects.

"It's procedure. I have to."

"But she lives here, Manny. She's cool."

"Standard procedure."

I grab Devin's arm. "What's going on?"

He steps toward the uniformed official, gets right in his face, and speaks slowly. "Manny, Nerissa is cool, trust me. We're here to see the sunset, that's it. I promise. So let's drop the standard protocol crap, okay?"

"All due respect, Devin." Manny speaks just as slow and with the same deliberate intensity. "I do trust you, and I know exactly who this young lady is." He shoots me a look. "But despite how *cool* Miss Nerissa John may be, I have a job which requires me to follow certain rules."

"Hey!" I say. "First of all, stop talking about me as if I'm not here. And second, I don't recall telling you my last name."

Devin looks at me, perplexed, and joins me in waiting for Manny's answer.

"Just doing my job, Doll."

That catches me off-guard. "And what exactly is your job?" I stammer.

"Emmanuel MacNamire, Senior Advising Bio-Horticulturist and First Officer of Security at Panacea Base One, to be exact. And it is my job to be well informed."

Great.

"Whatever I need to do, let's get on with it." I put my hand on Devin's arm. "Listen, I'm okay with the procedure. It's no big deal, right?"

"Thank you, Miss John. You obviously know how to play well with others."

"You're welcome, Mr. MacNamire. But please, call me Nerissa."

"Make it quick, Manny. I don't want to miss the sunset," Devin demands. "It's the whole reason we're here, remember?"

Officer MacNamire turns toward me. "Repeat after me. I, Nerissa John, understand that I am entering a government-protected facility."

I repeat the words, pausing before my last name.

"Under this declaration and the witnesses before me, I do solemnly swear to never communicate in any way the things I may see or hear at this or any other government facility on the islands of Panacea and/or Black Rock. I understand that should I breach this declaration, any communication is punishable to the fullest extent of the law, without exception."

No problem. You're dealing with a master.

As soon as the last words leave my lips, Manny waves his mossy-agate CNI in front of a small square on the wall behind him. As the wall swings away, the silent little room comes to life with the sound of lapping water and the smell of the sea. Beyond this holding room, in what is the back half of the long steel structure, appears a large open boathouse. Three identical FWG boats are docked in the dark water, with slips beyond for two additional craft. Just as in the previous rooms, this space has no windows and no discernible exit.

Manny jumps out onto a narrow pier, past the two boats closest to us, and stops at the farthest, which is numbered three, hops on, and disappears below deck.

Devin takes my hand. "Sorry for all that. It's so unnecessary and rude. Manny likes to puff up his chest sometimes."

"What exactly is the FWG so worried about me seeing? If it's so top-secret, why are we even allowed out here?"

"Yeah, that's exactly the point. There's nothing to see. The FWG works with Bio-Genesis, and they develop all the proprietary blends for the spas and restaurants and boutiques. They don't want anybody stealing their formulas."

"Oh! Well, the way the tourists practically swim in the stuff I spray on them, I guess I get it. I know they can buy the stuff to use on the island, but why don't they just charge more and let them take it home?"

"Because once again, they're afraid someone will steal the formulas. Besides, it keeps people coming back."

"The island is what keeps them coming back, not the stuff."

"It's both, trust me."

From some unseen place, Manny has triggered a loud metallic groan, and the wall to our right slides back, aligning with the front half of the structure. As the boathouse opens, Black Rock rises like a monolith before us, the dark, choppy water in the channel daring to be crossed. I suddenly feel small. And vulnerable.

"Impressive, isn't it?"

"It sure is."

"Come on, time to go."

We board.

"Why are the boats so small?" I ask Devin.

"They're designed specifically for this job. They're powerful and agile. A bigger boat wouldn't stand a chance against the channel, or any of these waters. There's countless wrecks along all the coasts."

"Yeah, I thought I heard something about that..."

Manny takes the controls, and we're quickly out of the boathouse and into the channel between Panacea and Black Rock, the open ocean on either side. I immediately feel the sharp, frenetic pull of the currents, threatening to either suck us out of the channel or capsize us.

It takes bravery to navigate this course. Either that, or stupidity. Because, should we capsize, these two sailors would be history. Maybe that's why they didn't bother to put on life vests—they know it wouldn't do them any good, even though they made me put one on, which ironically would be the exact thing to kill me before I could get it off.

Devin and Manny make a good team. They man the boat with authority as we forge ahead. Devin assures me this is the hardest part and that the ride back is much less perilous. Usually.

"All right, kids, here comes a big one," Manny shouts. "Hang on tight!"

Next to me, Devin reaches out to grip a metal bar running along the portside hull, leaning close with his arms on either side of me. The bar is designed exactly for this—holding on when the boat gets tossed about. An identical bar lines the starboard side. Just as I notice it, Devin reaches underneath the bar and grabs a thick yellow strap. He wastes no time wrapping it around my waist and clipping it back onto the bar. That's it, I'm trapped.

A giant wave hits us, and the boat lifts and tilts sideways. I'm breathless and soaked, my poncho offering nothing more than bright color against the dark, bleak background.

"Are you okay?" Devin searches my startled face. I wipe the saltwater out of my eyes and catch my breath. "Nerissa?"

"Wow! I wasn't expecting that, but yeah, I'm fine. That was, umm... fun."

He laughs.

"Why didn't you strap yourself in? You could have been thrown off."

"This ain't my first rodeo."

"What?"

He looks embarrassed. "Nothing. Remember, I've done this a thousand times. Don't worry, we'll be there soon."

The rest of the ride is better. We're hit with a few more big waves but none like the first few. Devin disappears for a minute and returns with a dry towel. I reach for it, but instead, he wraps it around my shoulders and frees my hair from beneath it. He doesn't speak. I watch his hands move to my waist and release the clip anchoring me to the bar. I try to unwrap the yellow strap myself, but he guides my hands to my sides and silently insists on doing it for me. He pulls me forward then back, freeing me from my bonds. He's strong but careful, his light-brown skin wet with the sea.

"You're shivering," he says.

"I am?"

He finishes unraveling me and pulls off his poncho. When he notices me watching his every move, a smile lifts his eyes. "Take off your poncho." I do as he says. "Now come here." He pulls me toward him and wraps his arms around me. He's a fortress. We're both wet, but he's warm and comforting, and I allow myself to accept his safeguard. It's nice in this place. I could get used to it here.

"Devin, we're pulling in," Manny shouts. "Watch the bow. We're moving fast."

We propel into the open slip. Two boats are moored in the spots closest to the rocky shore.

Devin and Manny make easy work of docking us, and before I can process everything that's just happened, Devin helps me off the boat.

"Thanks, Manny. Great ride."

"No problem, Devin. I'll be waiting for you."

"This way, my lady. We have some ground to cover, and we'll have to be speedy. Look." Devin points at the sky and the sun dipping behind the tree line to my left.

"Lead the way, sir."

We run down the dock, crossing a small wooden bridge onto a dark and jagged shoreline. There's only one way to go—up a steep metal staircase, which is barely noticeable under the cover of thick, thorny orange vines exploding with purple flowers. We climb and climb. When we arrive at the top, we're both breathing heavy but keep moving. Up here, there are some similarities to Panacea and Albatross—a few cacti, some bristly shrubs, and desert evergreens. But there are no regular trees and very little color, except for the vine that seems to grow everywhere. The ground is dense and dark. Volcanic. Besides the mystery surrounding it, I can see why this island is called Black Rock.

We wind our way through a maze of level walkways carved into the rock. When we finally turn a last corner before reaching the building, I stop to take it in.

It's enormous, made of white steel and glass, and looks incredibly out of place on the dark and heavy landscape. It's too sterile, too bright, and too damn perfect. At the top of the entrance are two names:

First World Government of Panacea Island
Bio-Genesis Wave Technologies

Why put the name on the door when the only people to ever see this place are those who built it and those who work here? It's the only building on the entire Rock. They know where they are.

We're also greeted by a sign like the one at the base entrance. Thankfully, this one doesn't promise to have some manufactured security creature threaten our lives upon arrival. How thoughtful. But we are being watched.

We step up to the front entrance, and Devin swipes his CNI over a panel flanking the door. "Devin Banks."

"Hello, Devin." A woman's voice surrounds us.

"Hi, Clarice."

"Who do you have with you, Devin?"

"This is Nerissa John, Clarice. Officer MacNamire has cleared her. Can you please let us in? We want to see the sunset."

Silence. We wait. It's maybe thirty seconds, but it feels like an eternity.

A buzzer sounds, and Devin grabs my hand. We fly through the entrance and turn left. We whip past an interior room with a small window, where a brunette woman watches us speed by. I assume this is Clarice.

Down a sterile white corridor with a dozen or more doors, we turn right, then pass through another. Again, a right turn, then a left. Through another identical hallway, we pass two sets of elevators, but Devin doesn't pause at either. Past numerous doors, we come to an abrupt stop at a third elevator. As Devin skids to a halt, he presses the up button.

The doors glide open, and once inside, Devin waves his CNI in front of the receptor. "Devin Banks."

"Hello, Devin. Where may I take you?" a beautiful, androgynous voice asks.

"Top floor, please. Observation deck."

"My pleasure. One moment, please."

Before I even blink, we've arrived, and the doors open smoothly, delivering us onto the observation deck. The fresh sea air rushes into the elevator.

We burst onto the deck, and I follow Devin to the waist-high stone wall facing the water. I'm breathless and speechless, in part because of our journey getting here but also because of what I'm seeing.

The clouds have lifted in the western sky, only a few floating on the fringes of the horizon, their soft transparent edges a clear yellow-orange. The sea is endless, the sun glittering on the waves as it descends. We've made it just in time, and I know I'm witnessing something magical that many never have the chance to see.

We pause side by side in silence and stare at the beauty before us. My breath and heart are still fast, but now for different reasons.

The wind coming off the ocean and up the cliff swirls all around us and sends my hair into a spiral flutter. We both laugh softly. But as the breeze carries Devin's now familiar scent toward my face, my giggle is replaced by a sudden and overpowering sense of urgency.

"So, what do you think?"

"It's amazing, just like you said. Even better."

"It certainly is." His brown gaze fuses onto mine.

Suddenly, there's nothing else. No sea, no sky, no sunset, no concrete beneath my feet. I have no body. There's just him and his eyes, looking past the place where my own can see. He has entered where no one has ever been allowed, his light filling the darkness of that lonely hollow space and branding himself deep inside.

Unexpected tears ride down my cheeks. I catch a flash of the barely-there sun sparkling off my own face before Devin leans forward and captures it with his lips. He tilts his head, his mouth centimeters from mine. I try to object, but I can't. A bigger part of me wants this more than I want oxygen, or sunshine, or even water.

"Nerissa..." he whispers, and I can taste his sweet breath. He puts his hand on the back of my head, spreads his fingers, and pulls my face to his. I don't stop him.

One... our lips meet, just barely. He's gentle and welcoming. I'm paralyzed as the world explodes behind my eyes. I taste my fallen tears on him just before his lips envelope mine. The kiss grows deeper, and he takes a sharp inhale as the rush of it overwhelms his senses.

Two... he digs in, powerless.

Three... I clutch at his shoulders, hungry for more.

Four... a small moan escapes him. In this frozen moment, his soul speaks in its entirety, and I know from this point forward, things can never be the same.

Five... it's now or never. I must stop or risk the consequences, and I'm torn between desire and intellect—a choice I've never had to make.

With an effort testing every fiber of my being, I pull myself back. A vacuum of air rushes in to fill the sudden space between us. Devin's eyes are unfocused, his mouth open, seemingly lost in a wild, breathless confusion. Or have I waited too long?

But he suddenly snaps back into focus. "What's wrong? Are you okay?"

"Are *you* okay?" I ask.

"Of course. What's wrong?"

"Nothing. Everything is right."

"Then..." He steps toward me, hunger in his eyes, and tries to continue our kiss.

I step back. He frowns and sighs.

"I just... I can't. I mean, I never..." I fumble in embarrassment, searching for an explanation. "I'm sorry, Devin.

I'm just not very experienced, and that was really intense." I hang my head, mortified by my own words.

"Hey," he whispers, his fingers at my chin, encouraging me to lift my head. I comply. And there he is again—beautiful, perfect, smiling that smile. "It's okay."

I try to breathe.

"Really, it's okay."

I exhale relief and smile back at him. We both lean in, and our foreheads meet. His fingers find mine again, and they lace together without effort. We stay here, swaying in sync to a silent but mutual melody.

"Are you telling me that was your first kiss, Nerissa John? Because if it was... wow."

I step back, my face burning with embarrassment. He's right in a way. I've never kissed anyone like this by choice. I've never wanted to. And I've never felt the way I did when our lips met. I never knew I would or even could. Of course I've kissed a man before, but it was with very different intentions and very different results.

So do I lie and say yes, it's the first time? Or do I say no, I've kissed someone before, but lie about the details? Either way, I'm a liar. And I hate myself for it. My pause grows, and one uncomfortable second ticks into the next. I can't stand it any longer, and I'm about to choose my lie.

"Never mind," Devin says. "I'm just kidding around. Forget it. It's not important. Sorry."

I can't seem to meet his gaze, looking everywhere but directly at him.

"It's okay, really," he reassures me. "Come on. We should get going before my father comes looking for me."

I finally settle back on his beautiful face. That's it. It's over. At least for now. He's his easy, breezy self again and just shakes off the awkward moment. He squeezes my hand, and we return to the elevator.

"Thank you for bringing me here."

"My pleasure. I'm so glad the weather cooperated for us. And thank you for joining me, because *that* was the best sunset ever."

I smile up at him, but my mind is a twisted mess.

The elevator doors close behind us. "Devin Banks."

The operating voice greets us again. "Welcome, Devin. Where can I take you?"

"Main level, please."

"Wait..." I interrupt.

"Hold, please." The elevator waits.

"You work here, right? Show me."

"Oh, it's nothing glamorous. Like I said, I'm mostly a servant for my father and his men."

But I want to make sure he knows how much I appreciate him bringing me here, and I don't want to end with the awkward moment on the deck. "I want to see. Show me around. I'm sworn in, remember? I promise not to take any notes or try to steal any formulas."

"Level two, please, Operator."

"My pleasure."

When the doors open, we step out into a sterile and deserted hallway. In front of us, a wall of glass reveals a warehouse-sized room with a dozen or more complex assembly lines. I instantly recognize the white and gold tubes being filled by the machines closest to us. The glistening lotion being pumped out in perfect increments is the Panacea Goddess sun care line—a less potent version of what I apply at the beach.

Next to that, another line squeezes a dark, clay-like mixture into cobalt-blue tubs. Another fills bottles with a buttery amber liquid, and yet another churns a soft-green serum into tiny, brown glass vials. My mother told me this also contains Wreckleaf. It costs more for that little bottle of serum than some people earn in a week.

"Kind of cool, isn't it?"

"Yes. Why is it running when no one's here?"

Devin seems amused by my question. "These machines are one-hundred-percent self-sufficient and can run all day, any day. But it's the beginning and end of the Season when they run almost non-stop. The tourists buy the stuff like their lives depend on it."

"At the end of the Season, too? I thought they weren't allowed to take it home with them."

"They're not. But come mid to late August, they start swimming in the stuff before they have to go all winter without it. One year, a housekeeper found a woman who had drowned in a bathtub she filled with..." He searches the assembly room, then points at the thick clay concoction going into the blue tubs "That one."

"No way. You're making that up."

"I swear, it's true. We had to put a warning label on all the products after that."

"That says what?"

"*'For external application only. Not intended for bathing, soaking, or ingestion'*," he recites.

"Ingestion? Really? People try to drink it?"

He shrugs. "I've heard a lot of stories."

"That is so pathetic."

"That's why we came out with the energy drink, so people could safely ingest some of the same stuff that goes into the beauty products."

"The energy drink?"

"Yeah, you know, the Aqua Tonic. AQT."

"Oh, your new favorite drink."

"Yep. As a matter of fact, I could use one right now. You should give it another try. It's really good and really good for you."

"No, thanks. I don't like it. But I do love the raw green smoothie at Concordia. The Island Green Infusion. All the resorts have one of their own. There's really nothing healthier. You should try that instead."

"Except AQT has added sea minerals that balance electrolytes and a natural stimulant that speeds up metabolism and aids in rapid cellular renewal. It's completely different, and the tourists can't get enough of it."

"Well, aren't you the well-rehearsed advertisement?"

He smiles. "Yes, Officer Banks would be proud."

"I know everybody seems to love it, but—"

"Yes, and it's all natural."

"So is caffeine, but too much of that isn't good, either."

"My father assembled the top experts from Bio-Gen to work with the government on this project."

"This is your father's project?"

"Yeah. He's into all sorts of things. They spent almost two years developing AQT. There's been a lot of research and money put into it. Trust me, the FWG knows what they're doing. We're seeing amazing side effects. I mean... just look at me!" He flashes his teeth and poses, his fingers spread around his face.

My eyebrows raise, and I play along, looking him up and down. "Pretty impressive, I must agree. But I'm sure the AQT had nothing to do with it."

I can sense he wants to lean over and kiss me again, but he stops himself. "Come on, I'll show you more."

We stroll down the corridor.

"That must have been the most expensive bath anyone has ever taken."

He clears his throat to hold back laughter. "She paid the ultimate price, didn't she?"

"The price of vanity. Someone needs to teach these people to be happy with what they've got."

"That's easy for you to say. Look at you, you're perfect. And did I mention those eyes? What's up with those? It doesn't really seem fair."

I know he's trying to be nice, but it's making me uncomfortable. I don't want this to be about my looks. Not this. Not with him.

"The grass is always greener on the other side, Devin."

I wait for his rebuttal, but instead, we turn a corner and stop. We're facing another glass wall fronting an even bigger assembly room.

"I present you with Aqua Tonic, health and happiness in a bottle."

I take in the huge space, and I'm amazed by the incredible volume of product being churned out. Some of the machines in this room are two stories tall and half as wide. Each has its job—one to line up the blue-green bottles, one to fill them, the next to put on the lids, the one after to seal them. Those move across a connecting conveyer belt to have labels applied, then on to be packed in their cases. After that, I can't see where the boxes travel next.

I look at Devin. His fingertips rest on the glass, his eyes wide. "What's wrong with you?" I ask.

"I've got to get some. Come on." He walks back around the corner from where we came and stops at a white steel door. He uses the crystal swipe, then a message displays on the panel, asking for a six-digit code.

"That's an awful lot of security for a drink, isn't it?"

"It's to prevent contamination." The door clicks, and he swings it open.

"Then maybe we shouldn't go in."

"I've got clearance. It wouldn't have let me in otherwise. I do it all the time."

"But what about me?"

"Come on, it's fine."

We pass through the thick doorway, and the sound inside is unbearable. The intensity sends vibrations up my legs and into my chest. As the bottles move along the belts, they tap lightly against each other. One on one, it would be a pleasant, solitary chime of glass on glass. But together, the tapping of thousands of bottles along their journey produces an ear-piercing, mind-numbing cacophony. I've inherited our breed's increased sensitivity to sound, which includes a rudimentary ability to echo-locate. I can't stand being in here.

I grab Devin's arm and plead with him, "Devin, it's so loud. Let's go back!"

But he signals for me to follow him, and deeper into the assembly room we go. We pass machine after machine. I have to keep my hands over my ears. We turn a corner at the back end of the giant room and follow what appears to be the last conveyer belt to where it splits into two. To the right, the cases of finished product disappear under a black rubber flap into the unknown bowels of the labs. To the left, the belt is empty.

"What are we doing!?" I yell.

"Hang on. Just four more minutes!"

I don't know what we're waiting for, but it doesn't appear as though I have a choice, so I take the opportunity to look around. It's funny, the way you can have an idea of something in your imagination, and then it's so different in real life.

"All right, we're in business." Coming toward us four long minutes later, split off from the main belt, is a single case of finished Aqua Tonic. It glides past us and disappears under another heavy rubber flap covering an opening to the far side of its twin. A door next to it reads, 'Quality Control' over a sliver of a window.

Devin opens the door, this time without any security requests, closes it behind us, and flips on a light to illuminate a closet-sized room with a second door on the back wall. Coming from the glaring, thundering, and cavernous assembly room, this room makes me feel like I'm in hole— or a coffin. It's much quieter in here, the overbearing noise somehow shut out. But my ears are ringing; I hope I haven't damaged them.

"May I offer you a refreshment?" Devin looks pale and sweaty. The noise must have gotten to him, too. He grabs the case of AQT and tears it open. "It's not cold, but it'll do the job." He pulls out two bottles and cracks open the tops, then chugs down a full bottle without stopping. "Ah... that's better."

"What the hell, Devin? Thirsty?"

"I just wanted to grab a couple bottles."

"Yeah, okay... but why did we have to wait for it? Why couldn't we just grab them from the other line and leave? It was so loud, I'm surprised I didn't go deaf in there."

"I can't just take AQT off the main line. It's really dangerous to put your hands near the belts, and it's not allowed. The line spits out one case every hour for quality control. Someone needs to inspect it. We got here at just the right moment."

"Well, lucky us. Why didn't we just wait in here?"

"Oh, I'm sorry. I just love watching the line and waiting for the test case to come rolling down at me." I'm not sure if he's joking. "I guess I'm just used to the noise. You sure you don't want one?"

"I'm sure. I really don't like it."

"Sorry, I'll stop asking."

"Can we get out of here now please?"

"Of course. We'll go through the back so we don't have to walk through the assembly room again."

"Oh, good. Thank you."

Before we leave, Devin takes two more bottles from the open case and shoves them in his pockets. Then he opens a tiny hidden drawer under the belt and removes a label that reads 'Inspected' and slaps it on the AQT case. He checks the 'clean' box on the label for Design, Appearance, and Taste, and finishes by writing the date and time.

We exit the tiny room through the back door into another sterile hallway. We pass through another door and walk by numerous others, never seeing anyone else. It's quiet now, but my ears are still buzzing.

"What are all these rooms?"

"These are research and study labs. And hallways to mechanical rooms and other stuff."

"What kind of research?"

"You know, the study of the plants and minerals that go into our products and the effects they have. Here, look in this room." He points to a door with a small vertical window just big enough to get a glimpse inside. I can make out rows of plants set on long tables under bright lights. The room overflows with a jungle of mismatched species.

I think I know the answer to my next question, but I ask anyway. "How do they study the effects?"

He doesn't answer and keeps walking. But seconds later, I catch him absentmindedly slowing and looking at the door of the next room to our right. I turn and move toward it.

"Nerissa, no..."

I ignore him and push my face against the glass. I'm met with exactly what I expect. Inside rows of cramped cages, stacked two and three high, are scores of imprisoned lab animals, each cage labeled with a number and a brief description of what's being tested, most of which I don't understand. Rodents, reptiles, birds, and rabbits, along with a few mammal-like creatures I don't recognize. I imagine them living out their tortured days in misery and confusion and most likely pain. I really thought human beings were advanced enough to perform research without sacrificing living, feeling creatures. They should just use their own kind. The world could spare a few. Hell, I bet some of the tourists would be happy to test the products if it meant they got to use one hundred percent more than the average amount. The sight chokes me up, but I can't pull myself away.

"Come on, Nerissa, let's go."

"Just a second." I stretch my gaze and see a large aquarium with a yellow turtle struggling to swim upright. Written directly on the glass in thick, black marker is: #13 Piper Methystican/Ashwagandha, 250 mg. Next to that is another row of stacked cages. A baby rabbit with long, soft-looking ears lies motionless, the label reading: #616 Myristica Fragrans (Max). A large, emaciated red bird paces out of control in the cage on top of the rabbit, its droppings falling between the grates, littering the unresponsive creature below. The manic bird is labeled: #237 Ma Huang/Rhodiala Amplificet. Next to them is a row of three animals I've never seen before. They all have pink, fleshy skin but resemble monkeys. They're small but aside from their size look almost human. The last in the row may be dead. Under each of their cages, a label reads: #s 475, 476, 477 C. Periculosis Abscondita, 10%, 20%, and 50% respectively.

I'm infuriated. A huge lump has formed in my throat, and tears are flowing. Devin pulls me away from the window, and I search his face like a scared child.

"Why? This is wrong, Devin. It has to be stopped."

"I know."

"How can you stand this? How do you agree to work here?"

"I don't have a choice."

"Everyone has a choice." Gabriel's words fall out of me. I bury my face in Devin's chest and try to wipe away the things I've just seen. But I already know they are things I can never un-see. He holds me close, rubbing my back.

"Sshh... it's okay. Take a deep breath." I accept his comfort and try to calm down. "Let it go... it's okay. You can let it go now." His words remind me of a childhood lullaby. My sister maids and I would lie close to each other, sometimes even falling asleep holding hands while we listened to our mothers sing. The song is so deeply ingrained, it's amazing how I can almost...

I pull my head from Devin's chest. "Did you hear that?"

"Hear what?"

"That song, that voice... it's coming from..." I thrash my head back and forth, frantically searching the barren hallway, certain I've just heard a woman singing the lullaby from my childhood. But that would be impossible. Wouldn't it?

"There's nobody here."

"I know, but what about in these other rooms? I heard it, I did, it's..." I plod down the hall, turning in every direction, desperately trying to recapture the faint and delicate voice. Devin follows me in silence. I'm sure he thinks I'm insane and is ready to get me off the Rock and home. I turn around, my cheeks hot, my hair everywhere.

"I heard a woman's voice, Devin. My hearing is really good. I'm not crazy."

"I know you're not. And there are women who work here."

"No, but the song was from..." I hang my head.

"You did say your ears were ringing. And you're really upset... I'm sorry, we shouldn't have come this way."

He's right. My mind's just trying to help me cope with the experience of seeing all those animals in such inhumane conditions. I let out a heavy sigh and move toward him. "You're right. Let's go."

He puts his arm around me, and we walk the rest of the corridor without looking through any more windows.

We finally come to an elevator, and Devin instructs the operator to take us to the main level. When the doors open, a large, tall man greets us. I haven't even had a chance to collect my thoughts when Devin forces out the words, "Hi, Father."

I try to follow Devin's lead. I know he wasn't happy when Manny told him his father was on Black Rock. I never stopped to ask him why.

"Well, good evening, son. On your way home?"

"Yes, I am. We are. This is my friend, Nerissa John. Nerissa, Officer William Banks."

"It's a pleasure to meet you, sir." I hold out my hand, which William Banks accepts with rough enthusiasm, pulling me out of the elevator. Devin follows. Still holding my hand, he leans forward and locks onto my eyes, staying there uncomfortably long before speaking.

"The pleasure is all mine, Miss John." He stares at me as if unable to look away. I'm used to being stared at, but this is different. His grey-green eyes bore into mine, and a shiver rolls over me. I have to look away. He releases my hand and turns to face Devin. "Take Miss John and return to Panacea. The building is shutting down for the evening."

"Yes, sir."

"Get home for dinner and tell your mother not to wait for me."

"I will."

"Good evening, Miss John."

"Good evening, Officer."

Our warm, fuzzy encounter is over. William Banks glides down a hall, where he unlocks a door and disappears inside without looking back.

"He's pissed."

"I hope it's not because I'm here."

"No. He just doesn't like me very much."

"He's your father. Of course he likes you."

"It's complicated."

We exit the sterility of the building and step back into the fresh sea air and the starlit night. I'm thinking about my own complicated relationship with my mother, and I know that she, too, doesn't always like me. The feeling is mutual.

As promised, the ride back to Panacea is easier than the ride out—still treacherous, but better. I'm thankful. It's been one hell of a day. But we still have to climb the limestone steps after we dock and part ways with Manny, a guy I won't be missing anytime soon.

Even without the rain, the steep ascent is challenging. As we reach the top and turn around the giant limestone outcropping, I'm aware of a low rumbling. It's coming from my right, but I see nothing other than one of the cottages, dimly lit in the darkening night. Next to the cottage is a small wooden structure that appears to be for waste and recycling but perhaps also houses some kind of machinery or generator. It must be something that runs itself, like the assembly lines at the lab.

The rumbling suddenly stops.

I return my focus to the path, but something at the structure catches my eye, and the sound begins again. Through the tiniest seam in the tall wooden slats, I see a flash of red. I stop and stare. There it is again. Devin notices I'm not behind him.

"What is it? Are you okay?"

I don't move. "Did you see that?" I whisper and wait. "Look, there it is again." With my breakdown at the lab, and now this, Devin must fear for my sanity.

"I don't see anything."

"Look... between the slats. There!"

"Oh! I see it."

"What is that?"

"I don't know. Let's find out." He doesn't hesitate for a second and heads straight for the structure. I have to leap twice to catch up with him.

When our toes are at the wood, we peer between the slats. The rumbling continues, and from this vantage point, it doesn't really sound mechanical. I spot the red flash coming to a stop in front of me. The sound grows louder while the red rises, wood being scraped on either side of me, from chest-height to shoulders and then above my head. The red flash stops above me and curiously morphs into two. I get the sensation of existing in slow motion as understanding slams into me.

I've come face to face with the FWG's security animal. It stands on its hind legs, clawed front feet holding it up against the structure on either side of my head as it looks down at me. Down. I'm paralyzed, knowing all that separates us is this flimsy wooden box.

"Nerissa, do not make any sudden moves," Devin whispers, trying to stay quiet and calm. Fido doesn't appreciate his considerations, and the growling grows louder. I'm quite certain that, should this beast decide to, it could break through with no effort and have me for dinner, Devin for dessert. An old saying pops into my head—*curiosity killed the cat.* In this case, the hybrid and the human.

A tiny whimper escapes my throat, and Devin whispers again, the urgency in his voice alarming me even more. "Do not look in its eyes." I drop my gaze but can now see through the slat into a mass of dense black fur, covering a thick-muscled body. I blur my focus.

"We are both going to step to the side very, very slowly so it can't see us anymore. Don't make a sound. And do not run." I feel his hand wrap around mine. The growling grows even louder, now mixed with snarling and what can only be teeth clapping together. We start to move to the left, and the creature gives us a brief moment of relief before it drops from its position, then jumps back up to meet us again. Up and down it goes, growling at full volume, snapping its fangs at us. We keep moving, but I'm horrified to discover that each of the boards have tiny seams between them. It can see us, and now the frenzied animal slams itself into the wood, the boards bending with the impact of its size. It's just a matter of when, not if, it breaks through.

I push against Devin, trying to make him move faster. The creature bashes itself against the box directly in front of me, letting out what resembles both the bark of a giant dog and the roar of an elephant about to charge. I scream—it's a reflex, and it just comes out. Devin grabs my arm and yanks me sideways. We fall to the ground as the animal comes crashing out of the structure, wood boards and splinters flying everywhere.

Devin throws himself on top of me, partially blocking my vision. All I can see is knotted, clumpy masses of dark fur and an angry mouth full of enormous white teeth. And I can't be certain, but it looks like the lower half of its legs are covered in scales, tipped with black shiny claws that could tear through anything in its path. I never imagined this is how I would die. I wonder if I'll be missed.

The grounds around us flood suddenly with bright light, and a man's voice cuts through the chaos. "Walter! No! Sit down, right now. Devin, do *not* move." Both of us freeze.

Did he just call that monster Walter?

"Walter, heel. Come on, boy, heel." Silence. "Good boy. Come here. Now, sit."

I hear movement and a softening of sorts, if that's possible. We stay motionless, and I'm aware now of Devin's weight on top of me, his face against my right arm, his breath moving forcefully against my skin.

I hear a chain and the clank of metal against metal, followed by loud chewing. "Good boy. Lie down." More silence. "Okay, it's over. You can sit up. Slowly, please."

Devin pulls himself off to sit beside me, and I exhale a huge sigh of relief. It's more like, *Yay! We didn't get killed and eaten by 'Walter', the vicious, manufactured security creature!*

I sit up next to Devin and look over to see an FWG Officer, Walter chained and obedient at his side. Even lying down, the animal's shoulders reach the tall man's hips. Walter chews on a bone the size of a horse's leg. He doesn't bother to look up at us, his red eyes locked on his prize.

"You all right?" Devin asks, never taking his eyes off the beast.

"Yeah, you?"

"I'm fine." He turns for a quick look at me, then back at the man and his loyal companion. "Why wasn't that animal in his regular cage, Klein?"

"He hates it. He paces and whines the whole time he's in there."

"That cage is designed to hold him. It's electrified."

"That's why he hates it."

"So you decided to put him in a waste surround without a roof? Or a lock?"

"I do it all the time. He's comfortable in there."

"Why didn't you keep him in your office with you until everyone was off the base?"

"You know he can't be inside. He'll destroy everything."

Devin's face reddens, and the veins in his temple bulge. "You almost got us killed! Did you ever think of *that*?"

"I'm sorry, Devin. I didn't expect you guys to walk right up to him. Besides, he wouldn't have killed you. He knows you. It's her he was upset about." He points at me like I'm just an unfortunate side effect. "And remember, the way to this big fella's heart is through his stomach. Just bring him a treat next time. Whole chickens are his favorite."

"This creature is required to stay inside the cage designed for him while there are employees or guests on the base or on the Rock. Do you understand?" Devin's voice grows louder, and now he's got Walter's attention.

"Walter wouldn't hurt any of the employees. He knows them all. And we don't get too many guests like her out here." Klein looks at me and shrugs.

Devin stands, and Walter follows suit. "Don't mess with me, man. Or her."

"What are you going to do about it?"

Devin takes a step forward. But if he thinks he's got a chance against a guy with Walter as his friend, he's going to learn some hard lessons tonight. I stand too and put my hand on his arm. Walter growls.

"Control that animal, right now."

"Nothing I can do. He doesn't like her."

Devin lunges forward, and I grab him from behind. Walter jumps on his hind legs, pulling against his chain, his handler unable to restrain him.

"Step back!" A booming voice echoes just past where the structure once stood. Officer Banks marches toward us with a huge rifle pointed straight in our direction. He pulls the trigger, and a shot rings out. Walter drops to the ground, his body limp but his legs still trying to escape. His wild eyes dart back and forth.

"No!" Klein throws himself on top of the animal, his face wracked with emotion. "Why did you do that? He wasn't going to hurt anyone."

My heart is racing, my eyes flicking from Walter to William Banks to Devin and back, my head spins, and I think I may faint.

"Relax, you idiot. It's just a tranquilizer." Officer Banks shoves the rifle in his subordinate's face, forcing him to stand and take it from him. "But he's going to sleep for a long time." Klein is clearly relieved.

"Gentlemen… and Lady, the evening is now over." Officer Banks circles around us. "Devin, you are to remove Miss John from the base immediately and get her home. Specialist Klein, see that this animal is placed inside its designated quarters. If this situation ever occurs again, he will not wake up next time. Are we clear?"

"Yes, sir, Officer Banks. Thank you for your mercy."

"Don't be such a suck up. It's disgusting."

"Yes, sir."

Just like earlier, Officer Banks turns his back and walks away without another word. He doesn't ask his son if he's okay. Or me. Right before he disappears into a cottage, he yells back at us, "Miss John. Remember, you are bound by an oath of silence. Do not break it."

Devin and I ride together all the way back to the Oval. I don't bother trying to convince him to let me ride home alone, not after the night we've shared. I'm happy to have him by my side.

As we get closer, I think about my own life and the decisions I made in order to join Devin on Black Rock. My mother is going to be angry with me, not to mention Kendra, but right now, that all seems small in comparison to the things I've experienced today.

We reach the Oval, and I'm happy to be home. I pull alongside the house and park my board in the port. Devin waits to say goodnight.

"You really know how to show a girl a good time." It's all I can come up with, and I force a small smile.

"Nerissa, I'm so sorry. There's no excuse for what happened back there."

"Which part?"

"Right. I understand if you never want to see me again."

I pause for effect. "Well, that would be little harsh of me, wouldn't it?"

He exhales.

"It wasn't your fault, Devin. And let's not forget, you saved my life, remember?"

"Hardly. I almost got you killed, after I caused your emotional breakdown."

"Oh, yeah, I'd like to forget about that part. Well, it sure makes a good story."

"You're under oath. You can't talk about any of it."

"Really? How strict is that for real?"

"It's very strict. For real."

"Okay. I guess we've got more secrets between us now."

He sweeps the hair from my face, watching the path his own fingers trace along the length of my cheek. "Nerissa, you are just so—"

"Tired. I am so tired. And hungry. Thank you for an adventurous day. Good night, Devin."

"Thanks for finally joining me, friend." He takes my hand in both of his and raises it to his mouth. He plants his lips between my index and middle fingers, right where their crease meets the knuckle, never breaking our eye contact. He's gentle and deliberate, and once again, I'm instantly intoxicated by him—and he knows it.

When he releases me, I don't move. He steps backward and gets on his board. "Good night, Nerissa John. I had an amazing, unforgettable day with you. And I can't wait to do it again."

11 – LET GO

MONDAY, JUNE 17TH

I'm going to get everything I deserve.

You're dreaming... wake up.

But I can't. I can't make it stop, can't wish it away—just like the night Anastasia disappeared.

One arm is wrapped around my waist, the other at my chest. I'm about to be raped on this slick white pier by a sweaty, drunken stranger. Laughing and clapping, his friends cheer him on.

A soft melody fills my head. *You can let go now, precious one...*

"We know exactly who you are now, little Doll," Tom whispers in my ear. "Or should I say *what* you are. You can thank your friend for that."

"Where is she? Where's Anastasia?"

"She's gone, and it's your fault. Don't worry, I'll take care of you, too."

I'm going to get everything I deserve.

...it's time to rest, your work is done...

"How about some of that magical weed?"

"It's not for you. You couldn't handle it."

...breathe deeply, you are not alone...

He spins me around to face him, his razor-sharp claws digging into my arms, his brow folded into an angry crease.

"Okay, maybe next time. You and I have a real future together, don't you think?" His head tilts back, and he lets out a deafening howl. His clothes turn to dirty black fur, his eyes to red lasers. The man growls and pants. "God, you're a real Beauty. Kiss me." The words appear above his head, then fade into the spreading darkness.

...always remember who you are...

I press my mouth against his. He responds, his sloppy, vile mouth covering mine. I feel his fangs and fight back the urge to vomit.

I deliver the kiss of a lifetime.

As I count to ten, our bodies sway to a beautiful melody.

...you are the Universe and that will always be....

Our lips part, and the monster searches my eyes. But now his eyes are my eyes looking back at me. They are sublime, unique, mine alone. I will not share. His hand darts to his mouth, where he tries in vain to form words.

"Still think you know me? Guess you didn't know everything. I didn't know everything, either."

A shot rings out, and Tom hits the pier, his color draining quickly, eyes already glossing over.

...you can let go now, precious one. It's time to rest. Your work is done...

Not shocked by their friend's collapse, the other two repulsive men aim guns at me and howl with laughter. They haven't yet realized their friend is dead. Did they kill him? Or did I?

I need to make my exit now, or these two animals will have to be next. I look back at the pathetic lump who dropped so easily under my power. But my victim is gone. The other two men are also gone. Someone entirely different stands in their place. I can't quite make out his face, but I know he is beautiful.

...you are not alone...

The blackness beyond the pier closes in. Somewhere, I can hear a clock ticking.

"Nerissa, why did you kill me? We are the same. I love you."

A stirring at the base of my stomach pulls at me. Then I hear my mother's voice. "Trust no one."

"I'm sorry," I whisper.

"You have nothing to be sorry for. I'm the one who's sorry."

"Yes, I do. I ruined everything." A cold tear falls down my cheek. I wait for him to kiss it away. Instead, he begins to fade into the darkness. My heart is being ripped in two.

"No. Don't go."

"I love you, Nerissa. Can you swim?"

"Of course I can. You know that."

A powerful shove topples me sideways.

...it's time to open your mind...

I'm launched off the pier and fall into the water, slapping the surface hard.

Wake up, Nerissa.

Saltwater floods my poison mouth. The world is spinning. I'm dying, alone.

You're dreaming. Open your eyes... Wake up now.

My eyes flip open. I'm in mid-scream, sitting upright in my bed, gripping the sheets as I fight off the terror. I'm drenched in sweat, shaking.

The room spins with the echoes of a delicate, haunting melody... and a delicate, haunting memory.

12 – CONSEQUENCE

MONDAY, JUNE 17TH

The news of the tragedy spread across the island like a devastating tidal wave.

Defeated by images from the dream and the day before mercilessly bombarding me, I rise before the crickets stop chirping.

I'm starving. When my mother brought down her fury last night after watching Devin drop me off, screaming at me about missing harvest with Kendra and the multitude of reasons why spending my time with a human boy is dangerous, I wasn't interested in the dinner she put in front of me. Instead, I pushed the food around my plate and half-listened to her rant. I didn't argue or defend myself. I knew it would be pointless. When she had exhausted herself, she left the kitchen. I cleaned up and went to my room.

It was Kendra's turn next. Words like 'traitor' and 'selfish diva' were thrown at me. All I could do was message back six words: *'I'm so sorry. Please forgive me.'* I didn't hear back from her before going to bed.

I won't start my day with any more negativity and decide not to check my messages. I'm too tired to deal with anyone right now. Coffee and Wreckleaf will help.

Outside my bedroom, a light coming from the other end of the house confuses me. Halfway down the hall, I start to hear voices. I reach the dining area to find my mother, still in pajamas, seated at the table with Giovanni and another woman I vaguely know. They all stop talking. The woman is crying but wipes her eyes and forces a tiny smile as soon as she sees me.

"What's going on?"

"Why are you up so early?" my mother asks.

"I had a bad dream. I couldn't go back to sleep. What's wrong?"

She looks down and doesn't answer me.

"Nerissa," Giovanni jumps in, "you remember Rebekah Charles, Lillian's mother?"

All Rebekah can offer is another small, artificial smile before looking away.

"It's nice to see you."

"Nerissa, Lillian suffered a miscarriage late last night," my mother says, and Rebekah lets out a muffled cry.

My heart is in my throat. "No. What happened?"

"We're not clear on all the details. When we are, we'll address everyone at the arena."

"I'm so sorry, Ms. Charles." My mother shoots me a sharp look. "Rebekah, I mean… I'm sorry. How is Lillian doing?"

She hesitates. "She's devastated, and weak. She lost a surprising amount of blood. But she's resting comfortably now."

I don't know what else to say except, "Please send her my best," which sounds so generic.

Giovanni gets up from the table. Her arms wrap around me, and she strokes my messy hair.

"Nerissa, please excuse us now," my mother interrupts. "We still have much to discuss."

"Of course." I'm almost to my room when I realize I never got coffee or Wreckleaf. I really need both. I'll be extra quiet. They won't even know I'm there.

Just as I'm about to step back through the doorway, I stop, listening.

"Please go over the details again." My mother's voice is flat.

"I found her just before midnight, lying on the bathroom floor. There was so much blood. I knew right away."

"You said she was quite unresponsive?" Gio asks.

"Yes. Not until after I got her to take a bit of Wreckleaf was I able to get her up and into bed. It was my last little bit. I don't know what I would have done without it."

"You would have messaged one of us or pounded on our door until we woke. Kendra and Cassidy harvested a beautiful bounty yesterday. And of course, we've got other medicinal plants on hand."

"You mean Kendra and Nerissa..." Gio says, confused.

"No, I mean Cassidy. Apparently, my daughter was too busy with her own affairs yesterday to take part in her harvest duties."

I'm suddenly glad I'm standing behind the protection of a wall. Facing their disappointment would be crushing.

"Kendra didn't tell me Nerissa wasn't there."

"I apologize for my daughter's absence. But Cassidy was an excellent replacement. Perhaps we'll call on her more often."

Guilt buries me.

"Rebekah," Giovanni continues, "forgive us, but we must ask a very difficult question. After you helped Lillian to bed, did you return to the bathroom?"

"Yes, of course, I had to clean up."

"Rebekah," my mother says, taking over, "was the child intact enough to tell its gender?"

My hand slams over my mouth to cover the audible gasp I can't contain. I think they've heard me, but then the grieving mother continues.

"I anticipated you asking that question." She pauses.

"And?"

"I considered the same thing I suspect you're thinking, that if it were somehow a male, something somehow went wrong to cause this. But I can say with absolute certainty, it was female, as usual."

"I assume you kept the body?"

"Lillian wouldn't let me take her. Would you like to see her?"

"No, that won't be necessary. You may prepare it for the funeral ceremony."

I've decided to skip the coffee. But I don't move.

"Well," my mother continues, "this is indeed a mystery. There's only been one other case of miscarriage. But it was the result of an accident that almost took the maid's life."

"I know our history very well, Tatiana."

"Rebekah, has there been anything different in Lillian's life?" Gio asks.

"Nothing that I know of. She goes to work, she comes home. She's been taking very good care of herself. Except..."

"Except what?" My mother is sharp.

"She's had trouble sleeping lately."

"Well, that's normal in pregnancy."

"True."

"Anything else you can think of?" Gio asks gently. "New food, new products at home or at work? Perhaps the tourists like to be injected with hormones of some sort now?"

"Nothing that she mentioned, except that the spa she works at now offers meals to anyone who's there during lunchtime, not just the all-day guests. So she started to eat their lunches instead of what she was bringing from home."

"And what sort of things are on the menu?" Gio persists.

"I honestly don't know. But she was impressed."

"We're grasping at straws, here," my mother insists.

"I suppose we are," Giovanni agrees.

"Matriarchs, if we're done here, I'd like to get back to Lillian."

"We're done. We'll proceed with ceremony on Wednesday at dusk."

I hear the chairs sliding away from the table and the sound of what I imagine is Giovanni embracing Rebekah one last time. Footsteps approach my hiding spot, and I make the snap decision to walk into the kitchen, as though I just arrived. I run right into my mother.

"Oh, you're still here. I hope I'm not interrupting."

"We're finished. I need to get ready for work." She turns down the hall to her room. "Nerissa, we'll be holding ceremony for the lost child Wednesday at dusk." She turns her back. "Do not be late."

I see Rebekah and Giovanni to the door, and only after they're gone can I truly breathe. Gio would never embarrass me in front of Rebekah, but I felt her disappointment. I'm thankful she didn't question me, because I don't know what I would have said. I can't exactly explain being out on Black Rock, watching the sunset and kissing a human boy, while my best friend was harvesting with a new partner just after a big storm—all while a sister maid was in the throes of a tragic loss. There's no explaining that.

WEDNESDAY, JUNE 19TH

Tuesday and Wednesday at Concordia come and go with the usual cast of characters and their demands. But Devin never shows, and I am utterly confused by his absence. I guess what happened between us Sunday ended there.

Kendra has spoken to me as little as possible. She's also made it more than clear that she and Cassidy can't wait to harvest together again.

The three of us finish our shifts and swim out to Albatross together. Kendra leads the way, followed by Cassidy. I take up the rear like a dog with its tail between its legs. When we arrive, Kendra and I do not sit together. She takes a seat next to Cassidy.

Tatiana and Giovanni stand at the front of the arena. This time, Lillian sits on a bench next to her mother. She looks hollow and drained, her eyes cold and lifeless. I've never seen a maid look like that. I've never been to a gathering like this one. A lump grows in my throat.

My mother rises. "We are here today to honor the unborn child of Lillian. It is with the deepest regret I must confirm the news that she has lost the child."

There are no gasps of shock or surprise. The news of the tragedy spread across the island like a devastating tidal wave. Everyone knows why we're here.

"It's been determined that the cause of miscarriage was due to a probable genetic abnormality from Lillian's Contributor."

I don't remember anything being said about that.

"As you all know, at no time in our breed's history has a maid suffered the loss of a child," Gio continues. "Except one. Decades ago, Jacqueline was the victim of a violent altercation, which took her baby's life and almost ended hers as well."

The arena remains silent.

My mother takes the lead again. "We will continue with our investigation of the Contributor's abnormality so that our efforts are not wasted with other men in the future."

It was a baby, not an 'effort.'

"We will continue ceremony at the water's edge." They gather Lillian and her mother from the front row, and we all follow like an obedient herd. We pass through the natural shelter of the arena and find ourselves on an uneven, rocky platform fronting the open water. There at the shoreline sits a large, ornate nautilus. It's covered in minute bits of sea glass, tiny shells of every shape and color, and sprinkled in some kind of gold dust. The nautilus sits atop a nest woven of twigs and driftwood. On each side, an arrangement of white lilies entwines with fresh Wreckleaf. The whole thing rests upon a gilded stand. The sight of it steals my breath.

Without speaking, we gather around the vessel. I haven't seen my breed in the grips of such deep sorrow since Anastasia's disappearance and our discovery. But somehow, this loss feels more poignant and insulting, like an unexpected flaw in an otherwise perfect blueprint.

"Lillian, have you given your daughter a name?" Giovanni breaks the silence.

"Yes." Lillian's voice is weak, carried away on the breeze. "Her name is Charlotte."

"Beautiful. Is there anything you'd like to say before we release Charlotte?"

She clears her throat, clenches her jaw, and swallows hard. "Yes. I would like to say thank you to everyone for your support and kindness." Her tears are wild, her voice trembling. "And I promise not to disappoint you again."

I want to grab her and say, '*No, Lillian! This isn't about you disappointing us or gaining our approval. This is about you and your baby, your daughter, your flesh and blood!*'

My mother reaches for the nest and lifts it from the stand.

"Wait! Wait..." Lillian stops my mother and retrieves a small pair of scissors from her waist pack. She lifts them to her head and cuts a huge chunk of her tawny-red hair all the way to the scalp. A few gasps rise at that. She tucks one end of the hair under the shell and with a gentle touch arranges it around the nest, mingling it with the flowers and Wreckleaf. She's shaking, her face frozen in a twisted smile. When she finishes, she surveys her work.

"I love you, Charlotte. Have a beautiful journey..."

Someone stifles a cry behind me. I turn to see Cassidy wrapped in Kendra's arms. I wish it were me in her embrace.

My mother lifts the nested vessel. This time, no one stops her. She walks to the rocky edge and, with her back to the rest of us, speaks one last time.

"May Charlotte find peace and safety in the arms of the ocean, with which we are one. May her energy return to its origins, and may she find wholeness in her transition back to Source. Let us also remember our sister as simply Charlotte, without ever having the burden and farce of a man's name attached to her. Charlotte is free."

She bends down and places the nest into the water. The current grabs hold of tiny Charlotte's remains and sweeps her into the open water. As the vessel becomes smaller and smaller, drifting out of sight and into the unknown, we all crowd against the shoreline and watch, desperate to catch one last look at what was to be a piece of our future.

Lillian has turned to stone, her stoic face unyielding against the wind. I rest my hand on her shoulder. She doesn't move, except to place her own cold fingers atop mine. Lillian's mother joins me, her loving touch on her daughter's other side. A hand suddenly falls on my own shoulder, and I turn to face Kendra. Cassidy's hand finds my other side. All at once, everyone joins in by placing one hand on the maid in front of them. We are an unbreakable chain. It's beautiful. I wish I could see this living lattice from above.

I turn back and follow Lillian's distant gaze for one last glimpse of baby Charlotte.

But she is gone.

13 - AFTERSHOCK

THURSDAY, JUNE 20TH

There's nothing more humbling or thought-provoking than unexpected, senseless death.

At 3:14 in the morning, I jolt out of a dream, unsure of where or who I am. In the dream, my tortured, jumbled mind makes me relive Charlotte's funeral. Except this time, it's held on the pier in front of Wave. Someone watches from the dark fringes as Lillian, Tom, and my mother dance in a circle, laughing and rubbing up against each other. I yell at them to stop, to help me look for Charlotte—she's disappeared with Anastasia and is in danger. We all are. But no one will listen. Maybe they can't hear me. Even though the words form above them, they can't see—or don't want to see.

The only way back to sleep is to cradle myself and sing. I imagine Lillian singing our lullaby to Charlotte, which makes me cry more. But sleep finally returns uninterrupted until my alarm wakes me for work.

I force myself to get ready. Like Kendra said, the tourists expect me to serve, no matter what. Divorced parents. Dead cat. Dead baby. Who cares? Get a new one, get over it, and get to work.

Despite my rough start, I'm here at work a few minutes early and alone on the beach, trying to get my mind right.

"Hey, what are you looking at?" Kendra breaks my trance.

"Oh, hi. Isn't it perfect?" I gesture to the horizon.

She waits a second. "It really is."

"You're here early."

"So are you."

"That was quite a ceremony, wasn't it?"

She doesn't answer, so I return my attention to the water. There's a long, awkward pause. When I can't take it anymore, I turn around to face her. "Kendra, I'm really sorry about Sunday. I put you in an unfair position. It was never my intention to hurt you. Can you please forgive me?"

She's silent, shifting her weight from side to side, staring into the distance.

"Kendra?"

She meets my eyes. "Yes, I forgive you. But don't ever do something like that again. We're a team. We have a system. Cassidy was great, but she's not you."

"I know, I'm sorry."

"You better have a really good reason for blowing me off. And you better be honest."

I'm under oath, but this is Kendra. "Oh, I have a good reason. And I'll tell you everything, but later."

"Tell me now."

From the corner of my eye, I see Marcus walking toward the beach pavilion. It's perfect. Kendra's back faces him. I wait just a few more seconds...

"So?" She's obviously impatient. "Where were you Sunday?"

Under my breath, I say, "I was on Black Rock with Devin Banks." Then with exuberance I almost yell, "Good morning, Marcus. How are you today?"

"Good morning, Ms. John. Ms. Lucas. It's going to be a stellar Concordia day!" He trots past us.

"As always, Marcus!"

Kendra pretends to adjust her uniform, her movements slow and deliberate. I watch her face and can't help but laugh. When she looks up at me, she shakes her head and mouths the words, 'No way.'

I nod.

Her lashes flutter and her jaw drops open. "Yeah, we're going to need more time."

Whenever we have the opportunity to walk alongside one another or refill our bottles, I give Kendra bits and pieces of my story from Sunday. We must not be overheard. It's improbable the guests could imagine what we're talking about and guaranteed they wouldn't even pretend to be interested. But I don't want to be reckless.

Devin is a no-show again. Good. He'd know exactly what we're talking about.

When our workday ends, I've only gotten to the part of my story where Devin and I take the elevator down to the assembly rooms. There's so much more to tell her. We message our mothers, telling them we're going to be late and giving ourselves more time to talk.

Two hours pass at the tree trunk along the river. I recap what I skimmed over at work, then describe the labs, my breakdown, our near-death experience with Walter, and everything else. When I finish and get up to stretch, Kendra looks the way I felt after Devin brought me home that night. Her eyes are distant, staring at nothing, and I can feel her mind working in a hundred directions.

"So?"

"I don't even know where to begin."

"I know, what a night, huh? It's exhausting to hear myself retell it."

"I'm sure. I mean... you've got the creepy plant guy, the crazy weather and the boat ride, the ominous Black Rock, and the labs with the animal testing. Then there's Devin's weird, disturbing father and the rabid monster that almost killed you. But wait, I didn't even mention the kiss!"

"Yeah, that."

"How was it? Was he a good kisser?"

"That's what you want to ask first? After all I've told you?"

"Yes."

"Well... since I really don't have anything to compare it to, I'd have to say he was an excellent kisser. But it would have been nice to have more than a few seconds."

"So, you would have kissed him longer if you had the choice? It was that good?" She gazes at me like a child asking her mother to confirm her favorite fairy tale is real.

"Yes, it was. I would have kissed him all night long."

"Wow, I can't imagine."

"I never had, either. It was so powerful, but I kind of surrendered control at the same time. It's hard to explain."

"I'll never let myself lose control over a man. Never."

"Never say never."

I couldn't have imagined finding myself in this situation, yet here I am. At least, there I was. Devin has made it clear with his absence and silence that the other night was a mistake. A part of me is relieved.

"So, what do you think about the part after the kiss and the sunset... when Devin showed me the assembly rooms and the labs?"

"What about it?"

"I don't know. Something's just not right."

"Well, the animal testing is barbaric. There's tons of programs for that kind of thing."

"Yeah, but there's something else. I can't quite put my finger on it."

"Forget about it. It'll come to you."

"You're probably right. I just wish I could go back and look around."

"Ask him to take you back."

"You're kidding, right? He obviously regrets the whole thing. He's been missing for four days. I don't think he had clearance for me the way he say he did. His dad was not happy I was there."

"Then let it go and move on."

"Okay. Come on, I'm starving." I pause. "Kendra?"

"What is it? Why so serious?"

"We're good, right? I'd be lost without you." She gets up and hugs me. I melt in her arms. "Okay, let go. You're squeezing the life out of me."

We ride back to the Oval in silence. Things are back to normal, whatever that is.

FRIDAY, JUNE 21ST

The Season is in full swing. The beach is nearly full when we step onto the pavilion. I see that even Devin's usual spot has been occupied. I wonder who's taken over his chair.

"I see Mr. Love is back," Kendra says.

"Who?"

"Mr. Love, Mr. Luscious-Lips..." She rolls her eyes at me. "Devin the Amazing Kisser, dum-dum!"

"Oh, no... are you sure it's him?"

"What's the problem?"

"What am I supposed to say to him?"

"Say whatever you want. You don't owe him anything. Just walk up to him and pretend like nothing ever happened. Be all business."

She's right. I grab my supplies and tromp toward him, kicking up sand in my wake. "Good morning, Mr. Banks. How are you today? We've missed you here at Concordia." My sarcasm is so obvious and thick that I wouldn't blame him if he just told me to shove off. That would make things quick and easy.

"It's so good to see you. I missed you, too."

"What can I start your day with, Mr. Banks? An application of slick bullshit mixed with exaggerated charm? Or how about a full rub-down of emotional manipulation served on the back of a deadly creature that will almost take your life? Sounds fun, doesn't it?"

He just stares at me. I don't give him a chance for rebuttal.

"When we're done with all that, I'll be happy to ring an attendant to bring you a heaping breakfast plate of steaming self-importance, along with a dozen or so Aqua Tonics, your one and only true love."

"What the hell is wrong with you?"

"I'm just cutting to the chase, Devin. Making things easier for you."

"You call insulting me and deliberately trying to upset me making things easy?"

"Aw, I hurt your feelings?"

"Nerissa, is this because I didn't personally message you?"

"Didn't message, didn't show up for days—like Sunday never happened. But it's okay, I get it. You need to leave your options open. Besides, I was busy with the inconvenient death of a loved one, but whatever, I managed."

"Well, I was busy with the exact same thing." His hard, sharp voice stops my rant.

"What?"

"Please tell me Marcus gave you my message?"

"What message?"

"Hold on." He jumps up from his chair and scans the beach. He spots what he's looking for and takes off. "Stay here!" he yells as he runs away.

He returns seconds later, pulling the breathless Marcus with him by his shirt sleeve. Marcus looks terrified, breathing hard and cowering.

"Obviously, Marcus neglected to give you my message, but he'll tell you now. Won't you, Marcus?"

"Yes, of course, Mr. Banks. My deepest and most sincere apologies, sir."

"Get on with it. Tell her."

Marcus clears his throat and closes his eyes, gathering the forgotten message to the forefront of his mind. Then he looks at me. "I was to tell you that Mr. Banks informed the resort he would be gone for a few days while attending a funeral on the mainland."

Devin barely lets him finish the sentence. "What else, Marcus?"

"I was to tell you that upon his return today, he would like to acquire you as his personal attendant for the remainder of the weekend."

"Don't forget the most important thing."

Marcus looks truly uncomfortable now, wringing his hands and leaning side to side. "Finally, Mr. Banks wanted you to know, I quote, 'that was the most beautiful sunset I have ever experienced, and I can't wait for another one just like it.'"

Devin releases Marcus from his grip. "Now get out of here."

"Sir, I am so sorry I failed to relay this message. Whatever you—"

Devin raises a hand to Marcus' face. "Shut up, man. Take a hike. Now."

"Yes, sir." Marcus hangs his head and skitters away. Devin doesn't look at me. He paces the length of three lounge chairs, searching the sand below for his next words.

I feel as though I've been watching a movie, like someone else just spewed the angry words I spoke moments ago.

Devin stops pacing and sits down. "Please." He gestures next to him. I flatten my uniform and sit down. The silence is unbearable, but we stay in it for many minutes, each of us trying to collect ourselves. "Is that really what you think of me?" The sadness in his voice cuts at me.

"I'm sorry."

"You're sorry because yes, that's what you think of me? Or you're sorry because it's not but you said those things anyway?"

"The second thing."

"Are you sure?"

"Yes. I thought after Sunday night, you were avoiding me for some reason."

"Why would I do that?"

"I don't know. Maybe you thought you made a mistake?"

"Nerissa, that was the best night I've ever spent on that island, or this one."

"Even the part with Walter?"

He turns and grabs my shoulders, forcing me to look in his eyes. "I would gladly face Walter ten times over to have experienced our night together."

"Is that so? Because I've got to be honest, I'm not so sure I would. That was scary!"

He puts his forehead to mine and lets out a sigh that turns into a small laugh. "Yeah, that was scarier than hell."

"Why didn't you just message me personally? We could have avoided all this."

"I wasn't sure how you were feeling, and I didn't want to push it. I almost got you killed. I wasn't sure that once you had the chance to think about it, you'd want anything to do with me anymore."

"So you left a message with Marcus instead?"

"Yeah, I knew Marcus would be freaking out if I didn't show up at Concordia for that long. So I figured I'd kill two birds with one stone."

"I hate that expression."

"You know what I mean. I had to get on a zeppelin early Monday morning. So I talked with Marcus. But now I want to kill that guy. What an imbecile."

"Who died?" I ask.

"My brother's best friend and his girlfriend, here on the island."

"Oh, no. What happened?"

"No one's quite sure, except that it was a murder/suicide. It looks like he poisoned her somehow and then took his own life. They lived life fast and hard... but still. The funerals were held on the mainland in their hometown. It was awful."

"I'm so sorry."

"Who died in your world?"

"A good family friend had a miscarriage. The baby's name was Charlotte."

"That's so sad. I'm sure your friend and her husband are devastated."

His comment catches me off guard. "Umm, yeah, she is, but she's not married."

"Oh, that must be even harder to go through alone."

"She's not alone."

He seems to think about my response. "Of course not."

We sit quietly for the next fifteen minutes. The news we've just shared has left us both numb. There's nothing more humbling or thought-provoking than unexpected, senseless death.

"Did you get in trouble for bringing me to Black Rock?" My question seems to startle him.

"No. Well, kind of. Officer Banks wasn't happy, but it's no big deal. I'm so glad you brought that up. I forgot to tell you something."

"What?"

"My mother overheard us talking—let me rephrase that. She overheard him reprimanding me."

"I knew it! I feel terrible."

"No, it's fine. Forget about that. She asked me a bunch of questions about you."

"Uh-oh. What did she want to know?"

"Don't worry, just things like your name, how we met... and what your favorite foods are."

"Why did she want to know that?"

"Because she'd like to meet you, and she's invited you to dinner at our house this Sunday."

"Oh."

"If you're available."

My mind goes into overdrive as I filter through a thousand things at once. I don't have harvest this weekend, but how will I get my mother to agree? I'll have to lie to her. On the heels of the funeral, she let me off the hook about last Sunday and said she didn't want to know details about where I was and what I was doing with the human boy. But she followed that by saying I better not let it happen again. Of course, I promised her it wouldn't.

"So what do you think?"

"Um..." I'd be standing in front of a firing squad. I'll have to re-study my identity papers. I couldn't afford to slip up in front of an Officer or his family. This is a bad idea. I can't. "What time should I be there?"

"Excellent. 6:30. My mom will be so happy. And don't worry, the Officer never shows up for dinner anymore."

"I wasn't worried."

"Good. It's just that he's not that charming, as you know."

"I guess you get it from your mother, then."

I think he's blushing. "My mother is a wonderful woman... who her husband doesn't deserve."

"Well, don't ever worry about your dad with me. I can handle myself."

"Yes, you can." He stands. "I'm going for a swim. Join me."

"No, I'd better not. I should keep things professional."

"Nerissa, after what Marcus did or didn't do, he'll agree to anything. If you want to swim, let's go. Hell, I could probably take you home for a while."

"Let's not get carried away."

"Okay," he concedes. "I'll be right back." But before he goes, he leans over and surprises me with a quick kiss, lingers at my face for a second, kisses me again, then heads toward the water.

I swing my head around to see whose watching. It surprises me to find no prying eyes on us, no one judging our spontaneous moment. I lace my fingers behind my head and slide further into the comfort of the now familiar chair. Before Devin gets too far, I yell, “Tell your mother anything but fish!”

14 – SEEDS OF CHANGE

SUNDAY, JUNE 23RD

Why did you come to my home today, Miss John?

"You know your story inside-out. Why do you need to review it?"

"I'm going to the house of an Officer, Mother. I need to be prepared."

"It's too risky an acquisition."

"I'm not enchanting him tonight. I'm just laying some groundwork. I'm not ready to be a mother. Besides, I'm not old enough."

"If you got pregnant a year early, no one would object, especially after losing Charlotte."

"We can't go breaking our own rules just because you're a Matriarch. What kind of example would that be?"

"Well, listen to you."

I smile. She's bought my story.

I couldn't look her in the eyes and lie to her about where I wanted to go. So I decided my only option was to play to her righteous side. My story is genius—a win-win. I get to see Devin, and she thinks I'm beginning to scout him—planting some seeds.

But I have no intention of ever tricking Devin into creating a new life.

"Why him, Nerissa? Why the son of that Officer?"

"Actually, Kendra made me see the brilliance in this. He's well-educated and well-bred. But mostly, it's the irony. Think about it... the son of an Officer. Who's controlling who, here? They think they have the upper hand, but *we* can have the last laugh."

"Your ideas are admirable. But remember that the Cooperative was signed only three years ago. There are Officers with intimate knowledge of our existence."

"I know, but Kendra explained to me there's only a few who know everything. And that none of their families would know. So, what are the chances?"

"The chances are slim but not impossible."

"What are you trying to say? Is there something you haven't told me?"

She doesn't meet my eyes, and she doesn't respond.

At the back of the living room, she moves a large, potted palm from its spot and waves her CNI—a dark, smoky quartz—over an almost invisible door. She reaches into the dark space and pulls out the only paper copy in existence of our assigned identities, a copy of the Cooperative attached to them.

"Here. Let me know when you're done." She hangs her head and leaves me standing there alone, confused by her behavior and holding the papers that changed our lives forever. I sit down and prepare myself. I haven't looked at these papers in a long time. This fictional version of myself is a tough pill to swallow. I inhale. This is not you, Nerissa. Always remember who you are, and who you're not.

Dolhuphemale Member: Nerissa, daughter of Matriarch Tatiana

Assigned name: Nerissa John

Age at integration: 14

Address: 216 Second Street, Southeast Sector, Panacea Island

Employment: Beach Attendant at Concordia on the Bay Resort

Background: Nerissa John, daughter of Mr. and Mrs. Henry and Tatiana John, was born in the rural village of Swain's Crossing on the Northeast Sector of the Mainland. There she attended school at Chippewa Elementary and was to attend high school at Northeast Four before she and her mother moved to Panacea. She is now enrolled with Panacea Virtual Preparatory. Nerissa's father Henry John, a wealth management entrepreneur, was killed in a private zeppelin wreck at the age of thirty-five, en route to visit an ill family member. Nerissa was eight years old.

The rest of this tall tale goes on to detail more about my mother, who is told to have been a stay-at-home housewife until my 'father's' death. With our arrival on Panacea, she acquired employment as a concierge, not because she had to, but because she wanted to stay busy and start a new life. It also details more of my childhood—some of my supposed friends, my family's history, my hobbies, like my love of modern architecture, boating, and sustainable energies and green technologies.

I knew nothing about any of that stuff, but along with my new last name came the responsibility to research, memorize, and own everything about my fake life. If the FWG took even a minute to get to know any of us before slapping these crappy identities on us, they could have imposed a more accurate set of details, which would have been more believable, not to mention easier.

I've regurgitated this story, or parts of it, more times than I care to remember. My mother is right, I know it inside-out. Still, I hope the conversations at Devin's house won't be all about me. I can't bear the thought of reciting this garbage, not to him.

Attached to my identity assignment is a copy of the Cooperative. This is another document I know verbatim. But here it is in a nutshell:

You belong to us, do everything we say, or die.

The two most laughable things about this contract are first, that it's called the 'Cooperative'... like we all sat down and negotiated the terms of this agreement. Second, the fact that they had my mother sign it, like it even mattered, as though her signature was the final thing that made it official, alongside the Officer that—wait. What? My eyes settle on the signature next to my mother's. I hold back vomit as my stomach flips and my anger ignites.

"Mother!"

I spring up and run toward her bedroom. When I burst in, I find her sitting in her blue chair, her feet up on the ottoman, crossed at the ankles. She seems unsurprised by my urgency. I know she knows why I'm here.

"Devin's father is Officer William Banks! He's the one who created the Cooperative!" I'm breathless, tears blurring my vision, the veins in my neck threatening to burst. "I knew I recognized that name from somewhere."

"I was hoping you'd remember on your own."

"Why? You could have spared me a little." My voice cracks. "That's so... you're so... awful sometimes."

"I'm sorry. But it's important you always remember where we came from, and how we got here, without me always having to remind you. You had to see his name again for yourself."

"But you didn't even want me to look at my identity papers. So why the sudden urge to impart some big lesson?"

"I did try to spare you. I urged you not to go to his house, to forget about him entirely. But you're so stubborn, Nerissa. Once I knew I couldn't change your mind, I honestly didn't have the heart to tell you whose house you'd decided to go to... who you've been hanging out with."

I feel like a trapped animal. Devin is the son of the man who designed and executed our capture and the life-or-death rules we must agree to forever.

"What do I do?" I don't wait for her answer. "I'll cancel. I'll forget I ever met Devin... I'll—"

"Hold on," she interrupts. "It's most likely Officer Banks believes you and Devin spending time together is coincidental. If he thought for a second that we were playing him, I would have heard about it."

"Well, that's good. I'll go message Devin and tell him I'm not feeling well."

"Wait."

"Why?"

"Officer Banks obviously knows who you are."

"Obviously, and I'm sure Devin and the rest of the family do, too."

"No, FWG Officers are sworn to an oath. Kendra was right. His family knows nothing about us. I guarantee it. And if Officer Banks was concerned about this dinner, he would have put a stop to it."

"So, what are you saying?"

"Don't cancel."

I'm so confused by her. There's no way I'm sitting at a dinner table with this man. No way. "I'm not going."

"You have to. Officer Banks needs to think you have no idea who he is and that Devin is the one who arranged this dinner."

"But that's the truth. Or at least it was."

"I know. So it's imperative that you make him believe you don't know him and that you lied to me about where you were going. That I know nothing about this dinner. He must continue to believe that you are alone in your decisions to befriend Devin. If you cancel, you won't have the chance to convince him. If he believes for a second that we put you up to this, with or without your knowledge, we could all be in great danger."

"No, I'm going to cancel."

"You can't. If you cancel, he'll probably realize you know who he is."

"Good, that's a show of respect."

"It just raises suspicions. You must use this opportunity to prove to Officer Banks that we eat, sleep, breathe, and live our assigned identities. That they're so ingrained in who we are, we can barely differentiate anymore. Or that we don't even care to because our lives are so perfect."

"So you want me to talk all about myself, as Nerissa John from Swain's Crossing and the charmed life I live as her, while I play stupid about whose house I'm eating dinner at?"

"That's right."

"No way."

She gives me that look of hers—the one she uses when she's disappointed with me and expects me to come up with a better answer than the one I've given. I make sure she understands me.

"No way, Tatiana. There's no way I'll do it."

"Officer Banks will just chalk the dinner invite up to his son having a summer crush on a pretty girl. And to you being a polite, integrated human—exactly as he expects all of us to act. And once you're gone, he'll somehow convince his son to dump you, and that's it, it's over. When you eventually acquire him, it'll be that much sweeter of a victory."

"What? You aren't making any sense."

"It makes perfect sense. You get to prove our loyalty to the Cooperative while simultaneously securing your future acquisition—son *of the* Officer William Banks—what a victory that will be for our breed!"

"A victory? This is just crazy and dangerous. And damn stupid!" I'm screaming at her now. "And I *will not* do it!"

I run down the hall to my room and slam the door behind me. I throw myself onto the bed and sob into my pillow. How can this be my life? How ... can *this* ... be my life?

Two hours later, I'm at the front door, primped and prepped and ready to go to dinner at the Banks' house. My mother won, again. I knew she would. And she knew I knew. That's why she let me scream at her, allowing me to believe for a minute that I was calling the shots.

"Remember, you must somehow make them believe that you've lied to me about going to their house."

"Yeah, that's going to make me sound like a real class act."

"I didn't suggest you boast. Make it seem like a slip of the tongue."

"Deceitful and stupid. Yay, me."

"All right, that's enough. You know what to do. Now message Devin and get going. Your board is working just fine, by the way. I checked it myself."

"Well, thank goodness for that." I follow her demands like a begrudged circus performer and send the message, 'On my way, see you soon.'

Devin instantly responds with, 'Can't wait,' which she reads over my shoulder. I walk out the door, mount my board, and ride out of the Oval.

On the main road, the wind whips up the cliff, blowing my hair everywhere. If the eye makeup my mother instructed me to put on survives my tears, it'll be a miracle. Between the hair, the makeup, and this stupid white dress, I must look like some kind of maniacal clown riding down the street. I don't care. I hope I scare the shit out of some passerby.

Devin Banks, son *of the* Officer William Banks. How is it possible? He was special, and different, and mine. And this was private. It was my secret oasis, a distraction at the very least. And now it's not. Now it's a test, a proving ground, an acquisition. Now he's nothing more than a future Contributor, and now I have to share him, share us, with everyone. I'm sure my mother will have a gathering at the arena to show off her trick pony, Nerissa. I should have lied to her. I should have made up a reason for being out tonight. Ignorance is bliss. I don't want to know all this. Never again will I feel guilty for lying to Queen Tatiana.

A short while later, I pull up to the Banks' property in the luxury sector. I rode right by this driveway the day Devin took me out to Black Rock.

I follow the cobblestone around a long, gentle turn to the right, then another to the left. The trees on either side are immense, and I feel like I'm navigating through a giant, tunneled maze. The house is still nowhere in sight, but I'm met with a fortress-like black gate, its fence spreading out in either direction as far as I can see. The camera at the top left corner of the gate buzzes into action and points directly at me. I offer a tiny little wave and immediately regret this ridiculous gesture. But it serves its purpose, and the massive gate hums and clanks and moves inward. I pass through and follow the driveway, taking one last turn before the house comes into view. I wipe under my eyes, smooth down my hair, and try my best to present myself "as usual" before proceeding.

I suddenly feel as though I've time-traveled back into the pages of a history book. This isn't Panacea's typical modern cathedral of a house. I'm paused before a one-of-a-kind Spanish revival—sprawling and impeccable. It's beautiful.

Before I can take it all in, the front door opens, and Devin appears, greeting me from across the courtyard with a smile. The house melts away. He looks like he's just stepped out of an advertisement; a white cotton shirt and gray pants that tie at the waist highlight every detail of his body. He walks toward me, his hands lazy in his pockets. His eyes never leave mine. Despite everything, I'm still paralyzed by him.

"Hi. Looks like you found it."

I think I forgot how to speak, and I'm not sure I'll ever regain the ability. I haven't moved, I just stand there, halfway on, halfway off my board as it idles in wait.

He realizes the effect he's having on me. "Come here."

His soft command unfreezes me.

"Turn off your board. You can leave it right here." I follow his instructions.

Devin puts his hand out, and I take it in reflex. Then he wraps his other arm around the small of my back and pulls me toward him. I'm pressed against his chest, our faces inches apart. He smells like fresh laundry and sunshine and himself.

"How are you?" He searches my eyes. "You look sad. Is everything okay?"

I take a deep breath, inhaling his aroma. "I'm good. Better now."

He smiles and hugs me tighter. "Good. I missed you. You look beautiful, as always."

"So do you."

He sighs. "I'm a fool for you, Nerissa John. You are going to be the death of me. Or at the very least, get me in some serious trouble."

"Never."

"Come on, my mom can't wait to meet you."

Holding hands, we stroll through the courtyard, under the entry arch, around a fountain, up the stairs, and through the giant rustic front door. Inside, I'm greeted by an ornate foyer, showcased by a grand, sweeping staircase wrapped in miles of intricate ironwork. Just as Devin closes the door, a small, stout woman rounds a corner and smiles at us.

"Nerissa, this is Esmerelda. Esmerelda, this is Nerissa John."

"Welcome, Miss Nerissa. It is my pleasure to be of service to you, Beauty."

"Thank you. It's a pleasure to meet you, too."

Her cheeks take on a rosy glow. "May I bring you anything? Or assist you otherwise?"

"Um..." I'm not sure what to say. I look to Devin.

"I'm going to show Nerissa around, but I'll let you know if we need anything. Thank you."

"Yes, sir, Mr. Devin." Then she clears her throat and looks down at our feet.

"You can go now, Esmerelda," Devin says kindly, but the woman doesn't move. Instead, she clears her throat again, looks down at our feet and back at Devin. When she sees he still doesn't understand, she points at my feet, and then at his, which are bare.

"Oh, yes. Thank you. My mother likes everyone to remove their shoes at the door. She's very particular about her home."

"Would your mom make an exception for me? My feet are so cold from my ride."

Esmerelda looks downright horrified by my request. "Oh, no, no, Mr. Devin. Ms. Leyla will not be happy. I'll get in trouble."

Another woman rounds the same corner from which Esmerelda joined us. I know immediately this is Devin's mother. I see him in her eyes, as well as in the line of her cheekbones. Her skin is darker than his and flawless, her hair black as a raven.

"Nobody is getting in trouble. Not on such a wonderful day. Hello, Nerissa. I'm Leyla. It's so nice to meet you."

Her voice is soft but assertive, and I'm comforted by her gentle, take-charge approach. Devin is definitely his mother's child.

"It's nice to meet you as well. Thank you for having me in your home. It's so beautiful."

"Thank you. I do love it. It's been a nice project for me. Devin, why don't you show Nerissa around and then come to the back courtyard for some appetizers. We can get to know each other a little before we sit down for dinner."

"Sounds good. It's okay if Nerissa leaves her shoes on, isn't it? Her feet are cold."

"Of course, dear."

I glance to the side, and I swear Esmerelda rolls her eyes the tiniest bit.

The next thirty minutes feel like a dream. Devin leads me on a tour through the house, and each room is more beautiful than the last. The grounds are just as impressive, perfectly groomed, and to my surprise include a stable with three horses.

"Can we go see the horses?"

"Sure."

"Can we pet them?"

"Of course. They're really friendly."

"Are you sure?"

"Yes. I ride these horses almost every day. Do you ride?"

"Me? Devin, I've never even touched a horse."

I can tell he's surprised by my answer, almost as though he thinks I'm lying or exaggerating. Or at the very least, he pities my deprived and uncultured life.

"Well, we'll have to change that. Come on."

We walk along a wooded path all the way to the charming stable. The dream I'm traveling through turns into a fairytale as we approach the enclosure.

Two of the Banks' horses wait to greet us. Ten feet from the pair, I stop. Devin walks ahead without hesitation.

"Hi there, big fella. How are you?" Devin sounds like he's addressing a three-year-old child. He reaches over the chest-high fence, rubs the side of the horse's face, and scratches under his enormous, bristly-haired chin. The glossy brown giant closes his eyes and puffs out a soft breath.

"How about you, Delia?" He addresses the smaller gray horse. When she hears her name, she pushes her big friend out of the way to stand in front of Devin and soak up his affection. "Come here," he tells me. "Delia and Goliath want to meet you."

Delia greets me with a snort, which makes me jump back, then giggle. "I'm not sure she wants me to butt in."

"Of course she does. She loves people, especially pretty ladies. Don't you, Delia?"

I step up and reach out my hand. "Hi, Delia. What a beautiful name you have." She responds by putting her head down and tilting it to the right, which I take as a request to pet her neck. Her fur is coarse and thick but still soft, and she seems to be enjoying what I'm doing because she doesn't move.

"My mother says that if I had been a girl, my name would have been Delia. This horse is hers, and Delia loves my mother."

"What about Goliath? That's quite a name."

He laughs. "Well, one interpretation of the name Goliath suggests someone who has ESP and the ability to reveal or uncover secrets."

"Ooo... how mysterious." I'm transfixed by him—his smile, his eyes—and he knows it. He turns to Goliath and leans in close to his face. He cups the horse's satellite dish of an ear, leans in closer still, and whispers something to him. I swear I see the horse's expression change, his eyes widen, as though he's been told something important. "What did you just tell him?"

"It's a secret for Goliath to keep. I'm sure you have some of your own?"

"Doesn't everyone?" I have to change the subject. "Hey, didn't you say there are three horses?"

"Yes, the other one is mine. He's out in the field somewhere. Would you like to ride him?"

"Ride him? No, thank you. Maybe next time," I lie.

"I still want you to meet him. He's an amazing horse." He lets out a quick, sharp whistle. Delia and Goliath both perk to attention, but neither moves. He does it again. The third time does the trick. At the far end of the enclosure, an elegant white horse saunters through an opening between two generous tree trunks, like a divine fairy emerging from a magical forest. If Devin were a horse, he would be this horse. He's refined, sophisticated, and well-groomed. But he's sexy and raw around the edges. And he seems to know how amazing he is, but also seems aloof and almost bored. He glides toward us, graceful and cool. But I have a feeling that this horse, if bent just slightly the wrong way, would turn primitive and uncontrollable.

"Nerissa, this is Neptune, the best horse that ever lived."

"No way."

"Yes way. Why? What's the matter?"

I'm at a loss for words as my heart fills up with bittersweet memories.

"Nerissa?"

"I had a cat named Neptune when I was a little girl. Best cat ever."

His smile is contagious. "Really?"

"Yep, imagine that. What a coincidence, huh?"

"There are no coincidences."

We spend another twenty minutes with the three horses. Devin is right, Neptune is amazing, not that I have anything to compare him to except Delia and Goliath. But he's bright and responsive and seems to have a real connection with Devin.

"You really love him, don't you?"

"I love them all, but yes, this guy's really special." He never takes his focus off the horse's long-lashed eyes. "We have a lot in common. We understand each other."

"What do you mean?"

"Never mind. It's stupid."

"No, it's not... It's beautiful." I move aside the lock of wavy, blonde-tipped hair covering his right eye. He sighs.

"Neptune is so much more than a possession. I don't own him. Nobody does."

"But let me guess, not everybody in your household agrees with that?"

"That's right. But this animal is no more an object or a commodity than I am. He can't be molded into something he's not. He can't be trained to ignore his instincts, and he won't stand for being anything other than who he was born to be."

Neptune has responded to Devin's energy by staring me down, as though I've upset his friend and will pay a price if I continue to do so.

"Are we still talking about Neptune?"

"Like I said, we have a lot in common."

We all do, don't we? "So, who was this horse born to be?"

"His very nature is freedom... in all ways." He turns back to Neptune. "This animal is a rare soul with a pure heart and deserves the best life I can possibly give him."

I place my hand on Devin's chest above his heart. "And who else is *this* rare soul meant to be?"

I've caught him off-guard, and his shoulders fall with the weight of my question. His eyes turn to the ground. "I don't even know anymore."

"Yes, you do." He looks up. "It's as plain as day. You're a writer, a poet. You carry that ratty old journal around with you like it's your only tether to the earth. And who knows? Maybe it is."

"My dad gave me that journal a long time ago. It means a lot to me."

"Really? That surprises me. Officer Banks doesn't seem like the kind of dad to give that type of gift."

"Officer Banks isn't my dad... not my real father."

"Excuse me?"

"That despicable human being is my stepfather. I thought you knew that."

"No, I didn't." I feel like I just opened a beautifully packaged present. "You always refer to him as your father. You have his last name."

"My mother took his name and made me take it, too. And she insisted I drop the 'step' and just call him my father. Same with my stepbrother Colton. He's simply 'my brother'."

"Well, this explains a lot! I thought you must really take after your mom, because you don't act like him or look like him at all, thank God." I catch myself. "I'm sorry, that was really inappropriate."

"No, you're right. If we were related and I did take after him, I think I'd do the world a favor and kill myself. I'm not a Banks. I'm a Navarre."

"Where's your dad?" Before I finish my question, I regret asking.

"My dad died when I was little. After about a year, my mother was struggling financially and—"

"I'm so sorry, Devin. You don't have to explain. It's none of my business."

"I want to tell you. Finally, someone I can talk to about it. You lost your dad too, in a way."

"Of course." I'm about to faint. I completely forgot that Kendra made up that ridiculous story about my parents' divorce, even though my papers say he's been dead for years.

As if disgusted by the story, or by me, and seeing his human friend in pain, Neptune abruptly turns, snorts, and leaves the oblong enclosure in a wake of dust, heading back in the direction from which he came.

"When money got really tight, my mother started working as a maid for some really wealthy families. She never complained, but she hated it. It wore her down, and I watched her spirit die. But one day, she came home and declared she had met a man who was going to make everything better for us."

"William Banks."

"Yes. William was going through a divorce when he hired my mother to clean his house. They were married three weeks after his divorce was final."

"Wow. How old were you?"

"I was nine when my dad died. Eleven when my mom remarried."

"So they've been married seven years. That's a long time."

"My mom will never leave him, even though he doesn't deserve her. He's a cheating, lying, controlling asshole. But she's tasted poverty, felt its suffocating grip... and now, she never needs to worry about money again. She'll put up with anything, and he knows it."

"She's got everything except an honorable man. Money isn't everything."

"You're right. We never had a lot of money when my dad was alive. But we were happy."

"So he gave you the journal. Did he teach you to write?"

"No, he wasn't a writer. My mother is—or was. He was a musician. And a damn good one."

I hesitate, then gently ask my burning question. "How did he die?"

"He got sick. Just like that. One day he was fine, the next..."

"I'm so sorry."

"He was such a brilliant, creative person. He taught me to question everything, to always think outside the box, because the lines that hold us can always be erased. But I'm not sure he really took his own advice."

"What do you mean?"

"I think all that creativity didn't have a big enough outlet and it got trapped and festered inside him. As happy as he seemed to be, I don't think he ever truly quenched his own thirst. He didn't erase his own lines."

"So you think he settled?"

"Yeah, kind of. I think the William Bankses of the world kept telling him to stop dreaming, to get a real job, just like he always tells me. That's why I keep my writing to myself. I think that's why my mom stopped writing. All that scrutiny and judgment... it's impossible not to take personally."

"Well, please, Devin, keep writing. You have to share it with the world."

He leans over and kisses me on the forehead. "You are the sweetest girl I've ever met."

"I mean it. I'm not trying to be sweet."

"I know. But the truth is, unless there's a creative-writing position with the First World Government, my art will die inside me, too."

"What do you mean?"

"I graduated this year, Nerissa. Officer Banks expects me to accept the position he's arranged for me after this Season."

"Doing what?"

"Doing what he does. A chip off the old block, just like Colton."

"Your mom won't let that happen."

"Actually, she expects it as well. She says we owe an unpayable debt to my stepfather for everything he's done for us and that I need to do whatever he wants."

"Just like her?"

"Just like her."

"It makes me think of the way they expect us to act at work. I'm constantly compromising myself, but hey, *whatever it takes, Beauty.*"

"At least you can quit if you want. It's just a job. I can't quit my family."

"It's not that easy."

"Sure it is. As a matter of fact, why don't you just quit and we can be together for the rest of the Season?"

"That sounds amazing."

"I'm serious."

"No way. My mother would never allow it. She doesn't even know I'm here today. I had to lie."

"Why? She doesn't like me?"

"It's not that. She doesn't think I should get involved with tourists who are only here for three months."

"So, you're not allowed to make new friends in the summer?"

"No, you know... romantic relationships." My face burns, and Devin bites his tongue.

He takes my hand and leads me away from the stable, back along the forest path. I think we're both relieved our conversation has come to an end. The smell of green leaves, damp moss, and black soil are distracting and intoxicating. It's like a wonderland in here, the springy dirt trail leading us into the unknown.

"What's that?" I ask. We come to a tiny, vine-covered cottage on our left. It's built in the same style as the house but looks like it hasn't been touched in years, thick ivy covering even its door.

"That's my mom's writing studio. Officer Banks had it built for her the first year we came for the Season. But I don't know the last time she was in it."

"Maybe you should use it, then."

"I don't think so. Come on, they're probably wondering where we are." He picks up our pace.

"They?"

"Yes. I'm sorry, but the Officer will be gracing us with his presence. Colton, too."

One last turn through the woods, and an expanse of perfect lawn opens in front of us. The back courtyard of the house sits just beyond, and I can make out Leyla and Esmerelda flitting about in preparation. As we cross the sea of green, my stomach turns, and a desert forms inside my mouth.

"You made it. We thought we'd have to send out a search party!" Leyla meticulously places the last pastry-encrusted bite among a myriad of other impeccably executed tidbits. Every food group is represented in this spread, all but one—fish.

"Please, dear, help yourself. William and Colton are running late, and we're not waiting."

"Thank you. It all looks delicious." I don't hesitate.

We spend the next hour enjoying the appetizers and making small talk. I compliment Leyla on the house, the grounds, and the stables. I ask about the artwork collections, the architecture, and the landscaping. I do whatever I can to avoid the conversation turning to me. I'm not ready.

"We've had the pleasure of much travel over the years. I'm just fascinated with other cultures, and I love collecting art pieces. My husband thinks the house looks like a museum."

"Well, I've never been anywhere, and I think it's all beautiful and mysterious. You should definitely have the things you love surrounding you. It's good energy."

"I couldn't agree more."

"Look, Mom." Devin reaches for my right hand. "Look at Nerissa's ring."

Leyla's eyes light up. "Oh, my. I can't believe I didn't spot that. It's extraordinary. Where did you acquire it?"

Here it comes—the first of the lies. At least this one is easy and a good warmup. "I was walking home one day and found it alongside the road, if you can believe it."

"Aren't you lucky? Do you know its origins or what it means?"

"No, not really." Devin doesn't call me out. Of course he doesn't.

"It's an ancient African symbol meaning freedom and independence. And the stone appears to be turquoise, although it could also be jasper."

"How do you know that?"

"The painting."

"I'm sorry?"

"The painting next to Devin's bedroom. Did you show it to her, Devin?"

He smiles at her. "It's a big house, Mom."

"Well, you must show it to her now. Go quickly. Dinner is ready in ten minutes."

He takes my hand. We pass through a pair of ornate French doors into the kitchen, then through a great room and up a staircase at the back end of the house. Along the stairwell wall hang a half-dozen photos, each one representing a year in the life of the Banks family. In each one, they're all posed on a beach in coordinating outfits, smiling and happy.

"Oh, look how cute you were!"

He stops, and I bump into him. "What do you mean, *were?*"

"I'm sorry. You're just as cute now." I can't help but giggle. "They're great. You all look so happy.

"They're only pictures."

At the top of the stairs, a long hallway turns both left and right. The floor is a dark, rich wood, the walls creamy ivory plaster. In front of us is displayed a bronze statue of a horse set on a simple, waist-high stand of wood. The detail is amazing. I wander over it, my eyes settling on an inscription at the bottom. *Delia.*

"Is this your mom's horse?"

"Yep. An artist friend made it."

"Wow."

We turn left and continue down the hallway. On our right, sun pours through window after window in splintered, diagonal streams. To our left, a railing separates us from the terra-cotta-tiled garden room below. It houses a fountain, a lush succulent display, and a half-dozen other unique pieces of art. A large bronze piece commands my attention—a life-sized dolphin jumping out of the water. At its tail, submerged to her waist, a beautiful, long-haired woman reaches upward, frozen in rapture. She's hypnotizing.

At the end of the hallway, a heavy wooden door stops us. Devin turns to his right and gestures.

My mouth falls open. The painting is large, nearly three feet wide by five feet tall, wrapped in a metallic-gold, chunky wood frame. It's an abstract fantasy painted in vibrant oil colors, depicting a woman going through some kind of spiritual, emotional transformation. On the left, she's crouched down, crumpled in a defeated heap. Tangled, lifeless hair falls around her twisted, pained expression. It gives me goosebumps. The colors behind her are clouded and dark. To her right, she takes on a much different form, yet it's clearly the same woman, still attached to her former self. She stands tall, arms outreached and spread wide. Her colorful dress blows all around her. Free of her hair, her streamlined head is held high, and her brown, glowing skin comes alive, illuminated by a light from within her. She gazes up and to the far-right corner of the painting, and her eyes seem to smile, as though she's observing something amazing or holds a secret no one else can know.

And behind her, there it is—the symbol identical to the one on my ring. It's translucent, swimming with the other colors in the painting but clearly there, and clearly the point of the entire piece. She is free. She has found her independence. Then I notice the small writing at the bottom of the canvas. *Emancipation Ignites Power and Fuels Responsibility.* A shiver runs over me.

I turn to find Devin staring at me. He knows how moved I am.

"She's beautiful, isn't she?" he asks.

"How is this possible? How is this here?"

"It used to be in a different spot, but I always loved it, so my mom moved it here."

"That's not what I mean."

"I know what you mean... I told you, there are no coincidences."

I return to the painting. I could stare at her for hours.

"Okay, come on. We better go back downstairs."

"Wait. Can I see your room? This is it, right?"

"Sure, but quickly. My mom cooked all day. I don't want to keep her waiting."

His room is an extension of the house—a showplace, really—with a huge, mahogany four-poster bed atop a bright tomato-and-white rug.

"What's with the giant vase?"

"You don't like it?"

"It's just a little unexpected. And I wouldn't have taken you for a chevron fan, either."

"A what?"

"A fan of chevron." He still seems confused. "On your rug, those zig-zag lines. That's called chevron."

"Oh. My mother decorated the whole house. She wanted everything just so, and I don't really care. But I do actually like the vase."

"Well it's a nice touch, but if you didn't tell me this was your room, I'd have no idea."

"All right, Miss John. We best get downstairs."

"Devin, I need to ask you a favor."

"Does it involve kissing you? Because I'd be happy to assist." He steps toward me and wraps his arms around my waist. "What is it? Is everything all right?"

"This is going to sound strange, but could you please not refer to me as Miss John?"

"Sure. Why not?"

I pause. "It reminds me of something sad. Just call me Nerissa, please."

"I'm sorry. Of course it reminds you of your dad."

I want to protest, want to blurt out everything about myself. "Thanks."

Downstairs, Devin leads me into the formal dining room, where Leyla and Esmerelda have put together a table fit for royalty. Everything is sparkling and perfect. I'm almost afraid to sit down and mess something up. Officer Banks and Colton haven't arrived, and I can only hope they're unable to join us after all.

"Please, make yourself at home."

"Thank you, Mrs. Banks. This is so beautiful. You didn't need to go to so much trouble."

"Please, call me Leyla. And it was no trouble at all. I enjoy entertaining."

"Well, thank you. Everything is so nice. And your house is amazing. I love all the artwork. You have an incredible collection."

"Do you like the painting?"

"Very much. I can't believe the coincidence."

"Seems meant to be, doesn't it?" Her eyes wander to Devin. He's smiling softly, looking down at his dish as he butters a dinner roll. "What else do you like?"

"Hmm... I think my favorite are the bronze pieces."

"Did you recognize my horse?"

"I did."

"I love that piece. I love that horse."

"It's great, but I think my favorite is—"

William and Colton enter the dining room, and the energy instantly shifts.

"Good evening, everyone. Sorry to keep you waiting."

"Oh, we didn't wait," Leyla says.

"Good for you."

Every muscle in my body tenses, reminding me why I didn't want to come here.

"Devin, introductions," Leyla prompts.

"Nerissa, this is my brother Colton. Colton, this is Nerissa."

"Pleasure to meet you, Colton."

"My father was right about you."

Devin shoots him an angry glare.

"Of course, you remember my father, Officer Banks."

"Hello, sir. Nice to see you again. Thank you for having me in your home."

"The pleasure is all mine, Miss John. It's nice to have such a Beauty in our house."

The heat rises in my face, and I fumble with my water glass, trying to act natural.

"Call her Nerissa. She doesn't like to be called Miss John," Devin corrects his father.

"Oh, no... that's okay," I protest.

The Officer lets out a quick laugh. "That is your last name, isn't it?"

"Yes, sir."

"Well then, I would encourage you to embrace your name with pride."

"It's complicated. Nerissa's father is gone, and she doesn't like to be reminded of him." Devin looks at me with apology in his eyes for revealing what he believes are my secrets. I look down, ready to pass out.

"I'm sorry to hear that, Nerissa," Leyla says.

"Let's change the subject," Devin insists.

"When we came in, you were about to tell my wife what your favorite piece of art is. Please continue."

"Umm, sure. I love the bronze dolphin in your garden room. It's incredible."

"Good choice. Bravo," Officer Banks says. "I happen to love that one, too. It has special meaning to me." His gaze is unyielding. "So, you really connect to it as well?"

I swallow hard. "Yes, I do. I've always felt a strong connection to dolphins." And before I can stop myself, I ask, "What's the special meaning it has for you, sir?"

His lips curl up. I don't know exactly what I'm expecting him to say, but his next comment nearly knocks me off my chair.

"That piece was commissioned three years ago, after I completed a very important classified project. It was given to me by the FWG as a thank you for a job well done."

My heart sinks. He must be testing me; he wants to see if I know who he is. I want to spit in his face, but instead, I keep pace with him. "How nice. Congratulations. But I'm sure that gift pales in comparison to the importance of whatever your project was."

Silence.

Esmeralda breaks the awkward moment by delivering us soup and salads. I've never been happier to be given leafy greens.

"Well, let's toast," Leyla proposes. We all clink glasses.

"Speaking of dolphins..." Apparently, the Officer isn't finished. "Colton, did they get that pod out of the marina?"

Colton lifts his face out of his soup bowl. "Not all of them."

"What happened?" Leyla asks.

"A pod of dolphins trapped themselves in the marina this morning. Stupid things couldn't find a way out."

"They're not stupid," I protest.

"Oh, yeah? Well they're not smart enough to realize they're all going to get killed if they don't get out, just like the baby."

"What?" I fight for composure.

"Stupid baby dolphin ran right into the propeller on the Andersons' yacht. God, what a mess. Mrs. Anderson was so pissed."

Officer Banks chuckles.

"Please, this is not good dinner conversation," Leyla objects.

"I heard the Andersons backed their boat right into that creature, not the other way around," Devin corrects his brother.

"Whatever."

"They ought to learn how to handle their craft. And they should be fined."

Again comes the chuckle from across the table, which I'm sure is mostly in response to the distress I'm surely wearing on my face.

"That thing had it coming... and so do the others if they don't leave. They won't survive the night if they don't. We tried to help the ignorant lot, but it's out of our hands now."

"The baby must've been separated from its mother and gotten confused. Then it swam toward the sounds in the marina." My voice trembles.

"Duh... like I said," Colton mocks.

I ignore him. "Dolphins are extremely social and have tight-knit families. The pod would have followed the baby into the marina knowing they were risking their lives trying to save it."

"Guess that didn't work."

"The mother's mourning. She won't leave without her baby. And the rest of the pod won't leave one of their own behind."

"How do you know so much about dolphins?" Colton asks.

"Like I said, I have a strong connection to them." I glance at the Officer. His eyes are ice.

"Well, I hope for my brother's sake you're not as dumb."

"Shut up, Colton," Devin snaps.

I clear my throat, look into Colton's eyes, and speak slowly. "Did you know that most human beings use only a portion of their brain capacity at any given time?"

"That myth was debunked eons ago. What does that have to do with anything?"

"I'm not referring to the ten-percent myth. I'm talking about the brain's potential. You know about the new savants... they're still rare, but their numbers are increasing."

"And your point is?"

"Even without having reached their potential, humans have large, complex brains and have accomplished a lot with their limitations, especially in the last century."

"And again, your point?"

"It's just like those big yachts in the marina. They're built for speed and performance. They're meant to cross seas. But they're only operating at a portion of their ability, being forced to stay within boundaries. They've got what it takes, they just don't use it."

Colton just stares at me, a tiny drop of orange soup on his chin. "What are you talking about?"

"There's only one remaining family of creatures—natural, pure-blood creatures with larger brains and higher intelligence than humans. They've utilized their brain's full potential, and they express it with advanced emotional awareness, highly complex memory, and extra sensory abilities. Can you guess the creature that leaves human beings in its wake?"

Devin's arm shoots up like we're in a classroom, and now Leyla chuckles from across the table.

"Yes, Devin?"

"Would it perhaps be the dolphin?"

"Ding, ding, ding! Yes, that is correct. All cetaceans."

"Wow, I didn't realize that," Leyla says. "Did you know that, William?"

"Fascinating."

"Imagine if all humans were utilizing their brain's full potential. What if we all had the extra sensory perception that kind of brain power would afford? You'd be able to anticipate and maneuver and hear things so much better. I think it'd be fair to say you'd have the ability to control things outside yourself. Even other people, to a certain degree. Of course, that's just scientific hypothesis, because none of us has ever experienced that. That would take some serious genetic engineering. Don't you think, Officer Banks?"

"Excuse me, Mr. William," Esmerelda interrupts. "There are two gentlemen at the front gate for you."

"Colton, go let them in. Bring them around to my office. I'll be right there."

"William, we're right in the middle of dinner. And we have a guest. Can't it wait?"

"Leyla, you know the answer to that."

But before Officer Banks makes his timely exit, I leave him and Colton with one last thought. "As great as it is being human, if I had a choice, I'd choose to be pure dolphin."

"Well, I just might join you, dear." Leyla smiles brightly at me.

Officer Banks stands from the table. "Excuse us. We have business to attend to. Miss John, thank you for joining us. Have a good evening."

"Thank you for having me."

The Officer spins around and runs right into Esmerelda, who carries a platter of meat and vegetables to the table. The serving dish crashes to the floor, and food splatters everywhere.

"Oh, I am so sorry, Mr. William. I didn't see you coming." The poor woman seems genuinely scared as she wipes at the food stains on William Banks' crisp white shirt.

"You clumsy oaf. Why don't you watch what you're doing."

I stand to offer assistance, but Devin puts his hand on my arm and guides me back into my seat. Leyla stands.

"Sit down!" William yells. "She'll clean it up herself."

"Yes, Ms. Leyla. I will do it. Please do not concern yourself."

"Don't be silly. It's no bother," Leyla protests.

William Banks freezes, then turns in his wife's direction. The room goes silent. "Leyla, you will sit down, now. This blind old simpleton will clean up her own mess. You are not a maid anymore, and I will not have you act as one. Do you understand me?"

Leyla's face reddens as she tries to compose herself. She reminds me of a resting volcano, bubbling quietly under the surface. Her hands wobble when she smooths out the front of her dress before easing herself back into her chair.

"Answer me, woman. Do you understand?"

Devin tenses next to me.

Leyla clears her throat and pauses before a tiny, forced smile forms at the edges of her mouth. She reaches for her wine glass and takes a long, thoughtful sip, making him wait for her response. "Yes, of course, William. Thank you for the reminder."

Esmerelda still swabs at his shirt, but he's had enough. "Stop. I'll go change. Just clean this mess up immediately."

"Yes, Mr. William."

With that, he storms out and down a hallway at the back end of the dining room. A few seconds later, a door slams somewhere else in the house. Leyla immediately gets up to assist Esmerelda. The two women work quickly side by side, no words between them.

"Mrs. Banks, let me help you."

"No, thank you, dear. And please, call me Leyla."

Devin takes my hand under the table, but even that can't soothe me. I'm crawling out of my skin, and I don't know what to do with myself. What a fun dinner this has been.

"Where's the bathroom?" I ask Devin.

"There's a powder room on the other side of the kitchen."

I get up and maneuver around the table, but Leyla stops me. "There's such a mess here. So much glass. You can use the one down the back hall, third door on your right." She points me in the direction Officer Banks went, but I hesitate. "Don't worry. He's in a meeting farther down the hall. You won't see him."

I retrace my steps, then turn down the back hall. After passing two closed doors, I arrive at the bathroom, slip inside, and lock the door behind me. It's a much-needed refuge. I stay as long as possible without making it obvious I'm stalling.

I wash my hands, splash my face, and do my best to focus on Devin. But the dream I felt I was walking through earlier has turned into a nightmare. I can't wrap my mind around the dangerous game I just instigated with the Officer. It's difficult to meet my own gaze in the mirror, but I give myself one last look—a cautionary reminder to keep myself in check—before exiting the safety of the bathroom.

Back in the hallway, I hear muffled voices. I do the unfathomable and turn in their direction. Officer Banks' angry tone carries, and it sounds like he's arguing with at least two other men. My mind screams for me to stop, but raw emotion propels me forward. I pass an open door on my right; another on my left is closed. In silence, I inch forward and peer around the corner. At the far end of the hall is the office of William Banks, the double-doors shut tight. I creep forward, and the voices become clear.

"Do you understand your orders?"

"I understand what you want, but with all due respect, sir, it's simply too much."

"I did not ask for your opinion, MacNamire! It is time to amp it up."

Amp it up.

"It's too dangerous, sir. It needs to be more progressive," says a third voice.

"Results to date are not enough. I cannot get approval without them. Make it happen. I will not wait another year. I need more funding, or we can kiss the whole project goodbye... and that is not an option."

"But the test subjects—"

"Those lab-animals?"

"No, sir, the—"

"I don't care about the test subjects. In fact, get some more."

"Sir... I'm not even sure that would be accurate."

"It's the closest thing we've got."

"Sir, I just think—"

"That's your problem. You think too much. Amp it up or hand in your resignations. And hurry up and figure out how to replicate growing conditions. We must be self-sustainable. The demands will be too high. It's that simple."

The room falls silent. I need to get out of here. I'm almost around the corner when the office doors open. I move quickly without a sound, passing the rooms on my right and left. I'll slip back into the bathroom, and no one will be the wiser. As my hand closes around the doorknob, his grip lands on my shoulder. He spins me around, and where I'd expected to find Officer William Banks, I'm instead faced with the bloodshot eyes of creepy plant-guy, Emmanuelle MacNamire.

"What exactly do you think you're doing?"

"I'm just using the bathroom."

He leans in close, tilts his head, and inhales deeply through his nose. "I can smell it on you, you know."

"Smell what?"

"The Wreckleaf... and your lies. Have you forgotten I'm both a terrestrial and aquatic horticulturist? I know that smell. It's the ocean and the rust."

"You're crazy. Let me go."

"Not so fast. Let's go have a little chat." He grabs my arm, squeezing hard enough to make my fingers numb by the time we round the corner and enter the office.

"Look what I found lurking in the hallway." Emmanuelle shuts the doors behind us.

"I was just using the bathroom. Leyla sent me down here because of the broken glass. I got confused and turned the wrong way."

"Mrs. Banks will need to be reminded of the importance of privacy. Colton, please show Officer Penn to the courtyard." The other two obediently follow his orders, gone from the room in an instant.

Office Banks gets up from behind a massive ebony desk, where he and the other men had pored over piles of papers and a holographic screen. His eyes are glued to mine. He seems repulsed and curious at the same time, like he's looking at a suicide victim—pity mixed with judgment. The expression is disturbingly familiar.

He stands directly in front of me and grabs me under my chin. He's not shy about letting me feel his strength and willingness to assert himself.

"You're hurting me."

"Why did you come to my home today, Miss John?"

"For dinner... because Devin and Mrs. Banks invited me to dinner."

"That was quite a little charade you put on at the table."

"I'm sorry? I don't understand."

"You know, I'm usually a fan of clever, intellectual contest, especially when no one but the players involved is aware. But this..."

"I don't know what you're talking about."

"This little game you're playing will not be tolerated."

"I'm not playing a game. I'm just here for dinner."

His grip tightens as he leans in, pulling my face up to his, our lips only inches apart. I swear he's about to kiss me. "Do not fuck with me, Doll... or I will crush you... and your entire family." He spits when he says *family.*

"You need me and my family, so don't fuck with me, sir."

He drops his hand from my face and actually laughs. "Not for long, you little ingrate."

The doors fly open and crash against the walls.

"What the hell is going on in here? What are you doing with her?" Devin charges into the room and stands between the Officer and me.

"Just giving Miss John a little tour. She lost her way back from the bathroom."

"A little tour with the doors closed?"

"Oops. Force of habit."

Devin spins around and eyeballs me up and down. He must not notice that his father was digging into my face, where hot, throbbing pain tells me red marks will soon appear. He closes his eyes and sighs. "Come on. Let's go."

Once we've stepped into the hall, Officer Banks bids us farewell. "Good evening, Miss John. It was so nice to make your acquaintance. Come back anytime."

I don't respond, and I don't look back.

15 – TANGLED

SUNDAY, JUNE 23RD –MONDAY JUNE 24TH

If you want answers, you've got to get them yourself.

Devin insists on riding home with me. I don't deny him. He knows something bad went down in that room. We ride in silence, and when we get to my house, I can't look at him, unsure of his thoughts, tangled in my own.

"I'm sorry, Nerissa."

That's it. He doesn't ask me what happened. I can't decide if I'm mad or relieved about that.

"It's not your fault." I turn and walk through the front door, leaving him no opportunity to respond and leaving me with the sickening feeling that those are the last words I'll ever speak to him. I can't quite understand the grip his stepfather has on him and his family—on this entire island, for that matter. After all, he's just a man.

"Hey, what's up?" Kendra greets me.

"Hi." I can't look at her.

"Why are we meeting here? I hate this place."

"I had to take care of something."

"Okay. You want to tell me what?"

I don't answer. I'm trying to wash the images of the grieving mother dolphin from my mind.

"Nerissa, are you all right?"

"I'm not sure."

"Listen… it's really late, and I had to sneak out to meet you. Tell me what's going on." She sits down next to me on the edge of the pier. I lift my eyes to meet hers. "Whoa. What happened to your face?"

"I had dinner at the Banks' house tonight."

"Devin did that to you? I'm going to kill him."

"It wasn't Devin."

"Who was it?"

I have to push the words out. "It was his father. His stepfather. Officer Banks."

"Why? What happened? Wait, he's his stepfather? Did Devin see it? What did your mom say?"

Her reaction makes me cry again. I spend the next hour telling her about the night, doing my best to keep calm.

"So you came down here to get the pod out of the marina?"

"I almost didn't. I haven't been down here since…"

"Since Anastasia disappeared."

"Yeah."

"Did it work?"

"Yes."

"Thank God."

"There were still people on their boats. There still might be, but I was careful. It took me a long time, but they finally followed me. They're safe now."

"What a night you've had."

"Yeah, what a night."

I had to lie to my mother, fabricating everything she wanted to hear. She seemed to believe me, even the part about slipping along the garden path; she knows what a klutz I can be. She retreated to her bedroom with glowing satisfaction. I snuck out ten minutes later.

Kendra and I sit in silence. It's a relief to have told her everything.

"I think I'm in love with him," I blurt out.

"I'm sorry, what did you say?"

I consider making her think she heard me wrong, but I can't. It's too late. "I think I'm in love with Devin."

"I think Officer Banks squeezed the brains right out of you. Don't be ridiculous."

"I'm serious."

"You're upset and exhausted. Devin Banks is nothing more than a prospective acquisition."

"He's a lot more than that, Kendra."

"He's a human man... and the son of the worst kind."

"That's his stepfather. He's nothing like him."

"Nerissa, come back to Earth. You *cannot* have a relationship with him. Besides, you have me. We have each other." Her voice drops. "We don't need men."

I bite my tongue and offer a small smile. "So what's next?"

"I think you need a hot shower, a cozy bed, and a good sleep."

"That's not what I mean."

"Then what do you mean?"

"I've thoroughly pissed off the man responsible for the Cooperative. I'm not sure I can keep all the lies I've told my mother straight. And I'm pretty sure I've put us all in danger because of it. Again. I need a plan."

"I think you're over-thinking things."

"How can you say that?"

"Your mother believes you, and what she doesn't know won't hurt her, and—"

"It won't hurt her only if Officer Banks decides it won't," I interrupt.

"Screw Officer Banks! He's not going to do anything. And that's probably part of what made him so mad. He knows he can't. He needs us, and he's not going to mess with a Matriarch's daughter. There's too much glorious money to be made, Beauty."

"But what about the part when he said he wouldn't need us for long."

"He's just trying to scare you."

"Well, it worked. He scared the hell out of me."

"Shake it off, Doll. Besides, and I hate to say it"—she can't contain her grin—"but you kind of deserved it."

"Excuse me?" I laugh. "Yeah... maybe."

We stand up. It's time to go home.

"What about Devin?" I ask her.

"What about him?"

"He'll never be allowed to see me again."

"Trust me, you haven't seen the last of him. You're under his skin now. And after what you went through tonight, you've got him wrapped around your finger. But only as a future acquisition." Her eyes grow big and she leans in close. "He'll do anything to make it up to you."

She doesn't get it.

"You're probably right, but I'm still worried about something."

"What?"

We start back up the long pier.

"Remember what I told you about the labs out on Black Rock? What I saw?"

"I remember."

"Well, between what I saw then and what I heard tonight... I don't know. I just have this feeling."

"What kind of feeling?"

"Something's not right there."

"Who cares? Since when have you been concerned about their idiotic endeavors?"

I pause to consider that thought. "I'm not. It's the animals and the secrecy. And that phrase Banks used—amp it up. I remember where I heard it first."

"Where?"

"It was Hermes, the bird that creepy plant-guy has at the base."

"It's a bird, repeating something someone said."

"I know, but that bird is ridiculously intelligent."

She starts laughing.

"Shut up. You need to meet him to understand."

"Okay, then." Kendra takes a long, deep breath. "Tell Devin he can make things up to you by taking you and your friend Kendra back out to Black Rock. Tell him you want me to meet the bird, and of course to see the sunset."

"Are you out of your mind?"

"Nerissa... for some reason, you think you're some powerless little flower. You're not. You owe nothing to any human being, and if you want answers, you've got to get them yourself. Besides, I've always wanted to see a real sunset."

"Devin got in trouble for bringing me out there. There's no way he'll agree. Especially after tonight."

"I think he'll do anything to win you back and anything he can to spite his stepdad... especially after tonight. Of course, I could be wrong."

We ride back to the Oval under a perfect, starry sky, and I message Devin. It's after midnight, and I don't expect a response, if any, until tomorrow. I get one almost immediately. Our conversation is short and to the point. Kendra's right. I'm under Devin Banks' skin, and he's glad to do whatever it takes to smooth over our grim fairytale of an evening. Kendra and I will be visiting Black Rock in two days.

16 – IMPOSSIBLE

TUESDAY, JUNE 25TH

There's no turning back now.

Kendra and I race out of Concordia's gleaming and opulent front doors.

Tap.

Tap. "Sixty-six."

Today couldn't come fast enough for her. She's giddy and a little annoying.

We've pored over the details of our visit to Black Rock, and I've made it clear how serious this is. She's assured me she'll stay alert and ask the right questions in the right way at the right time. She's got her assignments; I've got mine. I'm not leaving Black Rock without some answers.

We arrive at the base, where Devin's waiting. His skin is damp and pale as chalk.

"Where were you the last two days?" I ask. "Marcus is freaking out and won't leave me alone. Are you sick? You don't look well."

"I just wasn't in the mood," he says.

"You couldn't message me?"

"You could have messaged me, too."

"Can you just..." Kendra nudges him to the left. One step reveals the infamous red-lettered sign. She actually smiles. "Where's Walter today?"

"In his enclosure, which is electrified."

"Can we see him?" Kendra asks.

"No, thanks..." I say. "I don't want to go anywhere near that beast."

"You don't have to pet him," she tells me. "I just want to look." Then she turns toward Devin and bats her big eyes at him.

"Yeah." He sounds reluctant. "I guess we can walk by the enclosure... at a safe distance."

"Cool."

"What about your stepdad?" I ask him.

"He's not even on the island. He had some big meeting."

"Oh, good. What about everyone else? Will they be okay with us being here?"

"Don't worry. They won't question me."

"Even Manny?"

"Well..."

"Well what?"

Devin clears his throat. "We'll cross that bridge when we get to it."

"Don't worry. I'll take care of him." Kendra's nonchalance is starting to make me angry.

"Well, Officer MacNamire can be difficult," Devin counters.

"No problem."

"Okay... Let's do this. We don't want to miss the sunset." I try to mask my nerves with cheery focus.

Devin passes his blue crystal over the swipe and punches in the code. Kendra peers over his shoulder.

The gate opens, and we're on the other side. I watch Kendra take it all in, finding the moment surreal. I'm here for the second time, like it's just another day at the beach ... impossible.

"Come on," Devin says.

We walk between two red-roofed cottages. Inside the one to our left, a gray-haired man sits behind a steel desk and watches us pass, his sober expression unyielding. Past the stony witness, we continue down the manicured path; our footsteps make the only sound.

"I expected more people here today," I say quietly.

"Oh, they're here," Devin replies.

I briefly contemplate the sensation of being observed under a microscope, and the door to the building in front of us opens wide.

Out steps Officer Klein. "Devin, what are you doing here? With them?"

"Good to see you, too. Now that your pet is properly contained, my guests would like to see him."

Officer Klein snorts. "Oh, really? He's not some side-show freak, you know. And he doesn't like her." He points at me with a lazy hand.

"It's okay. I'll stay right here. I completely respect his, um... dislike of me."

"I don't think you know the meaning of respect."

"I do!" Kendra exclaims.

"And who the hell are you?"

"My name is Kendra."

"And I should care because..."

"Hey, Klein, these are my guests. And you need to show some respect yourself."

Kendra puts her hand on Devin's arm. "Officer Klein, I'm the one who wants to see Walter." Her words carry like a song. "He sounds like a magnificent animal, and I'm just fascinated by the hybrid technology the FWG is capable of. It's all so magical, so unreal." She tilts her head and twirls her hair with a long, elegant finger.

"Well it's real, all right. Walter is as real as it gets. I'm sure your friend would agree."

"Please, Officer Klein?" She's got him, and he can barely tear his eyes away from her.

"Yeah, okay. Come on." He gestures for us to follow him. "He's back here. Walk slowly, be quiet, and do not touch me."

"Excuse me, Officer," I say with a hush. "He can't get out, right?"

"I thought you were staying put?"

"Well... as long as he can't get out."

"He won't even try. Stay away from the fence, Beauties." We arrive behind a grouping of cottages, and Klein reaches up a back wall to flip a large lever with more red lettering on it. The massive enclosure before us comes to life with an audible buzz.

"That's supposed to be on all the time," Devin reminds him, his words sharp and loud.

"I know, but it's just cruel. And completely unnecessary."

"Do I need to remind you that he almost killed Nerissa, and me?"

"But he can't get out of here. Look at it. It's a damn fortress."

"Built that way for a reason."

"If anyone took the time to get to know Walter, they'd understand how to handle him."

"Aww, well, that's sweet. Maybe I'll ask him out for dinner and we can get to know each other better. But until then, keep the fence on, especially when there's guests on the base."

Klein's face drops, his eyes follow—but just for a second. He snaps up and looks squarely at Devin. "And if I don't, what are you going to do about it?"

As though he senses his friend's upset, Walter is suddenly visible at the far end of the enclosure. He's even bigger than I remember, like a black demon, his ears perked, red eyes scanning the grounds.

"Excuse me?"

"You heard me. What are you going to do? Tell Daddy that your guests felt unsafe during their unauthorized visit to the base, which he knows nothing about?"

"They have clearance. And you better not cross any further over this line."

"Let's stop pretending, shall we?"

"You've got a lot of nerve." Devin takes two steps toward Klein, and Walter is at the fence, his teeth bared and his low growl rising above the electric buzz. Devin faces him, and the animal growls louder. "You can't hide behind your hound now, can you?" He shoves himself up against Klein and grabs the man's shirt, jerking it up under Klein's chin. Walter lunges against the fence in response, instantly thrown back by the force of the shock. He lets out a horrible cry.

"No!" Klein melts in Devin's hold, sacrificing his pride. But Devin isn't satisfied, and he pushes and jostles Klein, who falls almost completely limp; the man clearly knows to show no further resistance. But Walter's instincts to protect his human override everything. He lunges at the fence, howling and snapping his teeth at Devin, and is thrown back in what must be excruciating pain. He does it again, and again, and Devin's twisted smile morphs into a sickening laugh.

"Devin, stop!" I scream, but he ignores me. Kendra throws herself on his back, desperate to end the animal's torture. Walter is relentless, the smell of singed fur and flesh rising in the air. Klein's eyes fill with tears. I'm paralyzed ... powerless.

The now muffled and exhausted whines of the loyal animal are about to send me running back to the gate and out of the base forever. Officer Klein meets my horrified expression with his own. I just barely make out the word "Please..." leaving his lips as he looks toward the back wall, then again at me. I follow his gaze and understand. I leap to the wall and pull down the lever. The drone of the fence stops and Devin's head snaps in my direction. His eyes are wild, his breath ragged.

"What are you doing?" he yells at me. "Turn it back on. It's not safe." He releases Klein and marches toward me. The Officer runs to the gate, unlocks it, and runs to Walter's side. Kendra's right behind him.

Walter lies in a heap, his breathing shallow and a quiet, constant whimper coming from his bloody mouth. Officer Klein strokes his coarse, charred fur, speaking softly.

"It's okay, Walter. You're going to be all right. I'm here. I'll fix you up. I'll bring you some chickens tonight. It's okay. You're okay." It sounds like he's trying to convince himself as well.

"What can I do to help?" Kendra asks, leaning in close.

Devin stands in front of me, my body blocking the lever. "Move aside."

"No," I tell him. "That's enough. Look at that animal."

"Are you two suddenly friends? It's not a pet, Nerissa. It's an engineered, manufactured lab rat. It's a freak. A monster. Completely unnatural!"

I want to cry. "But it's still a living, breathing, feeling creature. And it didn't ask to be created. Walter is just being what he was made to be. It's not his fault. And that was so incredibly cruel."

I can't tell if he thinks I'm completely insane or if he's never been more ashamed of himself. It seems as though every emotion a human being could ever experience ticks by behind his eyes at an impossible speed. When he can't stand it anymore, he turns and heads back to the front of the building. I let him leave. I'm glad he does.

Fifteen minutes later, Walter is stabilized, and Kendra and I have agreed—at first against her wishes—to continue out to the labs. I'm not giving up our visit to Black Rock. We need some answers. We walk around the building to find Devin sitting on a boulder, drinking an AQT. He sees us coming and jumps up.

"Well, we better hurry and get to Black Rock if we're going to see the sunset," I insist.

"Oh... you still want to go?"

"Of course. That's why we're here, right?"

"We can come back another day if you'd rather," he says.

"Devin," I say calmly. I need to convince him everything is fine. "It's pretty clear that we're not supposed to be here. We won't get this chance again. Your stepfather isn't here, the weather is perfect... and there's no time like the present. So come on. We're going."

"Okay, let's do it." He looks at his empty bottle. "I'm just going to grab one for the ride over. Do either of you want one?"

"No, thanks."

"Be right back..." He spins toward the building but stops and turns back around, "Um, how's Walter doing?"

I turn to Kendra for the answer. "Not so good. It's going to take some time. Hopefully there won't be need for a guard animal while he heals."

"But he'll be all right?"

"Eventually."

"Good to hear."

"Officer Klein's going to say that he got caught on the fence and couldn't break free." She sighs. "That was really awful."

"I'm sorry," he says. "I don't know what got into me. Why did Klein agree to that story?"

"Because I helped him realize the importance of allies."

"Okay," I interrupt. "Go get the drink, and let's go." He turns and jogs off, returning less than a minute later, looking like his usual self again.

We make fast work of descending the steep, limestone cliff. It's ten times easier without the rain, and I already know Kendra will make fun of me and call me a wimp for complaining about it. We clear the last bend, and the boathouse comes into view. My stomach sinks in anticipation of seeing Officer MacNamire.

We walk right up to the door, and Devin pounds on it. It swings open, and we're greeted by a very young, dark-skinned man who snaps his bootheels together and stands erect when he recognizes Devin.

"Hello, sir. Please come inside."

Devin shoots us a quick smile as we walk through the door, apparently just as surprised as we are by Manny's absence. Manny's bright-eyed replacement seems eager to please.

"Sir, I'm Cadet Drew Fenton. It's a pleasure to make your acquaintance."

"Nice to meet you, Drew. I'm Devin Banks."

"I know who you are, sir."

"Of course. You can call me Devin. These are my friends, Nerissa and Kendra."

We all say our pleasantries. Young Drew is already captivated by Kendra and me.

"So where is Officer MacNamire today? We were looking forward to catching up with him."

"Oh, sorry to disappoint. I believe he's on the mainland with your father. But you know, they don't tell me everything. I'm just filling in here today."

"Well then, lucky us. It's nice to meet a friendly face."

"So what can I do for you, Devin? Beauties?"

"The ladies and I need a ride out to the Rock. But we need to hurry. It's getting late."

"Oh, I'm sorry, sir—I mean, Devin. I'm not authorized to leave this post until midnight."

"No problem. I can captain one of the boats myself."

Drew's eyes shift between us and some unknown point of attraction on the wall. He takes a deep breath, then sighs. Then he does it again, trying to figure out his next move.

Devin finally attempts to relieve him. "Listen, this is easy. All you need to do is let us into the boathouse. We'll watch the sunset, come back, and leave. It'll be like we were never here."

I try to mimic Devin's breezy attitude and turn toward Hermes. "Hermes. I missed you!" I grab Kendra's hand.

"Hello, Nerissa. Good to see you again," Hermes answers me, and Kendra squeezes my hand so hard, it hurts.

"I told you this is no ordinary bird."

With our backs toward Devin and Drew, we listen to their conversation from across the room.

"Are you sure they were cleared? Nobody told me you were coming. I mean, I saw you on the cameras, but you were up there for so long, I stopped paying attention. I didn't realize you were coming down here until you showed up at the door."

Devin laughs casually. "Yeah, that figures. It's rough being the new guy. Don't I know it. They treat me like a kid and never tell me anything either."

"You didn't answer my question, sir."

"Yes, of course I'm sure they were cleared."

"Okay. I'll just call up there to make it official. You understand."

"That's not necessary."

"I'm afraid it is. This is a big opportunity for me, Devin. I have to follow protocol."

Kendra spins around. "Officer Klein is expecting your call. Remember, Devin? He said he bet the cadet will want to double-check our clearance?"

Oh no. No, Kendra. This is a bad idea.

Devin plays along. "I know, I just didn't want to embarrass Drew by making it sound like Klein was placing bets on him."

Perhaps a bit humiliated, eyes focused on the floor, Drew Fenton seems satisfied. He shuffles behind the desk, and I'm ready to watch the magic show as the wall disappears behind itself. But he stops abruptly and looks up at Devin.

"If Officer Klein and you were discussing me wanting to double-check your friend's clearance, why were you surprised to see me instead of Officer MacNamire?" He reaches toward a shiny glass panel on the desktop, ready to make a call.

"Let me explain..." Devin starts. But it's too late. Drew's touched the panel, and the line rings through a speaker.

"Yeah, this is Klein." His voice fills the room.

"Hello, sir. This is Cadet Fenton at the boathouse."

Silence.

"Sir, I have Devin Banks and two of his friends here, and they want to take a boat over to the Rock. They say they've already been cleared. Can you confirm this for me, sir?"

Silence again.

"Officer Klein, are you there?"

"Yeah, I'm here."

"Hi, Richard. It's Kendra. How's Walter?"

"He's doing a little better."

"Excuse me, Officer Klein." Drew does his best to take back control. "Can you please confirm or deny this group's clearance?"

"I told him you were waiting for his call, that you knew he'd need someone else's approval." Kendra's voice is sweet and sultry.

More silence.

"Sir?"

"Listen, you little dimwit," Klein's voice booms. "Do you know who's standing in front of you?"

"Yes, of course, sir."

"Well, I have a piece of advice for you, Cadet. And I'm speaking from personal experience. When the son of your boss tells you something, you best listen and not question it."

Drew's face blooms a deep red.

"Do I need to explain anything else?"

"No, sir. I understand. Thank you."

"Bye, Richard," Kendra yells. "See you soon!"

"Yeah, bye."

"All clear, Hermes?" Devin asks, interrupting the heavy, awkward moment.

"All clear. Time to amp it up, Devin."

Kendra and I both snap our heads back toward Hermes.

"Hermes, what does 'amp it up' mean?"

"Amp it up, amp it up, Nerissa."

"It's time to go. Now." Drew Fenton makes fast work of getting us out of here.

I pull myself away from Hermes.

We watch Drew repeat the exact steps Officer MacNamire took the first time I was here. The wall opens, and he leads us through the tiny concrete room into the boathouse. The cadet doesn't bother swearing Kendra and I in; I guess he's not qualified. Or else he's just had enough of us. Before we know it, he's secured us a vessel, and we're out in the channel, the water uncharacteristically smooth.

"That was fun," Kendra jokes.

"I'm going to make it a point to pummel that little imbecile if I ever run into him off the base."

"He was only doing his job, Devin. Take it easy." His eyes are bloodshot, his skin reflecting waxen off the black water. "Are you okay?"

He steels himself from his inner dialogue and flicks his gaze to me for a second, then back to the boat's controls. "Yeah, I'm fine."

But he's not. He's a live wire—a tormented bull on the edge of a charge. I regret continuing our journey today. I'm starting to regret a lot. But there's no turning back now.

Once across, we secure the boat and ascend the steep, metal stairway. At the top, Kendra says, "Wow! This just keeps getting better." I'm grateful for her enthusiasm; at this point, I couldn't fake it myself.

"You haven't seen anything yet," Devin says. A smile brings his face back to life. "Come on. We don't have long."

Exactly as we did the first time, we enter the reflective, sterile building and zip through the maze of hallways, finally reaching the correct elevator. We see a few people as we sprint by, but they leave us alone.

"Rooftop, please, Operator." We all try to catch our breath in the elevator.

I can't wait to see the view again, I can't wait to see Kendra's reaction.

A chime sounds, and the doors glide open. We step onto the observation deck to be greeted by the fragrant wind. The moment slows in silence as we advance toward the edge of the vine- and flower-covered wall. No words can do justice to the beauty before us. I turn to Kendra and watch her tears fall freely, sparkling in the orange glow of the setting sun, just like mine did when I stood here the first time with...

It's like I'm remembering something from a story I read or heard. Did that really happen to me? I swing my head around to meet Devin's piercing eyes, holding me in the truth of what we shared in this very spot. This is who he is, who I've fallen in love with. I don't know how I can be frozen and melting at the same time.

"Hey, you two... would you like me to leave?" Kendra snorts out an offended laugh.

We watch the last tiny sliver of light settle into the arms of the horizon.

"What'd you think?" I ask. "Amazing, isn't it?"

"I've got to hand it to you, you weren't exaggerating. That was spectacular. I don't know about the other stuff, but this? Yes, amazing."

"What other stuff?" I realize what she's doing as I ask the question.

"You know, the treacherous climb down to the boathouse and the dangerous channel crossing?" She's mocking me. "The ominous lab building with all the suspicious people and the big, giant production lines that nearly made you deaf?"

She's set it up perfectly. Back to business. What was I worried about?

"You're kind of a wimp, Nerissa John." *There* it is.

"Hold on," Devin says, coming to my defense. "It was pouring the first time we came, and—"

"No, that's okay," I say. "I know I can't re-create the weather conditions or how hard it was to get out here and into the building, but at least we could show her the production rooms, right?"

"Oh. Um..." He doesn't have to think about it long, especially when he sees the exaggerated anticipation on both our faces. "Yeah, of course. As a matter of fact, I could use a drink."

"Thanks for bringing us out here," Kendra tells him. "Nerissa was right about you."

Checkmate.

We take the elevator down to the assembly room corridor. Just like last time, it's deserted, and before I can question it, Devin reminds me by explaining to Kendra how self-sufficient the technology is.

"Oh, I know. My mom works in crystal technologies for the FWG."

"No kidding?"

"Yep. It's very possible she helped develop this exact production line. I'll ask her tonight."

"Oh, I doubt that. They keep this stuff pretty buttoned-up."

"Then why are we allowed to be here?"

"You Beauties are special."

"Well, thank you."

"You're with me, and I know you're not here to steal any formulas. Isn't that right?" He pokes his finger into my ribcage. "Because if you did, they'd destroy you..." He laughs and leans in to peck my cheek.

"Come on, Mr. Drama King. Show us around." I have to force a light-hearted tone.

Past the beauty care lines, we work our way down the long, hygienic hallways.

"Is it true that a woman drowned herself in a bathtub full of clay mask?" Kendra asks.

"Nerissa, you were under oath." He smiles.

"So it's true?"

"Every word."

We round the bend and face the Aqua Tonic assembly room. Devin's face lights up like a father looking at his newborn through the maternity ward window. The entire assembly still runs on what appears to be full throttle. The beautiful blue-green bottles are a million drones, lined up a dozen wide and forever deep in an unyielding march to their final destination. From here, it's still relatively quiet. But when I put my hands on the cold glass, I can feel the vibration of the ear-splitting madhouse within.

"Impressive, isn't it?" Devin sighs.

"I had no idea." Kendra sounds positively awestruck.

"Just a reminder... everything you see here today is one-hundred-percent classified."

"No worries. Promise."

"Seriously, I could get in a lot of trouble if people started hearing I was giving tours of the FWG's most prized project."

"Then maybe we shouldn't go in, Devin." My stomach burns with deceit.

"Well, we're here now, and I want some of the good stuff in there." He turns and looks at me with concern. "But I know you hate the noise. Do you want to wait here?"

"No way," Kendra insists. "I want to go in and see everything. Come on, Nerissa. Don't ruin it. Just cover your ears."

"Yeah, okay. I don't want to wait here alone."

Satisfied, Devin turns on his heels and goes about gaining access to the secure room, Kendra watching everything.

The door swings open, and the noise hits us with a discernible rush. Devin doesn't wait. We follow.

I cover my ears and keep my head down. It seems to take forever, but we finally arrive at the quality control room where the line splits. I run right into Devin when he stops and turns to face the line.

“What is this?” Kendra yells above the unescapable orchestra of bottle against bottle.

“The line splits here. Every hour, one case gets sent down this small line to be inspected. The rest are prepped for distribution. It’s my favorite place on this Rock.”

She gives him a thumbs-up.

“We’ve still got about ten minutes,” he tells me. “You can wait in there if you want.” He points to the closet-sized quality control room.

“Yeah. Come on, Kendra.”

“No way. I’m staying out here. This is too cool.”

“Your choice, but you’ll go deaf.” I leave them and enter the little room alone. It cuts the noise, and I feel like I can breathe again. One old metal chair with worn, white vinyl upholstery waits for me in the corner of the tiny, tired room. I plop down, facing the small window in the heavy steel door. I’m staring directly back at Devin and Kendra. They’re laughing and yelling above the noise, but he can’t hear her, so they lean in close. Kendra lays it on thick. He responds accordingly, his now recognizable blush of affection spreading over his features. He puts his right hand on her shoulder and leans over to speak something directly into her ear, lingering there a moment too long. She tilts her head and smiles, then laces her fingers through her honey-colored hair. I wonder what he said.

Just as I stand to rejoin them, a case of AQT rolls off the line, and they both jump to attention. I’m afraid nothing—or no one, not even a creature like Kendra—can hold Devin’s attention when Aqua Tonic enters the picture. Right now, I’m okay with that.

The two look like cheerleaders or amateur paparazzi, idolizing the case as it makes its way under the heavy black flap and into the tiny room to settle in front of me. The door bursts open, and they’re both buzzing with excitement.

He grabs two bottles and rips the tops off; one is at his lips even before he shoves the other in Kendra's direction. I watch him guzzle the warm liquid down, as though he'd been walking in the desert for days without sustenance. AQT spills down his chin, landing on his blue cotton shirt and spreading like an oil slick. He doesn't come up for a breath before the entire bottle is empty. It's repulsive.

"You know, I think the noise has gotten to me," I say. "Let's go, okay?"

He wipes his mouth with the back of his hand and grabs another bottle. "Yeah, sure. Just let me put a sticker on this... Cover your ears really well on the way back, and we'll run through."

"Let's just go through the back way, like last time."

"No way. I mean, we can't."

"Why not?" I clench my jaw.

"First of all, you had some kind of breakdown when—"

"No, it's okay," I interrupt and try to compose myself. "I just can't go back through that noise."

"I took a lot of heat from Officer Banks last time, Nerissa. He knew we went through that way."

"How?"

"How do you think? A lot of the corridors have security cameras. There's one just outside this back door."

"Why aren't you concerned about any of the other ones?"

"That back hallway is filled with laboratory rooms. They're kept as sterile and secure as possible. Those are the places where all the formulations and science are performed."

"Can't you just temporarily disable the camera in that hallway?"

"Well, yeah, I could. But I'm not going to. Sorry. We'll just run back through the assembly room."

It's clear what needs to happen, and I think I may be sick. I position myself right in front of Devin, leaning into him until our chests touch.

"Devin, please..." I hum, begging, my lips inches from his.

He takes my face in both hands and smiles. "You know I can't this time. But I'll carry you if I need to."

I don't think; I just act and begin counting as my lips fall onto his. Although taken off guard, he reacts just as expected and returns my kiss with craving intensity. Kendra never looks away.

I count only to two. But he wants more.

"Devin, I'd like to ask for transference." My voice is high and clear.

"What are you talking about?" He's sloppy and giggling.

"Transference."

"I don't know what that is."

"That's okay. Do I have your permission for transference?" I kiss him again for two more seconds.

"Um... yeah, sure."

I take his right hand in mine and put my CNI up against his.

"Say it. Say, 'You have my permission for transference,'" I sing.

"You have my permission for... transference. Now kiss me again."

My index finger burns hot and tingles, but I comply, and when I've reached a count of six, I pull away and examine his face. His eyes remain closed, his mouth slightly open, frozen in desire. I wait for him to sway so I can help him to the chair before he falls.

Instead, his eyes snap open, and he pulls my face back to his with such force, locking our mouths together with such greed, that I can't quite breathe.

"Impossible," Kendra mutters.

We've passed the ten second mark and entered uncharted territory. He's still standing strong, and I have to push myself backward with great effort to break his grip on me.

"Devin, stop." But he can't seem to hear me. "*Stop!*"

He seems lost, drunk with lust, and he's not going down.

Kendra pushes me aside and inserts herself between us, stepping on my feet. She grabs Devin behind the head and forces his lips to hers. They seem dead-bolted together, and I feel like I've entered a parallel universe.

Ten seconds, fifteen...

Hot tears run down my face. "Kendra, you're going to kill him!" She doesn't seem to care.

Twenty seconds...

His hands fall to his sides. I shove Kendra away, breaking their bond. Devin's eyes are slits. He loses balance and stumbles backward. Kendra steps behind him, attempting to hold him. I pull the chair from the corner and slide it under him as we ease him down.

Devin's skin is red, his breathing erratic and his face as hot as the sun. "What have you done?" I'm sobbing now, my voice catching in my throat. Devin starts twitching.

The back door to the tiny room swings open and hits me. I turn around to find a uniformed employee of the labs. His older, handsome face looks as surprised as mine.

"What's going on here? Who let you in and what are you doing?"

"Oh, thank God you're here." It's all I can think to say. "This is Devin Banks, Officer Banks' son. He's having some kind of seizure. Can you help?"

"Move aside."

Kendra and I squeeze ourselves into the corner of the tiny room and watch while the nameless man examines Devin.

"Is he okay?"

After a long, painful pause, the man finally stands and faces us.

"Is he okay?" I ask again.

"Have you three been drinking in here? Or doing anything else illicit?"

"No sir, of course not. Devin was showing us where he works, and he just collapsed." The lie comes with ease at this point.

"Well, you're both going to have to come with me, and I'll get someone to come collect Devin and let him sleep off whatever it is that did this to him. His father is not going to be happy."

I jump forward and take both of the man's hands in mine. "Thank you for coming to our rescue." He is without question a much weaker man than Devin, and the ease with which I enchant this victim of circumstance is a mere fraction of what it took to do the same to Devin.

My kiss lasts exactly six seconds, and our mystery man slumps to the floor. We prop him up next to Devin.

We stand side by side and observe them.

"Did it work?" Kendra asks me. "The transference? Did all his information load into your CNI?"

I can't look at her. But we have to move forward. "There's only one way to find out. Don't forget the camera."

"Got it." She takes off the man's shoe, reaches above her head, and smacks the camera in the corner of the back hallway until she's got it turned down toward the floor. We maneuver our way past it and agree to do the same thing to any more we find.

"Let's split up. The labs I told you about are down this hall. I'm going to see if I can find a control room for the assembly lines."

"Don't you think the control rooms will be on the main level?"

"You never know. Come on, we have to hurry."

We stop at the door to the laboratory hall.

"Here we go... Devin Banks." I run my finger over the swipe, and a green light appears. "You're in." I turn in the opposite direction.

"Nerissa..."

"Yeah?" I stop but don't look at her.

"Be careful."

“You too. Be back here in fifteen minutes. If you get caught, play stupid.”

We part ways. It may have been wiser to stay together, but I just can’t face the things I saw in the labs again. Besides, she’d think I’m crazy if she knew what I was really looking for. I wasn’t hearing things that day. I wasn’t having a breakdown. A woman was singing the lullaby from my childhood from somewhere deep in these corridors. I know I didn’t imagine it.

I reach the end of a long and otherwise door-less hallway to find an oversized, white steel entry with no windows. Nothing flanks it—no code pad, no crystal swipe. I look up and around. No cameras to be seen. Yet if I had to bet, I’d put my money on someone being able to see exactly who stands at this door at all times. I wave my CNI in front of the door. Nothing.

I wave it again just in front of the latch. Bingo.

The door buzzes, and I turn the handle to open it without effort. The sterile, shiny white behind me gives way to neon blue and black light as I stare down yet another long hallway. From somewhere deep inside, the mechanical buzz of who knows what awaits. I quickly make my way down the corridor.

Again, I find myself at a locked door, then another. With each passage, the temperature noticeably drops, and the air feels denser. Sound seems muffled, almost thick. And the color here—it’s comforting, reminiscent ... familiar, even. A wave of nausea rises in me, and my head spins as two words come slamming into my mind.

Silent.

Blue.

Silent blue.

The transference in my CNI opens what I already know is the last door I must enter. It swings inward, and the salty smell of ocean water hits me. The simulated color of the Wreckleaf fields bounces in waves off every surface. Even in the cool air, I’m sweating.

In contrast to the color and the smell of the ocean, an impressive network of machines and controls confronts me, the likes of which I've never seen. Pipes and tubes and glass control panels with blinking colored lights entwine with steel boxes, motorized parts, and shiny white desktops. A narrow, crooked walkway cuts through the crowded machinery and disappears into some unknown place beyond.

The clock is ticking, but I'm not going anywhere.

Soft singing past the machines pulls me into focus. The voice is barely discernible but undeniably female. I knew it. I knew I heard a woman singing. But I don't recognize her quiet melody.

Without a sound, I tiptoe and weave my way through the maze of churning, flashing contraptions, crouching, then standing, then crouching again. The undulating patterns of light and color seem to rock the entire room. I have to steal my mind back every few steps in order to remember this is not a dream.

I press my body up against a tall steel, vibrating box—the only thing separating me from whomever I heard that day here with Devin. With one last breath and the slowest movement possible, I peer around the cold gray shield.

Past my hiding place, the room opens into a tall, glass-enclosed semi-circle. At the far end stretches a dark, narrow corridor. To my right, a pleasant-looking, rotund woman cleans the floor, her back to me. Her dark, curly hair is held back by a red bandana, which stands out like a beacon against her crisp gray uniform and the cool blues of our surroundings. I watch her go about her business and notice she's wearing earbuds. Her singing continues, and I feel like a fool. Devin was right. All I heard that day was this woman—a janitorial servant of the FWG.

I turn my attention back to the room. Fifteen-foot-tall curved windows sit atop mosaic-glass-covered half-walls.

The windows curve inward at the top, forming a greenhouse of sorts. Although dark now, I assume they let in sunlight.

Under the windows, a room-length box gurgles, ten-feet tall and equally wide. It seems to be made of glass, but the side facing me is a dark, rusty brown and coated with some kind of material like worn resin or flaky metal. I can't be sure, but it appears the top of the structure is open. Everything inside of me wants to sneak into the room and see the side that's not visible from here.

The cleaning woman's back is still to me as she continues her routine. I make an instantaneous decision and dart to the other side of the structure. I go unnoticed.

Staring into the glass validates my worst suspicions. Wreckleaf sways in the simulated environment of the massive tank. The room starts to spin, and I have to remember to breathe.

"Hey, what are you doing? You can't be in here." I close my eyes for one last second, trying to regain composure. Play stupid. No ... that'll never work. Prepare to run or to take her down.

But she doesn't come for me, and I hear sudden laughter. It's a child.

"You know you're not allowed in here alone, Alakier. Where's your momma?"

"Mommy!" squeals the child. I hear soft footfalls coming down the hallway at the opposite end of the room.

"There you are, young man." A crystalline voice floats through the air like a feather.

"No nap, no nap," the child protests.

"Let's go. Sorry for the disturbance."

"It's no problem."

I hold my breath and peek around the tank to catch a glimpse of a tall woman in a flowing silk robe walking back down the hall from which she came. Under her fingertips prances a wobbly little boy with strawberry-blond hair, no older than two. They disappear.

Without another thought, I approach the cleaning woman. I don't give her time to speak or even think. I spin her around and press my mouth to hers and begin to count. Her startled struggle lasts but a second, and she succumbs with ease. I guide her to the floor and feel a pang of guilt for my tactics. But she won't remember a thing.

A familiar melody brings my attention back down the far hall. Now I know whose voice I heard that day.

"Let go now, precious one..." Her buttery tone spawns an impossibility in my heart.

"It's time to rest... your work is done."

I run down the hall and come to a carved, wooden door lying halfway open. Slowly, quietly, I ease it the rest of the way, my feet glued to the floor. Time stops.

In the warm, glowing light of what resembles a small home, the woman crouches with her back to me, her long, wine-red hair falling halfway to the floor, her silk robe gathered in a luxurious pool at her feet. She leans over the boy, singing to him as she tries to get him to fall asleep. "Oh, my special one, always remember who you are... you are the Universe, and that will always be..."

Yearning too much to think, I finish the verse with her. "The Universe is in you and you are free..." She doesn't move, but she sighs, and a small sob escapes my throat.

"Hello, Nerissa."

"Anastasia?" I whisper.

She stands and turns to face me. "Shh. He's such a light sleeper."

I can't move, can't breathe. I must be dreaming. This can't be real. Wild tears flood my vision as I try to soak up the sight of her and make sure she's truly here. I say nothing, plunging forward to wrap her in a desperate embrace. She places her hands around my back, loose and uncommitted.

"You're alive," I sob, tears and spit and snot mixing in a godawful stew just inches from her flawless face. "How is this possible?" I'm shaking. "And this boy. Who is he?"

"He's my son, Alakier." She beams with pride.

"Your son? Your real, blood son?"

"In the flesh."

"But..."

"I know. It's a lot to take in."

She takes me by the arm, and we leave the boy to his nap, moving to another room where we sit on fur-covered chairs.

"Ana, I'm going to get you both out of here." I jump up and pace the room. "They can't do this. We'll run, we'll fight!"

"Slow down. It's okay."

"Okay? It most definitely is not okay."

"Take a deep breath and listen to me. We don't have long."

I obey her like a scolded child, sitting back down and doing my best to slow my breathing. But the shaking will not stop. "Are you all right? Are you well? You look so pretty. So happy."

She considers my comments carefully.

"This is my home. They treat me like a queen, for the most part." Her voice catches. "It wasn't always that way, but after the boy finally came, everything changed."

"What do you mean, finally?"

"There were two girls before him. But I... I wasn't allowed to have them."

"They were never born," I say, overwhelmed by the truth behind that simple statement.

She doesn't respond to that but merely changes the subject. "Listen, you need to get out of here."

"It's just..."

"I know, this is a shock. I wasn't expecting you, either. But here you are, right in front of me, so beautiful, so full of life..." She strokes my hair and cheek. My mind can barely keep afloat. "Before you go, you need to know some things." She pauses and seems to organize her thoughts before she clears her throat. "Listen to me carefully. This will be hard for you to hear." She sounds cool and detached from her own feelings.

I suck in as much air as I can get in preparation. "I'm listening."

"First, the FWG is working around the clock to reproduce Wreckleaf. There is big, big money to be made. And William Banks won't let anything—or anyone—stand in his way. The beloved tourists, the ones so prized and treated like royalty? They're all guinea pigs, Nerissa."

"AQT. I knew it. How close are they to recreating the growing conditions?"

"I'm not sure. But what I do know is that every attempt has failed. So far. Every new batch hangs on a little longer. They've made incredible advancements. It's just a matter of time."

"I didn't think it was possible."

"Second, as much as I know you'll protest, I'm never leaving this place. This is my home now, and I'm not meant to return to my old life. I've been wrecked."

"You *can't* stay here," I protest. "We'll help you."

"*You* can't," she whispers, holding herself together by a string. "It's too late for me. My heart and soul are dead, my body is ruined. I'm unfixable." She hangs her head in shame.

"No. That doesn't matter..." I'm flailing.

"You don't understand. I'm physically dependent on a daily injection. The scientists concocted it for me when they first took me in. I'll die without it. They made sure of it. Trust me, I've tried to go without."

"Took you in?"

"Nerissa, please..." She's crying now.

"I'm sorry. They didn't 'take you in', they kidnapped you. They raped you and abused you and have held you captive for years!" I'm sobbing. "They told your mother you were dead! We all thought you were dead, but your mother..." I hang my head.

She leans over and takes my hands in hers. “I know. She’s gone. It’s okay.”

“It’s not okay! Stop saying that.” I can’t look at her. “I’ve been broken too, Ana. We all have. Things have never been the same since that night.” My voice is weak. “I can’t leave here without you. Without your son.”

“I can’t leave.” She shakes her head. “But Alakier still has a chance. They promised me they’d leave him alone, for now. But they’re going to try to duplicate him. I don’t trust they’ll wait too long.”

“What do mean? Like clone him?”

“Something like that. He’s special, Nerissa. Just like we are. If they can’t replicate growing conditions for Wreckleaf, they’ll need harvesters. The hybrid program is alive and well.”

“Yes, I’ve seen that firsthand. So they plan on replacing us with their own manufactured slaves?”

“If necessary, yes.”

“And if not necessary, it’ll be because they can grow their own Wreckleaf.”

“Yes.”

“So, either way, we won’t be needed.”

“Nerissa, you need to take Alakier and get out of here.”

“And what? Just walk out with him?”

“No... How’d you get in here, anyway?”

“I came with Kendra and Devin Banks.”

“Devin Banks? Is he here with you now?”

“It’s a long story.”

“I’m sure it is. But now you need to retrace your steps. Quickly. Very few people have access to these hallways. You shouldn’t run into anyone back here. But there are cameras.”

“I disabled the ones I could see.” I stand. I told Kendra to meet me in fifteen minutes. I’ve been here too long.

“Nerissa, be strong. And please, when the time is right, when you have a plan, come back for him. I’ll prepare myself to say goodbye.”

"He's your *son.* I can't..."

"I love him. And he deserves a better life than this."

"But things aren't the way they used to be. Everything's different now."

"I know how things are. So promise me you'll find a way. And don't wait too long."

I grit my teeth and hold back more tears. "I will. I promise. If it's the last thing I do, your son will have a chance at a happy life."

Anastasia leans in and kisses me on the forehead. "I always knew you were extraordinary."

I close my eyes, unable to fathom leaving them here. But I won't allow myself to be consumed by fear, not now. I shake my head, swallow hard, and look her in the eyes. "I'll see you again soon. I promise." Then I turn and run.

I don't focus on anything as I zip through the door, down the narrow hall, past the Wreckleaf tank, and through the hedge of controls. Back down the corridors, and through the steel-doored checkpoints, I'm unaware of anything physical except the temperature warming with every step.

I float down the final white corridor, images of my last night with Ana snapping relentlessly in my mind's eye. The lights, the dancing, the drinking. Her smile, her laughter. Then she's gone.

She's gone, and I'm alone.

But she's not gone. She's here.

She's here.

But I'm still alone.

I turn the last corner like a marathon runner crossing the finish line. I slide to a stop and bend over, racked with overwhelming emotion, then fall to my knees.

"Holy shit, Nerissa! Where were you? I almost left. Are you okay? Are you hurt?"

I've never been so happy to see Kendra, but it takes three tries for her to get a response out of me. I grab her arm and pull her toward my red, sweaty face. "She's alive, Kendra. She's alive." I can barely get the words out.

"Who's alive?"

"Anastasia. She's alive... and she has a child."

"Why would you say that?"

I look up at her. "I just talked with her. She has a boy."

Kendra takes a step back, inhales sharply, and covers her mouth with her hand.

"We need to get out of here. Come on, let's go wake up Devin if we can." I struggle to my feet and head toward the back door of the quality control room.

"Nerissa, wait."

"No, we need to leave and tell Devin everything." I keep walking.

"Nerissa, wait!" she yells.

I fling myself around to face her, annoyed by her delay. "What?"

"Devin's gone."

17 – INVERSION

FRIDAY, JUNE 28TH

I know who you are...do you?

Three days have passed since discovering Ana and her child. I would've never imagined the things we experienced that night, nor could I have foreseen the things that have happened since.

I haven't seen or heard from Devin since we left him behind in the quality control room with the unknown lab employee. It scares me to think we've injured him in some horrible way. But no one has come looking for us, questioned us, arrested us ... or killed us. Against everything inside me and at Kendra's insistence, I haven't told my mother anything.

After our escape from Black Rock and a sleepless night, Kendra and I swam to Our Beach to go over everything in private. Lying in the sand as the sun rose and life continued on around us, we pored over every last detail of the night before. Then we did it again. My head was thick with lingering questions, sadness, and deep regret. When I finally asked Kendra what she thought we should do next, her reply stunned me.

"Nothing. There's nothing we can do. And no one we can talk to about this. Not a word."

"What?"

"We're lucky to be alive, in my opinion. And Ana told you she wouldn't leave."

"She's drugged and scared and suffering from some kind of Stockholm syndrome. We can help her. And what about Alakier?"

"We can't help them. We can hardly take care of ourselves."

"Who are you? Not the girl from last night."

"Nerissa, I went to Black Rock to see the sunset. I played along with you because it was fun."

It's like a slap in the face. "Bullshit."

"You're wrong. I went out there for the thrill of it... nothing else. And then I was almost devoured by whatever that thing was in the channel."

"I told you the hybrid program has never been stopped. That creature is an underwater version of Walter."

"You told me that today. I had no idea last night."

"Really? You had no idea? After what you saw on the base and in the labs? What do you think all the little designer pets the tourists have are? They're hybrids."

"But those are harmless. They were never banned."

"You shouldn't have jumped in the water. You should have stayed in the boat. The channel is dangerous. You know that."

"We swim in dangerous waters all the time!" she yells. "I wanted to get the disgusting smell of the things I saw in those labs off my skin and out of my hair. Do not make me feel like it was somehow my fault I was nearly killed!"

"You knew this was no pleasure trip."

"Oh, you got that right. The cherry on top was dealing with that little weasel Fenton again."

"He was nothing." I try to regain composure, but can't. "What exactly did you think you were doing with Devin? You could have killed him."

"Oh please. If he had been killed, we wouldn't be sitting here. Don't be ridiculous, and stop with the jealousy. It's pointless."

"You were flirting with him all night."

"So what? I was doing what had to be done. What you couldn't do."

"You took it too far, and you know it."

"Falling in love with a human is foolish and dangerous. It's not meant to be. It's not even allowed. I wish you'd never met him. He doesn't care about you."

"Yes, he does."

"No, he doesn't. He will never love you. Stop wasting your time and stop putting us all in danger... again."

Her words cut deep. "You're not who you pretend to be, Kendra. And we're already in danger."

"I will never go back to that place. Ever. There's evil there. Those lab animals? Or whatever you want to call them... The dosage charts on their cages... those are oral doses, not topical. The beauty products the FWG is so concerned about keeping the formulas a secret for is a cover up for something much more insidious. I think the tourists may be ingesting something."

"It's the Aqua Tonic."

"That's my guess."

"It is. Ana confirmed it. We have to stop it."

"It's unstoppable. And what do you care? Let the humans destroy each other." She gets up and adjusts her swimsuit. "We've got to go to work."

"So that's it?"

"That's it. Go back to your life."

"That's what you're going to do? Go back to your life? Your enslaved existence that's been decided for you? What kind of life is that?"

"It's the only one I know, and the only one I've got. So please... let me live it. You should do the same."

"We're going to be obsolete one way or another. It's only a matter of time until your precious life crumbles in front of you!" She doesn't respond. She gets up, enters the water, and swims away. Selfish bitch.

That's the last time we spoke. We worked side by side for two full days without a word between us. Now, it's Friday morning, and I parade up and down the beach pavilion at Concordia in my clown costume. Another day in paradise.

I was close to breaking last night, close to telling my mother everything. But I didn't. Things have been quiet—surprisingly so. Maybe Kendra's right and I should keep my mouth shut. Except I can't stop the images of Ana and Alakier from assaulting me every few minutes. I can't just forget about them. It all feels like a dream. I wish it were.

Pulled from my fog, I see Marcus walking toward me like a soldier with direct orders.

"Nerissa, where's your girlfriend? She's late."

"My girlfriend?"

"Yes, Ms. Kendra Lucas. She's twenty minutes late. It's going to be a full house in another half hour. Message her right now and tell her she'd best get here if she values her job."

Yeah, why don't you do it, Marcus? I'm not her personal assistant. Or yours.

"Sure thing, Marcus. I'll do that right now."

He saunters along quickly, but I stop him before he disappears.

"Marcus? Hold on a second, please..."

He stops with a huff and turns on his heels, waiting impatiently.

"Have you heard from Devin? I mean, Mr. Banks? I haven't seen him in a few days."

His face crinkles up, and he sighs, and I know he thinks I'm incompetent. "Mr. Banks has been off the island attending to important business, but he's back." He points his nose down the beach, raising his eyebrows as if he's the owner of some classified information I'm not quite worthy to have but has decided to share with me anyway.

My head snaps to the left, and I see him. He's in his favorite spot, arms crossed behind his head, eyes closed.

"Marcus, were you supposed to leave me a message from him?"

"Not this time." He spins around and prances off, nose pointing to the sky.

I'm so relieved to see Devin's okay. We need to talk, but first I need to message Kendra.

'Where are you? Marcus is crawling down my throat. Hurry up and get here.'

I set my sights on Devin just before a young woman sits down in the lounger beside him. At first, I think it's a stranger settling in. But as I advance with caution, Devin opens his eyes and turns to look at her, a big smile proving my hopeful theory wrong. Maybe she's a cousin I didn't know about, or a family friend. But the sunny young woman with the chestnut waves and barely-there red bikini is more than just that. She tilts her head then lifts it in poised laughter, listening to whatever it is Devin's saying to her. The surf just barely drowns out their conversation; my hearing hasn't been the same since Sunday. A few steps closer should remedy that. I hope I don't regret listening.

"Why did we leave my club for this place?" she asks. "It's okay here, but..." She sounds like a spoiled child, her syrupy voice pleading for some expensive toy she saw in the store window.

"Carrie, sweetheart, this place has the best food! And their attendants are quicker. I'm sure you'll love it."

"I guess it's nice."

"Yes. Let's spend the day here. Me and you and that bikini..."

She giggles and throws her hair back. "It's new. I thought you'd like it. I know it's your favorite color."

I thought green was his favorite color.

"Come here." He pats the space on the lounger between his legs. Carrie jumps up with another giggle and plants herself right on his hand before he can pull it away. Then Devin giggles, shoving his face into her hair and nuzzling her neck. She closes her eyes and leans back, accepting the shower of public affection with total abandon.

"Mmm, Devin, these have been the best few days... Where have you been all my life?"

I guess Marcus was ill-informed of Devin's whereabouts.

"I'm here now, Beauty."

"Are you sure this is okay? They don't know me here."

"Well, they sure know me." He turns his head and sees me standing here, my mouth open, unable to look away. He locks on and holds my gaze but never pulls his face out of her blanket of shiny hair. "And they sure like my money here, too."

"Goodie. I accept." She turns to face him and glides her long, manicured fingers into his blond-tipped waves. He never takes his eyes off me. I can't breathe.

"Oh, look, baby. There's one now."

"One what?" She doesn't bother looking.

"An attendant. I'm ready for another drink. How 'bout you?"

"Sure, whatever you want."

"Watch this." Devin reaches behind him and finds the set of bells that have fallen into the sand. He has to break eye contact with me to get them, but as soon as he finds the one he's looking for, his gaze flies back to me, cruel and dark. He holds the bell high in the air and rings it hard.

"What's that for?"

"Just watch."

My feet are concrete in the sand. I can't move. I won't move. He rings the bell harder. I almost faint when I see Jade approach the couple.

"Good morning, Mr. Banks. Beauty. How may I be of service to you?"

He finally looks away from me. "My guest and I are thirsty. Bring us two Aqua Tonics, each."

"Sir, I will be happy to ring a server's bell for you right away. You have wrung a sprayer's bell, which I am happy to assist you with."

"Oh, right. Of course."

Jade rings a server, then begins the lotion application Devin has instructed her to perform on Carrie. Someone taps hard on my shoulder. I turn to meet Marcus' stony face.

"Ms. John, what exactly are you doing standing here?"

"I'm sorry, Marcus. I was feeling dizzy."

"Well, don't make a scene in front of the guests. Go to the locker room and collect yourself."

"Good idea." I bend over and pretend to fight back nausea. "Marcus, Jade and I don't normally work the same shifts. Why is she here today?"

"Because I'm short-staffed. Did you message Ms. Lucas? She's still not here. She'd better have a good excuse. Now go and splash some water on your face or something. Don't mess up your makeup."

Kicking up sand behind me, I run down the beach and through the employee entrance, past the portrait of Alexandria Bigelow. I burst through the locker room door and try to hold it together. Devin is just confused about the other night. This is all just a show...I'll tell him everything. Yes, he deserves to know. I splash cold water on my face. My makeup is fine, but my reflection seems unfamiliar.

After fifteen minutes, the locker room door opens. "Nerissa? You in here?"

I jump to attention and round the corner. "It's about time you..." But the voice doesn't belong to Kendra. The voice belongs to the towel girl. She's standing there like a mouse, her fingers in front of her mouth, her round eyes searching mine. "Oh, it's you."

"Marcus sent me to find you."

"Yeah, I'm coming." I straighten up and adjust the front of my bikini top. "How do I look?"

She looks me up and down with her sad eyes. "You're perfect, like always."

We make our way down the hall. As we pass the obnoxious portrait of 'Concordia on the Bay's Champion, Angel, and Fairest Beauty', I pretend to trip on some unseen object and knock into the ugly bitch, sending her frame into a deep, awkward angle. "Oops." I keep walking and Towel Girl looks both horrified and positively amused. She smiles up at me. "Come on," I say. "We can't keep these Beauties waiting."

"Ms. John, I trust you're feeling better." Marcus waits on the other side of the door, pacing and looking frantic.

"Yes, all better."

"Good. Get back to work. The bells are ceaseless."

He's right. The day is filled with never-ending demands. But for whatever reason, they seem a little more polite today, a bit less irritating. I work like a dog, but the day goes quickly. Still no word from Kendra.

Devin and Carrie lounge away the afternoon together, sleeping, tanning, swimming, and groping each other. I manage to avoid them. They each consume no less than my week's pay in food and drinks over the course of six hours. And each enjoy the thorough services of Jade—Carrie twice, Devin once. They're both glowing from the oils and the sunshine.

I've made up my mind. At the end of the day, I'm going to speak with him. Kendra may be right about some things, but she's wrong about him. I know he cares for me. This is just an act. We'll cut through it all when I tell him everything I know.

I wrap up my last application of the day. The guest's name is Emily, and she's the nicest, most normal tourist I've ever met.

"That was great. Thanks. What's your name again?"

"It's Nerissa. Thank you, Beauty, it was a pleasure being of service to you."

"Yeah, you can drop the formalities, Nerissa."

"Excuse me?"

"You know what I mean. I'm sure it's exhausting kissing everyone's butt all day. We can all be a little demanding."

"Oh, well you've been nothing but wonderful."

She looks up at me and grins. "Really, it's okay."

My fake smile falls, and I sigh. "Thank you. You have no idea."

"I don't, but keep your head up. Not everyone is so... you know, difficult."

"No, I suppose not. Thank you. Do you need anything else? Any snacks? A drink? I'll be happy to ring a server."

"No, thanks." She hands me a generous tip. "Nerissa, we're no different, you know. We're really just the same."

As much as I want that to be true, I'm afraid it couldn't be further from it. I look down and walk away. But I'll never forget her genuine smile.

Devin and Carrie are gone. I look left toward the pavilion, then right, past the junipers and into the gardens beyond. They're nowhere to be seen. All that remains is a pile of trash and too many beach towels for two people. The air rushes out of me.

Back in the locker room, the mood is somber. Only a few of us remain—Cassidy, Towel Girl, and myself. My hands are stained a golden hue from the oil and lotion, and my feet and legs ache. Towel Girl looks like she's been washed up onshore after a shipwreck.

"Hey..."

"Yes?"

"Are you all right?"

She smiles and looks around, making sure I wasn't speaking to someone else before she answers. "Yeah, I'm just exhausted."

"What a day, huh?"

She nods.

"Where's Kendra?" Cassidy asks out of nowhere.

"I don't know."

"Well, we're supposed to harvest this Sunday. She better not blow me off like you did to her."

My eyes bore into her. But she doesn't interpret the urgency. I glance sideways at Towel Girl and see the confusion on her face. "Don't worry, if Kendra's busy Sunday, I'll help you with your garden." Cassidy looks at me with a flash of annoyance before realizing I'm trying to cover her blunder.

"What do you guys garden?"

"I'm sorry, I don't think I know your name." I try to change the subject.

"My name?"

"Yes, your name. I don't think we were ever officially introduced."

"Hmm, I guess you're right. My name is Moriyah... Bigelow."

"Hi, Moriyah, I'm Nerissa John." I try to be playful.

"I know your name."

"Wait, Bigelow? Why does that sound so familiar?" My mind shuffles through distant information until a light begins to flicker. As soon as I grasp it, my mouth dries up, and I just want to run. The portrait. Shit.

"Alexandria is my aunt."

"I'm sorry I was so disrespectful earlier."

"Don't be. She's an insufferable bitch."

That wasn't what I was expecting. "Wait, if—"

"If Alexandria Allerton Bigelow is my aunt, why am I working here? Or working at all, for that matter... right?"

"Umm, right."

"Because Aunt Money-Machine insists we all must earn our way. We all must pay our dues."

"Well, I guess that's not a bad thing, is it?"

"Not in theory, but it's a complete and total change of philosophy from last year, the first time she brought me to this island for the summer. She tricked me, baited me."

"What do you mean?"

Moriyah plops down hard on the glossy white bench in front of a row of lockers and sighs. I follow her lead and sit down next to her. Cassidy takes the opportunity to escape her irresponsible slip and exits the locker room. Moriyah looks up and notices she's left, but she doesn't seem to care.

"Last year, I was invited to join my aunt here for the summer. I didn't want to leave my friends back home, but my parents insisted, and my aunt promised I'd love it."

"And?"

"And I did love it. I was treated like a princess. It was amazing."

"I don't remember seeing you here last year."

"You wouldn't. I never came here. My aunt went her way, I went mine, and we'd meet up in the evenings. I spent my days like a celebrity—on yachts, in spas, on beaches. I'd shop, and eat, and lounge. I was afforded anything and everything I could imagine. There were no limits, no budget, no rules."

"Wow. So what happened this year?"

"Well, when she asked me if I'd like to come back, of course I agreed. I'd made friends here. I'd had the time of my life. I couldn't wait to do it again. She seemed just as excited to have me return. She said she had some real surprises lined up."

"But not the kind of surprises you expected."

"Exactly. As soon as we arrived, it was like I was an inmate serving some kind of sentence. And she was the warden bent on making my time here miserable."

"I don't understand why."

"I don't, either. I still don't. She kept saying how she didn't get to where she is by taking the free and easy road. And she informed me I would be paying my dues this time. If I liked what I experienced last summer, it came with a price tag."

"But she didn't tell you ahead of time?"

"No. And that's the thing. I would have gladly worked to come here again. I'm not some lazy, ungrateful brat. My parents aren't rich like her, and I was never expecting anything from her. I didn't ask to come here. She invited me."

"So what do you do when you leave here?"

"I cook and clean. She's got a full staff in her giant mansion. I shouldn't have to do that. I'm so tired, Nerissa."

"Do you ever get any free time?"

"She gives me the weekend nights off."

"Good. We need to hang out sometime."

Her eyes sparkle with the tears she's holding back. "I'd love that."

"Where are the friends you made last summer?"

"Oh, they don't want anything to do with me anymore. I'm a working girl. I'm beneath them."

"Not that I want you to go, but why don't you just leave? Tell your parents and go home?"

"They already know. They said I have to stay." A tear slips out her eye, wiped away before it has the chance to invite more. "I didn't do anything wrong. I don't deserve this."

"No, you don't."

"I'll never come back here. I hate this place now. I hope to God I never treated people the way we're treated here."

"I can't imagine you ever did." I wrap my arm around her shoulder.

"I really thought my aunt was this great person. I didn't see her that much last year, but when I did, she was so nice to me. But now it's all different. At least I can see her for what she really is..."

"She's dangling her riches and power in front of you."

"It's like she got me hooked and then took it all away, just for fun. Just because she can."

"It probably makes her feel important. She probably really believes she's teaching you something."

"Oh, she's teaching me something all right. This whole place is. It's not the Utopia it's made out to be when you're on the other side."

"No, it's not."

She wipes her cheeks again and turns to face me. "What about you, Nerissa? What's your story?"

For the briefest, most fleeting second, I consider telling her everything. "That's a long, boring story for another day. And I really have to get home."

"Okay. Just one thing. You never answered me before."

"About what?"

"The garden. What's in your garden? I have one back home. Cassidy said harvest. It must be a big garden."

"Oh, we just joke around with that, you know, to make it sound better than it is. It's just a little vegetable garden we all agreed to help with."

"Yeah, it can be a lot of work. And if somebody doesn't do their share, it can be a nightmare."

"Exactly."

"Listen, I'd really appreciate if we could keep this between us. My aunt doesn't like sharing family business."

"I understand. My lips are sealed. Now let's get out of here."

We finish changing, gather up our belongings, and walk out the front door. Moriyah follows me.

Tap. I can't remember how many days are left. I only know what it feels like. "Ten thousand, five hundred."

"What?"

"Nothing."

Across the lot, we reach our boards and bring them to life. From behind, a voice rises from a dark hedge and scares us both.

"What took you so long?" It's Devin. He emerges from the shrubbery like a vampire—bloodthirsty and waxen.

"You scared me! What are you doing?"

"I was waiting for you."

"Where's your Carrie?"

"She's gone."

"Good. I want to talk with you. Moriyah, I'll see you tomorrow."

"Bye, see you tomorrow." She doesn't hesitate and promptly leaves.

"Devin, I have something I need to tell—"

He interrupts me with a sharp, stern voice, his eyes glazed over and emotionless. "Don't waste your breath or any more of my time."

"What?"

"I know you're not deaf. You heard me. In fact, you've got extra-special hearing, don't you?"

My heart is speeding up. "What are you talking about?"

"Stop pretending, Nerissa. Stop lying."

"Lying about what?"

He clasps his hands together in front of his face and inhales deeply. "What were you going to say to me when I woke up the other day? That is, if you had stuck around to make sure I was okay?"

"Devin, you fainted. We went for help."

"Is that what happened to Albert?"

"To who?" But I realize who he means even before I get the question out.

"Albert, the lab tech you poisoned and left for dead alongside me."

"Devin, I didn't poison you, I—"

"Stop lying!" He grabs my shoulders and shakes me.

"Let go of me, right now. You're hurting me."

"Do you remember who my father is? Who I am?"

"I know who you are... Do you?"

He disregards me. "When I woke up in the quality control room, slumped over with Albert on the floor next to me, everything was so foggy, and I was scared. I didn't know where you were. I thought we'd been attacked, or that we were sick..."

"Devin, wait. Please. Let me explain."

"When I was able to shake myself back to full consciousness, I started to remember. I thought I was remembering a dream. But the clearer it got, the more I knew it was real."

"You shouldn't have been able to remember. You shouldn't have even woken up that fast." I fumble in regret.

"Well, I did!"

"Devin... I'm sorry. Please..."

"I was so confused. I was so worried about you. At first. Do you know what I did then?"

I can't answer him. I can't look him in the eyes.

"Do you? Answer me! Do you know what I did then, Nerissa?"

I shake my head, still unable to look at him.

"I picked up poor, unconscious Albert, and I carried him to the elevator. We went down to the main level, and I alerted the front desk that we'd fallen ill."

I reach out to him, shaking, but he won't allow me to touch him. I lean in, and he steps back. I hang my head; my tears fall and follow a crooked path.

"They wanted to lock down the entire building as a security measure. But I wasn't sure if you were out yet. And even though that memory was getting clearer, I still wanted to make sure you were safe. So I lied and told them Albert and I had over-indulged, partied too hard, and there was no need to lock down."

I'm hardly breathing, my throat catching with every inhale and every exhale.

"We got Albert to the nurse's station and made sure he was stable. After a few hours, I left. I was glad there was still someone there to get me across the channel, since our boat was gone. Do you know Albert didn't regain consciousness for nearly six more hours? And the kicker... do you know what it is?"

"No."

"Oh, I think you do. But let me indulge you. The kicker is, he doesn't remember a thing. How convenient for me.

He believed my story, too, even though he barely knows me... and he doesn't drink. Then Albert got fired!"

There's a long, excruciating pause. I feel him staring down at me; I feel his resentment. He steps to the side and reaches into the bush where he was waiting for me to retrieve something. The familiar twist, crack, and fizz makes it unnecessary for me to look up. He makes no apologies, takes no measures to restrain himself as he guzzles the bottle of AQT nearly to its bottom.

"That stuff is the poison."

"Oh, that's a good one!" He laughs. "This stuff saved my life!"

"What is that supposed to mean?"

He ignores my question. "When I got home, I was really freaked out. I didn't know what happened to me or if I was going to be okay. So I did something quite unusual... for me, anyway."

He tilts his head back and throws down the last few sips. I finally look up at him. His eyes are bloodshot and sunken, the light I'd grown so accustomed to gone. And I'm filled with regret. A very small, maniacal smile pulls his mouth up at the corners.

"I messaged Officer Banks late that night." He's slow and robotic, almost as if he can't believe what he's saying. "I was so upset that I sought council from the great William Banks." His intensity falters for only a second. "It was a very enlightening conversation, to say the least."

My body has left the Earth, and I'm only aware of the pain in his eyes and the fear spreading into every corner of my being. He can see right through me—right into me. And to my surprise, tears stream down his cheeks.

"I was falling in love with you. Stupid me."

"No, it's not stupid..." I reach up to wipe his face, but he catches my wrist. He squeezes hard, and I try to pull away. "Let go." But he holds fast, gritting his teeth and breathing hard. He grabs my other wrist, pulling both up in front of us. Then he leans in and looks at me with such contempt, I wilt in his grasp.

"I know exactly who you are, Nerissa John. Exactly what you are."

"You know nothing, Devin."

This makes him angrier. "You are a liar. And a criminal."

"A criminal? Are you serious? Is that what your stepfather said? That I'm a criminal?"

"That among many other things."

"Well that's the epitome of hypocrisy! William Banks is the criminal, not me."

"You're dangerous. Your entire family is."

"Again... the pot calling the kettle black. *He's* the dangerous one."

"But you're the one who almost killed me, you and your bitch friend, you murderous liar."

"Devin, this is ridiculous. I would never do anything to hurt you. I swear."

"That's enough!" He shakes my wrists with enough force to throw me off balance. My body goes slack. He lets go of me. "This is from my dad." He reaches into his back pocket and pulls out a crumpled, sealed envelope.

"What is this?"

"I have no idea. But he insisted I hand-deliver it to you." I take the envelope and shove it in my pocket. "It's over, Nerissa, we're over. Do yourself a favor and leave me alone."

"Leave you alone? How about you leave me alone and stay out of my workplace with your whores?"

He pauses briefly. "Don't worry, I won't be back."

"Devin, before you go, please... I just want you to know something."

He regards me with detachment—a soldier who's crossed enemy lines. "What is it?"

"If you really know who I am, like you said, then you'd know this without a doubt. If I had wanted you dead, you wouldn't still be standing here making an ass of yourself."

18 – The Incomparable William Banks

FRIDAY, JUNE 28TH

This is a game you cannot win.

"Hi, Mom."

"You're late. Where have you been?" Something's up. She never waits at the kitchen table for me to get home.

"We were short-staffed at work, and it was such a crazy day, I just needed to decompress. I went for a quick swim in the river." I hope the water washed away my tear-battered face. "It's so peaceful there at night, and—what's wrong?"

"It's Kendra."

"Yeah, she didn't show up at work today, and Marcus was so pissed. She wouldn't return my messages. She's going to get fired."

"That's not what I'm talking about."

The hairs on my arms rise. "Then what are you talking about?"

"There's been an accident."

My stomach flips. "Kendra? Is she okay?"

"Hopefully."

"Hopefully? What does that mean, Mom!?" I yell at her, pleading for something more. "What happened?"

"There was a break-in at the house after Giovanni left for work this morning."

"A break-in? People don't do that here. What did they want?"

"They didn't steal anything. The only thing missing is Kendra's nautilus shell necklace. But that was probably just ripped off in the attack."

"Attack?"

"They raped her and beat her badly."

The chair behind me catches me as I stumble and collapse. "What? That's not an accident... How... why didn't she..."

"We don't know why she didn't or couldn't enchant them. They may have knocked her out first."

"They?"

"We think two."

"Mom!" I sob openly in front of her. I can't stop.

For the first time in such a long time—longer than I can remember—my mother comes to my side and embraces me. I crumble into her open arms and dissolve into a black hole of sorrow. She doesn't rush me. She just allows it. I stay there a long while, soaking in the comforting smell of oleander perfume on her skin. But now her scent will forever remind me of this inescapable darkness. And now I'm mad.

I push away and stand up, knocking the chair backward and onto the floor. "Who did this to her?" I demand, as though she's hiding something from me.

"We have no idea. They left some footprints, you know, tracked in some dirt on their shoes, but that's it. And we can't exactly bring her to the hospital for testing."

"But maybe we should."

"You know we can't."

"Is she going to be all right? Can I see her?"

"Giovanni's with her. She needs to rest now. You can visit her tomorrow."

"She'll never be the same," I whisper. "They've ruined her."

"Kendra is young and strong, and her body will heal. They cannot take her essence from her. No one can steal away who we are on the inside."

I want to join in her devotion, but I can't.

Tatiana walks me to my room and even offers to stay with me. It's tempting. I don't know when I'll ever be afforded the luxury again, but I want to be alone. I need to be. She kisses me on the forehead and encourages me to stay positive and to sleep. But I'm not sure I'll ever sleep again. My head is spinning, every thought vying for the front of the line.

I take off my clothes and get into the most comfortable pajamas I can find. I look like a drunken homeless person in my drab flannel pants and Devin's wrinkled green t-shirt. My red, swollen face tops it off. I grab my clothes off the floor to throw into the hamper, turning them right-side-out and emptying the pockets. Then my fingertips find the envelope from Devin's stepfather. I forgot it was there. A big part of me wants nothing more than to rip it into a thousand little pieces and light it on fire. But I have to open it. I need to see what that man could possibly have to say to me.

I climb into the safety of my bed and prop myself on a mountain of pillows. I slowly pull at the edge of the expensive textured envelope and peel it away from the black wax seal embossed with WB. I want to spit on it. I remove the thick, linen-like paper and take a deep breath. Okay, I'm ready ... I think. But nothing can prepare me for this.

Dear Miss Nerissa John,

I hope this letter finds you well. It has been brought to my attention that you have taken great interest in some of my official work with the partnership between the First World Government and Bio-Genesis Wave Technologies. Thank you for your regard.

I have also been informed of your second, most recent visit with your friend Kendra Lucas to Black Rock and the BWT laboratories. As you know, this is a highly restricted area and reserved for very select and recognized individuals. My stepson, Devin, has once again misunderstood his position. However, we are looking at this slip of judgement as an opportunity to set forth new guidelines and restrictions for everyone. Devin now understands the consequences of ignoring them. I'd like to thank you for assisting us in the clarification of these important standards.

As you are well aware, breaches in contractual agreements, whether verbal or written, carry with them hefty and non-negotiable disciplinary actions. However, because you and Miss Lucas were invited and escorted by an authorized individual onto the FWG base, as well as onto Black Rock and into the BWT building, you were not technically in breach of any contractual laws.

While I will not take any official action regarding this matter, it is my obligation to inform you this letter serves as a serious caution against any further bending of said laws. In other words, you and your filthy little friend stay off my base, off my Rock, and out of my laboratories. Stay out of my business and all other FWG affairs. Although I love partaking in a good, strategic game with worthy and comparable adversaries, this is not to be considered as such. If you take advantage of my generosity and continue to poke your nose where it doesn't belong, or if you discuss this or any of the things you are under oath not to disclose, you will come to regret your choices.

Devin has been instructed to cut you out of his life, and I suggest you do the same with him. You and your family's lives depend on you taking this with the utmost seriousness. If you do not, I will crush you. This is a game you cannot win. You have been warned.

Thank you. I bid you a pleasant evening.

Fondly,
William Banks

19 – THE SACRIFICIAL HERD

MONDAY, JULY 1ST—SUNDAY, JULY 28TH

It's a reminder that money cannot buy happiness.

The weeks trudge on—a pattern-less ebb and flow. I'm trapped in this prison of silence, this lonely place tossing me about without warning from one moment to the next. The sweet release of shouting everything I know to the world seduces me. What more do I have to lose? Nothing. And everything.

Kendra came close to dying, and she still won't see me. I can't remember ever going this long without her, under any circumstance. She told her mother she didn't want me to see her beaten beyond recognition. I begged Giovanni to let me see her anyway. But she wouldn't.

"I don't understand, either, Nerissa. But I can't force things. She's been through a lot, and they really messed up her head. Give her a few more days. Her wounds are healing. She's starting to get up and around, and I'm sure she'll be ready soon."

"Starting?"

She rubs my shoulder and sighs. "Those bastards beat her bad. They knocked her out. She had a concussion. They broke her leg and cut her up."

I can't breathe.

"They gagged her, taped her mouth shut, and took a knife to her face. Then they pummeled her with their filthy fists." The anger and pain in her voice is profound, but she somehow manages a smile. "No doubt my baby still put up one hell of a fight. Those boys probably didn't fare too well, either. She had their blood on her hands and under her nails."

I swallow her words and search her face. Did she really just say that? All at once, I'm thankful I haven't seen Kendra yet. But my mind can't stop its own train of thought. I don't want to ask, but the question spills out anyway. "Gio... did they destroy her... inside? I mean..."

"I understand. But the truth is, we won't know for quite some time. Not until she's ready to acquire... if she'll ever be."

There's no appropriate response. "Please tell her I'm thinking about her. That I love her. And I'm here whenever she's ready to see me. And that I'm so sorry." I just manage to get those last words out.

"Nerissa, you have nothing to be sorry for."

But I do. Kendra knows the same as I that her 'accident' was by design. And surely, just as I do, she blames me. At least in part.

William Banks wrote that letter like a proclamation. The twisted son of a bitch wanted to make sure I understand how serious he is. He's made it crystal clear. I just wish it had been me and not Kendra. It scares me to think about what else he's capable of destroying.

Any thought I had of talking to my mother is now out of the question. And I've resigned myself to the fact that I can't save Ana and Alakier. At least not now. But I swear, if I ever find out who carried out William Banks' orders to hurt Kendra, I will make sure they're paid back.

Devin has kept his word and stayed away from Concordia. My heart aches for him. He's left a space inside me that can't be filled by anything. Sometimes it catches me off guard, and I surrender to it. Other times, my sadness makes me angry. I think I'm losing my mind, and it scares me.

Devin and Kendra's absences at Concordia have nearly killed Marcus. I play dumb to both issues, keep to myself, and claim I know nothing. He doesn't believe me, and I don't care. It all feels so meaningless, and I'm so tired of everything and everyone. Mostly, I'm tired of myself.

"Hello? Nerissa?" My mother snaps her fingers in front of my face as she gets up from her seat across the kitchen table. "Are you going to answer me?"

"I'm sorry. What was the question?"

"All right, that's enough." She slams her coffee cup down on the table.

"What's wrong?"

"You tell me. I haven't been able to hold your attention for two minutes lately."

"You have it now."

"You are constantly distracted, and you've been sulking around for weeks."

"Sulking?" I scoff.

"Yes, and honestly, you really don't look good."

"Impossible."

"Apparently not."

"Thanks, Mom."

"I'm sorry, but something's got to snap you out of this funk you're in. What's wrong?"

Tell her, Nerissa. Tell her everything. Let it out.

"I'm fine. It's just..."

"It's just what?"

"I miss Kendra. I want to see her."

She exhales and sits back down. "She's gone through a lot. Surely you can relate." She leaves the table to go to the sink. "I notice you haven't mentioned that boy in a while. What's his name? The one you were scouting."

Is she serious? She knows his name. She knows it like she knows her own. "Devin Banks." It's the first time I've said his name for what feels like forever, and as it floats off my lips and forms in front of me like a vision, I have to close my eyes to hold in the pain.

"What happened to him?"

I clear my throat. "Umm, turns out he's not such a great catch." I can't come up with anything better.

"Well, easy come, easy go. All right. I have to get to work, and you need to get yourself focused for harvest. The water is a little rough from the rain last night. Use extra caution."

Talking to her is like riding a Ferris wheel. "Who am I scheduled with today?"

"Lillian."

"Oh, great. That girl's always late."

"Cut her some slack. She's also been through a lot."

"We all have."

She swallows one last sip of coffee, puts the mug in the sink, wipes the sparkly white counter with a towel, and leaves the kitchen without another word. We each retreat to our bedrooms to prep for our days in solitude. Tatiana will emerge dressed in a crisp white suit, ready to dazzle at work. I will don shorts and a tee, a bathing suit underneath, a sturdy waist pouch, and aqua shoes, ready to slip under the barrier ropes at Playa Rosa and swim to Albatross.

I can't ever remember a time when I wasn't looking forward to harvest. It's not that I'm usually anxious to provide the capitalistic pigs who head the FWG our precious resource. Nor do I particularly enjoy the businesslike approach we take toward the whole thing. It's the silence. It's the clarity. It's the stripping away of everything else and living in the exact moment, because if I don't, I could die. And of course, it's the color. But there's a first time for everything. For me, it's today.

As expected, Lillian's running late. I've been sitting on the beach alone for a hundred years. Behind me, a half-dozen resort brats have taken up a raucous game of volleyball. I don't understand why they're here polluting this beach. If I have to listen to their fake laughter and high-pitched squeals one more minute, I'm going to drown myself. Gabriel has come and does his best to linger as we wait for Lillian.

"Excuse me!" A volleyball has rolled down the rose-colored sand and comes to rest about fifteen feet to my side. "Excuse me, would you get that?"

I don't move.

"Umm, hello? The ball?"

I turn around slowly. "Are you speaking to me?"

"Duh! Get the ball. It's right next to you."

I turn back to face the water and falter in my disbelief for another few seconds. Then I stand and ever-so-slowly retrieve their ball, turning again to face them. One of the girls stands like a mannequin, her left hand propped on her hip, her head tilted. Another girl has her arms crossed, a deep scowl underneath her gold designer sunglasses. And the third one is simply too exhausted to be bothered and lies in the sand while the ball is recovered. Three tanned, muscled guys, each one looking identical to the next, stand in a huddle, watching my every move. Two have the stupidest smiles on their faces; the third can't keep his mouth closed. I walk toward them, their pristine white ball tucked under my right arm.

"Hello, little Beauty. Why so slow?"

Silence.

"Ball, please." The middle guy holds out his hands.

I am a statue.

"Hello? I'll take the ball. Now."

"Yeah, and I'll take a number-two spray." The sun-queen obviously recognizes me and barks her meaningless order.

I am an impending hurricane.

"Looks like somebody got cheated in the brains department, huh, fellas?" They all laugh.

"Good thing you're a hot little bitch," his friend flaps, "or you'd have nothing going for you." He doesn't have a chance to laugh again, as my hand is at his throat and my face just inches from his.

His friends move quickly, trying to pull me away.

A thick voice cuts through the insurgence. "Now, now, everyone relax! I've got the potion to end this commotion... ha-ha-ha!" Gabriel inserts himself between me and Mr. Big Talk. I hold my ground for one more second, then back off.

"What's your problem, little lady?"

"My problem, little man, is you and your posse, here. For your information, I don't work here. As a matter of fact, you're on my beach."

"God, you're such a bitch," mannequin-girl announces.

"And you are a lazy, insufferable, spoiled little brat. You all are. Go get your own fucking ball!" I rip the ball from under my arm and kick it as hard as I can. My shoe comes off and flies with it. Everything happens in slow motion as Gabriel steps in front of me, and I turn and run toward the water as fast as I can. I throw myself into the safety of an oncoming wave. I can only hope they all watched the ball and not me. No doubt they think I'm certifiable. I turn to face the open ocean.

A few minutes later, Gabriel stands at the water's edge, my shoe in his hand. "Here."

"Thanks."

"They didn't see anything."

"Okay."

"Remember, child, no one can take your power from you unless you give them permission."

"I couldn't help myself."

"You can always help yourself."

I breathe deep and exhale deeper. "It's just so hard sometimes."

"Come to the cliffs with my harvest tonight."

"The cliffs? Are you sure?"

"Yes."

"I will if Lillian ever gets here."

"She'll be here. Now, Gabriel must go quench the thirsty."

As soon as he's back up the sand, he has the crowd's unyielding attention. He's like a magnet—a superstar—and they can't get enough of him. Of course, the goods he's selling don't hurt.

I immerse myself into the liquid turquoise blanket and try to clear my mind. Damn Lillian for being so late. None of that would have happened if she were here on time. I look back at Gabriel and all around me. No one looks my way. I'm done waiting. I rip my shoes back off, shove them in my waist pouch, and I'm gone.

Swimming out to Albatross alone is the single best thing I've done in a long time. My last harvest was with Cassidy two days after Kendra was attacked. It was fine; I just don't really like that girl. There's something about her that rubs me the wrong way. She tried to apologize for her indiscretion in front of Moriyah. But the whole conversation was weird.

"I'm sorry for my slip in the locker room the other day."

"Don't worry about it, Moriyah believed the vegetable garden story."

"Nerissa, if she's the niece of that horrible, gross-rich woman, why is she working?"

"It's a long story, but let's just say things aren't always as they appear."

"Oh, come on. Tell me."

"Maybe some other time."

"Nerissa... what really happened to Kendra?"

I don't think twice, don't try to hide anything. "She was raped and beaten up really bad."

"Oh, no. The whispers were true."

"Who was whispering?"

"My mom and some of the others."

"Yeah, I'm surprised my mother didn't call a meeting."

"I heard that's happening in a couple days."

"Figures I'm the last to know. Well, let's see how she sugar-coats it."

"What do you mean?'

"Tatiana likes to bend the truth to suit the moment." In this case, she couldn't be blamed. She doesn't know the real reason Kendra was targeted.

"I just hope, for Kendra's sake, that they didn't render her incapable of getting pregnant."

"I hope you're right. But really, would it be so bad to not have one sole purpose in life? One that she didn't even choose?"

"I can't believe you just said that."

"It's not everything, Cassidy."

"It is in our world, Nerissa. You have no idea what it's like to be thought of as useless. It's a good thing I can carry out a good harvest—which, by the way, even after picking up the slack for you, I'm hardly ever assigned to anymore."

"I'm sorry. I—"

"I've been cast out, isolated, made to feel like nothing more than a burden to keep fed. I have to prove my worth constantly. It's exhausting."

"We all have to prove ourselves."

"It's easy for you to say. You're the daughter of a Matriarch."

"Let me remind you that I'm single-handedly responsible for our breed's discovery. The only one who doesn't resent me for it is Kendra." My voice caught as I realized I'd lost that, too. "You try carrying that around with you."

Cassidy was right. Three days later, my mother called a gathering to disclose information about Kendra's situation. It was quite possibly the most uncomfortable moment I've ever experienced, even worse than the service for baby Charlotte. Tatiana did her best, but it was awful.

The arena was in a hush. Giovanni sat in her chair next to my mother, silent and stoic the entire time. Tatiana had no trouble getting our attention. After her usual history lesson, she was short and to the point.

"Maids, the rumors you have heard are true. Kendra was attacked and raped by two men in her home last Friday. She sustained multiple life-threatening injuries and remains in a state of heavy sedation." Then the questions started.

"Why didn't she enchant them?"

"She was knocked unconscious and her mouth was taped shut."

"Are her injuries irreparable?"

"That is still unknown."

The gasps and whispers rose into the air like a cloud of toxic smoke.

"Who did this? Why?"

"At this time, we have no leads on the identities of the men, nor have we determined a motive. It is most probably a random act. We will keep you informed if and when we learn more."

"Is she going to live?" Lillian's sad and feeble voice pulled my attention off the floor and back to my mother's face.

"We foresee her regaining consciousness."

That answer has haunted me for almost three weeks. And what rides alongside it is the last thing Kendra said to me about her life. "*Please—allow me to live it.*"

Something catches my eye and rips me back to the moment. Was that a fin? I slow down and look around. Nothing. But then a large form materializes from the depths below, moving fast. The hybrid monsters that live in these waters are rarely seen, especially in the daytime. Some people believe they're a myth. But they're out there, and it'd be just my luck that today, they're out before dark. I'd have to surrender. I've got no more fight in me.

The creature moves closer, zips by inches from my face, and shoots out of the water into the air above my head. As it comes crashing down a few feet away, three more follow. They're dolphins, and we recognize each other at once. I couldn't be more thankful for their perfect timing. Laughter and joy replace fear, sorrow, and regret, and however temporary it may be, I welcome it.

We complete the rest of the swim to Albatross side by side. They know as I turn toward the in-tube that our journey together is done for now.

I glide into the caves with a renewed sense of strength. Inspired by my friends, I close my eyes and zip through the passageways. My fingertips graze the smooth walls of the enclosure. My accuracy confirms my hearing is back to factory settings. So confident with myself, I flip over and sail along with ease.

Just before the final breathing chamber, my shoulder collides with a passageway wall, and when I emerge, I complain to no one. I rub the top of my shoulder and laugh at myself. Best to keep my eyes open. I need to get serious and focus.

I descend the tube to the ship graveyard. Last night's rains churned things up a bit. The deep, rich blue is a bit dim and muddled.

I power out to the farthest wreck we harvest from and can taste the rust yards before I arrive. The Wreckleaf is tall and abundant here, glimmering in a frenzied dance. Dozens of fish scatter as I approach, no doubt intoxicated and numb. I go about my harvest, lifting the roots from their ancient host and pushing them deep into my waist pouch. The slip between my fingers is both sublime and electrifying.

Back at the chamber I transfer the Leaf to a pair of larger satchels. They'll both be full in two more dives. I'll be done before Lillian arrives, if Lillian arrives.

Back down the tube and into the muted indigo, I've saved the closest wrecks for last. I maneuver to the left, gathering the weed on a small primitive-looking vessel nearly erased by the passage of time and the shifting sediment. I make quick work here and am about to shoot back up the tube but impulsively decide to go to the last wreck instead. I've got plenty of air and enough room in my pouch to finish the job.

The last wreck is an obsolete relic, its enormous hull collapsed on top of itself like the fossilized ribcage of an extinct monster. It appears to have been some kind of research vessel, having come to rest on its side. Huge, ruined beams crisscross in a frozen pile of debris, and the skeletal remains of a possible communication tower lay broken and scattered across the sea floor to its side. It is one of the most productive growers but precarious to navigate.

I stay smart and remain on the upward-facing section of the hull where the current is smooth and the Wreckleaf grows thick. I float inside the slippery fronds, swaying and lurching with the ocean around me. It caresses my skin like a gentle lover, hypnotizing me with its subtle seduction. I could stay here forever. And now I wish I had gone for a breath so I could linger. I'll grab a few handfuls, then get some air and come back to enjoy the solitude.

I reach into the green carpet and pull up a handful. Then again. One more, and I'll take a break. My fingers reach blindly, and this time, my ring catches on something in the thick fronds past the roots. I pull back, but it's stuck. I relax to release myself, but it's no use. My ring is wedged tight, and at this angle, it's impossible to slide my finger out. A small panic creeps in; I'm going to need to come up for air. Soon.

I pull and push and pull again, my body thrashing and heaving in a fight for life. Turns out, I'm not ready to die. Like Kendra said, this is my one and only life—all I know. I'm not ready to give up on it. But it looks like the Universe has other plans for me.

I fight with everything I've got. But no amount of struggle will set me free, and the inevitability of the situation grows clear. It's time to allow things to take their course. I'm not afraid, just sad, regretful, and empty.

I can think of no other place I'd rather be as the light comes out of me—this sanctuary, this garden of perpetual life and death. It's poetic, really. And as I begin to surrender, I imagine becoming one with the Wreckleaf and the ships. I will forever belong to the place in which I found myself. It's beautiful. I absorb one last, sweeping gaze, then close my eyes.

"Nerissa! Nerissa, wake up!" Something jostles me, shaking me too hard. It really doesn't feel good, hurting my shoulder. Stop it. Stop. That hurts.

My eyes open. I spew an aquarium's worth of water out and roll to the side, retching against the salt in my throat. "Stop it. That hurts," I manage to choke out.

Someone laughs through heavy, frenzied breath. I turn over again to find Lillian's ghost-white face, her lips quivering in a small smile.

"Oh, thank goodness. Are you okay?"

I consider her question and look myself up and down. Everything rushes back to me, and then I feel the pain. I hold up my right hand. My middle finger is bent at an impossible, unnatural angle, swollen beyond recognition. My ring is not on it.

"I'm sorry. I had to break it. There was no other way except cutting it off. I hope you agree with my choice."

"Umm, yeah, of course. Thank you, I think."

"You're welcome. Nerissa, I'm so sorry I was late. Why didn't you wait for me? You would have died in another few minutes."

I'm not in the mood for a lecture. "I know."

"All right. Let's get you back home so that finger can get set."

"No. I'm going to Gabriel's."

"You really ought to have that taken care of first."

"Don't worry about it. I'll handle it." I'm short with her, which isn't the nicest way to treat someone who just saved my life. "What happened to my ring?"

"I don't know. It wasn't my priority."

"I'll be right back." I jump in the water and zip through the tube before she can protest. If I were her, I'd probably leave.

I swim to the spot where my life almost ended. I swish at the Wreckleaf with my other hand, trying to locate the exact spot I was trapped, pulling up Leaf and releasing it into the current. I waste at least an entire satchel-full before I finally concede. My ring is gone.

Lillian waits for me in the chamber. She doesn't speak another word. The look on her face says it all—her eyes so big they may pop, her lips and jaw so tight they appear to be sewn shut. We secure the harvest in silence and begin the return to Panacea. Lillian will deliver to my mother. I'm headed out to the caves to see Gabriel. I haven't been invited there in a long time, and I won't pass it up for anything.

Beyond the halfway point, we make out a floodlit commotion on Playa Rosa. We keep swimming, then pop up for a quick rest less than a hundred yards out.

"I wonder what that's all about."

"Let's skirt around to the left," she suggests.

"We can't. if someone sees us coming up out of the water there, it won't make any sense."

"It's too crowded and bright at our normal spot. If we want to come up there, we'll have to wait."

"I don't want to wait. Let's go left. Just be careful. And put your shoes on before you get out."

"Thanks for reminding me."

We exit the water at the far end of Playa Rosa undetected, just beyond the illumination of the emergency lights flooding the beach. Lillian and I blend in with the crowd of onlookers.

"Hi Nerissa." I turn to the left but can't quite place the pretty, familiar-looking young woman. "It's Emily, from Concordia... You were my attendant the other day, remember?"

"Oh, yes! Hi, Emily. This is my friend, Lillian."

"Nice to meet you."

"You, too."

"Were you girls swimming outside the barriers? In the dark?"

"Oh, yeah. There's a shallow spot where we collect oysters." I pat the stuffed bag at my hip and hope she doesn't ask to see my catch.

"In the summer? After dark?"

"Emily, what happened here?" Even though it's obvious, I point to where everyone seems to be gawking.

"Some moron lost control of their boat and drove it right up on the beach. You must have seen it. Or at least heard it."

"Did anyone get hurt?"

"Yeah, the driver, the three people on board, and the poor woman they hit."

"Was the driver drunk?"

"Drunk and high on something, along with everyone else on board. This will be fun to clean up."

"They'll make it look like it never happened." She stares at me. "What brings you out to Playa Rosa?" I ask.

"I like this beach. It's so big and open and... unpretentious. I've been here all day. I saw you earlier. That was quite a kick!"

"What does that mean?" Lillian asks.

"Oh, nothing, I just, umm, I..." I stutter, unable to form a sentence. What else did she see?

Emily laughs. "Nerissa had some salty words for a rude group of volleyball players."

"You said kick."

"Yes... she kicked their ball so far, I was sure they'd abandon it and just go buy another." Emily laughs.

My eyes fall to the sand. "I over-reacted."

"No, you didn't. Those little urchins deserved it. But then you just disappeared. Where'd you go?"

"I had to run an errand for my mom."

"Oh, okay. You vanished so fast, I thought you were upset."

"No, I'm fine."

"Good. I'm glad you're back. I have something for you." She retrieves a small, folded envelope from the pocket of her shorts. "Here. Devin Banks asked me to give this to you."

"He was here?"

"Yes."

In slow motion, I observe myself taking the envelope from her.

"What happened to your hand?" she asks with wide eyes.

"Nothing. I just ran into something."

"That's not nothing." Emily takes my wrist and stares at my mangled finger. "This is broken. In more than one place. Let me take you to the hospital."

"No, that's okay. I'm just going to bring these home and get them on ice. I live right up there." I point up the hill. "Then my mom will take me. But thanks."

She holds my eyes uncomfortably long. "Let Lillian take the oysters. I'll take you to the hospital."

"It looks worse than it feels, I swear. A few more minutes won't hurt." I break away from her. "Our boards are right over there. We'll be home in no time."

She stares in disbelief as we walk quickly away.

"See you at Concordia. Have a great night, Emily. Bye."

We hop on our boards and disappear onto the cool, dark road.

We ride along in silence. Up the hill at the cross street toward the Oval, we part ways with a simple glance. Lillian heads to the right, I forge straight ahead, continuing my ascent. I'm glad to be alone again.

This is a seldom-traveled road. It goes from a well-manicured, well-lit, perfectly landscaped route to a dark, dusty gravel path overtaken by the natural elements. But the moon is bright, and the simple beam on my board lights the way. I'm rather fond of this narrow trail. It reminds me of the one at the river. It's wild and serene, and void of the typical goings-on of Panacea. Except for the occasional ill-informed hiker, the far south side of the island is not a good place for people to explore, especially at night. More than a few lives have been lost here.

The brush closes in around and above me, and the ground levels out as I come to an enormous stand of sapodilla. I park my board against a craggy boulder and turn my attention to the tree, heavy with fruit, one of which I twist off its thick branch.

A narrow, hidden footpath reveals itself just past the rocks, where the black dirt is moist and spongey underfoot. I must navigate my way down the steep and treacherous trail with caution. The cliffside is dark and rugged and unforgiving. A fall from here would be fatal, without exception.

To my left, the heavy blue ocean stretches out as far as I can see, daffodil moonlight dancing on its shattered surface. There is nothing else out there. This is the edge of the world.

Down another precarious stretch, I see a faint light from somewhere deep inside the cliff. My heart speeds up with anticipation. I round the final bend with extreme caution, my hands skimming an ancient boulder hugging the cliff wall.

The smell of a fire welcomes me, as does the distinct aroma of the incense Gabriel is fond of burning. Moss, evergreen, jasmine, and tobacco flowers have come to symbolize this unique place he sometimes calls home. I reach the mouth of the cave and step inside.

"Nerissa... Greetings, child. It is good to see you." He embraces me, and I wilt in his arms.

"Thank you for having me. It's good to see you, too." I hand him the sapodilla fruit along with the satchel of Wreckleaf.

"Oh, thank you. Come. Sit down."

I sit on a wide, sturdy chair made from driftwood, facing the fire in the center of the space. I didn't realize how chilled I was until the heat of the flames warms me.

"So, how was harvest?"

"It was good, as usual."

"Good but not without consequence?" He looks at my hand.

"Ah, yes. I broke my finger."

"All right. We will fix it." I love that he asks no questions. He makes no judgements or assumptions. We'll fix it. That's it.

He gathers some supplies and goes about setting my finger. The numbness of shock wears off, and pain has set in. He finishes the dressing by wrapping a long, wet frond of Wreckleaf around it. Then he hands me a cup and instructs me to drink the muddy brown liquid. It's thick and sappy and reminds me of molasses. But the flavor is briny and sharp and makes my eyes water when I swallow it.

"What is this?"

"It's a reduction of medicinal herbs, including our favorite—Caulerpa Periculosis Abscondita."

"I'm sorry, what?"

"Wreckleaf. That's its scientific name."

"Oh! How'd you know that?"

"Gabriel is not just a peddler of mind-altering goods but a purveyor and scientific agent of all substances magical, restorative, and remedial. This island is home to everything one could ever possibly need to heal and thrive for what most consider an impossibly long life."

"So, how old are you, exactly?"

He considers my question in earnest. "Well, to be exact, I am definitely, specifically, unequivocally, on-the-button...

old." His mouth folds up in a million tiny creases, and his eyes follow.

"Come on. Really."

"Really, I don't remember. Ha-ha-ha. We will have to use our imaginations."

He gets up from another driftwood chair and stokes the dwindling fire until it comes back to life. The orange glow spreads out against the cave walls and lights up the eclectic collection of belongings Gabriel has displayed here. Everything is like the chairs we're sitting on—made from natural items found on the island. All but one oddity. Among the artwork cast in stone and shells, the collections of beach glass and feathers, the skeletons of cacti and bones of sea animals rests one unusual and out-of-place item.

"I've never asked," I say slowly, "but why do you have an old-fashioned shopping cart in here?"

"I keep it as a reminder."

"A reminder of what?"

"Some time ago, I came upon this cart late one night, deep in the Season, on the side of the road. It's a relic, and it caught my eye immediately. To my surprise, and for which to this day I do not have an explanation, there was a scantily clad, very over-served young lady inside it."

"No way. Who was she?"

"Incredibly, she had not lost the clutch containing her I.D. I recognized her last name and knew the location of her family's summer home. I pushed her across the island and delivered her to the front steps."

"What did they say when they opened the door?"

"Oh, Gabriel did not stay to find out. I picked her up out of the cart, rang the bell and ran, pushing that cart as fast as I could."

"Why didn't you just leave her in the cart?"

"I thought it was the most undignified way a person could be discovered. And she would already have a lot of explaining to do. Besides, I liked the cart, selfishly."

"Well that was awfully nice of you. She probably didn't deserve that much kindness."

He pokes at the fire again and allows me to think about what I've just said.

"We all deserve kindness. Every last one of us."

"Hmm." I'm not sold yet, but I'll think about it. "So you keep the cart to remind you of that night?"

"Not particularly. I keep it as a reminder of two things. First, that some designs were better left unchanged. And second, that money cannot buy happiness."

"Well, I'll agree with that. How'd you manage to get it here?"

"Let's just say I don't think anyone else could ever possess the stupidity it took to get it down the cliffside. How is your pain?"

I look at my finger, lovingly and expertly dressed. "It's much better. Thank you."

He smiles and nods.

Gabriel then busies himself with his Wreckleaf share. I watch for a bit as he divides and wraps it in portions, humming his own soft melody. The fire soon captures my attention, and my eyes grow heavy. I allow them to close as I begin to sift through the day. I imagine the volleyball game, the dolphins, zipping through the caves, and swimming into the wall. Even though I'm half asleep, my hand goes to my shoulder, and I smile. Then I feel the absence of my ring, and I recall my near-death experience in the ship graveyard. As I sink further, a mottled image of the boat accident and Emily morph together, and then she hands me something.

My eyes pop open, and I sit up. The letter from Devin. I stand up and retrieve my waist pouch from a small carved table. The letter is inside. I return to my fireside chair, never taking my attention off the folded envelope, as though it could walk away if not kept under constant surveillance.

I should just throw it in the fire. I don't think I can handle another letter like the one his stepfather wrote me. It couldn't be that bad, could it?

"Why don't you just open it, child?"

"Okay."

Nerissa,
Can we please talk sometime? Message me.
Devin

That's it? Is he kidding me? I don't think so.

"Everything okay, child?"

"Yes, Gabriel."

"Yes?"

"Well, no. Kind of. It's Devin Banks. He's asking to speak with me."

"And you don't want to?"

"It's complicated."

He turns to face me, the soothing fire between us. "I've got nowhere to be."

I tell Gabriel everything. Everything. It comes pouring out of me like an untamed river. I tell him about Ana and Alakier, and the letter Officer Banks sent me. I fill him in on everything we saw at the labs. I express my suspicions regarding Kendra's accident, and how I think it's all tied to us knowing too much about William Banks' projects with Bio-Genesis. I tell him that I've fallen in love with a human boy, and that I miss him desperately, even though I don't entirely trust him. And I tell him that I think he's addicted to the very Wreckleaf-infused product his stepfather and the FWG are testing on the tourists and that it has the potential to make ridiculous amounts of money for them. And that soon, they won't need us anymore.

Gabriel holds my gaze and listens to every word with genuine concern. He never interrupts or grows impatient with my rambling. He allows me to feel every detail of my story and sit with it in safety. I cry. I laugh. And I yell and shake my fists at the sky. I wring every last drop of it out of me. And for the first time in a long time, I feel better, lighter, acknowledged. Finally.

"You've had a lot on your mind."

His simple summary makes me laugh. "Yeah, I guess I have."

"I have just the solution to clear your confusion. A remedy for your malady. A fanciful flight to comfort your blight. A glass full of bubbles to end all your troubles." He's got me smiling now as he pours on the charm. "But seriously, child, Gabriel could use a drink after that story. How about you?"

"Why not?"

He fixes two bright-orange, tropical-looking drinks and hands me one. "This one isn't strong. But this one... for me? Yes, it is strong." We clink glasses, and I take a sip. The liquid is cool in my mouth but warm as it falls down my throat. Even though it's not strong, I feel its effects almost immediately, and I like it.

The fire lulls me, and I settle back into my seat. My eyes again grow heavy and close as I sip at the fruity, sparkly potion. The flavor is somehow distinct, though I can't quite place it.

All at once, with a powerful flash, I'm transported to Wave the night Ana disappeared. I can feel the bass thumping in my chest, the smell of musk and sweat all around me. Now I'm on the dock and Tom is whispering in my ear. I'm spinning, my heart racing. I kiss him, and he falls. I look at his two friends—there's also a third face, and it somehow seems familiar. It's farther away in the darkness, foggy. But I can almost...

My glass crashes to the floor right in front of the fire, smashing into a thousand little shards. "Oh, Gabriel, I'm sorry... I fell asleep." I bend down and attempt to gather the sharp pieces.

"Let me sweep that up."

The images are gone. I don't try to bring them back.

"What do you do with the Wreckleaf we bring you?" I've never asked him this, which now seems strange.

"I dry most of it for later use. But when I get a fresh delivery, I eat some and muddle some in juices. I smoke some... from time to time."

"You don't have any adverse effects, do you?"

"It's an incredibly medicinal plant, as you know. I've used it long enough and in the right ways that I reap its benefits. It fuels me, nourishes me."

"Well, that's what it does for us, but it's really a very toxic plant. It has the potential to kill. I'm surprised you can consume it the way you do."

"I respect the plant. I don't abuse it. What the mad scientists at the labs have done? Well... that's not respecting the plant."

"What do you mean?"

"They've taken the plant and refined it, extracted and isolated its strongest chemical components then condensed that, turning it into something far from what it was originally. It's not unlike turning wheat to white flour, or sugar cane into refined sweetener. By isolating the essence of the plant, they've created an entirely different beast."

"So, what was already dangerous on its own is now a super-version of its deadly self?"

"Yes, potentially. And by using science to formulate it further, they figured out how to take tiny little bits of this ultra-toxic substance, 'water it down', so to speak, combine it with other ingredients to buffer and prevent instant toxicity, and *voila*! They have created an incredibly addicting yet soon-to-be approved food product. It's like the historical case against high fructose corn syrup but worse."

"Hmm... it seems more like meth than corn syrup. It's making people crazy."

"Yes, I agree. There's a lot of strange, inexplicable behavior this Season. But you understand Gabriel, yes?"

"I do. You use Wreckleaf the way people use medical cannabis."

"Yes. It is a powerful elixir. A cure for many ailments when used appropriately. There are many, many substances like this in nature. Many on this island."

My mind stretches, seeking—lightbulbs flashing. A sudden, clear thought causes my mouth to run dry and my heart to pound. "So, Gabriel, would you consider yourself 'immune' to the ill effects most people would experience if they consumed Wreckleaf on its own?"

"Yes, child."

"Can I do an experiment?" I can't believe I'm saying this.

"And what is that?"

"Can I kiss you?"

He smiles. I think I even see a faint blush. "You want to enchant me, child?" His smile quickly fades as he realizes what I'm implying. He comes to my side and takes my shoulders in his hands.

"May I, dear one?"

"I'll stop at six seconds. I promise."

Our kiss is all business. There is nothing romantic or lustful about it whatsoever. I count to six and quickly pull away, searching his eyes, which remain open and alert.

"Nothing," he states with total clarity.

"Oh, my god."

"I'm afraid it's true, child."

"The Aqua Tonic makes them resistant to us." I hesitate. "Gabriel... do you think it will make them completely immune?"

20 – PERSISTENCE

TUESDAY, JULY 30TH

Nothing feels right anymore.

Gabriel made me promise not to make any emotional decisions in reaction to our conversation. I don't know if William Banks is aware of the accidental side effect of his experiment, but he can't find out. I need to decide who to tell what, and when.

"Ms. John..." Marcus comes at me quickly, waving something above his head.

Oh, no. Not again.

"Ms. John, I have something from Master Banks."

"You mean Mr. Banks, Marcus?"

"Yes, that's what I said."

"Which Mr. Banks?

"Mr. Devin Banks, of course. Here, open it."

I reluctantly take the envelope from his shaking hand. He stares at me in anticipation. "I prefer to open this in private, Marcus."

His shoulders fall in disappointment "Fine. But Ms. John... please, do whatever you can to bring him back. I would consider it a personal favor." He looks down, and I'm not sure, but I think I just saw the tiniest little bow.

"Excuse me, Marcus, someone is ringing for me."

"Yes, of course. Just one last thing... Why are you wearing that glove?"

I hold up my right hand, the white glove glowing in the bright sun.

"I broke my finger, and it was set and wrapped in a less-than-beautiful dressing. I thought this looked nicer with my uniform. And it needs to stay clean."

"Good thinking. Will this interfere with your applications?"

"Jade and I have already worked it out. I'm fine to do sprays, and she'll take my lotion apps."

"All right, carry on. Just don't get backed up and upset the guests." He turns and walks away.

Yeah, I'm fine. Thanks for your concern.

A few hours later, Moriyah and I eat lunch together. Then I excuse myself and climb up the rocks on the far end of the beach to read the note burning through my pack.

> *Nerissa,*
>
> *I need to talk with you. Will you please respond? Message me or meet me somewhere, anywhere you want. Please.*
>
> *I can't stop thinking about you,*
>
> *Devin*

No. No way. If it feels like a trap and sounds like a trap, it must be exactly that—a trap. If he were really sincere, he would have started with an apology.

WEDNESDAY, JULY 31ST

I'm having a nightmare.

"Alakier, no!" I run to him across the wavy blue room in slow motion and snatch the gun from his hand. We don't wake Anastasia. "This isn't a toy."

"Mommy doesn't like it here."

"But you would have hurt Mommy very badly. You could have killed her."

"I know."

A clock is ticking, and the walls start closing in around us. Alakier's eyes spill over with tears. Anastasia lies on her pillow like an angelic doll, her dark-cherry hair fanned out around the most serene face I've ever seen.

"It's okay. Everything is going to be okay."

"No, it's not. Everything is going to explode. Can I come with you?"

Riding out of the Oval, I'm not aware of anything except the persistent dread my nightmare left in me. I've been shaky since I jolted awake before 5:00 a.m. I couldn't breathe. I couldn't scream or cry. I just pulled my knees to my chest and rocked in silence until the first rays of light peeked through my sheer curtains.

I arrive at Concordia an hour before my shift begins. A clean-up crew of three men, who appear to be prepping for some kind of messy job near the side entrance, stop me as I try to pass.

"Sorry. This area is off limits."

"I work here."

"You'll have to go through the lobby."

"What happened?"

The tall guy sighs and shakes his head. He doesn't answer me. Instead, he pulls a cigarette out of the inside chest pocket of his white coveralls and lights it. He offers me one.

"No, thanks."

He blows a huge plume of thick gray smoke from his curled lips. "Some spoiled little buttholes made a mess of the building."

"How?"

He looks around, satisfied that no one is watching, his two co-workers still suiting up and gathering their equipment. "Have a look..." He walks me around the corner.

Splattered across the long white wall from one end to the other in blood-red paint is: 'Panacea is a lie!'

"Oh."

"Yeah, it's going to take us all day to cover this up."

"Any ideas who did it?"

"Nope."

Just as the word falls off his lips, sirens pierce the quiet morning, and we catch a glimpse of multiple emergency vehicles whizzing by just up the hill into the luxury sector.

"Used to be you didn't see too much of that... but lately..." He takes another long, casual drag of his smoke.

"Good luck with the clean-up."

"Thanks, we'll need it."

I turn and re-route. The lobby is totally void of guests, the front desk still quiet. I slip by without notice. In the empty locker room, I grab my uniform, head to a changing stall, and pull the curtain.

I'm nearly done lacing a shoe up my calf when the door to the locker room opens. The familiar sound of a locker opening is followed quickly by the clank and latch of it closing, as though the person changed their mind. I step out to see who's here. But I'm alone.

"Hello?"

No answer.

"Anybody here?"

Silence, except for the slight echo of my own voice.

I walk around the entire space, then circle back from where I just came. Nothing. I guess I'm hearing things.

At my locker, I pull up the silver metal latch. The door swings open. I cram my stuff into the narrow space, then freeze. Balancing on one of the hooks, a small, gray envelope stares back at me. On its front in familiar handwriting, I read, *'Nerissa, please open immediately.'*

I've had enough of this arrogant game, enough of his self-importance.

I tear open the envelope. But as I read, I get dizzy and hot and crumple onto the long steel bench. The world melts away.

She floated on a secret breeze
The air inside and all around forever changed.
Her silken flame became the fire that lights the way. That which without, I am lost; a nomad in a barren desert.
Every grain of sand I will count.
The rise and fall of the sun for an eternity I will watch.
To voice my admission, to taste her scent and to breathe the air that only she is,
My last breath I will save.

Please, without you, I am not living,
Devin

I wipe my tears and clear my throat.

No. This is calculated and manipulative—something William Banks put him up to. This cruelty is beyond what I thought he was capable of doing to me.

"Get up, Nerissa," I say aloud to no one but myself. "Go to work and forget about Devin Banks. He is dead."

FRIDAY, AUGUST 2ND

Two days have passed. Against my fiercest attempts to quiet them, Devin's words have worked themselves into nearly every thought I've had since reading them. I'm as distracted as I can possibly be. I've missed no less than three bells ringing for service. I misplaced my sprayers twice in two days, and last night, I didn't realize until I reached the Oval that I was still in my uniform. As a bonus, my dream last night was extra special. Instead of his regular script, Tom recited Devin's poem. I was so impressed by the lunatic's sentiment that I turned around and said, "I know I can't trust you, but sure, I'll be your girlfriend."

I'm so exhausted, I can't think straight. At least I remembered to change my uniform tonight.

Tap.

"One hundred thousand, six hundred, eighty-three."

Really, it's twenty-eight. It just feels never-ending. My life has been reduced to this haze of monotony. I wonder how many times I've walked through this parking lot. How many more? Is this really all there is?

I focus on the ground, and when I reach my board and look up, my stomach drops. Balanced on the control panel rests another small gray envelope.

I wrestle the paper dragon into my pack and ride home confused. And utterly alone.

SATURDAY, AUGUST 3RD

Even though I never have and probably never will again, today, I appreciate my job. I'm as busy as can be. The tourists are cranky and demanding, and for every minute I'm on duty, they hold my attention. The sun comes up, the sun goes down. I don't allow myself to feel ... anything. Jade and I are chummy. I'm starting to think this girl is clever and knows exactly what she's doing, exactly who she is. It's more than I can say for myself.

SUNDAY, AUGUST 4TH

Devin's latest letter sits unopened on my nightstand, tucked between two ancient journals. I can't even see it, yet it's commanded my attention since its exile over forty-eight hours ago. It watches me as I sleep, observing every move I make. It judges and critiques and evaluates every thought I think. Its pounding heart broadcasts into the wee hours of the night. It is the loudest, most demanding, irritating entity on the face of the planet. I just want it to shut up. But it will not cease.

At just before three in the morning. I wake from another ridiculous version of my dream. This time, Devin dances and sings as Tom holds me tight.

"I'll eat sand for you, I'll breathe fire for you, you are a liar and a coward and a freak. But I am the same and I can't live without you."

Then Tom forces me to drink a briny green liquid while Devin watches. I fall to my knees and say, "I love you. Rescue me."

Barely awake and blinded by the bedside light, I pull the letter from the nightstand.

Nerissa,

I am so sorry for hurting you. I miss you beyond description, and your silence is killing me. Nothing feels right anymore. Can we please start over, no disguises? If I don't hear back from you by Sunday at midnight, you have my word I'll never bother you again.

Devin

Sunday at midnight? Oh, no.

21 – SURRENDER

MONDAY, AUGUST 5TH

I will wait one hour.

Devin,

I know I'm nearly four hours late with this message. I'll be at the river at ten this morning. Meet me at the red pier... if you still want to. I will wait one hour.

Nerissa

22 – DISCLOSURE

MONDAY, AUGUST 5TH

No disguises...

Mother Nature is like a finely tuned, age-old orchestra. With the arrival of August, the morning air is thick, the change of light subtle. In a few more weeks, the tourists will depart, leaving the locals to clean up the impending frenzy of the last third of the Season. And the fall and winter tides and winds will come to own the island.

Devin did not return my message. I'll leave this meeting to fate. If he shows up, I'll hear him out. If he doesn't, I've got to let him go. The Season will end, he'll be gone, and I'll move on without him. I'll have to.

Just onto my forest path, I stop my board and lean it against a tree, then walk the rest of the way in silence. At the water's edge, I kick off my shoes and slide into the river. It's perfect, as always. The tension in my shoulders lightens with the river's cloak. With a big breath, I slip under the surface and reassure myself of my decision to come. I stay close to the shore, winding my way upstream.

The footholds of the docks come into view in front of me. I zip under the first, then the second, and float to the surface. The slated piers allow just a peek above. I scan the red dock next to me, stretching and craning. He's not here.

He's got one hour.

With every torturous moment that goes by, I try to summon the steely resolve that Devin Banks and I are not meant to be. Forgoing my hiding spot, I float freely in the middle of the river, mesmerized by the swaying canopy above. By the slight rise of the water, I know that more than an hour has passed. It's time to leave. I turn to go but notice the sudden absence of birdsong. From behind me, a thunderous gallop approaches.

"Nerissa!"

He emerges out of the deep green forest, a frantic white apparition, running up the trail behind the docks, mud flying and branches snapping in every direction. He trips and falls but gets up without pause, resuming his fevered advance. Unsure whether to be relieved to see him or terrified, I dive below and quickly swim underneath the red dock toward which he's headed. From underwater, I look up through the slats. Nothing. No movement.

I come up and look again from every angle. I don't see him anywhere. I swim out from under the dock and search left, then right, spin in circles twice one way, then the other. He's not here. He's vanished. Or I'm hallucinating.

I turn around again, and he rises out of the waist-high water two feet in front of me, breathless and wild-eyed. All the air is sucked out of me.

He doesn't speak or move. He just stands there, water pouring off him, our eyes locked. Time and space around us warps, holding us in a round, glass ball. The only existing light is in his eyes, and he's giving it to me.

"I didn't think you'd come." My voice trembles. The river drips out of his hair and glides down his face. "Devin, you're shaking."

He holds my gaze without speaking. I couldn't look away if I tried. He steps forward, narrowing the gap between us to just inches. I feel his body heat.

He takes my face in both his hands and holds me there, then tilts his head and lowers his lips to mine so they are just brushing. My eyes flutter closed, locking up my last feeble bits of willpower. Every part of me falls away involuntarily but with total relief and hungry abandon. I succumb to him. My head falls back, and his lips cover mine. We are liquid grace, passion-pure, blending together with the river's lilt and swell.

In that dark, secret, intuitive place, six seconds tick by, and I pull away against my desire. He pulls me back toward him. We exist in this tug of war for what feels like too long.

"Stop, Devin. I'm going to hurt you."

"I don't think so." I taste his words as he presses his lips to mine again.

I allow myself a few more seconds, then break his grip and step back. When he steps toward me again, I plunge into the water and stay there. He joins me, keeping his eyes open in the brackish water, and attempts to continue our kiss. But he's smiling now, knowing he's out of his element. He surfaces, and I give him a moment to cool off before joining him.

"I'm so happy you waited."

"I think you ruined your shirt." His long-sleeved, white linen shirt is smeared with black mud and bright green grass.

"I was having breakfast with my mother and didn't have time to change. I wasn't planning on swimming, it just sort of happened."

"So, you got my message?"

"Yes, about twenty minutes ago. I made it here as fast as I could."

"Why didn't you take your board?"

"I took it as far as I could up this side of the river." He pauses. "Nerissa... I'm so sorry."

"I think it's time we really talk," I say.

"Yes. Please."

"No disguises, right?"

"No disguises."

"Are you sure? Because once we cross this bridge, we can never go back."

"I'm not afraid, Nerissa."

"I am."

He takes me by the shoulders. "Nobody put me up to this. I'm here because I want to be."

"Our disclosure is dangerous. Seriously dangerous. It'll change everything. For both of us."

"I'm in love with you. All of you."

"If you say all of me, be prepared." I search his eyes.

"I am."

"It's what you have to give me in return. All of you."

"I promise."

Inhaling the river and the forest around us, I close my eyes and seal my decision. "Go home and put together a waterproof bag with some beach and swimming supplies. Meet me on Playa Rosa in an hour. But pretend you're alone. And don't talk to anyone."

"Okay. Why?"

"Do you have any compact dive equipment?"

"We're going diving?"

"Sort of."

"Yeah, we've got some, but it's small. More for emergency use."

"That's perfect. Meet me at the lifeguard stand. Sit down and wait for me. When you see me, don't get up, don't talk to me, and don't react at all. Just follow my lead, okay?"

"Yeah, sure." He laughs.

"This is no joke."

He straightens up and loses his grin. "Okay, I understand. I'll see you in an hour."

On my way to Playa Rosa, I have the fortunate coincidence of running into Gabriel and filling him in on my plans.

"Are you coming or going?"

"I have just finished my shift here, child."

"Too bad for me."

"The beach is easy today. I've gotten most of them thoroughly lit. But be extra careful. I don't think this is your best idea."

"I assure you, I've had worse."

"Ah, yes. I suppose so. Okay, Gabriel will be back on Rosa at four o-clock. Try to be here by then, and I will get you out."

"I'll make sure of it. Thank you, Gabriel."

Devin waits for me just like I instructed. When I reach him, I sit on the other side of the stand. He doesn't flinch.

I look straight ahead at the water and speak slowly and quietly. "In a few minutes, put on your goggles, get up, and walk into the water. Go almost to the edge of the ropes and stay there. Act casual."

Without looking at me, he responds, matching my volume. "What about my bag?"

"Leave it here."

"Then what?"

"I will get up with your bag and walk away. Do not watch me."

"Where are you going?"

"I'm just going down the beach a tiny bit farther, where I'll get in the water. I will swim to you. You will not know I'm coming, so don't be scared when you feel me touch you."

He clears his throat softly. "I promise you that will not scare me."

I ignore him. "You'll turn your back to the beach, and I'll hand you your regulator and tank. I'm going to pop my head out of the water in front of you. You have to block me completely. As soon as I go back under, that means we're clear. Don't hesitate. Go under without splashing and swim as fast as you can under the ropes. Don't come up until I tell you to."

"Where are we going?"

"To Albatross."

"What? We can't do that. It's impossible."

"I'll help you."

"The ocean will eat us alive. And I'm twice your size. How can you help *me*?"

"I'm pretty strong in the water."

"Well, that may be true, but the tank I have is for emergencies. I've got an extra cartridge, but there's not enough air for two of us."

"I thought you said you know exactly who I am."

"But I just—"

"Okay, you'll have to trust me. No disguises, remember? Now go."

I have to hand it to him, Devin follows instructions well. When I come up in front of him to scan the beach, he seems focused and engaged. I dive back under, and he follows, exactly how I asked.

Fifteen seconds under, Devin utilizes the tank. He's swimming pretty fast and getting winded, but we're not far enough to surface. He takes a couple breaths off the tank. I catch his eyes and ask him without words if he's okay. He nods. In the slow motion of underwater movement, I pitch my head back and direct my eyes to our un-seeable destination. He nods again. All at once, I take him by the hand, and we rocket through the water at double the speed. He wasn't expecting it, but to his credit, he slowly surrenders and gives way to the unknown.

He squeezes my hand, and I slow almost to a stop. He needs air. I wait, watching him fill his lungs, his blond-tipped curls bouncing in slow motion around his face. The movement of the water and the curve of his goggles play off the sharp lines of his jaw and the angle of his nose. He is sublime. He is art.

He manages an inconclusive smile, and off we go. We sail along for another good stretch and repeat our stop-breath-go pattern a few more times. I've convinced him to put his hands on my shoulders instead of me pulling him.

It's much easier for both of us, and I'm able to go faster. At just past the halfway point, I ease to a stop and surface.

He's breathing hard, sucking in the air. He rips off his goggles.

"Are you okay?"

He can't seem to speak and just searches my face for answers with big, wild eyes.

"I told you you'd have to trust me."

"Wow," he huffs. "I thought *I* was a good swimmer."

"Are you all right to keep going? We can come up as often as you want now. But the second half is harder. The water is calm today, but the currents are unpredictable out here."

"Well, we didn't come all this way for nothing."

"If you lose hold of me, stay calm. I'll get to you."

"I'm ready."

"Hang on tight."

We zip through the second half of the swim unscathed. The waves grow choppy and big for a small stretch as we approach the south side of Albatross, and I almost lose Devin when his left hand is ripped from my shoulder. But once we make the turn around the east side of the island, everything calms down again. We stop for one more rest, and Devin takes in the island.

"This is beautiful. But I thought it was dangerous and forbidden."

"Hmm, forbidden like Black Rock, I guess. And it's very dangerous, especially on the west side."

"Why'd you bring me here?"

"This is where I was born. Where I grew up."

His face lights up, and he gazes at the sheer cliffs dotted with green foliage.

"Come on, we're almost there."

We make our way to the tip of a rocky outcropping on the corner of the northeast point and climb out onto the rough, dark terrain. Devin's legs shake, and he bends over to catch his breath.

"You need a drink." I kneel down and open his bag, my hand finding a still-cool bottle. I pull it out and am dumbfounded. "Is this all you brought to drink?"

He can't meet my eyes or answer my question. But it doesn't stop him from reaching out and grabbing the bottle from me.

"You need fresh water."

"This'll do the trick."

"Did you at least bring two?"

He wipes his mouth and looks up. "Ah-ha! I knew you liked it."

"No. I don't want any. But you're going to need more than that before we go back."

"What about you?"

"This island will provide everything I need."

"Then I'll have what you're having."

"Be careful what you wish for. You might come to regret it." I laugh softly and look up at him. He's staring at me, looking like he's just seen a ghost, the empty bottle dangling from his fingertips. "What's wrong? Are you okay?"

"Your feet. I've never seen... your feet."

The hope I felt falls out of me in a sigh. He finds me hideous. "This is how I was designed." I drop the bag and turn away.

He's suddenly behind me, his hands at my shoulders, his fingertips trailing along my skin. With his lips against my ear, he whispers, "You are perfect." My breath falters as my head falls back against his chest. Tears spill freely.

I show Devin around the island. He seems enthralled with Albatross, and I'm surprised by how much he already knows.

"I'm so glad you brought me here. I was told stories as a kid. So much of it was made out to be folklore and fairy tales. It's nice to see that it's real."

"As real as it gets."

"And you're right, Black Rock is right in the way of a proper sunset."

"Told you."

"Take me into the caves."

"No way. It's too dangerous."

"I'm tougher than you think."

I return to the original topic. "So, your stepfather really told you a lot?"

"Yes. He thought I should know everything after the incident at the labs. Which, by the way, I know I shouldn't have told him about. I'm sorry."

"I'm sure he didn't tell you everything."

"Enlighten me."

We settle onto a soft, grassy patch close to the water's edge and sit facing one another.

"Do you realize that William Banks is the man responsible for the Cooperative? For forcing us to live under false identities or be punished?"

"I do."

"And what do you think about that?"

"I think William Banks is a cruel and twisted man and exists like a puppet under the control of capital gain and false power. And it's important to remember that there's no blood between him and me."

"Do you understand what's happening on the island?"

"Can you be more specific?"

I stand and run to where we left his pack. I scoop up the empty AQT bottle and rush back to him. "This!"

"What about it?"

"He's poisoning the tourists. He's poisoning you."

"What are you talking about?"

"This drink that you love so much has been carefully crafted to deliver a tiny amount of a concentrated form of the sea plant we provide. A plant that's toxic to humans. The thing that makes kissing me so deadly."

"Yeah, I know your saliva has something in it to cause some messed-up effects, but deadly? Am I dead?"

"That's my point."

"Sorry. I'm not following you."

"Aside from a lot of healing benefits, some of the compounds in the plant are toxic, but they're also addictive." I pause and take a breath. "There's a fine line between allergy and addiction. And the more you consume, the higher your tolerance and the more you want and need."

"What does that have to do with your saliva's effect on me?"

"You're growing a tolerance. Almost like an immunity."

"Because I drink a lot of Aqua Tonic?"

"Yes."

"I drink a lot. But addicted?"

"Yes! You know it's true. You can't go a few hours without it, can you?" He looks away. "They've created the perfect 'energy' drink... their 'elixir of life'. But what they're really doing is running an experiment on the tourists, on this select and isolated island, to see what kind of profit can eventually be made by widespread distribution. And the unfortunate side effect, besides the gross addiction, the mania, violence, and other unexplained events of this Season, is that they're rendering our only true defense useless."

"This is crazy, Nerissa."

"If you weren't drunk on AQT at the labs that day, we would have killed you. It took me exactly six seconds before Albert was unconscious and unable to remember a thing. But you remember everything, don't you?"

"Pretty much. But how did you..."

"I already thought something was going on. But the dinner at your house, when you found me in your father's office... I overheard them talking, and they pulled me in there to—"

"No, no." He shakes his head, resisting what he knows is the truth.

"That's what the secrecy at the labs is about. That's why all the restricted access and fear tactics about Black Rock. They're not concerned about the skincare formulas. Not anymore, anyway. They've got bigger plans, now. They're hiding the truth."

"Oh, my God..."

"That's just the beginning of it, Devin."

He hangs his head and reaches for me without looking up. I sit down in front of him and cross my legs. He looks up at me, his beautiful eyes full of pain. He knows I'm right.

"Tell me everything you know. Everything."

We sit in the same spot for what feels like forever in an instant and reveal ourselves to one another, vulnerable and open and unhinged as we share everything. I tell him about myself and my breed—our past, how we survived, and how we continue to do so. I talk about Officer Banks' wretched letter and my belief that he was responsible for Kendra's attack. I share our findings at the labs when we left him unconscious in the control room. His face twists in torment as I unveil the truths and horrors.

"I've seen the Wreckleaf tank. I didn't know what it was. I thought it was just another plant they use for the skincare products."

"They do use it in some of the skincare. That's how it started. Wreckleaf is really magical when used topically. But we warned them never to ingest it. I guess they wanted to see what would happen." I swallow hard. "I didn't think it was possible, but it's just a matter of time before they won't need us. What will they do to us then?"

He squeezes my hands. "The woman's voice you heard... it was real."

"Yes. It was Anastasia. I can't get her and Alakier out of my mind. I've even started dreaming about them. Have you ever seen them at the labs? She's seen you."

"No. Never."

I take a deep breath. "You know, it was my fault we were captured." I tell him everything about the night at Wave and nearly being raped by Tom. He's doesn't look at me. "I killed him, Devin."

"That guy was so drunk, he probably just passed out."

"No."

"So you thought Anastasia was dead?"

"That's what we were told."

"That's what he told me, too," he mumbles.

I must have heard him wrong. "What did you say?"

"Nothing." He clears his throat. "That's what the rest of your family thought, too? What they still think, right?"

"Yes. No one except Kendra knows. And look where that got her."

A warm gust of ocean air rises at our sides and delivers an unexpected soaking of sea spray.

"Well, that was refreshing." I laugh.

"I think that's our cue. My mother is expecting me. She's having a going-away dinner for the King and Prince Colton."

"Going away?" I ask.

"They're headed to the mainland for ten days. Business. Now I know what kind of business."

"You weren't invited?"

"I'm his stepson. He's only loyal to his own blood."

"I guess that's why he lets his stepson drink poison and spend time with killers. We better get going. I don't want him to get mad."

"Yeah and take it out on my mother. I've seen him push her around before. But I swear, if that monster ever touches her again, or you, I'll kill him."

"What time is it?" I ask.

"Four-fifteen."

"Oh, no... Gabriel was expecting us. Come on, we have to hurry." We gather our things, and Devin switches the cartridge on his tank. I secure his pack and lead the way down the rocky edge.

"We can't get out without Gabriel?"

"We can, it's just harder."

"You really like him, don't you?"

"I love Gabriel. He's like the father I never had. I'd be lost without him. We all would."

We descend into the deep water along the shoreline. The waves have kicked up a bit. "It's going to be a little rougher on the way back. And we need to move fast. Are you ready?"

"Now that I know what to expect... yeah, I'm good." But he looks nervous.

"And now that you know how strong I am?" I flex my bicep in the air.

"Yes, that too... Umm, Nerissa, what the hell is *that*?" He points behind me.

I swing around and see something large coming at us. "Devin, watch out!"

He covers his head and squeezes his eyes tight. I laugh softly. "*What* are you laughing about?"

"I'm sorry. That was really mean." The three gray dolphins stop inches from us. "These are my friends."

"Yeah... that *was* mean. I thought it was the Madoosik."

"The what?"

"The legendary sea monsters."

"Oh! I didn't know that's what people call them."

"They're real?"

"Yeah, but they only come out at night."

"Well, isn't that comforting?" But he apparently can't help but smile. "Wow, the dolphins are really your friends? Can I touch them?'

"Yes and yes. We go way back."

As though she understands perfectly, the large female dolphin slowly circles Devin, then pauses on his right side, turns to look him in the eye, and waits.

Devin reaches out. “It feels like a rubber ball,” he laughs. The childlike light in his eyes warms my heart like nothing I’ve ever felt.

“They’re like my family. I’m so happy you can meet them.”

“Me too.”

“But we need to go. They’ll swim with us for a while. Ready?”

“Yeah.”

We begin the return journey with impressive speed, the dolphins at our sides. It’s a helpful distraction for Devin as I challenge his strength and endurance.

After passing the point where we risk being seen, Devin seems to understand that I’ll slow down but not surface while he takes a breath from the tank. We repeat the pattern we developed on the way out and make great time. The pod stays with us.

He squeezes my shoulder again, this time harder than usual. I slow down, but he doesn’t cease. His fingertips dig into me. The female dolphin lurches suddenly in front of me, forcing me to stop. Devin stretches up and pushes his face above the surface. I follow him.

“What are you doing? We’re too close. We can be seen from here.”

He coughs and sputters. “The tank came loose and broke off. It’s gone.”

“Oh, no.”

“What do we do?”

“How long can you hold your breath?”

“I don’t know. But it still looks like we’re far.”

“I can have us to the ropes in thirty to forty seconds.”

“Can we rest a minute first?”

“Yes. If we don’t make it, if you come up for air and someone sees us on the wrong side of the ropes, we’ll have to make up a story.”

“Like I was drowning?”

"Yes, and I somehow got to you without anyone else noticing. Yeah, right."

The dolphins form a semi-circle around us, float there for a few seconds, then turn in the direction of the beach and speed away.

"What are they doing?"

"I think they've decided to be a distraction. Are you ready?"

"Yes. Count to three, please."

"One..."

"Two..." He takes an enormous breath.

"Three."

We head directly toward the lifeguard stand where we first entered the water. Eighty yards, sixty-five. Devin holds on for dear life, his grip tightening. Forty yards. Thirty. He's squeezing harder. Twenty yards, ten. I slow down and glide under the ropes. We surface in near silence, and Devin does his best to quiet his desperate gasp.

I don't think we've been noticed. All the action is to the right, where the dolphins have come into the swim area and made themselves comfortable with the tourists. Everyone is watching.

Except for one person.

Just past the commotion, standing at the edge of gawkers, Emily waves. I wait a few seconds to make sure she's meant it for me. Damn it. I return a timid wave.

The dolphins accept the shower of attention from the crowd of strangers formed around them. Devin and I exit the water and sit down at the stand. When I look back, I no longer see Emily, but Gabriel's voice rings through the crowd.

"Gabriel's got your drinks delish... to gander flowers, birds, or fish! Ha-ha-ha!"

"He's something else," Devin says, his admiration contagious.

"He sure is. All right, I'm going to relieve the pod."

We reach the crowd and approach Gabriel. He's fixing an already over-served man a fruity red drink.

"I'll have one of those," I say. Just like that, the show is over, and the dolphins swim away. Gabriel eyes me as he hands the man his drink. "Amazing creatures, don't you think?"

I smile. "Gabriel, this is Devin."

"I know who you are, sir."

"It's a pleasure to make your acquaintance, Gabriel."

"I'm sorry we were late," I whisper. "Now we need to get going. See you soon."

We turn to leave, and Gabriel catches me by the arm. He speaks slowly and quietly. "Be careful, child."

"I will be. Promise."

Devin and I return to our boards at the entrance to the beach. He blows out a huge breath. "Woah, that was..."

"Not something we can talk about right now, right here."

"Okay, yeah." He takes another deep breath and nods slightly. "When will I see you again? We're hardly done with our conversation."

"I'm working tomorrow."

"I'll be there."

"Marcus will be so happy, you have no idea."

"That guy is such a suck-up."

"Yes, which is why he'll be more than happy to accommodate your requests."

"Hmm? Are you thinking what I'm thinking?"

I nod. "See you tomorrow."

"Hold on." He steps forward and slides his fingers through the back of my hair. "Kiss me."

I don't argue, don't hesitate. I stretch up to his sun-kissed face and plant my lips against his. His other hand falls to the small of my back, and he gathers me to him. I allow myself to feel his strength, his lean, muscular build.

Then I pull away, breathy and red-faced. "Devin, this is..."

"What? Dangerous?"

I step back. "Promise me something."

"Anything."

"Promise me everything we talked about stays a secret."

"Of course it will." He frowns a little. "You can trust me, you know?" He kisses my nose, steps on his board, and rides away.

TUESDAY, AUGUST 6TH – SATURDAY, AUGUST 10TH

Marcus starts crying at the news of Devin's return.

"Just be cool, Marcus. He's been dealing with some personal stuff."

"Oh, of course. I will not do or say anything to upset Master Banks."

"He'll appreciate that."

"Ms. John?"

"Marcus, please call me Nerissa."

"Yes, Nerissa... thank you. Thank you for encouraging Master Banks to return."

"It's Mr. Banks, Marcus."

"Yes, thank you. I consider it a personal favor, and I'm very much indebted to you."

Let's see how long he remembers that.

The days roll by too fast. Concordia on the Bay has never been what it is to me this week. I've arrived early each day, waiting at Devin's favorite spot for him every morning. As planned, I'm his personal attendant for the week, and as best we can, we've shut out the rest of the world. Even Marcus has kept his word to leave Devin alone. We know we can't ignore the things we talked about, but just for now, for a little while longer, we both need to pretend we exist in a world free of corrupt men and their lies.

Saturday comes and goes before I know it. Lying side by side with Devin in the comfort of our now homey lounge chairs, the setting sun turns the sky pink.

"Will you ask Marcus to let me be yours for the rest of the Season?" I ask.

"I have a better idea."

"What's that?"

"We need a change of scenery. Spend next week with me out of the resort district."

"He'll never go for that. I think he'd sooner die than lose you again for any amount of time."

"I'm sure a generous donation to Concordia's Beach Pavilion would convince him."

"Well, you might be on to something. You should ask him."

"Nope. He told you he owes you. You need to hold him to it."

I sigh and roll my eyes. "Okay. I'll be right back."

Ten minutes later, I'm back at the juniper with the anxious yet trying-to-be-agreeable Marcus. Devin wears the most patronizing smile. Poor Marcus.

"Marcus, it's good to see you. I trust Nerissa has relayed my request to you."

"Yes, indeed, Mr. Banks. I just wanted to double check your requirements, sir."

"It's simple. I've got some personal business to attend to, and I need Nerissa to assist me. I'll have her back for her shift next Friday."

"And you will also return that day as well?"

"Yes."

"Well, we will miss you—and her, of course." Marcus shifts back and forth, then adds in a much quieter voice, "Ms. John mentioned a little something..."

"Yes, in appreciation of your generous cooperation and in the absence of your best attendant, I will leave the front desk with a substantial donation to the Beach Pavilion, as well as a little something extra for you, Marcus."

Marcus rises on his toes and claps his fingertips together in front of his face. "Oh, thank you, sir."

Devin stands and offers his hand, which Marcus takes like he's addressing royalty. "Marcus, please remember... my business is private. Nerissa being with me next week is my business. Do you understand?"

"Oh, yes. Of course. Not to worry."

The two shake on it, and Marcus leaves.

"Friday? Why will I be back next Friday? Why not Saturday? Or not at all next week?"

He smiles. "My stepfather will be back Friday from his trip. I'm not sure what time. I think it's best to play it safe and look as normal as possible."

"Normal?"

"You know what I mean."

As another Saturday spent on Concordia's beach comes to an end, we gather our belongings. Under our chairs, a large array of plates, glasses, and bottles have collected.

"How many AQTs did you drink today?"

He shrugs. "How many bottles are there?"

"Too many. Devin, you have to stop drinking that. It's poison."

He turns to face me and captures my eyes like only he can do. "I've cut back, I promise. But I will never stop completely. I don't care what it does to me."

"Why would you say that?"

He doesn't answer me with words. Instead, he leans over without hesitation, without concern, and delivers a long, deep, wet kiss. And in an act of defiance—of long-awaited rebellion—I return his kiss.

A million years later, back in our own galaxy, we release each other. His eyes are glossy. "Damn, girl. You're going to be the death of me."

"Not funny. Come on, it's time to go."

We walk along the sand toward the building.

"Okay. What would you like to do tonight?"

"I'm sorry. I'm having dinner with my mother tonight."

"After."

"I can't, I have harvest tomorrow, and she'll want me to stay in."

"Too bad. I was going to suggest we go dancing."

"Dancing? You've seen my feet, right?"

"Ha! Oh, yeah. Okay, take me to harvest tomorrow."

"Absolutely not."

"Why not? I'll replace the tank I lost. No problem."

"We really pushed our luck the other day. And trust me, that was easy. The water isn't usually so calm. Spend the day with your mother. I'm sure she'd love your company."

"You're probably right. I'm just not sure I can pull her out of her studio."

"She's writing again?"

"Yes, since the Officer left for his business trip, I've hardly seen her."

"That's great."

We've reached the end of the pavilion, and I turn toward the employee door.

"So I have to wait until Monday to see you again?"

I pause, not sure I should say my next words. "Do you remember where I live?"

"You want me to come to your house?"

"No. Ride past the Oval, up the hill. Go as far as you can till the road ends. I'll meet you there tomorrow at five o-clock. Don't be late."

23 – ALL OF ME

SUNDAY, AUGUST 11TH

So this is what real joy feels like.

"Greetings, Beauty. You're late," Devin gurgles through a mouthful of fruit. "This is delicious, by the way."

"Grab a ripe one… and I apologize for my three-minute tardiness."

"Here you go."

"It's not for me. It's for Gabriel. And this." I pat the large satchel at my waist. "Come on, this way." I gesture toward the cliffside. "Watch your step."

"We're going to walk down there?"

"Umm, *walk* probably isn't the most accurate word."

"Great."

"You'll be fine."

"Hey, when we're done with this, how about we do a little base-jumping? Or shark-hunting?"

"Sounds fun. Don't forget the bull-fight I scheduled."

He wipes his fruit-stained hands on the back of his pants and exhales. "Let's go."

MONDAY, AUGUST 12TH

The cool, mineral-green river has never felt sweeter. Luxuriating in procrastination and denial, Devin and I while away the hours in unrestricted peace, soaking in the temporary escape.

"Thanks for letting me come with you to see Gabriel yesterday. It was so oddly fantastic."

"Gabriel's pretty protective of me. I want him to trust you."

"Do you think he does?"

"I think he does now."

He takes my hand underwater. "Do you? Trust me?"

I don't answer.

"Nerissa?"

"I wouldn't be here if I didn't." But I know I took too long. "I certainly wouldn't have taken you to see Gabriel."

"He's a real character."

"Did you like his stories? He really likes telling them."

"Yes. I had no idea how involved scouting is. It sounds like he had a successful day yesterday helping your sister maid find the perfect, umm... acquisition?"

"He knew exactly how to get her in the right place at the right time with the perfect match."

"So let me get this right... Once scouting is complete and a Contributor is chosen, he will be enchanted and then acquired?"

"You're a good student."

"It sounds like hooking up with a stranger for a drunken one-night stand that you don't remember in the morning."

"That's exactly what we'd like our Contributors to believe." I smile.

"Ah. Of course. Except that the goal is pregnancy. Acquisition?"

"Exactly. So Master Banks, what do you have planned for us tomorrow?"

"Well, my skin is pruning from all the water activities. Do you remember how to get to my house?"

"Your house?"

“The Officer and Colton are not back until Friday afternoon, and my mom spends every free minute in her studio. We'll have total privacy. Be there at ten.”

“I'm supposed to be at work tomorrow. I need to keep up appearances for my mother. I'll be there at eight-thirty.”

“Excellent. We'll have breakfast together.”

With few words, we swim and float and stare at one another for hours. When we dry off on the red dock, our skin warming in the soft breeze and speckled light, Devin writes in a journal. He doesn't let me read it. I don't mind, I just watch him. He's exquisite, his hand a catalyst, the energy of worlds moving through his pencil.

The trees above sway in a silent melody. The gentle lap of the river and the birds accompany in perfect harmony. When I finally look outside my utopian bubble, the shadows grow long and the river has swelled.

“The fishermen will be here soon.”

“Let's buy some fish. I'll have Esmerelda cook it for lunch tomorrow.”

I squish up my mouth and eyes and try not to seem impatient—and disgusted. “Nothing that had fins, remember?”

“Sorry, no fish. Damn, I love fish.”

“You eat whatever you want.”

“Absolutely not.”

“Well, good. Thank you. Because I wouldn't have kissed you for a long, long time.”

“Then I'll never eat fish again. But you know you can't resist me.” He reels me in and tickles my sides till I laugh out loud.

“You're right. I can't resist you. Kiss me.”

TUESDAY, AUGUST 13TH

Fifteen minutes early, I'm not even at the massive black gate when it slowly swings open. He was waiting. And watching. Everything looks just as I remembered—the sprawling house, the immaculate grounds. But the air feels different, lighter. It feels safe.

Just like my first visit, Devin materializes at the front door like a magical creature, hypnotizing me into a state of euphoric oblivion. I'm in a dream again, traveling in slow motion, unable to move at the speed I want. He's become a drug I can't absorb fast enough, an addiction over which a part of me fears I have no control.

"Good morning, my sweet Nerissa." We wrap each other in a fluid embrace, and I'm instantly relieved, filled up, complete.

"Good morning. It's been forever."

He squeezes me tighter. "I couldn't sleep last night thinking about you."

I return his gesture and breathe in the smell of him. "So what are we doing today? Swimming in the pool?" I smile.

"No more water. First, let's eat. Esmerelda made breakfast." He takes my hand and leads me around the house. "I hope you're hungry. She's laid out a feast for us."

"What's on the menu?"

"You know, all your favorites. Sushi, smoked trout, seafood chowder."

"Very funny..."

We turn a corner and arrive at the same stone patio where we enjoyed appetizers with Devin's mom. Esmerelda is waiting for us.

"Greetings, Miss Nerissa. Please, enjoy breakfast. I hope it's to your liking. Let me know if there's anything else I can provide."

"It's good to see you again, Esmerelda." She tilts her head and smiles. "Thank you so much. It looks like you've outdone yourself. And I have everything I could possibly need." I hug Devin's entire arm before we take our seats at the perfectly dressed table she's set up for us.

Esmerelda beams. "I will not bother you."

I gorge myself on homemade waffles, fresh fruit, and black coffee. Devin eats an enormous cheese and mushroom omelet, three waffles, and a giant bowl of fruit before he comes up for air.

"Wow. You've got one heck of an appetite."

"Yes, I do. I was up all night writing. I guess all that mental work gets me hungry."

"When can I read something?"

"Hmm... soon. But for now, our next adventure awaits." He stands and grabs three apples from the table.

"Do tell."

"We're going to ride Neptune and Goliath, maybe Delia, if she's in the mood."

"No, we're not. I mean, I'm not."

"Oh, yes you are. If I can agree to nearly being drowned while you drag me through the ocean, then scale down a sheer cliff wall and back up in total darkness... you can get on a gentle, loving horse."

"I'll watch."

"Come on."

We cross the lawn to the wooded path leading to the stables. At any moment, I expect to be greeted by a living garden gnome, or a fairy, or better yet, a unicorn.

As we pass Leyla's studio, Devin puts a finger to his lips. We continue without conversation until we've put the studio a good distance behind us.

"I didn't realize she was in there. How'd she get in? The door is still covered in vines."

"Yeah, I'm not sure how she managed, but I'm pretty certain she kept it that way on purpose."

"So nobody knows she's in there?"

"Exactly."

"How did *you* know?"

"She told me."

Around a final curve, the black, springy dirt changes to brown, dry dust, and the stable appears in front of us. Enjoying the morning sun, Goliath, Delia, and Neptune stand like three friendly sentinels against the fence of their enclosure, heads held high, eyes bright, and ears at attention. They knew we were coming long before we arrived.

"Good morning, my friends!" Devin squeals.

Goliath snorts and startles the other two.

"They seem a little jumpy."

"They're happy to see us."

"Devin..." I do my best to sound the least amount of wimpy as possible.

"Oh... you're really scared, aren't you?" I must have a horrified look on my face. I nod. "I promise they're all very friendly, and Goliath in particular is really easy to ride."

"I believe you, but... I'd rather just watch you. At least for now."

He lets out a little sigh. "Okay. Let's consider this a learning day. You watch, take notes, and get to know them. And then you ride tomorrow?"

I nod in relief.

"All right, let's start our lessons."

He's a natural—a master, really. I've never witnessed this kind of relationship before, this deep, mutual respect and trust between human and animal. Devin clicks and grunts and taps his hand on his chest or shoulder, and the horses respond. Then Devin says something to one of them as though he's answering.

"Yes, Goliath, my friend. I'm going to put your saddle on, now. Turn to the side, please." The horse positions himself just as requested. Devin steps onto a wooden box, up three stairs, and hoists a giant, brown leather saddle onto the horse's back.

"Am I going to have to do that too?"

"Why? Are you worried you're not strong enough?"

"You can't expect little me to pick up that heavy thing all by myself. I need a big strong man to help me."

"A big strong man like me?" He plays along, sporting a stupid grin, posing and flexing, turning right, then left, like he's just won a gold medal.

"Oh yes, just like you..." I blink up at him.

He turns all the way around to show off his backside but missteps and tumbles off the box, hitting his head hard on the edge. He crashes into Goliath's side, landing directly underneath the giant animal. With one wrong step, Devin could be crushed.

I jump off the fence. "Woah, Goliath. Stay still, big fella. Don't move." I step slowly and carefully into the enclosure to Devin's side, under the horse's enormous legs and soft belly. Devin seems woozy, his head bobbing, and is very slow to get up. Goliath doesn't flinch. I help Devin up and out from under the horse.

"I'm okay," he says. "Just a klutz."

"I think your posing days are over, big strong man. Let's sit here for a few minutes."

He raises his head, looking a little embarrassed, and peers over my left shoulder. "I think you've got a new friend."

I turn to have my cheek nudged by Goliath's giant, velvety-soft muzzle. I startle just slightly, and he puffs out a big, warm breath at me. It smells like hay. I can do nothing but giggle and accept the shower of affection the mammoth offers.

"He's very grateful," Devin says.

"You're welcome, Goliath... yes..."

The other two horses join us to see what the commotion is about.

I'm back in my bubble, surrounded by three loving, beautiful animals—who are really no different than either of us—and the man I'm falling deeply in love with at my side.

So this is what real joy feels like.

WEDNESDAY, AUGUST 14TH

The gate swings open ten minutes after eight. Esmerelda has turned out another impressive, scrumptious breakfast. Devin and I pull our chairs as close together as we can, then delight in another satisfying feast.

"I brought you something," I tell him.

"What is it?"

"You need to know that it's not without its dangers."

"I'm intrigued." But he must have worked it out by now.

"You don't have to if you don't want to."

"Nerissa, let's have it."

I grab my pack and retrieve a small baggie from it, which I set on the table in front of him. "This is Wreckleaf. The real thing, not that gross, processed, bubbly crap."

"And what do I do with it?"

"You eat it."

"Just like this?"

"Yep."

"No offense, but it looks like slimy green worms."

"You probably shouldn't eat it anyway. Never mind." I grab the bag, but he covers my hand with his to stop me.

"Hold on. I didn't say I wouldn't try it. You said it could be dangerous."

"Yes. It's toxic. You know that. This would be an experiment. But I think you'll have a minimal reaction, if any."

"Because of the AQT?"

I nod. "The same reason you can kiss me."

"Then let's have some." He pulls the baggie from me and opens it.

"Hold on—"

"Nerissa, if you thought for even a second that this would seriously hurt me, you wouldn't have brought it."

"If you can handle this without any serious reactions, it would be worth considering transitioning you off the AQT and onto this."

"Like Gabriel?"

"Exactly."

"Will it make me feel the same?"

"Wired? Hyper? Manic? Explosive? I hope not."

He shoots me an impatient stare. "Full of energy."

"Well, that's what it does for me... and it's really medicinal. It just might not be as instant or noticeable. And we'll have to take it slow."

"Does it mean I can still kiss you?"

"I hope so. That's the goal."

"So I really just eat it like that?"

"Yes, but just a tiny little bit to start with."

He reaches into the baggie, pulls out a slippery frond, and brings it to his lips. "Wait," I say at the last second.

"It's going to be fine."

"But what if it's not? I could never live with myself if I hurt you."

"Then you'll have to bring me back to life. You know mouth-to-mouth resuscitation, right?"

"Stop."

"Look, this tiny little bit"—he rips off a centimeter-sized corner—"will not kill me."

"What if you get sick?"

"Let's find out." He pops it into his mouth before I can stop him again, and his face contorts.

"Are you all right?"

He swallows with great effort. "That. Is. Disgusting."

"How do you feel?" I watch him, examining his pupils, my fingertips moving to the pulse point at his wrist.

"Do you really like that stuff?"

"I love it." I slurp a huge frond into my mouth, close my eyes, and swirl it around before it glides down my throat.

Devin's hand darts to his chest, his eyelids flutter, and he tips back in his chair.

"Devin!" I lunge forward as he falls, unable to catch him before I drop to his side. "Devin, talk to me..."

"Quick, I need resuscitation." A wicked smile spreads across his face, and one eye squints open. "Oh! Are you crying? I'm sorry."

"That was so mean, and so not funny."

He sits up. "I'm sorry, I didn't think you'd believe me." He obviously can't help but let out a little laugh.

I punch him hard in the arm.

"Ouch!"

"Serves you right."

"You're right." He rubs his arm. "Consider us even."

"For what?"

"For thinking I was going to be eaten by a monster the other day."

"Fine."

He leans in and kisses me lightly. I can't stay mad.

"Seriously, how do you feel?"

"Fine. Honest." He pauses. "Actually, I feel really good."

"I knew it!"

"Come on, it's time to ride." He leaps up, grabs my hand, and we head for the stables.

The cool shade of the wooded trail is so refreshing. "Hey, once I get the hang of it, can we bring the horses on this path?"

"Of course. They like it in here."

We stroll in silence for another few minutes. When we approach Leyla's studio, my mind wanders to more serious matters.

"You know, we're going to have to talk about... What are you doing? I'm serious, stop fooling around." He's stopped almost ten feet behind me, his face blank, his eyes vacant. "Devin, seriously."

His fingers graze his lips, and his eyelids droop.

"That's enough. I'm not kidding!"

"I'm not either," he slurs, then falls forward onto the mossy path, landing on his knees. "So many stars..." He crumples on his side, curls into a fetal position, and grips his stomach.

I run to him, expecting to see some tortured, pained expression contorting his perfect face. Instead, he sports a sublime, relaxed grin, his eyes open in their own smile.

"Okay... you've gone too far. This is *not* funny," I yell, shaking him. But he doesn't flinch; his expression never falters. "Devin! I swear, if you're kidding around, I'll kill you myself."

But he's not kidding this time.

Leyla emerges from her studio and runs to my side, her voice riddled with fear and desperation. "What's wrong with him?"

"I don't know."

She drops to her knees and examines him, turning his face back and forth in her hands. "Nerissa, go into my studio. Wet a towel and grab a bottle of water. Hurry."

I do as she commands, moving as fast as I can. When I return seconds later, Leyla puts the towel on Devin's head and slips her hand under his neck to gently lift him up. He accepts a tiny sip of water, then seems to partially regain his focus.

"Look at me, sweetheart."

"Mom?"

Leyla and I both sigh. The tears I was holding back finally spill.

"What happened? Did you faint? Have you eaten?"

He manages to sit up but grips his stomach again. "Umm... yeah, I ate. I think that was the problem."

"Was something bad?"

"It must have been the omelet."

She strokes his face and holds his eyes. "Such an unusual reaction. Did you throw up?"

"No."

"Maybe you have an allergy to something. We better get that checked out."

"I think I'm fine, Mom. Maybe I'll just come back to the house and rest."

"I'll run ahead and get your room ready. Can you walk?"

"Yes."

"Nerissa, will you please help him?"

"Of course."

"I'll let Esmerelda know about the bad eggs."

"Mom, wait. It's not her fault... about the food."

"Of course not. Now take your time and let Nerissa help you."

Leyla jogs off, her petite form disappearing quickly down the path.

"Follow my finger," I say. He watches it clearly as I move it from side to side. Once again, I feel his pulse, this time at his neck.

"What are you doing?"

"Wreckleaf is a complex and toxic plant. I want to make sure you're okay."

He stands but stumbles. "I'm fine, really."

"You're not fine."

"I am." He turns to face me. "Besides the stomach pain, which was a little intense for a few minutes... that was a totally enjoyable experience."

"Are you kidding me?"

"No, it was rather euphoric."

"Tell me what happened, exactly."

"I was fine. Then my lips started tingling. Then they went completely numb, and so did my hands and feet, and my stomach felt like it was in a vice. But then everything started twinkling and dancing, and the pain was gone. It made me feel so happy—like I could die and it'd be okay."

"That explains the grin. And honestly, you're still a little loopy."

"Well, if that's what the horrible, toxic Wreckleaf does, sign me up."

"Umm, yeah. I don't think so."

"You mean for now?"

"I mean indefinitely."

THURSDAY, AUGUST 15TH

"Are you ready to ride today?" Devin asks me.

"Are you?"

"I'm great. Slept like a baby last night, how about you?"

"No... not so good. Bad dreams. You're really okay?"

"Completely fine. And my mother's been watching me like a hawk."

We dig into Esmerelda's cuisine, minus the eggs.

"So... are you excited to ride?"

"I'll ride, but I can't quite say I'm excited," I tell him. "You know, we're going to need to talk about a plan. The Season's going to end before we know it."

"No, no!" He covers his ears.

"I'm serious... we've put this off too long."

"Just give me one more day to not think about anything except you." He grabs hold of me with his piercing gaze, and my skin tingles.

"Okay, you win." I lean toward him, and our foreheads meet.

"I always do."

We finish our breakfast and walk toward the stable.

I can hear the horses snorting and snuffing by the time we pass Leyla's studio. "They're excited to see us," I say.

"How do you know?"

"I can hear them... and... *feel* their thoughts."

"Oh, yes, you and your extra-sensory perception. So you read their minds?"

"I'm not a mind-reader." I laugh. "I have enhanced perception."

"What's the difference?"

"We're all just energy, right?"

"Right..."

"Thoughts and emotions are like a broadcast of energy. A vibrational frequency. I can feel and interpret them. Almost like an image. We all can, actually. I'm just better at it than pure-humans."

He stops and faces me. "Can you feel my thoughts?"

"Sometimes. I used to be able to all the time."

"What happened?"

"I think it's the AQT. It dulls your vibration."

"No kidding?"

"No kidding."

We reach the stable, where the horses are waiting for us. Devin enters the enclosure, and I follow.

"No more accidents today," I tell him. "All right?"

"Agreed. I need to get you up on this big boy." Devin leads Goliath next to the stair box, and the huge horse waits. "You know what to do."

I retrieve an enormous saddle off the stable wall and schlep it back to the steps. It's a lot heavier than I expected.

"Hey, Muscles, you having a hard time?"

"My strength is in the water."

"Need some help?'

"No." I heave the saddle onto Goliath's back, but my skills at attaching it are pitiful. Devin steps up to take over, and I move out of his way. This is his world.

When Goliath is finally ready for me, I put my foot in the stirrup, count to three, and lift myself up. I'm on, but I feel a little shaky. I must be ten feet tall. "All right, pretty boy. You and I are friends," I tell the horse. "I respect you. Please, be nice to me." Goliath slowly drops his head forward and exhales a deep, fluttering breath through his nostrils.

"Show me what I taught you," Devin instructs.

With a firm but gentle voice, I command Goliath to walk forward, turn left, and then right. He stops and starts and moves exactly as I request.

"Good job. I'll get Neptune geared up and meet you at the other end. We'll take them into the field." He disappears into the stable as Neptune waits alone at the stair box.

"Okay." Without prompt, Goliath walks until we reach the back edge of the enclosure, then stops. "You're so amazing," I say. He huffs and nods, turns to look at me, then flicks up one husky lip. He lowers his head and walks through the opening. Just like that, we're on the other side of the tree-lined enclosure in a massive, open field out of view from the stable.

"Let's wait here, big boy," I say softly to the massive horse.

A gentle wind blows tall grasses and a sea of wildflowers in soft waves. Goliath tilts his head to the side again, grabbing a quick look at me. I pat his shoulder lightly.

He breaks into a gallop.

"Nerissa! Where are you?" Devin screams from somewhere far away. I surprise myself with a smile.

Goliath's hooves pound the earth ... faster and faster. I'm not scared, I'm electrified. It's magic. He moves like water, or air, and I'm a part of him. We're flying, soaring ... free. Emotion catches in my throat. I close my eyes and feel tears flying off my cheeks. I lift myself up, put one arm out to the side, and get my balance. Then I let my other hand go and grip the immense animal with just my legs. He and I are one.

There is nothing else.

I am a shadow, gliding atop a rhythmic galaxy. We are tethered to nothing and everything, attached by a swirling green tentacle of light above and below. I know without a trace of doubt that I am safe. I am loved. I would rather die now than to never feel this way again.

Behind us, a small sound grows stronger and stronger until it becomes a roar. Against raging internal protest, I'm forced back to the earth and met by Devin's wild eyes as he rides frantically beside us.

"Woah, Goliath. Nerissa, take his reins. Now!"

I hear him and understand him. I just don't want to. Goliath doesn't need to be controlled. He is a meteor, and I am his passenger.

I finally do as Devin commands, and as soon as I touch the reins, the beast's omniscience responds. We gradually slow, and eventually, he comes to a stop. Devin and Neptune flank us.

"What are you *doing*? You could have been killed!"

I wish I could see myself in a mirror right now. I've never felt calmer, but I imagine I've never looked wilder. "We were totally safe." I lean over and stroke Goliath's tree-trunk neck. My arms are covered in rust-colored dirt.

Goliath's breathing slows. I feel he knows what he just did for me. "Thank you," I whisper in his ear.

"You've never ridden a horse?"

"Never before today."

"I don't believe you."

"I swear. I wish it wasn't true. That was incredible!"

"Well it's time to take it down a notch." He takes the reins from me and holds them loosely at his side. Then he clicks his cheek twice. "Come on. We're taking a break." We turn back and saunter along in silence. My smile is eternal. I will never be the same.

We're quickly back in the enclosure, where Delia takes a long drink from a black tub of fresh water. She doesn't bother to look up as we pass. Devin leads me to the stairs, and Goliath turns to let me dismount. I get off and step around to face the horse, then reach up to place my hands on either side of his face. He blinks his thick, mile-long lashes, and he and I are forever entwined.

"Nerissa?" Still astride Neptune, Devin points down at my feet. Completely unaware, I find myself standing in a muddy quagmire made from the water basin's runoff.

"Oops."

He clicks twice, and Goliath steps back and away from the steps and the mud.

I glance up at Devin again, noticing what's not there. "Where's Neptune's saddle?"

"You didn't exactly give me a chance to put one on."

"Sorry. It wasn't my fault."

"Whose was it? Goliath's?"

"Of course not. Does it hurt?"

"To ride bareback? No, I actually like it."

"I meant the horse? Does it hurt Neptune?"

"Oh. Well, I don't make a very regular habit out of it, but I think it's probably more comfortable for him, too."

Delia wanders away to the far end of the enclosure, and Goliath follows her.

"They can just leave, into the field, anytime they want?"

"They always come back."

I look down at myself. My clothes are covered in red dirt, my boots in black muck. I unbutton my purple plaid shirt and toss it over the fence. Somehow, even my tank-top is dirty.

"Do you want to try it?" Devin asks.

"I'm sorry, what?"

"Bareback. Would you like to try?"

I turn to face him. "I thought we're taking a break."

"You're obviously a natural." He guides Neptune to the edge of the steps. "Get on."

"With you?"

"I'd like to be a little more in control this time. And Goliath's busy." At the far end of the corral, Goliath and Delia stand side by side, their heads both hanging over the fence. Something has captured their attention.

"Okay." My boot hits the first step, and I'm quickly reminded of my filthy condition. "Hold on." I step down and remove my boots. "Is this okay?"

He smiles. "Sure, as long as they don't stink."

"My feet smell like roses." I walk up the steps. "How do I do this?"

Devin flexes his foot hard and lifts his lower leg slightly. "Step here and give me your hand." I do as he says and step up easily before sliding into place in front of him. "You sure you never rode before?"

"No, sir."

"If you say so."

"Can we go onto the path?"

"Yes, I'm boiling." He peels off his shirt and tosses it to the ground. We leave the enclosure and enter the cool shade of the wooded path. Pressed up against Devin's warm, muscled body, I find my senses on sudden overdrive.

Sharp pine and lush green waft up with every step Neptune takes. My bare feet rub against his wiry white hair, and I'm thankful for my long pants. He is a magnificent animal, sleek and sculpted, walking with pride and grace and who seems eager to please. But his energy feels wild and untamed. He definitely reminds me of Devin.

"So all this weight is okay for him?"

"He's not as big as Goliath, but he's very strong. This is no problem for him."

"Okay. Good."

"But you know what's not okay?"

"What?"

"This hair in my face."

"Excuse me?"

"Your hair. Woah, boy." Neptune comes to a stop and takes the opportunity to munch on a patch of rich green grass. "Do you have a hairband?"

"No."

"How fond are you of your shirt?"

"Not very. It's kind of trashed now anyway. Why?" He grabs the bottom hem of my tank and pulls hard. "What are you *doing*?" I ask. He tries to rip my shirt again but can't. So he lifts the shoulder strap to his mouth instead and tears a hole in it with his teeth. He rips the fabric some more, yanking me back and forth.

"Got it. Sorry about the shirt."

I look at my bare shoulder. "Yeah, thanks."

"You were hot anyway."

He's right, and I'm happy feeling my bare skin against his. Then I feel his hands on either side of my head. "What are you doing?"

One hand over the other, he bundles and smooths my wild hair away from my face. His touch softens as he works, his fingers lingering at the skin along my hairline with each pass. "You're so soft," he says.

"You're so gentle."

He continues until he's gathered an ample ponytail, then winds the strip of my shirt around and around before tying it off. "There. All done."

"Are you sure?" My breath is quick. I close my eyes.

His right hand returns to the front of my neck, his fingers skimming along my collarbone until goosebumps rise all over me. Then his lips are on my skin, working their way down to the bend of my bare shoulder. His other hand inches slowly up my thigh.

He moves the ponytail, and his mouth finds the curve of my neck. I reach up behind me, winding my fingers in his hair. But my eyes pop open, and my head snaps forward. "Stop."

"What's wrong?"

No disguises...

I exhale and fight back a tiny sob. "Lift my hair up off my neck... all the way." He does it, and I feel him go still. "You see it?"

He takes a deep breath. "Yes."

"Read it. Out loud."

"No."

"Devin, read it. This is what I am. This is what we're dealing with, and we're going to have to face it. We can't keep ignoring it. Pretending it doesn't exist."

"Did he do this to you?" His voice is weak as he runs his fingers along the scarred, raised skin.

"Read it!"

"Property of the FWG." He can barely get it out. "That is *not* what you are. Not *who* you are!" He roars at the treetops, and Neptune startles.

I pet the back of the horse's head. He walks in place, picking up each foot and tamping it down hard. He snorts and whinnies and huffs, swinging his head from side to side, but stops suddenly as something down the path catches his attention.

"Devin, someone's coming."

Leyla rounds the trees in front of us, her face pale and slick with sweat. Devin peers out from behind me.

"Mom, are you okay?"

"I heard voices," she says. "Are *you* okay?"

I curl my feet inward as far as I can, but it's no use. There's nowhere to hide.

"I'm fine, Mom. How long have you been here?"

She just stands there and looks at my feet, her face void of all visible emotion. I let go.

"Mother! How much did you hear? What did you see?"

"Enough."

24 – BLOOD LOYALTY

FRIDAY, AUGUST 16TH

Everyone is trapped in their own cage of disbelief.

"I hate being back here."

"I could talk to Marcus," Devin offers.

"I can't keep lying about going to work when I'm not. We're lucky we got through the week with only one of our mothers having their world blown. How is she?"

"Not as bad as you'd expect. She knows what kind of man her husband is, what kinds of things he's involved in. She's been pretending for years."

"I can't blame her."

"Me neither. Oh, no, here he comes..."

Bounding across the beach pavilion, Marcus looks like a dog about to be reunited with his human after years of separation. "Master Banks! It's a pleasure to have you back on the sand at Concordia. On behalf of all of us, I'd like to thank you for your generous donation to the beach pavilion. I assure you it will be used to benefit all our guests."

"You're welcome."

"Sir," Marcus adds, lowering his voice, "many thanks for the personal gift as well."

"Nobody deserves it more. And I insist you spend that on yourself."

"Well, if you insist."

"Now Marcus, if you don't mind, Nerissa and I are going over some of the business she assisted me with."

"Oh, of course. Hello, Ms. John. I will send over all your favorites, Master Banks. Please enjoy your day. And I assume Ms. John will remain your assistant this week?"

"How accommodating of you," Devin says. Marcus clasps his hands behind his back and swings his leg along the sand. "Do you know what I'd really like, Marcus?"

"Anything..."

"Regrettably, only two short weeks remain before the Season is over. I would like to assure Nerissa's services for the remainder. Of course, another personal gift may find its way into your hands before I leave the island."

Marcus' eyes bulge with restrained tears. "Your wish is our command. Enjoy your day." He raises his hand above his head and turns, offering Devin a backward wave, then leaves.

"Poor Marcus." I sigh.

"What a fool."

SATURDAY, AUGUST 17TH

I've overslept, and I'm late. I grab my waist pack and run down the sand to the junipers. Devin has made himself comfortable, having taken off his shirt and shoes. He's ordering drinks from a server.

"Oh! There she is... get her a couple also."

"Yes, sir. My pleasure."

"What are you ordering me?" I stop to retie my laces.

"Mr. Banks has requested two Aqua Tonics for each of you."

"And don't forget the rum!"

"Yes, sir."

"I'll just have water, thanks."

"Bring it all!"

The server hesitates. I meet his eyes and give a slight nod.

"Yes, sir. I'll be back in a few moments."

Devin jumps off his chair and grabs my arm. He wraps his other arm around my back and yanks me to him, sloppy and unbalanced.

"Are you drunk?"

"So?" He leans in and kisses my neck, his breath heavy with alcohol.

"So, it's not even nine in the morning."

"Are you trying to embarrass me?" He gropes me with rough, clumsy hands.

"Stop it," I say, but he ignores me. "Let go of me!"

He tries to focus on my face. "You're so beautiful. You just need to remember that you belong to me when you're here."

The server returns with the order, and Devin snatches the bottle of rum out of the server's hand. He takes a big, long swig, then pours another half glass. He fills the rest with a freshly cracked AQT and stirs it with his finger. Holding the drink up in front of his face, he looks at it like it's a glass of liquid gold riddled with razor blades.

"Here's to health and happiness." He brings the drink to his lips, closes his eyes, and tips his head back, not bothering to stop until it's gone.

The server looks at me and mouths the words, 'You okay?'

I nod again, and he walks away.

"Wait!" Devin stumbles after him and slaps a wad of money into his hand. I'd bet it's the biggest tip he'll get all day, maybe all Season.

Then Devin mixes another drink. It's like watching the aftermath of a crash—horrible and disturbing, but I can't stop staring.

He stands upright and faces me, barely able to focus. "Come with me." He grabs my wrist and pulls me forward.

"Where are we going?" He doesn't answer. "Devin, you're hurting me. Let go." He pays no mind and we trod through the sand like drunken zombies.

We reach his desired destination—a beach cabana, trimmed with flowing white curtains. Inside, a luxurious, inviting gold bed lies piled high with pillows of every shape and size.

"You think I'm going in there with you?"

"Yes, you are." He pulls me into the cabana and forces me onto the bed. "You are my attendant, remember? You belong to me."

Just as he's about to fall on top of me, I stand up and slap him across the face. "I don't belong to anyone!" The force of my strike has spun him around. Then I see his right shoulder is covered in a large, angry bruise and a swollen red scrape.

He turns back around, his head hung low. His hair covers his face, but I can't miss the shine of tear-filled eyes. He's shaking. "I'm so sorry." He falls to his knees and lets out the desperate moan of a dying animal. Then he wraps his arms around my legs and clutches at me, trembling. "Please, Nerissa. Please forgive me... I'm sorry." His body heaves.

I want to pull away—to run away. But I can't leave him like this. I sit back on the bed, slowly reach out, and lay my fingers on his injured shoulder. His breath halts, then the rest of the armor falls away, and he completely lets go.

I'm able to coax him off the floor and onto the bed beside me. He sits for a few minutes, then succumbs to the heavy cloak of emotion and drink and lies down. I rub his forehead with a gentle touch, and he takes my hand. "Nerissa, I'm so sorry." His voice is weak, his words slurred. "I don't deserve you or your forgiveness, but I can't lose you." He finally manages to look at me through puffy, bloodshot eyes.

"I can't lose you, either." I lie down facing him. "I forgive you. What happened?"

He closes his eyes and swallows hard. "He hit her. That bastard hit her right in front of me."

"Your stepdad? He hit your mom?"

"He got home yesterday. When I got there, they were arguing. He found something in the house, something of yours."

"Oh, no. I'm so sorry."

His brow folds. "No! You've done nothing wrong."

"Is she okay?"

"He hit her right in the face."

"And then he got to you?"

"I went crazy." He clenches his jaw. "I jumped on his back and pummeled him... until he threw me off."

"You're hurt."

"I'm fine."

"How did it end?"

"He accused her of dishonoring him and his name and warned her never to cross him again. That it was his final warning. Bastard. Then he left with Colton and said they'd be staying at the labs for a while."

"How did she take *that*?"

"She's devastated. But she let Esmerelda take care of her and went to bed early. I've been up all night."

"Clearly."

I move closer to him and position my arm under his neck, his face at my chest, and I wrap myself around his body. He lies like a child in my arms, and I find myself humming. Just when I think he's drifted off to sleep, he asks the thing I've been wondering for weeks.

"What do we do now?"

I rub the back of his head, losing my fingers in his soft locks. "The Season is over in two weeks. It's time to go to the Matriarchs and tell them everything."

He falls asleep a few minutes later. I stay with him a bit longer, then slip away to let him sleep off the alcohol and grief. No doubt he'll be here a long time. Before I leave,

I watch him sleep for a few minutes and send him a message.

Devin,

Join me at the coffee shop on resort row tomorrow morning at ten. I'll ask the Matriarchs for a meeting at eleven. Get some rest tonight. And don't worry, everything is going to be fine.

Nerissa

PS ... Don't go home, Devin. I love you. Stay on the island with me forever.

Just before I send it, I delete the PS.

SUNDAY, AUGUST 18TH

On my board, I cross the bridge and turn right. The sun bounces off the rooftops and sparkles in the distant waves. I draw in a deep, cleansing breath. The familiarity of this island, which has bred more than just contempt, suddenly feels like an old acquaintance. It may be arrogant and boring, yet it's somehow reliable and strangely comforting. And it's all about to change.

Down the road, the coffee shop comes into view. I can also see Devin. He's sitting at a patio table having a drink, and I can tell even from here that it's not coffee. Out of nowhere, Colton appears at his table and slaps the drink from Devin's hand. Devin stands, toppling his chair backward, and people turn to stare. I stop my board and listen.

"What the hell is your problem?" Devin shouts in his stepbrother's face.

"I told you not to drink that crap, Devin."

"What do you care, Daddy's Boy?"

Colton lowers his voice. "It's poison, man. It's making people crazy. It'll make you crazy, too."

"Well, you're playing your part in that, aren't you?"

"You know I don't have a choice. And you know I can't stop him or change things."

Devin grabs Colton by the shirt collar and slams him against the coffee shop wall. "But you could have told me the truth. You knew all along."

"I didn't know everything."

Devin pushes harder. "You lied to me, man. I *know* you knew it was her."

What does that mean?

"I was under oath."

Devin gives him one last shove, then releases him. "You know what you can do with your oath, don't you?"

"Don't do this, brother."

"Shove off... brother." He turns his back, and Colton walks away, crosses the street, and disappears.

I'm a tree rooted in the middle of the street.

Devin paces with manic steps. I better get to him before he sees me standing here. I force a weak smile and zip toward him.

"Good morning!" I pull up and park my board.

"Oh, hey."

"How are you feeling?" I sit down at the tiny table. "Did you get some sleep?"

His face is gaunt, his hair everywhere, dark shadows under his eyes. "I'm fine. Nerissa... I want to apologize for my inexcusable behavior yesterday."

"You already did."

He attempts a smile. "What would you like to drink?"

"Black coffee is perfect, thanks."

"Be right back."

"We can wait for a server to come."

"No, I got it." He disappears inside the shop.

I take a deep breath and allow my thoughts to wander into the world around me. The distraction is surprisingly welcome. People pass, on their way to whatever their charmed day on Panacea may bring, and I try to imagine being in their shoes—living a day in the life of a tourist. My attention is suddenly caught by two women across the street who have just stepped out of a boutique.

“Thanks, Mom. I love it.”

“You deserve it, Beauty.”

The pair lean against each other, and then I see it—hanging from the daughter’s arm, a white, fur handbag. The young woman strokes the bag, and the tail ‘wags’ in response. They both giggle. I never see the front of the bag. I never want to.

“Good morning, Beauty. What can I bring you?” A server interrupts my thoughts.

“Oh, good morning. That’s okay, my... friend... he went inside to order. But thanks.”

“Well, if you’re going to sit here, you could at least let me do my job.” She leaves in a huff. Devin passes her in the doorway.

“Here you go.”

“Thank you.”

“So, what’s the plan?” He falls into the chair beside me.

“The plan is, you let me do the talking—at least at first. My mother especially is not going to be happy to see you, and less happy to have you in her house.”

“Great.”

“To them, you’re a direct extension of Officer Banks.”

“That’d be the other *brother*.” He mimes quotation marks in the air.

“They’re going to be shocked and angry with everything we say.”

“Join the club.”

“You can’t add fuel to their fire. We need to stay calm and present the facts we know.” I search his eyes. “All the facts...”

“The whole truth and nothing but the truth. I’ve brought notes.” He holds up his journal and slaps it on the table. It’s stuffed with loose papers, all torn and crumpled at the edges.

"Is there something you haven't told me?" I ask, looking up from the stack.

"They're just notes."

I sip at my coffee until it's almost gone. We don't talk.

"Okay, you ready?" I finally ask.

"Let's go."

Normally, I wouldn't dream of leaving my trash on the table, but today, I not only leave it, I gently tip over the cup before walking away. Let that waitress bitch do her job now.

We ride out of the resort district and up the hill. The wind drifting up off the ridge is strong, and I turn to the left to face it. Out in the distance, beyond the ropes, the waves look formidable. I'm glad I'm not harvesting today. Yet as I contemplate what I'm about to do, perhaps I wish I was. Devin seems just as nervous. He doesn't speak a word or look at me once as we ride into the Oval. My mouth turns to cotton.

We enter the house and hear voices in the kitchen. I take Devin's hand and step toward the hallway, but he holds still. I turn around to face him, afraid he's changed his mind. He pulls me to him and wraps his arms around me like it's the last time, and I lock onto him.

"Devin, whatever happens today, I need you to know something..." I play a fast-motion tug of war inside my head, but my heart finally wins. "I love you."

He inhales my words slowly. Our eyes are glued together, and for a brief flash, we're back on the observation deck, the first time he took me to Black Rock and I knew I couldn't live without him. For just one glorious second, everything falls away, and it's just us again.

"I love you, too. I always have."

"Nerissa? Is that you? We're in the kitchen," my mother calls out.

We don't move, each of us trying to absorb the moment before it dissolves forever.

"You did tell them I was coming, right?"

"I did, but they're still not happy about it."

"I don't suppose I'd be either."

"We're coming!"

We walk slowly down the hall, and each of us knows there's no turning back.

Giovanni sits at the kitchen table, her hands wrapped around a steaming cup of coffee, Wreckleaf staining the rim. My mother leans against the counter, her arms crossed in front of her chest. I knew they wouldn't be happy to see Devin, but they both look like they've been up all night. My mother looks terrible. And that's not something I've ever thought before.

"Hi. Thanks for meeting with us." No response from either of them. I guess I should just dive in, but I can't help my curiosity. "I thought I heard three voices. Is there someone else here?"

They glance at each other, then both look past me.

"Just me."

I spin around to find myself facing Kendra. I gasp, then throw myself at her, burying my face in her hair and bundling her against me. I can't get enough, and I can't let go. "I'm sorry, Kendra, I'm sorry... please forgive me..." She puts her hands on my arms and unlatches my grip, pushing me back far enough to see her face.

"You have nothing to be sorry for," Giovanni insists.

I don't acknowledge Giovanni. I just stare at Kendra. I can't look away. She doesn't retract, doesn't hide at all. She allows my eyes to wander along her scars.

The knife sliced her from the outside corner of her left eye down to the curve of her jawline. Then again from her ear, where it removed half her lobe, all the way to her collarbone. She follows my eyes. "That's the one that almost killed me."

I bite my lip so hard, I taste blood. "I'm so sorry. They'll pay for this."

"Please don't," she whispers.

"Nerissa!" I turn to face Giovanni. "You are not responsible for this, and you will not seek retribution. This was a random act of violence."

"No, it wasn't." Here we go. "That's why we're here. Well, that's part of why we're here." I look at Devin, then back to Gio and my mother. "We have a lot to tell you, and it's going to be hard to hear."

My mother steps forward. "Whatever you have to say will have to wait. We have news that must be discussed immediately."

"No, Mom, this can't wait."

"It has to."

My face grows hot. "Are you kidding me? This cannot wait! I've asked to address my Matriarchs in our home, with a pure-human at my side. Don't you think that means it's pretty important? I will not be ignored by you anymore. We're here to speak, and you will listen!"

"Gabriel is dead."

"What?"

"Gabriel is dead. He was found early this morning. It appears to be a drug overdose."

No.

The Earth stops turning at the same time my heart stops beating. Time freezes, and every sound, every sight, every thought ceases to exist. I am being buried ... crushed alive. I can't move. My mouth becomes a wide, deep chasm, but I can't draw in any air. I can't push any out. The pressure grows—a force from my chest that must escape but is trapped. I feel myself melting, dissolving, when finally the space at the back of my throat rips open, and the shriek of a thousand tortured souls escapes, dropping me to my knees.

Devin catches me as I slam onto the floor. I grip at him like a patient in an asylum, pushing and pulling and wailing, demanding he relieve me. I search his face, pleading without words. But he cannot help me. Every part of me vibrates, but nothing connects. I am spinning, descending. Nothing is real.

Kendra falls to my side and gathers me in her arms beside Devin to cry with me. We rock back and forth through our grief and panic, and we stay here for a long time. She is my only tether to this world. She doesn't speak, doesn't offer any words of hope or condolence, because she knows it would mean nothing.

Eventually, I'm helped up off the floor and guided into a chair at the table. Someone puts a glass of water in front of me, then hands me tissues. I stare at the table for an indistinguishable amount of time. When I look up, I drink the entire glass of water, wipe my face with my sleeve, and clear my throat.

"Gabriel didn't overdose. They killed him, just like they attacked Kendra." Kendra looks down and closes her eyes.

"They who?" my mother asks.

"The FWG. Specifically, William Banks."

"You're overcome with emotion, Nerissa. You don't know what you're saying."

"I know exactly what I'm saying. And now, it's time for you to listen."

"That's your father she's accusing, Devin."

"He's my stepfather."

"Still, that's an awfully big accusation, don't you think?"

"It's true, Tatiana," Devin confirms.

"Are you sure you want to do this?" my mother asks, her voice low.

"Yes, I am."

Tatiana settles back against the counter.

"Excuse me," Gio asks Devin. "Am I to understand that you know who we are?"

"Yes, I do."

"How long have you known?" my mother asks.

"I've known a long time. A very long time." His words draw me out of my tunnel.

"How long?" I ask, suddenly confused.

"A lot longer than you think. Let me explain."

"Please do. You have our attention." Gio's voice is as sharp and cold as ice.

"Yes, please do," I say. I allow Devin to take the reins and explain everything we came here to reveal in hopes of my mother, in particular, finally listening and believing. But something else whispers at the back of my mind.

"My stepfather is not only responsible for the Cooperative, he's also lying to you and everyone else on this island. He's using the Wreckleaf you provide him with—which, by the way, he will not need you to do for much longer—to develop and mass-produce an incredibly addicting product."

"AQT," my mother interjects.

"Yes. Everyone on the island is a test subject. Even me. He's gathering data for his associates on the mainland, hoping for approval for mass production and distribution back home. The problem is, he's far surpassed what the regulators have declared are safe formulations. So he's lying to his superiors and his investors—"

"So he's blatantly ignored our warnings about ingesting Wreckleaf?" Gio interrupts.

"Not at first. Originally, it was only used in some of the skin care. But he was always running experiments behind closed doors."

Hearing Devin speak this truth to the Matriarchs—what I've been carrying around with me and what I've wanted to scream to the world for so long—is incredibly sobering.

"The experiments... they were done on lab animals?" Gio asks.

I look up at my mother and know her mind is working, the wheels turning behind her hardened gaze.

"Yes," Devin continues. "Some were natural-born animals, some were made... There were others." He pauses, unable to look up at any of us.

"Tell them," I insist.

Devin hangs his head. "Anastasia. They're using her to see how far they can push the levels. Her and her child... even though it's not an accurate measure."

Giovanni stands and drops her cup, spilling coffee across the table. "Did you just say Anastasia? Our Ana?"

Hearing Devin say my friend's name with some strange sense of authority, as though I'm the one he's revealing it to, causes a weight to drop in my gut. But I realize it's more important to help Giovanni now, while I can. I stand and take her hands across the table. "Anastasia is alive. They've had her all this time. She has a son. His name is Alakier."

Giovanni's legs give out from under her, and she flops back on her chair. "What?" she whispers.

"It's true," Kendra says. I want to turn to her, to wrap her in my embrace and relive the last day I spent with her as my best friend, untouched by the cruelty she'd endured at William Banks' command. But then my mother's voice cuts through the kitchen.

"Devin, how long have you known?"

"A long time, but let me be clear. I've known about the testing for a while. I didn't know *what* they were testing. I mean, I didn't realize the finished product was the AQT. But I did have my suspicions about the woman I saw in the lab about a year and a half ago."

I turn to look at him, feeling my heart race and my face grow hot with confusion. "You told me you had never seen Anastasia." I wait, hoping he has a good explanation. But he doesn't answer me. "Now you're saying the first time you saw her was a year and a half ago?"

"No." He looks down and draws in a quick breath. "The first time I saw her was *three* years ago... the first time I saw you."

"*What?*"

"The night you and Anastasia snuck onto the island, before the Cooperative, Colton was one of the guys you went into that club with. He didn't stay long, but he didn't come home. I was sent to find him, and then I saw Ana being dragged away by two other guys just outside of Wave. I wanted to do something, believe me, but I... I didn't. I was just about to leave when I saw you walking down the pier, and that idiot and his friends were following you."

I'm time-traveling, swirling in a black hole, afraid of where I may come out. "You were there?"

"I was there. I saw everything. I'm the one who pushed you in the water. Others just like Tom, just like my stepfather were coming, and they would have taken you, too."

I'm about to be sick. I sit down. "You? You pushed me in the water?"

"Yes."

"After you asked me if I could swim... right?"

"Right."

I'm not sure any of this is real. I'm not sure I'm here, in this room, living any of this. "So all this time, you knew exactly who I was?"

"No." He shakes his head and begins pacing, his words spilling out quickly. "I had my ideas. I asked a lot of questions about what I saw that night, and everything was just explained away. Then I saw Anastasia in the labs a year and a half later, and thought I recognized her. That summer, I saw you at the beach too. I recognized you, but I didn't dare open that can of worms."

I'm a tea kettle ready to blow. "Then why this year?"

"When we were at the river, that first day... I just... I don't know. I—"

"You wanted to see if you could land your own legendary Water Doll. Your own perfect Beauty."

He halts abruptly and turns to me. "No—"

"But all along, you knew... You knew everything."

The air rushes out of him, his shoulders fall in surrender, and he shakes his head again. "I didn't know everything... but she did." He points at my mother.

Tatiana steps forward. "You watch yourself."

"What does that mean?" Gio demands. "She did?"

"She knew all along about Anastasia. Officer Banks told me. He said that because she's the Matriarch, she knew she had to accept the loss of one of her kind without a fight in order to preserve the rest of the breed."

Both Gio and I are out of our seats again and bearing down on my mother. "Tatiana! Is this true? Did you know Anastasia was alive and being held prisoner? Did you know she had a son?"

Everyone holds their breath, waiting for her answer. But her silence speaks even louder, and I'm not sure I remember how to breathe anymore.

"I did not know about the boy."

Gio rushes toward her, gets right up in her face, and hisses out her disgust. "We all mourned that child. Lives were ruined!" She slaps Tatiana across the cheek. "That's for Ana's mother."

The stony Matriarch barely flinches, accepting the punishment.

"I thought she was dead, Mother!" I scream. "I thought I killed her!"

Tatiana readjusts her position, setting her feet firmly in place. "I did what I had to do, what I was told to do in order to keep the rest of us alive and safe. He told me it was easy for him to take any one of us at any time. He said no one would miss us. I agreed to keep my mouth shut, and I made him agree to never touch you."

"So that's why he went after Kendra instead of me."

"No. He would have never gone after you." Tatiana's face slackens, and her nostrils flare with her next exhale.

"Why not?"

She stares at me, unblinking, her fists balled at her sides.

"*Why*, Mother?"

"Because you're his daughter, Nerissa."

Hot liquid rises in my throat, and I turn my head to splatter vomit across the kitchen floor. I'm certain I'm about to faint as the room spins around me. No one comes to my side, everyone trapped in their own cage of disbelief.

My head fills with the sound of my own blood rushing through my veins, my heart pounding at the back of my throat. The silent room bears down on me, then faint laughter breaks the warped moment. I wipe my face with the back of my hand and look over to find Devin crumpled onto the floor, knees pulled to his chest, rocking and staring at nothing. He laughs again. I crouch next to him and put my hands on his knees.

"Devin, it's okay."

But it's as though he's entered some semi-catatonic state. He's gone, unreachable, and he just keeps laughing. I turn to my mother. "When were you going to tell me?"

"Honestly? Never." She won't look at me and just stares at the soiled floor. "I didn't want to burden you with it."

"You didn't want to burden me? That's ironic. But you know what's worse? You always tell me to trust no one. I didn't realize that included you."

"You're my sister," Devin whispers.

I turn around. "What?"

"You're my sister. I have no business being here." He stares straight ahead at nothing, his eyes glossed over.

"No, Devin, that's not true."

"I'm going to leave now. This..." He twirls his finger in circles, pointing at the pathetic room and the circumstances contained within. "This is too much to deal with. I need to be done. With all of it."

"We'll figure it all out." My voice is shaking. "We'll make a plan."

"No."

"Devin, don't. Don't leave."

"I can't be in love with my sister."

"I'm *not* your sister."

"I can't be in love with that monster's daughter!"

One more blow, and I will float away and never come back. "I am *not* him. I'm nothing like him!"

Devin stands, fighting for balance, and sweeps the room with his sad, confounded eyes one last time. "I can't be a part of this." He exits the kitchen, but I follow close behind.

"Devin, stop. Please." He doesn't slow down; he doesn't consider me at all. "Please! Don't leave."

He reaches the front door and turns toward me. "Tell them they don't have long. Tell them your father will make sure you're all obsolete... very soon." He walks out, and I run after him. I try to grab him, but he doesn't yield.

"Devin, no. Don't do this. I love you!" I stand in front of his board and put my hands on the holds. He looks down at me, and the resolve in his eyes shatters me. He reverses the board and pulls away, ripping from my hold. Then he rides down the street, out of the Oval, and is gone. Just like that.

Deep in the farthest folds of my being, a terrified voice rises out of my own darkness. *You're never going to see Devin Banks again...*

I spin around, run through the house, and crash through the kitchen door. Only my mother remains, cleaning the floor. "Where did they go?"

"We're just leaving." Kendra and Giovanni come around the corner from the bathroom. "I needed to splash some water on Mom's face. She's a little emotional." Kendra makes no attempt to buffer her sarcasm or contempt.

I can't stand still. I round the room three times and push over a chair. My fist meets the wall, and then my angry foot follows. "Why did you keep that from me?" I scream at my mother. "How can he be my *father*? Why did you tell me now? Here? With Devin and... Gabriel... What are you *thinking*? He wouldn't attack me, so he went after Kendra! Lucky me!"

"Kendra was attacked by strangers," my mother says.

"Stop it! Stop defending him. You know that's not true. Kendra was attacked because we went to Black Rock and saw the test animals and found Ana. We enchanted Devin, but he wouldn't drop because the AQT's making him immune to us. It'll make all of them immune."

"You didn't." She stops mopping and looks at me, apparently more upset by my confession than by what we discovered.

"I did. Twice. And William Banks—" I swallow hard and fight back the urge to be sick again. "He warned me not to anger him... the day Kendra was attacked. He didn't come after me because I'm his blood. Devin told me he's only loyal to his blood. Then they killed Gabriel because I told him everything and I took Devin to see him. Somebody must have seen us."

"You did *what*?"

"Don't you dare scold me, Mother!"

"Are you happy, Tatiana?" Gio asks.

She lets out a small, sarcastic laugh. "Happy? No."

"How could you keep all this from us?"

"I didn't know about the testing and the Wreckleaf being used like that. I swear."

"But you knew the worst of it." Giovanni grips Kendra's arm to steady herself. "You knew about Ana. We could have rescued her. We still can."

My mother sits and scoffs. "You can't stop this. All of us put together can't stop this. This is bigger than just William Banks."

"It doesn't matter anyway." My voice is drained of everything.

"Why not?" Gio snaps.

"They're not going to need us for much longer. My guess is a couple of months. They're close to recreating growing conditions... in a simulated environment. The

Wreckleaf tank. When they do, they'll get rid of us. They'll make their own Wreckleaf. They'll make more tanks."

"That's absurd!" My mother slams the mop handle to the floor. "I don't care what kind of technology they master... they cannot recreate the conditions of the ship graveyard."

"I've seen it," I say.

"You've only seen their feeble attempts at Mother Nature's perfect design."

"You know about the tank, too, Tatiana?" Gio's voice is weak now.

"No."

"Then you have no idea what they're capable of, Mother."

"I do know," she says. "That's why we have to cooperate with them. They'll destroy all of us if we don't."

"What are we going to do when they can grow their own Wreckleaf?" I ask. "Or let's say they can't... What about when all the tourists are immune to our toxins and we can't enchant them anymore?"

"Not everyone drinks that stuff."

I get right up in her face. "They'll put it in something else. And if it's not that, it'll be the hybrid drones they create to harvest instead of using us. They're going to clone Alakier."

"Don't be so sure about that."

Unbelievable.

"Wake up!" Giovanni seems to have mustered the strength to yell. "This is happening. We have to take action."

"No."

"I'm not kidding around," Gio says.

"Neither am I. We do nothing, and we live."

"This isn't living." I've only seen Giovanni cry on two occasions before now. This makes three. "Either way, they're going to eliminate us. Stand with me, sister. I beg you."

Tatiana rises from her seat and smooths down her shirt, then surveys her cleanup and swallows hard. “I will stand by you within the laws of the Cooperative.”

Gio takes Kendra by the hand, and they turn to face me. “Sweet child, we will see you at ceremony tomorrow evening.”

“Ceremony?”

Giovanni strokes my cheek with the back of her hand and offers a tiny smile. “For Gabriel.”

The hole grows deeper.

“Gio, don’t leave.” My mother steps up behind her as Gio comforts me, placing only her fingertips on her friend’s shoulder. Giovanni turns abruptly, not allowing my mother any relief. “Please, my sister…” Tatiana pleads, her eyes wide and glossy, her voice broken at last.

“We are done, Tatiana. Goodbye.”

25 – GABRIEL

MONDAY, AUGUST 19TH

Emancipation ignites power and fuels responsibility.

The newest version of my dream is like a carnival ride—no, a freak show.

Tom holds me, tightening his grip and panting in my ear.

"Hey, Tom, old buddy. I'll take it from here." Devin appears out of the dark. Tom releases me and dissolves.

"What are you doing here?" I ask.

"I want to show you something." Devin walks to the edge of the pier, stares out at the black water, and waits. When I reach him, he holds out his hand. I place mine in his, and a million stars fill the night with blinding light. I have to shut my eyes.

When I open them, I'm standing solo in the cool blue labs, the Wreckleaf tank in front of me.

"Hello, child." There Gabriel stands, a scruffy white cat with two different-colored eyes at his side.

"Gabriel? You didn't say goodbye."

"I have not left, dear one. I'll always be with you." He strokes the purring cat.

Behind him, from down a narrow, dark hall, Anastasia and Devin appear and join Gabriel. Devin holds a white, blanketed bundle in his arms, and the tiniest squeak makes him giggle.

"It's a girl," he says and hands the baby to Gabriel.

"I know." Gabriel accepts the child but never takes his eyes from me.

"When do I get a chance to hold her?" Anastasia asks.

"Soon. You'll get your chance soon, child."

I blink, and the room changes. The wavy blue walls fall away, replaced by enormous fields of Wreckleaf. We are all enveloped within the monstrous green fronds. Something catches my eye, and I see my ring sparkling against the dark floor. I reach for it. When I'm inches from retrieving it, a large, heavy foot steps on my hand, crushing my bones. The pain blurs my vision, and I know my ring is gone.

Devin walks to the other side of the room and joins two people whose faces are not yet clear. They each extend an arm, inviting him to settle between them as they come into focus.

My mother stands on Devin's right, William Banks on his left. They're all smiling.

"One big, happy family," Devin says, his chin raised, standing tall.

My eyes dart from the three of them back to where Gabriel and Anastasia shower the baby with love and affection. I can still hear the cat purring. Back and forth, back and forth, I flip between the two. The room spins as I stand motionless in the center. They whirl past me, over and over. Gabriel's voice fills the room.

"Nerissa, no one can tell us who we are."

Spinning and spinning and spinning...

"You are exactly who you expect and want to be..."

Spinning ... endless spinning...

My eyes open, and I'm blinded by the sun. I roll to the side and vomit.

When I force myself to my feet, I brush off the dirt and grass that gathered over me as I slept. Everything hurts.

My night on Albatross wasn't the escape I'd hoped it would be. But anything would have been better than staying on Panacea last night—even the sweet escape of death. I entered the pitch-black caves twice but knew if I went to the shipyard, there would be no turning back. I'm not entirely sure what stopped me, except perhaps for the cloudy images of Alakier and Ana bouncing around in my head.

My mother called for ceremony to begin just after sundown. I'll remain on Albatross until then. In fact, I may never leave.

After a long and lonely day, I sit on the patch of grass where Devin and I revealed our inner selves to one another and watch the sunset. It's almost reached the top edge of Black Rock, where its final journey to the horizon will be blocked from view. I imagine the observation deck and wonder if anyone is there enjoying the privileged sight. I wonder if they know how lucky they are, or if they even care.

Another hour ticks by and the first of the maids arrive. It'll be a while before everyone is here. Tatiana gave strict orders to come no more than two at a time, spaced at intervals. Typically, Playa Rosa clears as darkness approaches, but without Gabriel to assist, gathering for ceremony will prove to be trickier.

When I'm sure I can wait no longer, I leave my dark, private spot and join everyone in the arena. I squeeze next to Kendra.

"I like your wreath. Did you make it?"

I touch the grass and flower wreath at my head. "Yeah, I've been here all day. It helped me pass the time."

My mother rises from her chair.

A hush spreads, and Tatiana holds us all in the inescapable silence. She skips the formalities and jumps right in; I can hardly breathe.

"Maids, it is with great sadness that I bring you confirmation of Gabriel's death." Just hearing her say the words makes my stomach flip and my eyes spill over again. Kendra takes my hand.

"Life as we know it will change. Without his assistance, scouting will become a collaborative effort. We will work on details through trial and error. However, what we do know is that Matriarch Giovanni and I will need to pre-approve potential Contributors."

The arena buzzes, and I am numb.

"Gabriel's death has come at a most unfortunate time. We have reason to believe that there exists a widespread genetic mutation, perhaps even a virus, among this generation of potential Contributors. The very same that caused Lilian to suffer a miscarriage. Therefore, it is imperative not to attempt acquisition or even enchantment without prior approval."

I hear her, I just can't believe what's coming out of her mouth. And when I look at Giovanni shifting in her seat, eyes wide, I imagine she and my mother did not agree to these lies.

Hands raise.

"Questions... yes?"

"How did Gabriel die?"

Go ahead, Tatiana. Tell them the truth.

"We suspect a drug overdose."

Liar.

"How do we know who has the mutation? Or the illness?" another maid asks.

"Good question. Yes, there are certain characteristics. Avoid anyone who seems unusually manic or who you observe consuming large quantities of alcohol or stimulants of any kind."

"Isn't that a normal precaution?"

"Yes, of course. Just be extra diligent. This anomaly seems to give them a propensity for addictions."

"How did you determine this?"

"We are fortunate to have reliable inside sources, which of course I cannot reveal."

Unbelievable.

Kendra raises her hand.

My mother seems to pretend not to see her right away. Perhaps she's worried someone will actually speak the truth. "Yes, Kendra?"

"Matriarch, may I address the arena?"

Giovanni immediately stands, regarding her daughter with soft eyes and a gentle smile. Tatiana seems caught off guard, turning quickly toward Gio, then back to Kendra. "Well, I... umm..."

"Yes, of course," Giovanni answers instead. "Come to the front."

Kendra squeezes my hand, then joins her mother. Whatever she's about to say, I'm thankful for the interruption of my mother's lies.

Kendra turns toward us. "Thank you. In light of the tragedy of Gabriel's death, I have news that may bring a small spark of hope and joy."

My mother seems to have won a huge jackpot of good fortune and perfect timing, making her lies so much easier to deliver. I'm locked onto my best friend's face; we all are.

"Please. We could use some good news," Tatiana says.

"Thank you." Kendra clears her throat. "I'm happy to announce, through unusual circumstances, that I'm pregnant."

I'm pretty sure my heart just stopped beating ... again. I close my eyes and wait for it to start.

The arena erupts in applause.

I shake my head until it hurts, trying to wake up from what must be a nightmare. But when I open my eyes, the reality hits me—everyone else is happy about this abomination. I stand and look at Kendra. She meets my gaze across the arena, her laser focus threatening to destroy me if I ruin her moment. I open my mouth to protest.

'Unusual circumstances?' I want to scream. *'This is a bastard child conceived out of the violent act of rape. They almost killed you! You can't be happy about this. How will*

you look at your child with love, knowing its father intended to ruin you?'

But instead, I sit down.

The celebration thunders on around me. I hang my head and cry. Gabriel's voice rings in my ears. *'Above all else, know that you are already free, because you always have that choice.'*

I lift my head, and Kendra is still somehow looking at me. I force myself to smile. She smiles back, but inside, I die a little more.

My mother wrangles everyone's attention once more. "Maids, this is a bittersweet evening. But know that our future always remains bright and that I stand gratefully by your side in good times and in bad. Nothing can break us."

The arena comes to order, and we file out into the starlit night to the place where we released baby Charlotte into the sea. We have nothing of Gabriel's. Instead, we line up, and the Matriarchs hand each of us a floating candle. We'll light them at a torch by the water's edge, pay our last respects, and place them into the ocean, where the current will carry them away.

When I reach the front of the line, I look my mother in the eyes and whisper, "Why didn't you tell the truth? They deserve to know."

"I told them exactly what they needed to hear. Now be quiet and move along."

"I think you underestimate us. All of us."

She hands me a candle. At the water's edge, I light it, then stand there for many moments, unsure how to let it go. I suddenly remember my dream from this morning. Gabriel's words find me again. *'I have not left you, dear one. I'll always be with you.'*

"I will always be with you, too, Gabriel. I love you." I bend down and place my candle in the water. I will my fingers to release it, and in an instant, the water whisks it away. I stand and watch the flickering lights dance on the surface, some filtering out, others going strong. I have no more tears left to cry. A hand rests on my shoulder.

"I'm so sorry, Nerissa. I know how close you were to him."

"Thank you, Lillian."

As the last of the lights drift into the darkness and disappear, I resolve that Gabriel's free spirit—his wisdom, light, and love—will live through me. And somehow, his death will be avenged.

When the evening on Albatross is over, I linger, unsure whether I want to return to Panacea. I watch my mother and Giovanni speak with the few remaining. They stand side by side, poised and perfect, and to the unknowing eye, all remains the same. Kendra stands at her mother's side, smiling and accepting congratulations. She sees me staring at her and breaks away.

"I'm glad you're still here."

"Congratulations. You'll be an amazing mother."

"I know you're not happy for me. You think this is awful. I felt the same way at first."

"Kendra, I—"

She raises a hand to stop me. "But I've decided this is a good thing. The only thing that's saved me from checking out of this life forever. Those men took a piece of me that I can never get back. Ever. But this baby... we're the same. Neither one of us had a choice in this. And it's neither of our fault. But here we are, and the only way either of us is going to survive is with each other."

All I can do is nod, and what I thought was a dried-up well overflows again.

"I know it's not the way things should have happened," she continues, "but it's the way they did. I accept your concerns and even your disapproval, but I need to ask you—beg you—please... Don't blame my baby. Please just love and accept this innocent being."

Nothing can justify any hostility or resistance. I melt. And I gather her up in my arms. "I love you, Kendra. And I will love your child just the same." I feel a sigh of relief escape her.

"I have something for you. I wanted to wait for the perfect moment."

"What is it?"

She reaches into a neat waist pack and pulls out a small black box. "Here. I knew you were missing this."

I open the box, but I don't understand.

"I had it made."

I remove the ring from its cushioned slot inside the beautiful, shiny box and slip it on my middle finger. It's perfect, an exact replica of the ring that was lost again to the ocean—the ring that almost ended my life.

"I don't know what to say."

"Do you like it?"

"I love it." I think of all the pain she's been through, all because of me. "I don't deserve this."

"Of course you do."

"Thank you. It's even more special than the original."

"You know what it means, right?"

"Yes."

She takes my hand. "Lead us to freedom. To independence. Lead us to truth. I will stand by your side."

My heart is suddenly racing. She dives into me and swims around inside my head until my vision clouds and my thoughts blur. The painting by Devin's room flashes in my mind. I look down at my right hand.

Emancipation ignites power and fuels responsibility.

26 – RETRIBUTION

TUESDAY, AUGUST 20TH

This is for me.

I considered calling in sick but decided late last night that, while I figure out what to do next, the gross and irrelevant distractions of Concordia will be a good thing. The beach is crowded, people anticipating the closing of the Season. The bells ring all day. I barely get a break. It's fine by me.

Poor Marcus nearly fainted after he asked me where Devin was, and I couldn't answer him.

"But you are his girlfriend now, aren't you?"

Turns out I'm his sister.

"No. Our relationship was purely professional."

"Was?"

When I can't answer him, he stomps off in a fluster, gripping at his chest and waving the other hand above his head.

I perform a lotion application on a middle-aged man who starts snoring halfway through. He's had so much to drink, he won't know I didn't bother to wake him up, flip him over, and finish. I hope he turns over and gets the worst sunburn of his life. I gather my bottles, and another bell rings.

"Oh, hi, Emily. How are you?"

"I'm wonderful, Beauty. How are you?"

"Great, thanks."

"I'm not convinced. Come and sit down for a minute."

I make sure Marcus is nowhere in sight before I sit. "My feet are killing me."

"Take your shoes off for a few minutes."

"Oh, that's okay. They're so hard to get back on."

I hear Marcus' voice and jump up. Emily handles it completely. "How about a Number One spray? And please, take your time."

"It is my pleasure to serve you, Beauty."

"So, hey, that was amazing the other day... on Playa Rosa, wasn't it?"

My mind sifts through the past number of days; I can't settle on what she means. "Umm..."

"The dolphins!"

"Oh, yes."

"Seems like you're rather skilled in the water yourself."

My hands stall on her shoulders a second too long. "I love your suit. You're always so... chic. Is this new?"

"Thanks, I bought it yesterday."

"You always have the coolest stuff."

"We should go shopping sometime."

"Yeah... sure." I finish her back, and she flips over. I do my best to avoid eye contact, but she watches me the entire time. "Relax, Emily. Close your eyes."

"Where's your friend today?"

"She's taken a leave of absence."

Emily sits up, forcing me to look at her. "You know who I mean." She waits.

"Devin and I had a little argument, and he's decided to spend some time at the other Big Six." I sit down without being asked. "Please don't tell Marcus."

"My lips are sealed."

"Thank you."

"All right, I need a drink... One of those orange cream freezes. How about you?"

"That was Gabriel's fav—" The word gets trapped in my throat.

Emily puts her hand on my arm. "Oh, I can't believe how insensitive I am. I heard about Gabriel. You were close to him, weren't you?"

"Yes." I hang my head.

"I'm so sorry. He was so terrific, such an icon. He'll be missed."

"Well, you may be the only person who feels that way. He's gone, and nobody seems to care. All anyone is concerned about is where their drinks will come from and who'll entertain them when they arrive. It's like he never existed."

"You know, I'll just order an Aqua Tonic. Would you like one?"

I want to tell her, to warn her. She has the right to know she's a guinea pig. They all do.

"No, thanks. I'll ring a server for you." I fasten my pack to my waist. Emily hands me a generous tip. "You don't have to do that," I say. "I didn't even finish."

"Take it. And Nerissa, let me take you shopping after work."

"No, I couldn't."

"Then dinner."

"My mother is expecting me. I'll see you tomorrow. Thanks anyway." I walk away before she can offer anything else. Her persistence reminds me of Devin. I wonder where he is, what he's doing. I just hope he's safe, buried in his writing and away from his stepfather.

WEDNESDAY, AUGUST 21ST – FRIDAY, AUGUST 23RD

The steam has risen nonstop off Black Rock the past few days. The assembly lines are no doubt churning out the beauty products—and the Aqua Tonic—at triple-speed. The tourists grow anxious, and with the weirdness of this

Season, I wouldn't be surprised to hear of another accidental drowning in Wreckleaf-infused potions, another murder, or some other act of violence or insanity.

Businesses are booming across the island—at the resorts, the clubs, the spas, the stores. Likewise, the designer pets pop up everywhere as people acquire living mementos from their summer holiday on Panacea. Yesterday, a woman sported a hat with a red parrot hybridized into the woven fabric. She asked for a Number Two spray but refused to take off the hat. I did my best not to asphyxiate the poor thing, slipping it bits of her sandwich while I worked on her back because I'm sure the woman doesn't feed it. She probably also doesn't realize that, although modified, this 'hat' will have to eliminate as well. I hope it shits in her hair. A lot.

Our services are in higher demand than ever, and money gets thrown at us. It's amusing to watch the cash waved in the air as they attempt to lure us to their chairs like dogs to a juicy bone. I happily collect the gross daily sums, tucking it away for Kendra's charity or a rainy day.

Even Emily went overboard when she greeted me with a pretty silver bag—inside, the exact black and gold bikini I complimented her on two days before.

"Really, you shouldn't have."

"I wanted to. I know you can't wear it here, but I hope you get a chance to enjoy it before the Season is up. If he sees you in that, he'll be sorry he broke up with you."

I shoved the bag in my locker, where it will stay.

I haven't had a bad dream since the weird nightmare I woke to on Albatross. In fact, I haven't dreamed at all—nothing. My sleep is black, my waking thoughts a haze. I don't want to think, don't want to feel. I just want this Season to be over. Then I can breathe. And without the chaos of the tourists and their superficial frenzy of demands—without *him*—I can figure out what to do next. I can figure out how to save Ana and Alakier... and my breed—a debt I vow to repay at all costs.

The closest I've come to a normal conversation with my mother since Sunday was at the awkward breakfast we shared this morning.

"You're on for harvest this weekend."

"I know. Who's joining me?"

"I think Cassidy, but she hasn't been feeling well. We may need a replacement. Remember to exercise extreme caution at Rosa."

"I'll go out Saturday night and sleep there. Just please remind whoever it is not to keep me waiting on Sunday."

"I will, but Nerissa..."

"Yes?"

"Even if they're late, don't harvest alone."

"I won't."

As I hit the beach this morning, perfectly groomed, angel wings perky, and bottles filled with liquid gold, habit still takes control. I automatically look down the pavilion at the junipers, expecting to see him waiting there for me, smiling and beautiful. But of course, I'm only reminded that he is gone. The truth is, Devin was lying to me. And I need that reminder as often as I can get it. Because with every thought of him that slices through the fog and flashes in my mind, the blades of regret and confusion cut deeper into my already bleeding heart.

"Good morning, Beauty." I wave and smile at Emily as I pass her.

"Good morning. Come back when you're finished."

"Ring your bell."

I service a gentleman who must be in his eighties or even nineties sporting the tiniest man-bikini I've ever seen. Three times, I suggest a spray application, but of course he insists on lotion. I work as quickly and gently as possible, afraid his ancient skin may peel off under my fingers or his bones may crumble with any amount of my strength. He moans the whole time. I'm not sure if it's in pleasure or pain.

"Well thank you, pretty lady. You have a delightful touch." He graciously extends his hand to offer me a tip.

"I told you your money is no good here," a woman says, stopping him.

"I can do what I want."

"No, all your expenses are met." The woman stands in front of me. "Thank you... That will be all."

"Alexandria, if I want to tip this fine young woman, I will."

"Uncle Whitaker, this woman is employed at the finest establishment on the island. It is her job to serve guests, and she is paid handsomely to do so. She does not need to be compensated further."

"If you say so." He sits up and juts his hand out again to shake mine. "Thank you, dear. What is your name?"

I take his hand. "I'm Nerissa, sir, and it was my pleasure to be of service to you."

"You are just the prettiest thing I've ever seen. My name is Whitaker Bigelow, and it would be my pleasure to service you." He winks at me.

Alexandria turns back to me. "You may leave."

As I walk away, I can't help but smile. That was disgusting and inappropriate and excellent.

A bell rings. It's not Emily. A different woman eyes me now, and I have no choice but to tend to her.

"Greetings, Beauty. How may I be of service?"

"I would like a Number Two spray. And one for my daughter." She motions toward the chair next to her, and I suddenly place the two familiar women—the white fur handbag with the wagging tail.

"My pleasure. Allow me to ring another attendant so your lovely daughter doesn't have to wait."

Jade joins my side in an instant. She takes the daughter while I work on the mom. When she flips over, I open my mouth, and the question escapes before I can stop it. "How is the white handbag doing?"

She opens her eyes, shielding them from the sun. "What?"

Jade stares at me, wide-eyed.

"You know, the white fur handbag you bought your daughter the other day. I saw you... Are you enjoying it?"

"Are you stalking us?" the daughter asks.

"Of course not, Beauty. I was having coffee across the street, and I saw you come out of the shop. I just fell in love with that bag. Is the care easy?"

"That bag was very expensive."

"Of course. But is it difficult to care for?"

"As difficult as throwing it into my closet." They both giggle.

"Enough chit-chat," the mother instructs. The feeling is mutual. When I'm sure her eyes are closed, I dribble a generous amount of oil into her tableside cocktail.

When I finish, Emily sees I'm free and rings her bell. Jade walks toward her, but I beat her there by three seconds.

"Good day, Beauty. How may I be of service to you?"

"How's your day going?"

"It's crazy."

"Well, I require a very lengthy application today. I have on a new suit, and I must make sure my newly exposed skin is protected."

"Of course."

She lowers her voice. "You know I'm just kidding. Well, not about the suit."

"Another new suit, Emily?"

"A girl can never have too many suits. Besides, it's my birthday."

"Happy birthday! Why are you all alone?"

"I like it that way. I'll meet up with my family and a few friends for dinner. They like to do their thing, I like to do mine."

"Like what?" I don't really care. I'm just filling space.

"Mom is all about the tennis and golf. And my dad and brother are yacht-rats. Well, mostly my brother. He's on my uncle's yacht all day, every day. I'm not into that stuff. I like the beach."

"So... what did you get for your birthday?"

"Let's see, I got that bag down there." She points at a gold leather bag with crystal-encrusted handles. "It's a little flashy, but I like it. And the shoes down there... I really like those."

"Yeah, those are cute." I stop myself. "But please, you don't need to buy me a pair."

"I like buying gifts. What size do you wear?"

"I don't know."

"Try them on."

Nothing would make me happier than showing her who I really am. "Absolutely not." I finish her back and instruct her to flip over.

She pushes her hair out of the way, and her fingers settle on a chain at her neck. "Oh, I also got this..."

I bend over to get a closer look, completely unprepared for what I see. I inhale sharply and slam my hand over my mouth.

"It's beautiful, isn't it?"

Fireworks explode inside my head, and everything blurs—everything except the shiny, golden, nautilus-shell pendant dangling on its delicate herringbone chain. Kendra's necklace.

"Who gave this to you?"

"My brother, which is shocking. He's usually so self-absorbed. Isn't it special?"

"One of a kind." I force myself to take a controlled breath. "Your brother... what's his name?"

"Tommy."

Breathe in. "Do you know where he got it?" Breathe out.

"He didn't say. I can find out."

"No, that's okay. I wouldn't want to copy you. That gift is too personal."

"Aw, thanks."

"So, where is the birthday celebration tonight? On the yacht?"

"No, it's at home. My mother hired a chef. I don't like spending time on *Easy Money*. I get seasick, even when we're in the marina."

"*Easy Money*?"

"Yeah, stupid name for a boat, right? Hey, you should come to the party."

The absolute last thing I want to do is accept this invitation. But I won't pass it up for anything. There's work to be done. And I may never get this opportunity again.

"Sure. What time?"

"Really? You'll come?"

"Why not? I could use some fun."

"Great! It's supposed to start at seven. But everyone in my family is *always* late. Wear your new bikini. It's a pool party."

"It's a little sexy for a family get-together, don't you think?"

"It's not just family."

"Okay. I've got until seven?"

"At least."

"Great, see you then. Leave directions to your house with the front desk. I've gotta run. The bells are ringing."

"I'll message you. Give me your info."

"I've got to go," I say. "Marcus is going to kill me." I leave quickly, don't look back, and never return to her chair the rest of the day.

When the last of the guests leave the beach, I head to the locker room. I take my time showering, toweling off, and brushing my hair.

"Goodnight, Nerissa," Moriyah says; she's the last person to leave before I'm finally alone. "Have a good evening."

"Goodnight."

I go about primping and prepping like never before. I need to be perfect—exactly who they would expect to show up. I know I won't disappoint.

The finishing touch waits in my locker. I pull out the bag and peek inside. I can't believe I'm going to put this thing on, but it's the right thing to do. I slip into the barely-there suit and face the mirror. I will be irresistible. I'm ready to choose my life and ready to embrace my freedom.

I grab my cover-up, shoes, and a long-tailed metal comb from the vanity. I leave everything else in my locker. Time to go. But I have one short detour to make.

I run down the dark hallway leading to the pavilion. I'm alone. When I reach the portrait of Alexandria Allerton Bigelow, I stop and regard her doggish face.

"Alexandria, you're right. I don't need to be further compensated for getting your decrepit, horny Uncle off. This will do, and a promise is a promise..." I raise the shiny silver comb and stab it right between her eyes. The canvas is thick, but I pull the comb down as hard as I can, and it rakes through her face, leaving a gapping, ragged tear.

"Well, Beauty, the fairest of them all, it has been my pleasure servicing you. Bitch."

I turn around and make my way to the lobby, but I don't stop at the front desk for directions. I know exactly where I'm going. Out the massive doors, I drop the comb in a garbage can.

Tap. "Eight."

I hop on my board; I don't have far to go.

The night is electric. The breeze blows soft but steady, the temperature perfect. Adrenaline fuels me, and I feel more alive than I have for days. I reach my destination and park in a dark, shadowy spot.

For being blatantly conspicuous, I blend right in. I walk down the stairs and pass a giant, lit sign—'Welcome to Panacea Yacht Club and Marina'. I cross the main walk-way and begin my search.

There are an untold number of vessels to investigate. I know nothing about the boat I'm looking for except its name, and time is not on my side. I stroll along the walkways through an endless maze of identical ships. They vary in size, shape, and infinite detail, and despite my identity assignment as somewhat of an aficionado, they're all the same to me—gleaming white, high-tech, and simply ridiculous. They bear names that reveal something about their owners, names like, *Sex Sea*, *She Got the House*, *Wet Wiley*, *Tip-Sea,* and *AquaHolic*, to name a few.

I approach the end of a long, quiet walkway and pass a dark, unoccupied boat called *Nauti Girl.* No one appears to remain in this section, and I'm about to turn around when I spot *Easy Money* at the very end. It's dimly lit, and I see no movement. I hope I'm not too late.

I climb aboard the stern, step quietly across the deck, and am surprised by a young, dark-haired man.

"What the hell do you think you're doing?" He turns and shouts, "Tommy!"

"No need to yell. I'm looking for Adam. Is he here?"

"I don't know any Adam. Tommy! Get out here!"

The door to the cabin swings open, and the man I presume is Tommy comes stumbling out. "What do you want, Bradford, you obnoxious idiot? *Oh*! Well hello, little Beauty. Who are you?"

"I'm looking for Adam." I lurch forward and fall into Bradford's arms.

"Someone's a little tipsy." Tommy leans over, his salty breath in my face.

"Is Adam here or not?"

"Sorry, darlin', you've got the wrong boat."

"Oops." I turn around and allow my cover-up to fall off my shoulders.

"You don't have to leave. How about you stay and party with us?"

"But I have to find Adam."

"You can call me Adam."

"Oh! You're funny." I spin around and giggle, the cover-up falling farther down my torso. "Okay, why not? I'm tired of looking for him."

"His loss."

"Yeah, his loss," I slur.

"How about a drink, little Beauty?"

"Yes!"

Tommy disappears for only a minute. He puts on some music and returns with a bottle of Tequila and three shot glasses. "Cheers."

We all drink. The hot liquid burns my throat going down.

"Can we dance?"

"Yeah, baby. Come here. Let's dance."

My cover-up falls to the deck. I glide my fingers across Bradford's face, over a still-pink scar, and cup the back of Tommy's neck under his blond hair. "This is a nice boat. Is it yours?" His thoughts are starting to follow his lust, and I reel him in. "Whose big, special boat is this?" I sing.

Bradford answers. "It's his uncle's boat."

"I'd sure like to meet the man who's got such good taste."

Tommy's hips are grinding against me, the music, the liquor, and the hormones taking over. "Uncle Tom isn't here. But let's toast to him. Bradford, pour us another drink." Bradford does as he's told.

"Thank you, Bradford." I lean over and kiss him on the cheek, close to his mouth.

"Here's to Uncle Tom." They both raise their glasses, and I follow. "Rest in peace, Tom. You are my hero."

"Oh, no. He's dead?" I pretend I care. "I'm so sorry. What happened?"

Tommy takes a handful of my butt in his right hand. "No worries, Beauty. That dumb-ass died a few years ago doing what he did best. He got super wasted at some night-club, passed out, and had some kind of seizure on the pier. His stupid friends were so drunk, they couldn't help him."

I stop dancing, freeze, and scan his ginger-blond hair, his sunburned skin, his suddenly striking familiarity.

"What's the matter?"

"Nothing, I just... that's just so sad. What nightclub was it?"

"Huh? I don't know. Bradford, you remember?"

Bradford hands out three more shots. "Wave."

"Yeah, that's it. Wave."

I put the shot to my lips and drink it down fast. "Can I use the bathroom?"

He pulls himself away, disappointed by having to stop dry-humping me.

"Come back quick, Beauty. Our night has just begun."

"I'll be right back. Bradford, pour us another drink."

I stagger into the cabin and find the bathroom. I lock the door, lift the toilet seat, and throw up. I'm spinning, vibrating. I may pass out, or explode, or die. I splash my face with cold water, then stare at myself in the mirror, searching my own eyes for a way out of this storm. But there is no way out, only through. I take three deep breaths and open the door.

When I exit the cabin and step back onto the deck, something catches my eye. Tucked along the portside edge, covered by deck rags and plastic sheets, a shiny silver wire frame pokes out. I'm hypnotized, in a numb trance, powered by forces outside myself.

"Hey, where are you going, Beauty?"

"I just want to see..." I speak so quietly, I'm sure they don't hear me. My disembodied hand reaches out. The only reason I know it belongs to me is because of my ring. I grab hold of the plastic sheets and pull. The music masks my whimper. I close my eyes to hold back hot tears and know I have about three seconds to pull myself together.

One.

Breathe in.

Two.

Breathe out.

Three...

"Where'd you get the old shopping cart from?"

"Cool, isn't it?"

"Really cool. I've never seen anything like it."

"Come here, Beauty. I want to dance."

"Me too. Time to dance."

The three of us meet in the middle of the open deck, where Bradford shoves full shot glasses at us. The two men swig their shots, and I pretend to sip mine but stumble into Tommy and spill it down his chest.

"Oh, I'm sorry. Let me help you." Starting at the top, I unbutton his shirt one button at a time, first with my fingers, then with my teeth, humming as I work. Tommy slides his fingers in my hair. I return to his face. He's breathless and hazy. "How'd you get those scars on your chest?" I ask. "Looks like you had a fight with a werewolf."

"Yep... she was a real bitch. Come here, Beauty."

I lean in and put my lips on his. Only three seconds. Then it's Bradford's turn. His face is red with anticipation. He grabs my chin and slams his lips to mine. Three seconds for him, too.

"More drinks, boys!"

"More drinks!"

I repeat this pattern two more times each, first Bradford, then Tommy. I increase by a second with each turn. It's time to see who's been drinking Aqua Tonic. I kiss Tommy for six long seconds, then pull away to look at him. He's drunk, no doubt, but not from me. I try again, lingering at his mouth until I'm sure it's no use. I rake my nails lightly along his face then put my finger in the air, signaling him to wait, that I'll be back. Then I lean into Bradford. Pressing against his chest, I take his face in my hands. On my tiptoes, I plant my lips firmly on his. He responds aggressively, squeezing my arms then trying to pull my top off. Tommy stands behind me, groping every inch of my body. I'm suddenly afraid I might not get out of this. But

Bradford sways, and I know it's working. I put my lips next to his ear and whisper slowly.

"Do you remember Kendra?"

His dusky eyes grow large. He tries to speak—to warn his accomplice, I imagine. But I cover his mouth with mine, and when I finally tilt my head back to look at him, his eyes have rolled, and he's lost his ability to stand.

"Woah. I think your friend has had too much to drink." We ease Bradford onto a long bench at the portside edge of the stern. He collapses against the fiberglass, landing face-down with his arm hanging off the side.

Tommy falls to the deck, laughing so hard, he holds his stomach. "Guess you're going to miss my sister's party tonight, Bradford... Good. I'm sick of you hitting on her... idiot!"

I'm a bull trapped in a ring with a red, flag-waving opponent. But this fight is unfair, because the matador doesn't realize that although this bull feels empathy and regret and guilt, this is still a fight to the death—one he will not win. I push aside my thoughts of Emily.

"Do you know what I want to do, Tommy?" I coo.

"Anything you want, Beauty. Your wish is my command."

"Oh, ha! That's a good one... perfect!"

He smiles in confusion, the irony of his comment lost on him. "What's so funny?"

"Let's go skinny-dipping."

"Yeah, sure. The hot tub is all fired up."

"No, not in the hot tub. Out there." I point to the darkness beyond the boat.

"In the ocean? It's a little..."

"Private." I reach behind my back and unhook my bikini. It falls to the deck in front of me, and Tommy's eyes smile. He starts mouthing the words to the song playing through the speakers and walks in rhythm toward me, snapping his fingers. Stupid.

"Wait," I say. "One more shot first. Hell, just bring the bottle."

Tommy is an obedient puppy, never taking his eyes off me. "Here you go, Beauty."

"Thanks." I pretend to drink, then step up onto the bench. I gesture to his shorts. "Your turn." He wastes no time stripping down. I hold out my hand, and he steps up, kicking Bradford's foot out of the way as he joins me. We face the water.

"It's kind of a far jump. We could get hurt."

"I like danger."

"And I like your style. Okay, ladies first."

"No, you first. I insist." I raise the tequila bottle high in the air behind him and swing it down as hard as I can. The glass shatters into a thousand tiny pieces across Tommy's head. He falls forward, easily clearing the edge of the boat, and hits the water below. I jump in after him.

He loses buoyancy quickly, but I hold him up. "Not yet, Tommy. Open your eyes." I splash his face, and he sputters and moans. He touches the back of his head, then looks at his blood-covered hand, his eyes out of focus.

"What... did you... do?" He's barely coherent.

"I'll tell you exactly what I did, what I'm doing, and why. I want you to know what's happening to you."

He squints, trying to hold onto consciousness.

"My name is Nerissa, in case you were wondering. And I'm here because you and Bradford—who is also going to die tonight, if he hasn't already—have been very bad boys."

"Go to hell..." he manages to spit at me.

"Hmm, actually, you're going to hell. A lot sooner than you realize. You can join your Uncle Tom." I grab his hair and push him under the water. He fights hard at first, squeezing my arms and tearing at my flesh. I almost let go a few times, the pain immeasurable, but a hard kick between his legs does the trick. When I pull him up, he's choking and gasping, water pouring from his mouth and nose.

“That was for Kendra. And oh, by the way, one of you is going to be a father. Congratulations.” I push him down again, and he puts up another fight, but he’s growing weak. I bring him right to the edge of death, and when I feel him begin to give in, barely hanging on, I pull him up.

“That was for Gabriel. He was like a father to me. Nothing will ever fix the hole you’ve made in my heart. So this?” I tighten my grip on his hair, some of it ripping out with the force of our life-and-death game. “This is for me.” I dive under and drag him behind me. Besides a few last reflexes, the fight has completely left him, and he floats along in fluid animation, his arms splayed at his sides. The light from the marina makes his body a black, ghostly silhouette behind me. It’s ironically beautiful. I bring him under the hull of the boat, where I contemplate him one last time—he got exactly what he deserves. I leave him there and swim to the top.

Back on the deck, I put on my swimsuit and scan my surroundings. The boat next door remains quiet, and Bradford is where we left him. I drape the rest of him over the siderail, then push and pull and tug until he finally flips off the boat and slaps the water. I hang over the edge and watch him until his lungs fill and he sinks. It doesn’t take long.

One last thing before I go.

I return to Gabriel’s shopping cart and rip all the sheets and rags off it. Then I hoist it up and heave that, too, into the water.

27 – A MOTHER'S LOVE

SATURDAY, AUGUST 24TH

Help me be like you, help me be brave.

The alarm is louder than usual. My mouth is sawdust; inside my skull is a heavy, buzzing chainsaw, my body a train wreck. It can't be morning. I climbed into bed five minutes ago.

When the ceiling comes into focus, I attempt to sit up. My hands and arms protest first. A blurry survey reveals a maze of deep red scratches and dark, loud bruises. My ears are ringing. My head *hurts*.

It takes a minute before I realize I'm covered in loose papers. They're all over my bed, some spilled onto the floor. Why am I buried in trash? But recognition soon rises. This is Devin's handwriting. I push past searing pain and grab the one closest to me, forcing myself to focus.

This frozen wheel keeps turning
Returning me to this place in time
Where the pools overflow and spill out
Onto pink velvet
How fragile is this paper heart
Folded in two like a good old book
Waiting to be opened by a hand
Turning on itself
How long? How long can this excuse justify?

Again and again...
The cry of the past into future... and now
Solidly joining till all will collide
With no hope of return
As seasons change and tumble back
The seed I feed will grow
Choose well which one to plant
Which one to harvest
Tonight in this place I turn within
To open the channels clogged by fire and ice
Fueled by blood and breath
To recreate
Again and again...

My eyes blur again, this time from sad, lonely tears. He's in pain. I'm in pain. And nothing will change unless I do.

Tommy's dead face flashes in my mind. I can't push it away, can't undo what's been done. I wonder how long before they're found. Or if the sea and its creatures will find them first.

I gather up the papers in a neat stack, swing my legs off the side of the bed, and squeeze a fistful of blanket to quell the sudden nausea. I need some coffee and some Wreckleaf.

I put on a robe and head toward the kitchen. The coffee is made, the kitchen empty and quiet. I fill a giant mug. Then my mother appears at the door, blocking the way back to my room.

"Good morning, Nerissa. How are you feeling?"

I can't meet her eyes. "I'm fine. How are you?"

"You don't look fine. And you weren't fine last night."

"What are you talking about?"

"Let's not play games. I saw you stumble in. You were drunk, weren't you?"

"Maybe."

"Nerissa, I know the past few weeks have been difficult."

"The past few weeks? How about the past few years?"

"Please don't turn to alcohol to numb yourself."

"It was a one-night thing, I swear." I take a long sip of coffee. "I feel awful."

"Good. Now get yourself ready for work. You don't want to be late."

"I'm going to call in sick."

"Absolutely not. There's only a week left in the Season, and this will be the busiest day of the year. Go pull yourself together."

I try to pass her.

"I assume you saw the papers I left on your bed."

"You left them?"

"I found them on the floor behind the plant in the kitchen. I thought you'd want to have them."

I try to work it out in my hazy thoughts. "Devin must have dropped them the other day. He had his journal with him when we were all in the kitchen talking about..."

Out of character, she tries to comfort me with a sudden embrace. I wince and pull away, the wounds from last night shouting. I cross my arms in pain.

"What's wrong? Are you hurt?"

"No, it's nothing."

"Let me see."

"No, it's... I just... fell off my board because I was drunk."

She grabs my robe and yanks it off my shoulders. "What happened to you?" she demands.

"I told you, I fell off my board. It's embarrassing." I try to pull up my robe, but she refuses to let me.

"These are scratches. Somebody did this to you."

"I fell into a cactus."

"Why are you lying to me?"

There's nothing more to say. I look her in the eyes and wait for whatever fury she's about to unleash. She holds me there and searches my face. Her brow creases. She inhales deeply, and I brace myself.

To my utter surprise, she let's go of me and walks toward her room. "Go to work." Before she closes the door, she adds, "I'll leave you something to heal those wounds. It should work quickly."

As promised, after I shower and dress, a muddy green salve waits for me in the kitchen next to a glass of bright-green liquid. But she's gone, and the house is quiet. I spread a layer of the potion over my arms, neck, and at my waist. It soothes the fire instantly. I chug down the juice and feel it coating my insides. Relief.

When I arrive at work, I find Marcus before I get into my uniform. "Marcus, I had a little accident last night and I may need to alter my uniform today." I show him my injuries.

Marcus gives me the once-over with scrutinizing eyes and pouty lips. He's clearly disgusted, then holds his index finger to his mouth. "Message to Concordia Spa and Salon: I am sending Nerissa John to see you. She needs full body and face makeup." He looks at my head. "And hair. I need her done quickly."

"There are no cuts on my face," I protest. "And my hair does not need to be done."

"This is the busiest day of the Season. Let's wow them, shall we? Now, I trust you know where the salon is."

"Yes."

"Get in uniform, go to the salon, and let them work their magic. And hurry back."

Two hours later, I step onto the sand. I'm a caricature of myself, and I'll be surprised if all the makeup doesn't melt off in the sun. Marcus is more than pleased with the results of his orders, but the pavilion is a frenzy, and he makes it clear I've kept the guests waiting too long.

"It's not my fault, Marcus. This was your idea."

The last regular Saturday of the Season lives up to expectations. People sway between the manic, anxious determination to absorb every last bit Panacea has to offer and the cold, emotionless oversaturation by nearly three months of indulgence. Either way, the bells ring constantly. By noon, every server, sprayer, activity coordinator, and equipment handler have serviced two days' worth of guests. It's exhausting but distracting, and the fuzzy memories of last night almost fall out of my thoughts entirely. Until I see Emily.

When she spots me, she waves, then picks up her bell and rings. I'm surprised to see her and unsure if I can stick to the story I devised.

"Good afternoon, Beauty. How may I be of service to you?"

"Well, you can start by telling me why you didn't show up last night."

She doesn't know.

"I went to the front desk, and they said they had no idea what I was talking about."

"You're *kidding.*"

"No. You did leave directions, didn't you?"

"Of course, and I was explicit about making sure you got them."

"Well, they looked at me like I was crazy. And when I asked for your info so I could message you, they refused, saying they were forbidden to give out private client information."

"Unbelievable. I knew we should have exchanged info. What's your code?"

I can't deny her request any longer. "It's NJturq@the-ovalP.FW."

"Got it. Okay, so how about a Number One spray, please, my Beauty? I need it. I feel like I was in a hurricane."

"Me too."

She looks up at me. "Really? You look great. As a matter of fact, you've never looked better. You must have had a good night even though you missed my party." She sighs and pouts her lips.

"How *was* the party?"

"It was pretty lame. Everyone was late, my girlfriends were all having some stupid bitch-fest drama, and my brother never even showed up. Which, honestly, I don't care about. But he was bringing his friend Bradford, and I really like him."

I squeeze my eyes shut and clench my jaw. "Gee, I'm really sorry I missed it now."

She laughs. "It would have been more fun if you were there. I stole my parent's tequila and got drunk."

Just the word tequila almost makes me sick. "Well, I don't drink, so you would have been on your own. Okay, time to flip over." She follows my direction. My eyes pull like magnets to the nautilus strung from around her neck.

How fragile is this paper heart?

I look away and get the job done. "All finished. And no more tipping. We're friends now."

The next few hours drag on. I'm walking through mud, my head navigating through dense fog. The makeup has held up well in the heat and sun. Thank goodness I don't look the way I feel.

"Marcus, I need to run to the ladies' room."

"Be quick."

I'm not quick. I take my time. At the sink, I splash cold water on myself without thinking. I blot myself with a towel, the creamy makeup transferring to the soft white cotton. My CNI pings.

"Display."

It's Emily already. I open the message.

'Some big, mean guy is here looking for you.'

What guy? But I'm afraid I already know the answer. I run out of the locker room and down the hall. Only a faded outline remains where Alexandria's portrait once hung. I reach the exit and peer out the tiny window to the pavilion, but the angle won't allow me to see far enough down the sand. I open the door and to find Towel Girl's cautious expression. With just her eyes and a few choice nods, Moriyah warns me to stay put—or better yet, to turn around and hide.

I follow her gape down the pavilion and, unsurprised, see Officer William Banks towering over Marcus, glaring down and demanding something of him.

"Sir, it's a true pleasure to have you here at Concordia's beach pavilion, but I'm sorry, I'm unsure of Ms. John's whereabouts. May I offer you a beverage? Or better yet, an application from my star attendant, Jade?"

"Listen, you little ferret... you know exactly where she is, and if you don't bring her to me, I will crush you."

From here, I can see the shiver his warning sends through Marcus. "Sir, please, there is no need for threats. I'm here to assist."

William grabs Marcus by the waist of his shorts and yanks him up hard. "That was not a threat. It was a promise."

"Is someone looking for me?" I yell down the beach, and both their heads turn in my direction. I pretend to adjust my uniform as I approach them. "I'm sorry I disappeared without telling you, Marcus. I was having a major wardrobe malfunction." Officer Banks releases him, and Marcus exhales.

"Not at all, Ms. John. I'm going to fetch Officer Banks a cold beverage." He turns and jogs off the sand.

"What do you want?" I spit.

"Where were you last night?"

"Why?"

"Answer the question."

"It's none of your business."

Officer Banks bends down, his face inches from mine. As I stare into his eyes, it finally occurs to me why they struck me so much the first time I met him. It's like I'm staring at myself. And for a split second, I believe he feels the same.

"You have a lot of nerve, little Doll," he hisses and squints.

"So do you."

He grabs me by the arm, and the pain makes me gasp. "Something wrong?" He scans me. "What happened to your arm? And your neck? Looks like it hurts." He squeezes me harder, but I don't let myself flinch.

"Let go of me, right now."

"Why should I?"

"Are you really going to make a scene... right here, in the middle of the pavilion, on the busiest day of the Season, with everyone watching? Because I could make it really entertaining for everyone and really interesting for you."

"You have no idea what you're doing. I will crush you."

"Yeah, I've heard that one before." I lean into him. "And I know exactly what I'm doing, Daddy."

I'm certain he's about to rip my head off, but a tiny woman steps up behind him.

"William, I think it's time for you to go." She speaks softly yet firmly.

He loosens his grip, then turns toward her. "Alexandria, this doesn't concern you."

"Oh, but it does. This is my place of peace and tranquility. I don't expect to be pampered on your base. You should not be here expecting to conduct your business. You need to leave."

"Fine. We'll take this elsewhere."

"No. This girl is working, and the pavilion is at full capacity. If you take her, it will disrupt all the guests, including me."

He sighs. "Of course, Alexandria."

"William, you go back to Black Rock and do what you do best. I've invested a lot of money in you. Now go and make the next best thing to keep me looking this good."

He doesn't answer her but turns his head back toward me. "We're not done."

Just before he clears the pavilion, a piercing shriek comes from down the beach. Everyone stares. A woman stands next to Emily, rubbing her back as Emily bends over in what looks like severe pain and anguish. They're both crying.

Someone has found the bodies.

I look for the Officer. He stands a few feet from the lobby door, watching the tragic scene play out along with everyone else. He meets my gaze one more time and lingers, then turns and leaves.

You're right, William Banks. We're not done.

I scan the pavilion and find Alexandria. She's lounging comfortably again, unaffected by the world around her.

"What do you want? I didn't ring for you."

"I just wanted to thank you for standing up for me."

"You have a job to do here. I couldn't care less what affairs you and William have. I was merely ensuring my investment runs smoothly."

"You invest a lot on this island, don't you?"

She tilts her head up slightly, raising her eyebrows behind her sunglasses. "And in what way is that any of your business?"

"It's not, of course."

"Correct. And it's time for you to get back to work."

I try a different angle. "I hope the rest of Officer Banks' investors are as dedicated as you."

"Ha!" She rises halfway from her chair and lowers her head to look at me over her glasses. "Well, if you mean dedicated as in how much money they've put toward current projects, those other little stragglers are weak."

"You're his number-one supporter, aren't you, Ms. Bigelow?"

She scoffs and adjusts her position. "You have no idea." She waves her hand at me like she's brushing away a fly. "Now get back to work."

"Have a good day, Beauty. Please ring me if you need service."

Even the strongest of us are beaten down by the time the day ends. But we're almost done.

Tap. "Seven."

I'm actually scared to ride home alone. So it's time to do what should have already been done.

When I'm far enough away that no one can hear me, I speak my message out loud. "Mom, I don't want to scare you, but I think it's time to gather everyone and leave for Albatross. William Banks came to see me today. He's out of his mind with anger and threatened me. I know you don't believe he's responsible for Kendra's attack or Gabriel's murder, but I know he is. And he knows I know. It's only a matter of time before he's done with me. With all of us."

I'm about to send the message when a shadow moves behind me. I twirl around, ready to defend myself, and from behind a tall shrub steps Devin's mother. "Leyla! I almost hit you. You scared me."

"I'm sorry."

"What are you doing here?"

"I believe you, Nerissa."

"What?"

"The message you were just composing. I believe you." A shiny tear slides down her cheek from under the blue frame of her sunglasses.

"It's almost dark," I say. "Why are you wearing those?"

She pulls the glasses off to reveal a large purple bruise surrounding her right eye, yellow faded remnants under the left. "He came to see me today too."

"Oh, no."

She points at my arm where the makeup has finally quit. "Did he do that?"

"No, that was my fault. Where's Devin?"

Her face crumbles, and she can't contain her tears. "He's got him."

"What do you mean?"

She puts her glasses back on and composes herself the best she can. "Let's speak someplace more private."

"Good idea. Where should we go?"

"Come to my house. I'll leave before you. Wait five minutes, then join me there."

"Your house?" I ask. "That seems reckless."

"It's the last place he would think to find you. And he's already returned to Black Rock with Devin and Colton. They're not leaving there until next week when the last zeppelins fly out."

"Devin is with him?"

"I'll explain everything. Message your mother and let her know you'll be late. But don't send that first message... yet." She disappears behind the shrub, and I do as she instructed.

A short while later, I pull into the Banks' driveway, and the gate opens at my approach.

Esmerelda greets me at the front door with an unexpected hug. When she releases me, I pull off my shoes and arrange them neatly among the rest. Her eyes grow wide, but she doesn't look away, doesn't falter.

"Right this way, Miss Nerissa."

She leads me to the back patio. The courtyard is lit with tiny white lights and a gentle, glowing fire. I plop down in a large, cushioned chair and rest my bare feet on the coffee table in front of me.

"What can I bring you to drink?"

"What's your favorite drink, Esmerelda?"

"Oh..." She looks left and right, then smiles. "I like pink sparkly wine."

"Then bring that please. And three glasses."

She nods and leaves me waiting alone.

Leyla joins me a few minutes later. She sees my feet on her table and doesn't react. She's dressed in the most comfortable-looking clothes I've ever seen. And I'm jealous that the soft ivory material isn't wrapped around my own body, embracing my tired muscles and painful skin.

Esmerelda returns with a beautiful bottle of powder-pink wine and three crystal glasses. She pours each of us a glass and sits down. Under other circumstances, I'd say this evening is perfect—the house, the courtyard, the stars above, and the company. But...

"Nerissa, I need your help."

I pick up a glass and hold it to the light. The facets sparkle and shine, and everything inside me wishes I could just admire this glass all night and ignore everything else. "Let's toast," I say. "To new beginnings."

We all raise our glasses. "And to freedom," Leyla adds.

"To freedom."

We clink glasses, and I sip at the delicious liquid. It's like a deceitful promise on my lips. I know it's not real, but I can't resist its seductive allure. I drink the entire glass. Esmerelda refills it immediately.

"Tell me everything." I settle into the chair and give Leyla the floor.

"William Banks is a wrecking ball. He's convinced not only Colton but now Devin that their future will be determined by the success of Aqua Tonic and other Bio-Genesis projects. He's persuaded Devin to assist him and, with the huge profits they'll make, assured him he'll be free to do whatever he wants with his future."

"Is he still drinking it?"

"Yes. More than ever. He's sick. He can barely function. But he's doing work for William at the labs every day. He hasn't been home since Wednesday. When I questioned William about it, he said, 'Why should I care? He's not my real son.' He said Devin makes the perfect voluntary test subject."

Esmerelda refills Leyla's glass, then her own.

"Nerissa, I'm done with William Banks. I know exactly who he is, what he's done, and what he's capable of. I've turned my head for too long, and now he's crossed a line with my son. It really is true that money can't buy happiness."

My head is spinning. "So... you know who I am?"

She looks at my feet. "Yes. And I know that William has some Godlike power over you and your family."

She doesn't know everything. "And you accept me for who I am? You accept my family?"

"My son loves you... for all that you are. If he loves and accepts you, I do, too."

"I'm not so sure he does."

"He's under the stronghold of a powerful addiction and a manipulative, angry man."

"So, we need to break the addiction."

"I don't know how."

"I do."

She and Esmerelda both tense in their seats. "How?"

"We take down William Banks. Destroy the labs, every last drop of Aqua Tonic, and their ability to make more."

She smiles at me. "And how do you propose we do that?"

"Well, that's the complicated part, isn't it?"

My head swims in emotion and alcohol, and Leyla convinces me to message my mother and stay the night. I lie to Tatiana and tell her I'm staying at my friend Emily's house. Leyla suggests we reconvene in the morning, and Esmerelda shows me to the guest room. I get my wish to be swaddled in soft fabric as I slide into the downy white robe left for me.

The guest room is like the rest of the house—nothing overlooked, no detail or expense spared. The bed is fit for a queen, with white and gold linens and a protective canopy. I'm beyond tired, but sleep doesn't come. I lie there staring out the window into the dark night, my mind a blurry tangle. The hours tick by, and I visit and re-visit the bathroom without actual need. This time, I don't return to bed but leave the guest room in search of something.

The house is a maze of long hallways, room after perfect room. But I remember exactly how to find her. Once I pass the bronze statue of Delia, the only sound I hear is my own soft footfalls. The silence is so deep when I reach her, her image creates its own kind of noise inside me. The woman in the painting captivates me as much as she did the first time I laid eyes on her. Her beauty, her heroic-feeling transformation, steals my breath and makes my heart race. Against the darkness, the painting's vibrant colors are alive and light up the dim hallway with an energy of their own.

"Help me be like you. Help me be brave."

I crouch down before her and try to recreate her pose. I rise and open my arms, look to the sky, and force a confident, content expression. I imagine she feels great pride, and this causes my chest to broaden and lift, even though tears have started to fall.

"Freedom," I whisper. I crouch back down and repeat the movements three more times.

"Freedom."

"Freedom."

"Freedom!" I yell the last one and catch myself. I don't want to wake anyone, to scare them. If they see me, they'll think I'm insane. I open the door to Devin's room and duck inside.

I press my ear against the door for many minutes, listening. No one is coming. I'm alone in his room, and this realization makes my heart sink and flutter at the same time. I take a second to gather my thoughts and a few deep breaths. My head is fuzzy, and for a brief, terrifying moment, I imagine turning around to find William Banks lying on Devin's bed, yelling, "Surprise! Now I will crush you."

Of course, no one's there. Like the rest of the house, Devin's room is unreasonably perfect. It's just the way I remember it, just the way it sometimes appears in good dreams. Mini memories flash in my mind of the first day I came to the Banks' house and Devin and I stood in this exact spot together. I feel cold. Neither the robe nor my thoughts of him help.

The bedside clock says 4:05 a.m. Knowing the time suddenly makes my utter exhaustion real, and I can think of only one logical thing to do. I pull down the thick grey covers on Devin's bed with a twinge of guilt for disturbing such a masterpiece. But I climb in, pull the blankets half-way over my head, and sink into the deep, luxurious lin-ens. I'm in a soft, warm cocoon, where I'm hidden and safe. With bittersweet recognition, I close my eyes and gather up the pillow to my face. I can smell him.

Soft tears fall, and I quietly cry myself into a deep, dark sleep.

SUNDAY, AUGUST 25TH

When I wake, it takes me a few seconds to figure out where I am and what day it is. When the rush of awareness hits, I sit up. It's 9:30. It appears I didn't move an inch once I succumbed to sleep. I'm sure I can remake the bed to look as though I was never here.

I get up and pull the covers to their original position. But I stop when I reach the pillow. I bring it to my face again, breathe in deeply through my nose, and hug it like it's a person—like it's him. I wait for his strong arms to draw me in, for the firm, protective wall of his chest to en-velope me. I yearn to run my fingers through his springy, blond-tipped curls and to taste his whisper on my lips. But mostly, I miss his eyes—the sublime, stained-glass win-dows to his soul, his beautiful soul. He knew how to look inside me to depths no one has ever seen. I have to force myself, but I release the pillow and finish making the bed.

I linger in his room for just a few more minutes. I may never find myself here again, and I want to brand it in my memory. I turn slowly in a circle, absorbing every detail. Facing the window, I can see the wooded path at the far end of the yard—a place where magic truly happened.

Devin's desk sits under the window in front of me, and I lower myself into the black leather chair. I can't imagine too much writing happening here. It's too contrived, too expected.

I open the top drawer, hoping to see or hold a tangible piece of him in my hands. But it's empty except for a package of the pencils with which he insists on writing. I rifle through every last drawer. And with each one, my disappointment grows—loose paper, a few other simple supplies, but nothing personal. I open the package of pencils and take one. I know it wouldn't make sense to anyone else. But to me, it's all there is.

I place the opened package back where I found it, and a white envelope tucked in the far back corner of the drawer catches my eye. I try to pull it out, but it's caught in the seam of the wood. Finally, I manage to release it, and my stomach flips. I recognize it instantly.

William Banks disguises his crudeness in attempted formality and elegance. If I didn't know better, I'd be charmed by the style executed within his beautiful, handwritten notes. I'm shaking and consider tucking it back where I found it.

Instead, I rip it open, tearing the top third halfway off. I piece it together and read.

Devin,

Read carefully and respond immediately. You will report to the base to join Colton and I for the remainder of the Season. My deadlines are fast approaching, and I need all hands on deck. We will be conducting a tour for the investors the Sunday after Season's end. I have arranged for our private zeppelin following the tour.

I will require your services for approximately three months back home once we gain approval for mainland distribution. Once things are set into motion, you will be released from obligation and compensated generously. At that time, you can do anything or go anywhere you wish. If you decide to waste your life in that journal of yours, you will have the freedom to do so. Until then, I expect your full cooperation. The health and wellness of your mother, yourself, those horses the two of you worship, and that petulant little Water Doll depend on your enthusiasm and dedication.

Have a most pleasant day,
William Banks

I close the desk drawer, stick the note back in the envelope, and fold it into my robe pocket.

The guest room is quiet and undisturbed. A fast shower and the freshly laundered clothes laid outside the door get me going. Down in the kitchen, Esmerelda's prepared her usual bounty, and she greets me with warmth and kindness.

"Black coffee, Miss Nerissa?"

"Yes, thank you."

"Mrs. Banks—Leyla is in the courtyard. I'll bring you both breakfast."

She hands me a cup of hot coffee and I step outside to join Leyla. She's tending a lush rosebush, and I watch her for a moment before making my presence known.

"Good morning."

She turns around. "Good morning, Nerissa. How did you sleep?"

I shrug. "Um, so-so."

"Hmm... same. Come." She gestures to the table where Devin and I shared many meals. "Sit down."

The chair is hard and cold, not the way I remember it. Esmerelda brings pancakes and fresh fruit. She refills my coffee and disappears back into the kitchen. Leyla and I eat in silence for a short while.

"So what do we do now?" I finally ask.

She puts her fork down and laces her fingers together above her plate. "Well, I think it's time to talk with your mother."

I shake my head.

"But surely, she needs to know—"

"She does," I interrupt. "She's known for a long time. Not everything, but a lot."

We invite Esmerelda back to the table, and I tell them the rest—about the Cooperative, Anastasia and Alakier, the attack on Kendra, and Gabriel's death. If Leyla hated her husband before, she despises even the idea of him now.

"What about the other Matriarch?"

"Giovanni, Kendra's mother."

"Yes. Perhaps we should contact her."

"I was thinking the same thing."

We finish our meals, then seal our agreement with a nod. I pull up my display and compose my message out loud.

"Giovanni, I need to speak with you immediately."

We wait only sixty seconds. Her voice is loud and clear. "Where are you?"

"I'm at the Banks' house, with Mrs. Banks—Leyla. She knows everything. She needs our help."

A slightly longer pause occurs, and I imagine Gio considering my last comment. Finally, she replies, "Give me directions. I'm on my way."

The longest half hour of my life ticks by, and I can't sit still. I pace the length of the courtyard, back and forth. In those thirty torturous minutes, I silently declare myself insane. One minute, I'm filled with relief and gratitude that

I'm finally able to shed the lies, though still not all of them. The next minute, I'm convinced I've ruined everything, again, and that I need to retract all I've said—to pretend I was wrong or mistaken. My mother's face floats just behind my vision, telling me I should have left things alone. Then it's the woman in the painting, filling me with the promise of freedom. Then it's William Banks, his eyes that are my eyes, laughing and assuring me he'll 'crush me'. I'm a whimpering child, then a raging dragon, then a flightless bird. I'm hot in the sun, then cold in the shade. I just can't do this. Yes, I can. I can do this and a whole lot more.

When I've convinced myself the waiting will literally kill me, Giovanni finally arrives. She and Leyla step onto the patio, and as soon as I see her, I fall into her open arms and melt into a puddle. She strokes the back of my head and sways ever so slightly. Both Leyla and Esmerelda stand behind me, and each put a hand on my back. This trio of caregivers, of strength and courage, allows me to cry until my tears decide to quit.

We all sit down. Gio takes out a small package. "How long has it been since you've had any?"

"Too long. Thank you." I devour the contents.

"That's the Wreckleaf, isn't it?" Leyla asks.

"Yes." I slowly regard the last of the fronds. "This is the troublemaker."

"I'd like to try it."

"Absolutely not," Gio inserts.

"Yeah, Leyla. I'm sorry to tell you that the day Devin fainted on the path... that wasn't food poisoning. It was Wreckleaf."

"*What*? Nerissa, what were you thinking?" Giovanni demands.

"I knew it wasn't my food." Esmerelda smirks.

"I'm sorry. To all of you." I go on to explain our reasons for trying it.

"So that would suggest they're not entirely immune to us yet," Gio says.

"Yet is the key word," I say. "Some are more than others, but if things continue the way they're going, it's only a matter of time."

The four of us pore over every last detail. Each of us has a turn speaking, and along with the gathered facts, we have the opportunity to express our feelings, hopes, and fears. We all feel betrayed in one way or another. We all fear for our futures and our loved ones. And we're all grateful for the opportunity to lift the burden of truth from our shoulders and be heard, understood, and accepted. Our greatest desire, collectively, is to be free from the chains binding us all.

All at once, I'm on the beach again with Emily. *'We're no different, you know. You and I are really just the same.'*

Then Gabriel... *'We all want the same things. Every last one of us.'*

Then with Devin... *'We all have our scars...'*

I didn't believe any of them at the time. But now...

"So... we all agree?" Leyla begins. "We will destroy the Bio-Gen building. The labs, the testing facilities, the tank, and the assembly lines?"

"Yes, and all the computer systems," Gio adds. "Next Sunday, after the sun goes down."

"But then Leyla and Esmerelda will be stuck on the island another month. The last public zeppelin leaves Saturday night. Officer Banks is giving a tour of the facilities on Sunday. We need to do it before his investors see anything."

"How do you know that?" Leyla asks.

I reach into my pocket and pull out the letter from Devin's desk. "I found this. I don't know when he got it, but it might help explain his choices." As I hand the note over, I know she recognizes the envelope. I watch her read, her eyes filling with tears. She passes it to Gio, who then offers it to Esmerelda. When we've all read the man's threatening words, Leyla leans forward and prompts us to join hands.

"Please, help me recover my son. And I will do anything I can to help you and your family. Anything."

My crystal pings. "I have a message from William Banks."

"Why does he have your code?" Gio asks.

"William tends to get what he wants," Leyla reminds us.

"Should I open it?"

"Once you do, he'll know you've seen it," Gio says.

"Okay. I'm going to the bathroom. Let's think about it a few minutes before we decide." I find the powder room and lock the door. "Display."

The hologram lights up the small room. I select the message from William Banks, expecting another tyrannical rant ending in an ominous warning. Blah, blah, blah. But instead, a photo pops up. It's a bit fuzzy, but it was obviously taken outdoors near the water. I enlarge it, and as the details come into focus, I need to grip the edge of the sink to hold myself steady.

There, on a lonely strip of sand, two bloated, partially eaten corpses lay glistening in the Panacea sun. At the bottom is a brief message.

Miss John,

Look what washed ashore! Although I can say with certainty that the world will be a better place without this human garbage, please understand you will not have the last word in our little game.

Have a most pleasant day,
William Banks

P.S. You have such accommodating acquaintances, and I was very thorough in thanking Emily Alvarez for giving me your code after she was in-

formed of her brother's death. She was just as gracious as Allison Greenwald was when she pointed out Kendra Lucas' house to the dearly-departed Tommy and Bradford. Best.

I will myself to keep from throwing up my breakfast, then take only a few minutes to gather my senses and rejoin the women outside. Gio's eyes are glued to me. I try to act as normal as possible.

"So we think you should open the message right now."

"I think I should wait. No need for him to know I read his words, whatever they may be. Let's at least give it a day or two. We all need to stay focused."

Giovanni knows I've read it. But she plays along. "You're right. Let's not muddle our heads with his nonsense."

"I agree," Leyla adds. "Nothing he can say or do will change our plans. And his words are meaningless to me now."

"Good. What *is* our plan?"

We spend the next three hours going over our strategy and intent for Saturday at sundown. We agree to conduct ourselves with as much normalcy as possible in the preceding days. This is the last week of the Season, and we just want things to appear as they always are, with no attention drawn to us.

"What about my mother?" I ask. "We have to tell her, don't we?"

"You leave that to me," Giovanni says. "I will address her as a fellow Matriarch just before taking the base."

"You don't want to prepare her a little sooner?"

"No. That way, we'll know immediately if she stands with us or not. I don't want to leave any room for her to contrive her response."

I take a deep breath. It seems a bit unfair, but I understand. "Okay." I've lied to her before, I can do it again.

"Can we meet here again on Wednesday evening to touch base and go over things one more time?" Gio asks Leyla.

"Of course."

We all have our assignments for the next few days. The meeting is over, we say our goodbyes, and Gio and I leave one at a time.

It's hard to go. I felt safe under Leyla's loving care. I'm at least grateful the sun perches at its highest point and I'm not riding home in the dark. I'm scared to find out what William Banks' next move will be to ensure I don't have 'the last word.' But he has no idea how loudly I'm going to finish this 'game.'

When I reach the Oval, Gio is waiting on the side of the road just before the turn, a handful of lavender and wildflowers in her hand. I pull over next to her.

"What did he say?" she asks.

"What did who say?"

"Nerissa, if we're to be successful and come out of this alive, you need to be completely transparent with me."

I hold up my CNI. "Display." The bright day makes the picture difficult to view, but she gets the gist, especially after reading the message.

"Did you do that?"

I nod, never looking away from her. "It was for Kendra and Gabriel. Those men were the ones who carried out William Banks' orders."

"How are you sure it was them?"

"I just am." I'll spare her the details. "You'll have to trust me."

She holds my gaze for another few seconds. "Okay." We ride into the Oval together, then go our separate ways without speaking again.

MONDAY, AUGUST 26TH

I don't leave the house today. I tell my mother I'm not feeling well, and she leaves me alone. At dinner, she asks me if I heard about the two tourists they found.

"No. What happened?"

"Looks like they partied a little too hard and either went for a swim or fell overboard. One of them hit his head really bad. They're pretty sure that's what killed him. No foul play is suspected. Stupid humans."

"There's been a lot of death on the island this Season."

"There sure has."

TUESDAY, AUGUST 27TH

The air feels different at Concordia today. It feels different across the entire island. I know it's partly because the winds are changing along with the tides. But it somehow feels internal, like I'm generating my own energy that affects everything.

When I step onto the sand, I'm relieved to find Emily's favorite spot unoccupied.

"Ms. John. Ms. John!" Marcus shouts from the other end of the pavilion. I wait for him without taking a step. When he reaches me, he conducts his standard survey of my appearance. He pauses at my tousled hair but doesn't comment. "Ms. John, one of our team members, Ms. Cassidy Robert, has messaged in ill. There couldn't be worse timing."

"It's always bad timing, isn't it?"

He tilts his head. "Why, yes, it is. I tried my best to get her to come anyway, but I guess we can't have the servers puking on the guests."

"I suppose not."

"Anyhoo... Taren will be working double-duty. I'm trying to bring in backup. But I haven't been successful yet. So just be aware and help him out if you're able."

"You got it, Marcus."

"Carry on. Oh! I hear a bell!"

WEDNESDAY, AUGUST 28TH

"All right, so you know where to go?" I ask the quiet girl standing beside me, hoping she hasn't changed her mind.

"I do. I'll meet you at the gate at six."

"Remember, don't let anyone see you."

"I won't, I promise."

Just as planned, we gather again at the Banks' estate Wednesday evening for a follow-up meeting. This time, we join in the great room facing the courtyard. A fire burns and candles glow. The room feels cozy and inviting after riding in the brisk rain that began a couple hours ago. When I step into the room, everyone is already there, looking confused and concerned.

"Everyone," I say, "this is Moriyah Bigelow."

"And why is she here?" Gio thrusts her hands in the air, clearly displeased someone new has joined us.

"I'll let Moriyah tell you." I sit in a chair by the fire and leave the girl standing at the front of the room, facing the women like she's about to pitch some new product.

"Hi. My name is Moriyah Bigelow, and I work at Concordia on the Bay with Nerissa. My aunt is Alexandria Allerton Bigelow, and she is Concordia's biggest financial supporter."

"And you're telling us this because?"

"Hold on, let her talk," I insist.

"In addition to being Concordia's biggest financial supporter, she is also Bio-Genesis Wave Technologies' biggest individual investor. In particular, my aunt pours enormous amounts of money into the beauty care lines produced on

Black Rock and sold on the island. So far, her investments have proven to be extremely profitable. When she was given the opportunity to invest in a new product that would expand the island's use of its naturally medicinal plants into an ingestible, promising to be the fountain of youth in a bottle, she had to jump in. Her money made the product come to life."

"And so was born Aqua Tonic," I say, completing her setup.

"My aunt is a tough woman," Moriyah continues, "in all ways. No doubt she loves being wealthy and is ruthless in the pursuit of it. But she maintains strict personal morals. She hates being delayed, she hates excuses, and she maintains a ridiculously high work ethic. But more importantly, she despises dishonesty."

"So, you believe your aunt may not know of William's testing and research methods?" Leyla asks.

"She knows the AQT launch is a trial run, but she thinks what she's drinking is stable and consistent and safe. I'm pretty certain if she knew people were being used as guinea pigs, herself included, Aqua Tonic would be long gone. And if for some crazy reason she were okay with that, if she found out Officer Banks was lying about his test results, fabricating favorable conclusions without tangible evidence, it would be over."

"What exactly are you proposing?" Gio blurts. "And am I to take it that you, too, are aware of who we are?" She waves a finger between her and me.

I stand up and step in. "I was in the right place at the right time when I accidentally learned of Alexandria's investment position. I approached Moriyah because we've gotten close working together this Season. I thought it was necessary to divulge all of myself so she could trust me. So the answer is yes, she knows who we are."

Giovanni lets out a long, resolute sigh. "So, Moriyah, you're proposing what?"

"I'm hoping that once we deliver this information to her, my aunt will not be happy."

"What if you're wrong?"

"Then we'll stick to the original plan and destroy the labs," I say. "But wouldn't it be easier if we didn't have to?"

"If for some reason both options fail," Moriyah says, "we have one more idea, but it will only buy a little more time."

"This was all her idea," I say.

"I'll fake an accident just before the tour on Sunday. She's a businesswoman, but she's also invested in her family. She'll postpone the tour until she knows I'm okay."

We all take a collective breath and pause in consideration.

"I will prepare a detailed message for Alexandria," Giovanni finally says.

"Send it to me, and I'll forward it to my aunt," Moriyah offers.

"How will we know if she's put a halt to the program?"

"I'll message you as soon as she responds."

"Thank you, Moriyah."

"Gio?" I ask. "Were you able to obtain the blueprint of the Bio-Gen building?"

"Yes. I went back into my records and found the layout that was current when I joined them and updated their systems. I imagine all the control rooms are still in the same place, but other things have most likely changed. You probably know the building better than anyone at this point."

"You worked in the Bio-Gen building?" Leyla asks.

"Yes," Gio replies. "And five of the Big Six, setting up their systems. I have a... gift."

"She's a wave-tech goddess," I brag. "Gio's the one who taught me transference."

"Transference?"

"Yes, the transferring of information from one CNI to another."

"I thought that was impossible."

"It's impossibly simple, if you know Giovanni."

"Speaking of that, Nerissa..." Gio adds, "the chances of codes not being changed on the base and at the Rock are slim."

"English, please!" Leyla shouts.

I attempt to fill her in. "When Kendra and I went to Black Rock with Devin, I performed transference on his CNI while he was under the influence of my toxin. That was how I was able to access the locked corridors and rooms. The tech picked up the signal as if I were him."

"So it's a really thorough and sophisticated identity theft."

"Yes. Exactly."

"And you still have his transferred information in your CNI?"

"Yes, but it's not like I can somehow see into his world now or anticipate his thoughts or actions. Transference is about information, codes, passwords... that sort of thing."

"All the things that keep us safe." Leyla sighs.

"If the access codes have changed," I say, "I'll enchant and perform transference on someone else on the base."

"If that becomes necessary, choose someone with clout," Gio says.

"Well, it'll be whoever we can convince to open the gate. Because if we can't get in, the whole plan is shot."

"Esmerelda?"

"Yes, Ms. Leyla?"

"You know your part?"

"Yes. I will message Mr. William at six o-clock Saturday evening and inform him there's been a break-in and that two men are in his office going through his files and attempting to access his computer."

"Yes. Tell him to hurry, that you're scared because they're threatening to kill us." Leyla frowns.

"What is it, Ms. Leyla?"

"He'll care a lot more about the break-in than about us. As soon as you send that message, you run or hide. Just get away and stay away."

Esmerelda sighs and hangs her head.

"Once he's off the base," Gio adds, "we'll go through with our plan. Thank you for your assistance, Esmerelda."

"It is my honor, both to assist you and to know you, Ms. Giovanni. I thank you."

I ask what everyone is thinking. "What if neither plan A nor plan B works?"

Gio nods and inhales. "Then our friend Moriyah has an accident."

"It won't be too hard," Moriyah says. "I'm a natural klutz."

"Don't go overboard," I plead. "Promise me."

"And that will buy us some extra time to... do what?" Leyla asks, still obviously unconvinced.

"If we get to that point," Gio says, "it buys us time to evacuate. That's it. The breed will be instructed to make an emergency exit off Panacea and onto Albatross. Which, unfortunately, won't protect us for very long this time."

"What about Leyla and Esmerelda?" I ask.

"Nerissa, don't worry about me." For the first time at this meeting, I see hard resolution behind Leyla's eyes. "I'm not leaving here without my son."

28 – HOW BRAVE YOU ARE

SATURDAY, AUGUST 31ST

I am exactly where I'm supposed to be.

I'm the lone pebble thrown into glassy water. I may not be changing the whole world, but I am changing mine, ours, and that change will have profound effects. Somehow, I've always known it was up to me—a debt I carry. I'm a hybrid, a novelty, a toy left to fend for myself. I'm not even supposed to exist, yet I do. And I asked for none of it. Or did I?

The rain has been relentless, but it's the perfect backdrop for my last few hours at Concordia for the Season—or forever. The last of the tourists finally conceded and began their departures. They'll all be gone by sundown, and for any stragglers, the last public zeppelin for a month will fly out at 10:00 p.m.

When I walked out Concordia's front entrance, I tapped the door one last time. "This is for you, Kendra. Zero and done!" Then I stuck my middle finger up as I walked away. On my ride to the Oval, the rain finally ceased, allowing one last bright ray of sun to slice through the clouds and rest in the distance over Albatross.

We've waited since Thursday to hear from Alexandria Bigelow. Late last night, Giovanni received a message.

'I fail to see how this information is any of my concern.' That's it. I guess Alexandria Allerton Bigelow doesn't have

the level of integrity Moriyah believed she did. We'll go through with tonight's plan. There won't be a tour for Alexandria to take tomorrow if the building no longer exists.

I look in the mirror and run my hand over the copper buzz that was my long hair only moments ago. My fingers skim the brand on the back of my neck. Now the whole world can see who I am. No more disguises, no more lies. *Freedom.* Big things are about to happen. And no matter what the outcome, I will have unchained myself.

I kiss my ring. "To freedom."

The house is so quiet, it's eerie. I survey the place I've called home the past few years for what may be the last time. Nostalgia sneaks up on me, and a pang of regret spreads inside.

I slip out into the light purple twilight. The wind is kicking back up; our night will turn stormy again. I ride along the ridge and out of the local district. Over the bridge into the luxury sector, the streets are empty, the houses all dark. It seems everyone is gone.

Past the mansions and down the road, I pull off at our meeting point. Down an almost invisible dirt path, behind the cover of giant trees, Giovanni and Kendra wait.

"I didn't know you were coming," I say to Kendra. "Is it safe for you and the baby?" They both just stare at me. "Oh, yeah." I rub the top of my head. "You like it?"

"It's different." Kendra smiles. Then she leans in and embraces me, and I absorb her energy like it's my last breath.

Giovanni isn't fazed. "I tried to convince her not to come, but she insisted."

"If you think I could let you do this without me, you're crazy. I'd be a wreck."

"But a safe wreck," I say. "What if something happens to you?" I definitely don't like the idea.

"What if something happens to *you*?"

"I'm not carrying a life inside me. Gio, what about my mother?"

"I presented her with everything this morning."

"And?"

"I guess you can ask her yourself." She nods and looks behind me. I swing around to face my mother, Lillian standing beside her.

"I like your hair."

"I'm glad you're here, Mom."

"I don't like this plan, but I stand by my daughter and my breed."

"Thank you." I hold her gaze. "You brought Lillian."

"I miscarried because of that drink. It was too much for Charlotte to process. They can't get away with murder."

Leyla appears behind Tatiana. "Hi, everyone."

"Good. That's everyone. Is Esmerelda ready?" Gio asks.

"She's waiting for my message."

"Are you ready?"

"Yes," Leyla says.

"Giovanni, have you heard the news?" my mother asks.

"About what?"

"Two more maids are missing."

Gio doesn't seemed shocked. "What about Cassidy?"

"No news."

"Hold on," I interrupt. "Marcus told me she called in sick."

"That's the last time anyone's heard from her," Gio says.

"Why wasn't I told?"

"You've had more than enough to deal with," my mother tells me, her voice soft.

Gio gathers our attention. "What we're about to set into motion cannot be undone. The dangers are great, for all of us. Does everyone understand?" We all nod. "Okay. Leyla, whenever you're ready, message Esmerelda."

Leyla steps away briefly. "Done."

"Remember," Giovanni continues, "our plan is not foolproof. In the event of failure, save yourselves and go to Albatross."

I turn to Leyla. “What are you going to do?” I can’t stand the idea of that monster getting hold of her again.

“Esmerelda knows our meeting place,” she says. “We both know what to do... under all circumstances.”

My head feels strangely detached from the rest of me as Gio addresses us one last time. Moments into her final instructions, she slows and stops, listening. Then I hear it, too. William Banks is coming down the road. And he’s not alone. I put my hand on Leyla’s shoulder, my finger in front of my lips. We all stand perfectly still and don’t make a sound.

I can make out the soft hum of three, maybe four boards. There’s no talking, and the boards zip by us fast. When we’re sure they’re gone, we all exhale and unfreeze.

“That was quick,” I say.

“William must be out of his mind,” Leyla sneers.

“Who else do you think was with him?” Gio asks.

“I’d guess he’s got Colton and Devin.”

“I heard four boards,” I say.

Kendra catches my gaze and seems to read my mind. “Creepy plant guy,” she says.

“What?” my mother asks.

“Emmanuel MacNamire. He’s Officer Banks’ puppet.”

“All right, it’s time.” Gio reaches out to her sides, and we find each other’s hands, forming a circle. We have only seconds, yet time freezes in this moment of reverence, where no words exist to represent our bond and the journey we’re about to take.

The base entrance is just down the road. We stick to the edges of the forest on foot. When we reach the mile-high fence, Lillian leaps up and climbs the chain link with little effort. She reaches her mark and pulls a thick, fibrous cloth from her waistband. I watch in awe as she slips it over the camera looking down on the gate and hops back to us.

"Who the hell are you?" I chuckle.

"Kendra, Nerissa, you're up."

We face the keypad and crystal swipe, and we're eye level with the infamous red-lettered sign. My stomach drops. "What about Walter?"

"Got it." Kendra pats her pack. "Three raw chickens—his favorite."

"Gross."

"I'm sure Walter will share."

"Devin Banks." I speak clearly, then swipe my crystal. Green light. Kendra punches in the code she committed to memory weeks ago. Another green light. The gate unlocks.

We're in.

Giovanni punches in a new code. "That should keep them out for a while."

Kendra and I lead the way down the gravel path. Just as we're about to descend the limestone steps, Officer Richard Klein appears from behind the last building, gun in hand and Walter chained at his side, growling and snapping.

"Stop right now, or I will release my security animal." We do as we're told, but Kendra turns toward him.

"Hello, Richard. How are you?"

"What are you doing here?"

"We came to see you. I wanted my family to meet Walter."

"You're a bad liar."

"I'm not lying." She reaches for her pack, and the Officer cocks his weapon. Walter growls. But Kendra proceeds to pull out a chicken. Walter's nose twitches frantically, his neck stretching to get closer to the smell.

"See? Here you go, fella." She stretches forward. "I'm so happy you're all better." She tosses the chicken to him. Walter snatches it off the ground and devours it. Bones crunch like pretzels, and little bits of pink chicken flesh fly out the sides of the animal's mouth. I can't pull my eyes away. Officer Klein watches his loyal beast, a satisfied smile lighting his face. Kendra steps closer, and I fight with myself not to pull her back.

She brings out another chicken, and Walter is hypnotized. She holds the bird to Walter's mouth. I shut my eyes. I hear the snap of his teeth as he grabs it from her. Officer Klein laughs. "You are one brave girl. I'd never get that close to his mouth."

"Richard, I'm so happy to see you." Kendra steps right up to him and puts her hands on his chest. Walter growls but continues eating.

"What happened to your face?" he asks. "Somebody give you some trouble?"

"I'd love to tell you all about it." She's inches from him now, and he's fighting his desire. She doesn't give him any time for consideration and puts her mouth to his. Six seconds later, Richard Klein sways but still doesn't drop.

"What are you doing?" His words are slurred. She keeps going. After another six long seconds, she eases him down to the ground, his grip on Walter's chain loosened.

"Kendra, the chain."

She takes the chain, the combination of that and his master's unexpected behavior agitating the animal. He leans over to sniff Officer Klein, who remarkably is still trying to speak. "Help... I... know..." Walter seems satisfied his human is okay and turns toward Kendra's waist pack. She opens it and holds up the last chicken.

Without turning to look at us, she says calmly, "Walter and I are going to his enclosure. Go to Black Rock. I'll make sure the Officer is secured here, and I'll check for others."

"We're not leaving you here alone."

Giovanni puts her hand on my shoulder and nudges me.

"Come on, Walter. Let's go for a walk." On all fours, the animal is nearly as tall as her. And he's putty in her hands. Until the chicken is gone. She walks away from us, Walter following her with perfect obedience, then rounds the building and disappears.

"Nerissa, lead the way," my mother instructs. I shake myself, turn, and begin the descent to the boathouse. The rain starts again one-third of the way down. Once again, Kendra won't experience these stairs under difficult conditions. But she's got her own battle to win above. I hope I get the opportunity to tease her about how easy she had it.

My mind drifts back to the first time I came here with Devin. I imagine him in front of me, trudging down the slick rock without an ounce of grace in his step, the rain soaking his hair and pulling out the curls. I hold out my hand, pretending to lace my fingers with his as he guides me further and further into the unknown.

My brief fantasy is interrupted when I turn a corner, look up, and find an enormous, armed man standing in front of me like a statue. For a second, I think I'm hallucinating, the stress finally taking over. I almost run into him.

"Who are you and what business do you have here?"

Leyla pushes her way in front of me—quite a feat on the narrow, treacherous stairway. "What is your name, son?"

Silence.

"I'm Leyla Banks, Officer Banks' wife."

The nameless man lifts his weapon and slams it into her. She topples backward. I catch her as she falls, only inches from the steep edge. Giovanni appears at my side, steps over Leyla, and puts herself in front of the aggressive, impatient man.

"Why did you do that?"

"Just following orders. You want to be next?"

Giovanni lunges at him, grabs his face in both her hands and forces her lips against his. Unaffected, he slams her to the ground. Then the man throws himself on top of her and wraps his hands around her neck. Giovanni chokes and flails, trying in vain to hit him and kick herself free. My mother climbs over my back and comes down hard on the man's head with a huge rock. He goes rigid, then drops to the side, blood pooling where his head has landed.

Gio sits up, coughing and rubbing her throat. She sputters a few more times, then stands. "Let's go."

We step over the man, one by one. My foot lands in his rain-diluted blood. It runs down the dirt, forming a quick red river. We continue down the path, my mother assisting Leyla.

When we reach the bottom, I'm still as awestruck by Black Rock as I was the first time I saw it from this perspective. It's even more menacing in the dark. We all stand and stare, catching our breath. The door to the boathouse swings open. A head peeks out, then pulls back. I walk quickly toward the door to catch it before it closes.

"Hey, who's there?" I try to sound bright and positive. Someone peers out again. "Hi, Drew. Good to see you."

Cadet Drew Fenton steps outside. He looks like a child preparing to be scolded, his face a mix of defensiveness and fear. "Where's my man?"

"What man?"

"The guard I sent up the cliff to apprehend you."

"Apprehend us?"

"Yeah, you're not supposed to be here."

"Of course we are. And there was no man. Are you all right, Drew?"

"Then what happened to her?" He points at Leyla.

"She fell. And she's bleeding, so we need to come inside and get out of the rain." I walk toward him, and the other women follow me. Drew shifts, fidgeting and unsure. I press myself against him and hum. I glide my finger along his jawline and smile as the others walk past us into the front room of the boathouse.

"You look different."

"Do you like it?" I lean into him.

"Um, yeah."

I put my lips to his and count to six. It's just as easy as last time. Dragging the cadet behind me, I push my way through the front door.

"Well, you didn't waste any time with him. Bravo," Lillian says.

"How's Leyla?" I ask.

"I'm fine." She hobbles out from behind a wall. "Is he dead, too?"

"No, just unconscious."

"Hello, Nerissa." A clear, crisp voice makes me spin around, all of us ready to respond.

I exhale. "Hello, Hermes."

"It's good to see you again, Nerissa."

"Good to see you again, Hermes." I go to his perch and offer him the last slice of mango from his bowl.

"Nom-nom, thank you."

"Okay, we have to go," Gio prompts.

"Well, ladies, this is where I leave you." Leyla falls onto the velvet sofa, blood staining her left shoulder.

"You can't stay here. It isn't safe," I protest.

"It doesn't sound much safer on Black Rock. Besides, I think I may have broken or at least dislocated something. I'll only hold you back."

"What if Officer Banks gets back in the base?"

"It's not if, it's when," Gio corrects me.

"Well then, when William gets back," Leyla says with resolve, "you're going to need someone to keep him from coming out to the lab."

"Do you think you can stop him?" Tatiana asks.

"If Devin is with him, I think he and I can stop William together. But I'll kill William Banks if I need to."

"Release the boats."

We all freeze and turn toward the perch at the far end of the room.

"What did you say, Hermes?"

"Release the boats," Hermes repeats.

"Of course," I say. "Let the boats go into the channel. The current will carry them away."

"How many are there?" Gio asks.

"There's five altogether." I remember the spaces. "But that doesn't mean they're all here. And it'll be tricky and time-consuming to maneuver them unmanned into the channel."

"I'll do it," Leyla says plainly.

"And how are you going to do that? You can barely move," my mother reminds her.

"Don't worry about me. You all need to get going. I'll get it done."

That's it. Deliberations are over.

"Thank you, Hermes. You're a good boy."

"You're welcome. I'm a good boy, I'm a good boy."

"You've got to love this bird," Giovanni swoons. "Let's go."

"All clear, Hermes?"

"All clear. Time to amp it up."

"I guess you could say that..."

We gain access to the concealed boathouse with memorized codes, the contents of the transference, as well as the pull of the antique book.

Four of the five boats rest in their slips. Someone is on the Rock.

Leyla takes my face in her hands. "Promise me you'll be careful."

"I promise. You, too."

Tears fall down her cheeks, and she pulls me into her, wrapping her good arm around me. "I promise." She steps back. I see Devin in her. "Let's stop this monster from ruining any more lives."

I nod and fight back what I know could easily turn into ugly sobs. She leans forward and kisses my forehead, just like Gabriel used to do. "I love you, Nerissa."

"I love you, too."

We board the closest boat, leaving three for her to maneuver into the channel. I'm not sure it's possible. If she falls in, she'll be swept away and eventually drown, even if she can manage to swim for a bit. Or the hybrids will take her. I look back at her one last time.

We pull out of the slip and into the channel, the water black and churning, the rain pelting us sideways. Tatiana surprises me by handling the boat with precision. The waves are huge and strong, but she manages them. I look over the edge into the charcoal water, and something flashes right under the surface. Then again. As I look up, we're blindsided by an enormous wave that tilts the boat. I grab the yellow strap just in time. When we right ourselves, I look around. We're all on board.

"Look!" Lillian yells and points. Leyla has released the first boat, and just as predicted, it's instantly caught in the current. It disappears into the dark in under twenty seconds. One down, two to go.

"Hold on!" I yell above the wind and rain. The wave hits us even harder than the last, the boat lurching and heaving. My feet leave the deck this time, but I've wrapped the strap around my hand, and I'm not going anywhere. But when I look up, Giovanni is gone.

"Giovanni! Where are you?" I scream. My mother can't leave the controls. Lillian and I search the water. "Giovanni!"

"There!" I glance at where Lillian points and take a deep breath. Gio swims alongside us at a comfortable distance; she seems fine. I scan the water for hybrids.

Another wave hits us, and another. I lose sight of Gio. I lose sight of almost everything. I don't know how my mother manages to steer. We're battered over and over again by the monstrous waves. The boat rattles and shakes.

"Giovanni! Where are you?"

After an endless, torturous journey, my mother finally yells, "Prepare for landing!"

With little control, we hit the dock hard, sending the three of us fighting for balance. When I regain my footing, I see Giovanni standing on the dock, helping to steady us into the slip. The other boat is here, bouncing in the chop. When we're secured, I hop out, slam myself into Gio, and squeeze her tight. "Are you okay?"

"That was refreshing."

"Are you injured?" my mother yells.

"No, I'm fine."

"Did you see them?" I ask.

"See what?"

"The sea monsters. The Madoosik."

"No."

"Well, I did. They're out there. You got lucky."

We waste no time and ascend the slick metal staircase. They follow me without question. Only when we reach the top do we slow to take it all in. All around us, the vines hang in heavy, wet curtains. Down the rain-soaked trail, the building stands like a white, glimmering shrine, a beacon in the dark night. But it's a lie. All of it.

At the front door, I pray everyone has gone home—for the night or the weekend, home until next year. I suspect four unauthorized visitors showing up out of nowhere on a dark, stormy last night of the Season would raise some concerns.

To my relief, the swipe works just as it did at the base, and no one's here to stop us. In great contrast to the first two times I entered this building, everything is dimly light, only small emergency exit signs lighting the corridors. I hear nothing, see no one. The smell is sterile—a mix of medicine and cleaning fluids.

"Lillian and I will go to the control rooms and disable the computer network as soon as we retrieve as much information as we can," Giovanni whispers.

"I'll take my mother upstairs."

"I won't stop the lines until you message me. Prop open the doors. Once the system is disabled, the building may go into lockdown."

"Remember, save yourselves no matter what," my mother reminds us.

"I'm not leaving without them," I say.

Gio puts her hand on my shoulder. "Just be careful. All of you, be careful. Now, it's time. See everyone back at the boat."

In one final nod of solidarity, we all meet each other's eyes in silence, then part ways.

I start through the maze of hallways, my mother at my heels. I remember every detail, never faltering for a second. We turn into a windowless corridor where the bright strobe of lightning disappears, but the booming thunder still rumbles overhead. Every new clap startles me, like someone is shaking the building or running down the hall toward us.

I spot the elevator we need, but a door just in front of it stands ajar, a shadow moving through the soft light inside. I take a deep breath, then slowly pass the door and stand beside the elevator. My mother and I nod at each other, and she repeats my actions precisely. We've slipped by undetected.

I touch the elevator's call button.

It's answering ding is way too loud.

One second ... two.

The shadow moves inside the room. The elevator door opens. We step inside.

"Devin Banks," I whisper.

Three, four seconds.

The light from the room grows; the door's been opened.

"Greetings, Devin," the operating system blares, coming to life. "Where may I take you?"

A hand stops the door from gliding shut.

"Rooftop! Rooftop!" I yell in vain reflex. The burly man stomps his way into the elevator and grabs my mother by the neck. The door closes behind him, and we're trapped.

"How did you get out? Come on, I'm taking you back to the lab."

Taken completely by surprise, I watch Tatiana play along in a game to which she doesn't know the rules. "All right," she says, "but just one little favor first?"

"What position are you in to be asking for favors?"

"I'm not. You're in charge. But please, I haven't seen a real man like you in ages. Would you kiss me? Just once?"

It seems as though he's about to grant her wish, but the elevator door opens and the cold air rushes over us. We're on the observation deck. Wet, wilted purple flowers litter every inch.

"Oh! You almost had me, little Doll. But I know your tricks."

I dart out of the elevator onto the deck, the rain and wind blasting off the ocean in near-hurricane force.

He lets go of my mother and follows me. "Oh, no you don't."

I move toward the rock wall, the flowerless vines matted together in a chaotic mess.

"Don't you jump," the man growls. "Not on my watch!"

I face him and step back, inching toward the wall. He mirrors my pace, trying to coax me to come toward him. When the backs of my legs touch the wall, I turn around to face the horizon and close my eyes. I feel him getting closer. Just as he's behind me...

"Move," my mother says calmly, and I step to the right.

I hear a sick, muffled shove on my left; a terrified scream, the crunch of branches or bones, the crash of a body on rock, and the rush of air coming out; one last, desperate moan, quieter and quieter, and then a splash—the most delicate, disproportionate splash.

I open my eyes. The only proof he was here is a tiny scrap of his blue shirt stuck to a broken vine. Tatiana stands at my side. We don't speak. What's done is done. Where once I reveled in the uncompromising beauty of the setting sun, alive and hopeful with the innocence and spark of new love, I now stare at blackness, faced with death. It surrounds me as far as I can see. It fills every inch, inside and out.

"What was he talking about, Mom?"

"I have an idea, but I pray I'm wrong..."

I don't want to know. She follows me back to the elevator. I'm drenched and shaking, but I feel nothing.

"Devin Banks."

"Where can I take you, Devin?"

"Laboratory level, please."

"My pleasure."

When the elevator door opens, I hear it in the distance. I feel it—that awful, encompassing vibration; that ear-splitting torture chamber of insanity and lies.

"The AQT lines are running."

"How do you know?"

"I'll never forget that sound."

The total silence of the skin care assemblies makes the sound even more discernable. The giant room is still and dark. Through the glass, we gaze at the sterility of it, empty and buttoned-up for the winter, as though it only existed in my imagination.

We walk past the glass walls, down the next hall, and around the corner. The vibration grows, and a shiver runs up my back. The AQT room is as bright as the blinding sun, its secrets calling out like a siren song through the shrill tapping of bottle on bottle.

"I can't wait to make that noise stop," I say through gritted teeth.

"We have to assume as soon as the lines are disrupted, they'll know we're here."

"Oh, they already do." I point to the camera tilted at us.

"Let's hope Leyla got all the boats out."

"She did. I know she did."

"Still," my mother says, "we'll stop the lines last, just before we leave."

"Giovanni will stop the lines in the control room. We need to make sure they never run again. That there's nothing left to run."

We reach the steel door. "Devin Banks," I say clearly. I swipe my CNI and punch in the code, and the door clicks open. "You might want to cover your ears." Without hesitating, I step inside the room. My mother follows. I could be imagining it, but it seems there are even more bottles.

We round the massive line and head toward the tiny quality control room just past the split. Inside, we both find reprieve from the torturous racket.

My mother shakes her head and blinks hard. "You weren't kidding."

"On the other side of this door is the area I told you about."

"Right."

"I'll get you in the hallway, then you go to the labs."

"I'll destroy as much as I can."

"And please, let the animals go," I say. "We're leaving the doors propped open. Maybe they'll stand a small chance."

She raises her eyebrows.

I sigh. "Then at least put them out of their misery. Please." I open the back door. Standing in front of us is another armed guard. I lunge at him without thinking, and before he can react, my mouth latches onto his. He grabs me by the waist, and I have to fight to stay on him. For about three seconds, his massive hands squeeze my ribcage with extreme force. Then they fall to his sides, and he succumbs. I pass six seconds, and my mother's hand comes down upon my shoulder to pull me away. I stay locked onto him.

At eleven seconds, he falls to the floor. He'll be our door prop here. I take his weapon and his shoes, and we leave him.

"Nerissa, he was done at six... You should have stopped then."

I don't look at her; I don't respond.

We reach the door to the labs. When it opens, Tatiana steps through and places the guard's shoe as a prop. Then she straightens and looks at me. "Go get them. Bring them back to us."

I nod, forcing back tears. "I will."

"I'll meet you in quality control. If I'm not back, go into the assembly room and do what needs to be done. Then get them out."

"I'm not leaving without you, Mom."

"Just in case. You know the plan."

I can't help it anymore; the tears fall. "Just make sure you're there."

She cups my cheek in her hand. "I'm sorry… for everything." She swallows, battling her own tears. "I love you. And I'm so proud of you."

"I love you, Mom."

"Now go." She turns and disappears, the door falling almost shut before resting on the black leather shoe.

I start my journey down the first long hall on my way to Ana and Alakier.

Just like the first time, past each doorway, the temperature cools, and the light changes from white to blue. I pass no one. I have the guard's weapon and pray I don't have to use it.

When I open the last door, the color somehow takes me by surprise, as though I'm seeing it for the first time. It's captivating and strikes a melancholy pang inside me. Then it lights an angry fire, because it's also a lie. This is the light of deceit, of betrayal—a cancerous growth dressed up in a pretty package. They've ruined my silent blue.

I weave my way through and make it just beyond the machinery at the front end of the room when she steps out of the dark, narrow hallway at the other end.

"Nerissa? Is that you?" She's barefoot, dressed in a flowing white gown, her hair a tangled mess. Even from here, I see Anastasia's eyes are hazy and out of focus.

"Yes. It's me. It's time to get you and your son out of here."

"Alakier?"

"Yes, go get him. We're leaving."

She returns a moment later, the boy limp in her arms. "Please, take him."

"What happened?"

"They've been testing on him, just like the others."

"What others?"

"The others in the labs." She can barely speak, her words sloppy and difficult to understand.

"Can you carry him? If anything happens, I have to be able to protect us. And I have to do one more thing before we leave."

"No, Nerissa. I told you, I can't leave here. I'll die."

"Ana, you'll die if you *stay*. We're going to destroy this place. You have to come with me."

She stands in front of me, her child dangling between us. "It wasn't your fault, you know."

My heart races. "Don't."

"It was my fault. I should have never brought you to the island that night." She struggles for balance. "I was a fool who thought she was above it all."

I shake my head. "No, I shouldn't have killed that man. It's my fault."

"You did what you had to do to survive. I'm the one who exposed us, not you. And I got what was coming to me."

"You didn't deserve this!" I thrust my hands in the air. "No one deserves this. Come on, we're leaving."

"I'm not leaving. Take my boy. Give him a good life. Give him his own life."

I don't answer her, stepping away toward the Wreckleaf tank to face the glass. Inside, the plants look perfect—tall and healthy and abundant. The water moves furiously, then calms. Tiny bubbles form a spiral, then lift to the top and disappear. The Wreckleaf dances just as it does in the shipyard.

Ana joins me. "He said you'd come."

I pull my eyes from the tank to search her face. "Who said that?"

"Devin Banks. He said you'd come back for me and Alakier."

"When did he say that?"

"When he brought Alakier back. About half an hour ago."

My breath stops, my feet glued to the floor. "He's here? Now?"

"Yes."

I point the guard's weapon at the tank.

"What are you doing? Are you crazy?"

I grab her arm and drag her back around the machinery and toward the door. "Wait for me on the other side. If I don't come right out, go to the assembly room and meet my mother. Do you understand?"

"He loves you, you know. Devin Banks loves you."

The door closes, and I'm left standing alone, the world spinning inside and around me.

I return to the glass front of the tank to admire it one last time. It's impressive. It's impossible. And I'm honored to be the one to destroy it.

Just to test the weapon, I point it at a slick gray desk on the other side of the room. I pull the trigger, and the barrel emits a bright white beam followed by a loud, electric crackle. Like an impossibly hot knife, the light slices through whatever it touches. I try it on a glass screen, and when I touch the screen afterward, it's still hot. It cracks at the slightest pressure, and glass falls in two large, clean pieces. I need to be sure this will still work on something larger.

I turn to the huge garden windows, step back as far as I can, and aim. Directing the beam to the top right corner, I draw a two-sided square, the ceiling and window frame serving as the other two sides. I can see the cracks, but nothing happens. Perfect.

I round the front of the Wreckleaf tank and take my aim. This is it. I make another two-sided square at the top left edge.

A huge lightning bolt fills the sky just outside the building, followed by an enormous clap of thunder that rattles the windows. I look up just as my square pops out at the top. I hold my breath, waiting ... Please, no. Two seconds later, the window comes crashing down. I only have time to crouch to the floor, cover my head and face, and take the beating as sheets of glass fall and shatter everywhere, showering me in razor-sharp shards cutting and lodging into my flesh.

When the assault is over, I look up at the tank. Chunks of glass have fallen inside, bending and slicing the plants. A large, jagged piece rests halfway inside, just atop my square. It must weigh a ton. The water seeps through the lines I carved. My body can't move fast enough as I rise and watch the square pop out and fall to the floor. A steady torrent of water follows, and while I run to the door, time seems to have slowed.

Then comes the final, terrifying creak and split of the tank breaking, thick glass crashing everywhere, the deafening roar of water rushing out and swallowing everything in its path. Through the machinery, crackling and electric sparks race behind me. I turn right, then left. My shirt grabs a metal corner and tears, slowing me down for a half-second too long. My hand is on the latch. With all my strength, I rip open the heavy door and throw myself into the hall. The force of the water slams the door closed behind me, knocking me to the hallway floor. My knee splits open.

Breathe ... breathe, Nerissa.

There, in a lifeless ball, Alakier lies alone, his clothes and hair soaking up the water squeezing under the door. I stand and spin, looking for Ana. She's gone. I loop my head and arm through the weapon's strap, push it around to rest at my back, and scoop him off the floor.

Alakier bounces in my arms, a slack, inanimate mannequin weighing me down. But we exit through the next door, then the next. The building is somehow alive, watching me as I run in fear, mocking me in its silence and calm.

As I approach the last door, I slow down, try to calm my breath, and gain control of my racing heart and mind. I balance Alakier in one arm and open the door. Down the long hallway, things remain impossibly quiet. I move forward. Nothing but this last corridor and a final turn separate me from the back door of the quality control room. I expect someone to appear in front of me at any second, to either kill me or force me to kill them. Please, don't let it be him.

At the end of the hall, I peek around the corner to my right. The door to the labs is shut, the shoe just in front of it. The other way, the unconscious guard still lies where we left him—a motionless prop. I step over him into the quality control room. My mother isn't here. I peer back into the assembly room through the tiny window. The lines are still running, and I don't see her anywhere. I put Alakier down on the chair and try to make him as comfortable as possible. A groan escapes him.

"Alakier? It's okay." I stroke his hair away from his face, then engage my CNI and try to make contact. "Mom, where are you?" Almost a full minute ticks by with no response. "Gio, have you heard from my mom? I'm ready". Ten seconds pass.

"Nerissa, I'll stop the lines from my end. Start without her." Gio's voice comes through strong and clear.

I turn to Alakier. "I'll be right back."

Just before I open the door to the assembly room, I notice the case of AQT that made its way to quality control while I was gone. The package is perfect, the pretty blue-green bottles all primed and ready to make their way into the lives of the unsuspecting consumer. I pull open the small drawer under the belt, and take out a sticker and pen and scribble:

Warning: the beverage you are about to enjoy is poisonous and may cause extreme side effects, including mania, violence, debilitating addiction, and death.

I slap the sticker on the toxic brainchild of William Banks, then swing open the door.

As I step into the assembly room, the noise consumes me. But this time, I don't hide from it. I listen. I allow the sound to fill every cell of my body, every tiny space inside my soul. Images float behind my eyes—Kendra's scarred face, the shopping cart, Anastasia tortured and alone. I grasp the weapon and take aim at the packed line directly in front of me. When I pull the trigger, I don't hear anything anymore, even though I'm sure I'm screaming.

I sweep the weapon back and forth. The bottles melt and explode under the beam's slicing heat, throwing glass into the air. Translucent blue-green liquid sprays everywhere.

The images continue—Tom, his dead nephew under the boat, Concordia ... the Cooperative, Leyla Banks, the woman in the bathtub, the graffiti on the wall: Panacea is a lie!

When the assembly lines slow, I think I'm imagining it. I'm not. Giovanni has shut them down. Almost instantly, a bright-red, spinning light begins flashing, flooding the entire warehouse-sized space with inescapable warning.

I jump atop the line in front of me and marvel at the vast emerald-blue ocean of bottles now at a permanent standstill.

"This is where it ends!" I spray the room with electric white light. The destruction is massive. I walk along the line, firing and screaming, the tears pouring freely down my face. I'm a wild horse running free.

I jump to another line and repeat the devastation—again and again. The rubber conveyers split into unrecognizable shreds, bottles tumbling and crashing to the floor. Cardboard crates dissolve into nothing.

I train the beam on a control panel high up the metal base in the middle of the room. Lights flash everywhere. I aim and fire, and the metal burns black. The lights go out. Grey smoke sifts through the charcoaled steel.

The snake ring, the parrot hat, the white fur bag ... the nautilus shell with baby Charlotte's remains floating away...

The huge windows suffer next. They shatter and fall, and—oops—the sterility of the room has been compromised. I hop down and work my way through every inch of the huge space. There won't be a single bottle left when I'm done.

The Wreckleaf tank, the hybrid program, the lies, the deceit ... my father, William Banks...

I jump from belt to belt, destroying everything in my path. Ready to survey my work, I leap across the broken blue wasteland to one final belt, but my foot slips on a layer of glass. I slam to the floor, landing on my side, searing pain shooting up my left arm. A serrated, broken shard has wedged itself into my flesh. Blood spills freely, but the beautiful scrolled font etched into the glass is still clear—'The Elixir of Life.' All I can do is laugh.

I yank it from my arm. The room starts to spin, then everything slows down. I close my eyes, and pleasant images replace the painful ones—Our Beach, the Wreckleaf fields and my silent blue; Gabriel's smile, my ring, the dolphin pod; riding Goliath, Devin's eyes...

I never imagined a bed of glass as a final resting place, but I'm so tired, I feel like I could lie here forever, like I could end things in this moment. As my mind drifts, I grow aware of a new sound. The rattling of the bottles has forever ceased, replaced by some kind of siren. I force open my eyes and note the synchronicity of the red light and the siren bursts. In the spaces between them, a robotic voice announces, "*Warning: Security Breach. Warning: System Failure.*" This repeats after every flash of light, and while I recognize the words, I feel indifferent, unconcerned.

I close my eyes again and let myself float away. There's only peace now. I travel back in time to Albatross.

I'm a child. My mother is singing. Neptune the cat and I are playing in the sand. Then I'm standing at his shrine, pulling whiskers from his perfect face. A twinge of guilt almost stops me, but I must have a piece of him forever.

A familiar but faraway sound travels faintly across a vast distance. I imagine the AQT-glass-covered sea I've created. A door opens. I listen. Then it closes.

Tatiana?

"Mom. Mom, I'm here!" Through dizzying pain and exhaustion, I will myself to sit up, then stand and trudge through the wasteland, glass and debris crunching underfoot. The assembly room is destroyed, and I look around at my work. One single, lonely bottle lies untouched on its side. I take aim, and it becomes a part of this history-in-the-making.

I stagger toward the quality control room and struggle to pull the door open and reunite with my mother. But she's not here. And Alakier is gone. I step over the guard and peer down the hall. A long-haired, familiar-looking woman gains access to the laboratory doors.

"*Cassidy*?"

She freezes, no doubt terrified.

"Cassidy, it's Nerissa. We need to get out of here!"

She turns slowly to face me, Alakier in her arms. She looks right at me—right through me—for only a second, then she turns, walks through the door, and pulls it shut behind her.

"What are you doing? This way!" I stagger after her, and my CNI pings.

"Gio, what's going on? Where are you? Is my mother with you? I just saw Cassidy!" I realize she can't hear me; there must be interference, and I'm forced to stop and read her message.

'I'm about to shut the whole building down and destroy the system. Make sure to prop the doors. I don't know if the swipes will work. Get out of there.'

I open the door to the labs and replace the guard's shoe. The lights go out when I step into the corridor. A few seconds later, the fluorescent white is replaced by a neon, emergency blue, which only does a fair job of lighting the way. Even the siren bursts and the robotic warning have ceased. The building comes to a humming stop, and all at once, everything falls silent—total and complete and eerie silence.

My ears are filled with my breath and my heartbeat. Outside, the storm rages. Every few seconds, a rumble of thunder shudders its vibrations through the walls and up my legs.

A cry rises from a room down the hall. I shuffle toward it and peek through the tiny windows on each door. Nothing, nothing, and then, in the last room, where I saw the animal experiments, shadows dance. I hear the cry again, then burst into the room, my head snapping to the far-right wall.

"Mom?"

"Nerissa, get out of here." She's tied to a chair, her face bloody and swollen. I throw the weapon to the floor, rush toward her, and work at the knots in the ropes holding her down.

"Who did this to you?"

"You're hurt."

"I'll be fine." I get the first knot untied.

Our faces are inches apart, and she whispers through pained breath, "Nerissa, please, get out of here.

"Not without you. Who did this?"

"I did." I spin around. Cassidy glares at me. She looks worn and used and finished with the nonsense responsible for useless emotion.

"You did this?"

"Nerissa, you think you're the only one who's lived a painful life..." she seethes, squinting at me through hateful eyes. "They recognize that I'm not useless, that I have a real purpose."

"They? You mean the FWG and William Banks?"

"Officer Banks is a good man."

"He's a liar and a thief and a murderer! What has he convinced you of, Cassidy? That you're somehow contributing to some great cause?"

She's like a statue, frozen in place. Her lips hardly move when she speaks. "He has a vision for the future. He sees things beyond this island, beyond the tiny little lives we live."

"You know what he sees? Dollar signs. That's it. What did he promise you? A life full of adventure and fame and riches? Have you seen Ana?"

"Anastasia is an experiment, just like the others."

"What others?"

She steps aside to reveal her purpose in the labs. Contained within two glass enclosures are our sister maids, Cecilia and Rena. Both are unresponsive, in some kind of suspended consciousness. Clear, plastic tubes protrude from each of their arms, small adhesive electrodes attached to their chests and necks. Next to them, Alakier lies on a table, curled into a fetal position, shaking. Behind him, the stacked cages are filled with animals, some of those I saw the first time I was here now gone, replaced by new, tortured individuals.

"You're drugging your own kind? You're torturing lab animals and children?"

"They're not in any pain."

"How do you know?"

"Because I get a little bit of the same thing every day. It's quite wonderful, actually."

"You're crazy." I push past her and slam my fists into Rena's enclosure. She doesn't move. I look for a seam, a door to open, a latch to release. My own blood smears the glass as I search in vain.

Cecelia's confines are the same—no visible way in or out. I go to Alakier and move to pick him up.

"Leave him," Cassidy snaps. "He's staying here."

"The hell he is." I lift him in my arms and turn to face her. There she stands, twisted and confused, holding the guard's weapon that just helped me destroy the assembly room. "What are you going to do? Kill me?"

"If I have to."

"Then get on with it. Just make sure to do the same for everyone here, including yourself. Because if you think this is living, Cassidy... if you think he'll take care of you... You're wrong. He's a monster, and you'll end up in one of those boxes. Or worse."

She holds the gun high and aims it directly at me. I close my eyes and draw Alakier close to my chest. It'll be quick, and a tiny part of me anticipates the relief.

"No!" I look up just in time to see Cassidy falling to the floor. Her face slams into the cold tile, her chin splitting and spraying blood. Anastasia jumps on her back.

"My boy is leaving this place!" She holds Cassidy down, pushing the woman's face into the floor with the force and fury of a rabid animal.

My crystal pings.

"Everyone needs to get out of the building. The assembly room is on fire and it's uncontained. Get out now!"

I look at my mother, her leg still bound on one side, but she works the ties with determination.

"Mom..."

"Take Alakier and get out of the building."

"No." I rush toward her.

"Go now! I'm almost free. I can manage the rest. Take Alakier and remember the plan. Go."

We hold each other's gazes for one last second, then I turn, hoist Alakier in my arms, and run.

The smoke already fills the hallway, drifting through the propped-open door. I can't go back the way I came, so I turn right. When I enter the main corridor on this level, the smoke is thick enough to make me cough. I search for a stairway sign. Nothing. I don't know how to get out. I only know where the nearest elevator is.

Up and down the hall I run, Alakier still unaware. Then finally, I spot it. We burst through the door and fly down the stairs. The farther we descend, the easier it is to breathe. On the main level, I run as fast as I can and crash through the front doors. I try to catch my breath as the rain washes off the smoke and blood and sweat. I look up at the building.

Come on, Mom. Hurry.

Two more deep breaths.

Now go.

I run through the maze of rock in near-total darkness. At the metal staircase, I carefully navigate our way down. It's impossible to descend with any speed while holding Alakier and being mindful of my footing on the wet steps. It feels like forever, but I'm finally back on solid ground.

There doesn't appear to be anyone at either boat. I expected Lillian and Gio.

"Remember the plan, Nerissa. Come on, we can do this," I say aloud, trying to steady myself.

I'm almost unaware of my feet, slipping and sliding along the dock, until they come out from under me and I land hard on my tailbone. This is what finally jostles Alakier awake, and he looks up at me, confused, blinking back the falling rain. The scream that escapes him terrifies me.

"It's okay, Alakier. I've got you." As though his scream took every last bit of him, his eyes roll and flutter, and he's out again. Pushing through new pain, I get up and head to the boat in the farthest slip. I carefully climb on board and lay Alakier on a bench.

The substantial rope on the stern unties easily, but it's slow and heavy work. I leave it draped along the dock for a bit more control as I untie the other docking lines. It's taking too much time.

I finally release the bow and hop on board. I'm about to take the controls but stop when I look up, convinced I'm hallucinating.

Devin stands on the dock, holding the stern's rope. He's almost unrecognizable in the pouring rain. His hair lies straight and flat against his head and face, and he's grown a short, messy beard. He doesn't move, dead-looking, his eyes black and without expression.

My boat drifts away from the dock, but Devin's got a tight grip on the rear rope.

"Devin! What are you doing?"

He doesn't answer, doesn't move. He just stands there, staring at nothing, a lifeless zombie unaware of his surroundings. Unaware of me.

Behind him, up the cliff, smoke rises out of the BioGen building. Two figures run down the stairs.

"Devin, let go!" A wave hits the bow, tipping the boat and slamming us back into the dock. Alakier tumbles off the bench. I head to the controls. If I pull out and Devin doesn't let go, he'll be dragged in and swept out into the channel instantly. Another wave shoves us into the dock. Devin doesn't move.

"Please." I search his face for something—any little spark of light. "Devin. You need to let us go," I scream. "Let me go!"

Alakier tumbles back and forth on the deck of the vessel. If he hadn't woken a few moments ago, I'd think he's dead. I start the engine.

Just as I'm about to pull away and risk dragging Devin to certain death, he lowers his hands. One fist slowly releases the rope.

"Come on, Devin. I know you love me…" I mutter, hoping. "Let me go…"

He looks up at me. I can see his pain; I can feel it. His tears pour out and mix with the rain.

This frozen wheel keeps turning, returning me to this place in time...

Another wave slams us against the dock, which falters under the siege.

Where the pools overflow and spill out onto pink velvet...

For one last second, our gazes fuse together, and we are all that exists. If my life ended here, I would know he loves me as much as I love him.

A blinding white light fills the darkness behind him, making him nothing more than a black silhouette. A loud, electric crackle rises above the thunder and surf, and before I know what's happening, Devin lurches forward and drops to his knees. The rope falls from his hand, and he collapses face-first. Behind him, Anastasia stands, the guard's weapon still glowing in her grip.

"No." I rush to the boat's stern and stretch over the siderail. "Devin!" He doesn't move. "Devin, get up." My voice is whisked away in the wind, and the current grabs us. We move quickly, and Devin grows smaller and smaller as the distance between us quickly widens.

In a blink, he's gone.

My body heaves and quakes, and I vomit into the water with such force, I almost fall overboard. I drop to the deck, Alakier at my side, and I sob so hard, I'm sure my heart will explode and my bones will shatter and my skin will peel off.

This can't be real. This can't be happening. He can't be...

He's gone.

Alakier opens his eyes and looks right at me, but he doesn't scream again. All I want is to lie here next to him and let the ocean take us where it will. I'll wrap him in my arms, and we can die together.

"Nissa? Where's Mommy?"

He has the most beautiful face. Her face.

"Nissa..."

"Mommy's helping some friends. She'll meet us later."

Get up.

Get up. You're not done.

Get. Up. Now! And finish this.

A switch flips inside me.

This moment, all this pain, somehow becomes nothing more than an object I imagine wrapped in a soft gold cloth. I place it in a box and put the lid on tight. Up on a high shelf in my mind, I rest it. I'll get back to this later. Now get up.

I stand, instantly alarmed by our surroundings. We're shrouded in thick, dark fog, the rain still pelting down on us. I can't see anything past a few yards, but I know the boat is drifting fast in the wrong direction. A wave hits us, and I have to catch my balance. Alakier has huddled into the crook of the hull beneath the siderail. I need to strap him in. Another wave slams into us.

I jump to the controls and restart the engine. It sputters once, twice, then catches. I turn the boat and aim us in what I think is the right direction. The waves seem to come at us from every direction. The boat rises and falls with each approach, then the crash of every wave sends water up and over the bow, along the sides, and off the stern. But I've got this. I have to believe that.

We move along at a steady clip. I'm really cold. Alakier must be freezing. He's still in the same place, curled into a ball. I can see him shaking from here. I'll leave the controls for just a second, wrap him in a blanket or a poncho, if I can find one, and get him secured with the straps. I step away from the controls, and the boat lurches under the force of another wave. We shift directions immediately. I need a new plan.

I grab the yellow safety strap from the starboard side and unclip it. Then I rig it to the helm so the wheel stays in position and the boat stays its course. Once I'm satisfied, I step away. This time, we hold. I wait for the next wave to hit; it's working.

A hinged supply bench holds a bright yellow, plastic tarp. It'll have to do. The waves push and pull and challenge my footing, but I reach Alakier and encourage him to stand.

"Here, I want to wrap this around you." He complies, tucking his arms along his body as I swaddle him like a baby. He looks over my shoulder and his eyes grow big. "Nissa..."

I turn around just in time to be hit with a huge wall of water. It knocks us both down. Alakier spins helplessly inside the flooded boat like a fish bobber.

"Nissa!" He's headed toward the stern, and another wave hits us. The water rises higher, and I lunge forward to grab him. My fingers find the edge of the plastic.

"I got you... I got you..." I grip the tarp, but my fingers slip. I grab it again and finally catch a solid handful. Another huge wave batters us, drenching everything and blinding me. I never lose my grip on the tarp. But when the water clears from my vision, I see the whole thing has unraveled, and Alakier is gone.

"Alakier!" He's not anywhere on the boat. "Alakier!" I pull off my shoes and dive over the siderail.

The water is so dark, churning and frenzied. I spin in circles, searching. Rising, I scan the chaotic surface and notice the boat disappearing quickly as the current pulls me the opposite direction.

"Alakier!" My head snaps to the left. What was that? Did I hear... "Alakier! Where are you?"

The tiniest voice carries over the broken surface. "Nissa!" My eyes dart back and forth, squinting and fighting against the rain and saltwater. "Nissa!" There—fifteen yards in front of me, a tiny figure. He raises his arm. I speed toward him, scoop him up, and hold his head above water.

"Are you all right?"

He nods and blinks.

"Are you sure? Can you say something?"

He nods again. "Hi, Nissa."

I can hardly breathe. "How are you okay? How did—"

"I'm a good swimmer," he says perfectly.

I'm dumbfounded, but only for a second before realization dawns. I reach under the water, hold up his foot, and take off his shoe. Of course. "You're the son of a Dolhuphemale. Let's get rid of these shoes."

My relief dissipates when I look up and find myself staring into an oncoming wave. It batters us, pushes us under, and pulls us farther in the current. But I manage to hold onto him, and we're both fine.

"Can you hold your breath a long time?"

He nods.

"Okay. Looks like our ride is gone. You hold my hand and squeeze when you need a breath. Understand?"

He nods again. "Yes, Nissa."

"All right. On the count of three. You help me. One, two..."

"Three!"

As I expected, the lift of the swell and crash of the waves are easier to navigate under the surface. We both have much more control, and despite my mangled body, we move at a surprising yet comfortable speed. I'm pretty sure I can just hear water crashing into a still-distant shoreline ahead and to our left.

Alakier squeezes my hand. We slow and rise to the surface.

"Doing okay?"

He breathes deeply and nods.

Submerged again, we go even farther this time before he needs air. We slide into a rhythm—swim, surface and breathe; swim, surface and breathe—without any lengthy pause above water. I can sense we're not too far. I just don't know exactly where we'll land.

Alakier squeezes my hand, and we rise for a fast breath. But when we dive back under, he keeps squeezing. His eyes are wide and full of fear, and he points at something. I follow his gaze but don't see anything.

I bring us to the surface again, where we're immediately pummeled by another wave. I almost lose him. "What is it? What's wrong?"

"Monster."

I whirl back and forth, scanning the surface for movement. I see nothing. I duck under the water and spin around. Still, I don't see anything. But then a cloudy form materializes, and I recognize it instantly. I breach the surface again and exhale hard. "Alakier, it's just the dolphins. We're safe."

There are five of them, all their fins above the water, and they circle us where we bob in the choppy current.

Now I'm scared.

Dipping under once more, I look around and finally spot it. Just visible, between us and where we need to go, the enormous hybrid waits. Its skin is jet black and shiny. The only features discerning it from the black water are a dozen long white tentacles illuminated in an elegant dance all around it, glowing white fangs, and eyes flashing electric green. It must be fifteen feet long or more. It floats like a dark, malevolent fairy in wait, then a friend joins it—the creatures are twins in every way except the second stretches ten extra feet. The Madoosik.

I pull Alakier close. Above the surface, I frantically search for any sign of land. Through the lifting fog and rain, I see cliffs. We're close.

I take his face in my hands. "Listen to me carefully." He blinks hard, and I so regret the terror I'm about to instill, even though I'm afraid it may be the only thing that keeps us alive. "You're right. There is a monster. There are two. The dolphins are here to protect us. So you must watch them and me very carefully. Do not let go of my hand."

"I'm scared, Nissa."

"Me too. But we can do this. We can do this and a whole lot more. If we get separated, you keep swimming fast, that way, with the dolphins." I point. "Ready?"

He nods. I hold my fingers out and graze the pod leader as she swims by me. She dives, and the rest stay with us. Then we go under and move.

The large female dolphin heads directly toward the hybrids. They first respond only with simple observation. Then without warning, tentacles snap forward in a synchronized move. She's fast and avoids the attack. Then a second dolphin joins her. He whistles and flees. Confusion reigns. The two hybrids size up their competition. The rest of us manage to skirt around them and gain a head start, the other three dolphins forming a triangle around Alakier and me. I can see nothing but the water in front of us now, but I hear the whistles, chortles, and clicks behind us. We don't stop.

Three dolphins become two, and an unnatural squeal pierces the water. Alakier squeezes my hand, and we catch a quick breath. We dive back under, and I steal a glance behind us. One of the hybrids is impossibly close, and the two remaining dolphins flank us. Without warning, Alakier screams under water and yanks on my arm, stopping us both. He twists and convulses, his mouth open, eyes squeezed tight; he's been hit by a tentacle.

Behind us, the monster merely observes, resetting its deadly appendages. This is it. I close my eyes and wait for the pain. But it doesn't come—only muffled cries and clicks. I open my eyes and watch one of the last two dolphins struggle in the web of poisonous arms. The other hybrid is nowhere in sight, nor are the other three dolphins. The last of our escorts rams into the monster, attempting to free his pod-mate. But the grip on his friend remains unwavering, and his attempts are futile. The monster pulls the seizing animal closer to its core, all dozen of its lacy tentacles wrapping and twisting. The fight for life is useless. The last of the pod cries out in grief.

Alakier floats motionless next to me. I bring him to the surface, where his reflexes take over, and he inhales. It's small, but it's a breath. I dive under again and don't look back. I can see the island.

Seconds later, the last surviving dolphin joins us and escorts us safely the rest of the way. Somehow, we make landfall only fifty yards or so from the boathouse. I kiss our hero. "Thank you... I'm so sorry." He looks at me and swims away. The wind steals my mournful cry.

"Alakier..." I shake him. He's covered in red welts already seeping yellow fluid. His skin feels almost electric to the touch, a faint vibration under his skin. "Hang in there. It's almost over."

I force myself to stand and hike across the rocky terrain, carrying Alakier over my shoulder. The pain is mind-numbing. When we reach the boathouse, I call out, but no one answers.

"Leyla, where are you? I need help..." The door is open. We step inside, and I set Alakier on the chair beside the still-burning fire. Cadet Fenton lies exactly where I left him, blissfully unaware of the world around him. Everything seems undisturbed. I run to the boat room and find it empty. She did it, but I'm scared Leyla might have fallen victim to the channel.

Then I remember Hermes. Of course. The bird will know if someone was here or if Leyla left.

"Hermes, where's Leyla?" I walk around the wall toward the perch. The beautiful bird lies under his swing, his head completely severed and propped upright in a pool of his own blood.

I turn around, lift Alakier back over my shoulder, and leave the boathouse.

The rain has settled into a fine mist. I trudge up the stairs. With every step, pain shoots through me like red-hot fire. I fight for balance as I step over the guard who injured Leyla. His skin glows bluish-white, every drop of his blood long since washed away. If we meet another man like him, we will die.

The journey to the top of the base feels five times longer than it actually is. I'm dizzy, everything blurry and pulsating. I fight for consciousness more than a few times. When I reach the top, I lay Alakier down and lean against the giant boulder. My left arm throbs, bleeding again. I rip my wet shirt and tie a shred of it around my left shoulder. I don't know if it'll help.

I allow myself ten more seconds.

I peer back across the channel just beyond the boulder. A light fog still covers Black Rock, but I can see the fire from here, glowing orange against the dark. My eyes spill tears with abandon. Please let them be okay.

I inch along the gravel path, my feet plodding and dragging under Alakier's weight. As I pass the red-roofed cottages, I try to imagine a simpler, easier life. It's hard to recall if there ever was such a thing—if there ever could be again.

The gate looms ahead to the left, the final cottage to my right. The door swings open, and like an angelic apparition, Leyla emerges. Her shoulder is dressed with a large silver wrap. I exhale a huge sigh of gratitude. But her wide eyes and clenched jaw do not match my relief. Then I spot the gun pointed at her head.

She moves aside, and William Banks steps out next to her. I'm paralyzed as the two walk toward me; the gun never leaves her temple.

"Good evening, Miss John."

"You can call me Nerissa."

"So... Miss John, are you pleased with the outcome of your evening?"

"Yes, actually."

"Well, the night isn't over yet, is it?"

William Banks no longer scares me. I no longer feel any fear or pain—physical or otherwise—and I've never felt calmer or more absolute in my entire life. I found my purpose, Gabriel. And you were right. I am exactly where I'm supposed to be.

"Are you actually capable of shooting your own wife?" I ask. "She's not the one you should be concerned about. I am. You knew I knew everything. But you like playing games, don't you?"

"How dare you? You think you can just take this child from my possession? You think you can just take whatever you please? Who do you think you are?"

"Like father, like daughter, I guess."

Leyla looks at him sideways, then back at me. "Nerissa?"

William grabs her arm and walks toward us. Leyla winces under his grip. "Well, Leyla, this little hybrid, this filthy little Water Doll..." He stops right in front of us, grinning. "She's my daughter, my offspring. Just like this one." He pokes the back of Alakier's head. The jab wakes the boy, and he starts crying, no doubt in excruciating pain from the stinging, electric tentacles of William's monsters. I will not indulge this man with the knowledge of our narrow escape.

I glance at Leyla and watch the resolve drift over her like a veil, hardening her as the silent tears of the abused and betrayed fall down her face. I hold my breath and wait. "William," she says evenly, "why don't you allow me to comfort your son? I'll quiet him down so you can speak with Nerissa."

I hold Alakier toward her, and she reaches for him.

"Do you think I'm stupid?" William rips the child from my arms, and Leyla struggles to pull him away. They jostle Alakier back and forth like a rag doll.

A shot fires.

They freeze. Alakier screams, and my heart drops. As I lunge forward to help him, Officer Banks points the gun at me. Leyla drops to the ground. She grips her left side above her hip, blood seeping through her fingers.

Alakier will not be consoled in his father's violent grip. William looks at his son with disgust and drops him. The boy lands with a thud on Leyla. She moans in what must be agony but wraps her good arm around him and pulls him to her chest. Alakier buries his face in her shoulder and wraps his arms around her neck. Leyla looks at me and musters the tiniest nod.

I step back. Then again. William moves toward me, and I continue to lead him away from Leyla and Alakier until I back into a large rock. He presses into me, his twisted smile as bold and cheap as a neon light. I hold his gaze but can see past him in my periphery. I can't imagine the strength she has summoned, but Leyla somehow rolls over and struggles off the ground with Alakier, comforting him as she rises. He quietly maintains his grip around her neck.

"You like to play games, don't you, William?"

His smile widens. "You can call me Daddy, Doll."

"Okay, Daddy... What do we do now?"

His face is inches from mine, his body pinning me against the rock. "Well, I think somebody needs to teach you a lesson." He grabs my chin and shoves the gun into my neck. "God, you're beautiful. Kiss me."

I'm falling through a dark hole, time rushing past me, behind me, in front of me. The world spins, and I'm ready to get off this ride. Please, just pull the trigger. I will not put my lips on his.

I don't know how much time passes while William taunts and threatens me. It could be an hour, or a minute, or a year. But when I stretch my gaze to the side, Leyla and Alakier are gone. Relief spreads over me, and my torture finally halts when a massive explosion erupts across the channel. A hot wave of energy hits my face. Black Rock looks like a pool of red lava in the distance, my heart burning at the center.

William shudders, visibly shaken by the blast, and pushes his weight into me. "You have destroyed me, you irrelevant hybrid slut. Now I will crush you." He grabs my head with both hands and slams it into the rock behind me. A million tiny stars light up behind my eyes, then everything goes dark and numb. I hear the cock of the gun's hammer, then feel the cold press of the barrel against my forehead. I'm ready.

"Nerissa, move!" someone yells, their voice sliding deep and thick into my awareness, and my eyelids flutter open. A huge, dark figure flies through the air just behind Officer Banks and crashes into us. I crumple to the ground like a puppet cut from its strings, where I watch a blurry, surreal movie play out a few feet away.

Officer William Banks—my father—lies pinned on his back, moaning in pain. Walter snarls, his snapping fangs inches from the man's face, one enormous paw on either side of his body. White, foamy drool oozes into William's hair.

"All right, Walter. Heel." Richard Klein steps up to the fallen William Banks and holds him in place with his boot. Walter growls, deep and long, then heeds his human. Officer Klein points a rifle directly at William's leg and fires. William Banks lets out the loudest, longest scream I've ever heard. My head spins, and the scream morphs into a song.

'You can let go now, precious one. It's time to rest, your work is done...' The lullaby and darkness court me..

William is crying, Walter's low grumble comforting me as Richard looks down on the helpless Officer Banks.

"Relax, you idiot. It's just a tranquilizer. But you're going to sleep for a long time."

A soft light in the sky, just outside the base, catches my eye. The last zeppelin of the Season lifts off into the night. I know Leyla and Alakier are on it. I just know it.

I close my eyes.

29 – MY BEAUTIFUL DEATH

SUNDAY, SEPTEMBER 1ST

It's just the beginning.

Death is beautiful. Death is release. Descriptions of the cold, lonely darkness—the sinking, faceless, stony void of the end of life—it's all wrong.

Death is warm, inviting, and luxurious. It's a long nap on a bright, clear day. It smells like white flowers and green earth and the sweet, salty ocean. It's a lullaby rocking me in eternal sleep. I'm not afraid. I'm at peace, relieved. The struggle is over, and I'm free. Finally.

'You can let go now, precious one…'

Death is comforting. Death is familiar.

'It's time to rest, your work is done…'

Death is a welcoming melody.

"Nerissa, wake up." A cool hand strokes my forehead. "Come on, wake up, now."

Eyelids fluttering, I struggle for focus against a glaring white light, now aware that my head rests in my mother's lap. She smooths the hair from my face with the tender touch of days long gone.

Death is sentimental and nurturing.

"Hi, Mom."

"Hi. You're finally awake. I thought my singing might do the trick."

Death is playful.

"I'm so happy you're here, Mom. Death is beautiful."

"You're not dead," she says. "I'm not, either. We're both very much alive."

"That's impossible."

"It's true."

"But... it's over. Isn't it?"

"No."

"I thought this was the end."

"No, Nerissa... It's just the beginning."

Thank you for diving into Nerissa's world.

If you enjoyed reading *Wreckleaf*, please consider

writing a positive review at your place of purchase.

Enjoy this sneak peek of the compelling and powerful sequel to *Wreckleaf*,

SILENT BLUE

PREFACE

I had my fantasies about leaving this place—living some kind of normal life. But I should have known I'd never really leave. I belong here. This is home, like it or not—where it all began, and where it will end.

This island and me, these people ... we're all the same. We're all one. A terrible Beauty.

1 – WHAT I DESERVE

WEDNESDAY, SEPTEMBER 4TH

It ends here…

Three days ago, I woke up with my head in my mother's lap. I thought I was dead—convinced, really. But it wasn't the end, at least not for me. Part of me, a bigger part than I want to acknowledge, wishes it had been the end.

Matriarch Giovanni is dead. And on this perfectly beautiful, sunny afternoon, we are gathered on Albatross Island, at the arena, for her funeral. Our sister maids, Cecelia, Rena, and Cassidy, all perished as well, along with the countless test animals who were sentenced to a life of torture in the laboratories on Black Rock.

The fire I started in the assembly room after blasting through the warehouse full of bottles and destroying a control panel spread quickly, too quickly. The sea of spilled Aqua Tonic—William Banks' toxic and addicting energy elixir—proved to be quite the conductor of flames. We don't know the details, but I imagine Giovanni tried everything she could to get the others out, even after my mother begged her to come with her and Lillian, out of the building and down to the water.

Anastasia's whereabouts are unknown. But we assume she, too, is dead. By the time my mother and Lillian reached the dock and surveyed the situation, she had disappeared. But Devin still lay where Ana had caused him to drop. I will never, ever, be able to stop replaying that scene in my mind—his final resolution as he decided to let me and Alakier go, then his look of pain and terror as the white-hot beam from the gun Ana fired shot through him and crumpled him to the ground like a fallen soldier.

My mother and Lillian had no choice but to leave him there, to leave without Gio. They had to take the remaining boat and get away from the island as fast as they could, knowing the inevitability of the destruction to come.

The currents stole their boat severely off course, then eventually swallowed it. Fortunately for them, the Madoosik had already eaten, and the terrifying hybrid monsters did not make another appearance.

They came upon shore far from the gatehouse, fighting the tail end of the night's ravaging storm as they trudged across the broken landscape. They reached the bottom of the stone stairway leading to the base just as the night lit up with the explosion on Black Rock.

After we witnessed the destruction from the top of the base, and he realized the labs were gone—along with all the Aqua Tonic within—William Banks took my head in his hands and slammed it into a rock. The lingering effects still catch me by surprise, blurring my vision and my thoughts. With the residual pain of my battered body, but mostly because of the pain in my heart, I don't know if I'll ever be the same. How could I be? After everything I've done, after everything I put into motion ... I'm not sure I deserve to feel anything but this devastation.

To make things feel even more unstable, it's been eerily quiet the last few days. As planned, the entire breed retreated to the relative safety of Albatross, and we know nothing of what is going on back on Panacea. There has been no word from or about Leyla, Alakier, and Esmerelda. I feel confident they escaped unharmed. It seems as though we collectively silenced William Banks, his scientist-cohorts, and the rest of the greed-driven monsters of the Panacea Island Branch of The First World Government. But there is no way to really know. I offered to do some investigating, but my mother will not let me do anything until I'm completely healed. I begrudgingly agreed to wait, but only because I want to keep my eyes on my best friend.

Kendra is nearly inconsolable. She has moments of clarity and what seem like acceptance and calm. Then she dissolves. Back and forth—an ebb and flow of sorrow and grief for her mother, like the waves spilling onto the rocky shore where we will release our loved ones to the ocean. I try to gently remind her to be strong for her unborn baby. It helps, for the briefest of moments at a time.

Now at ceremony, for the first time in a long time—maybe ever—my mother, Matriarch Tatiana, has very little to say. She is grieving as well, and her grief has trapped her voice inside of her. But it's now that we need her the most, to console us, to guide us. *What will happen next? Are we safe?* But she just can't.

After the shortest of announcements, she forces herself to say the thing we've all been dreading. "Please follow me now for the release." The catch in her throat is an audible reminder of Giovanni's permanent absence.

The arena is silent. We all stand and slowly make our way outside, like the sacrificial herd we have become. There, on a long, gilded stand, four adorned nautilus shells resting on their own beds of grass, driftwood, and Wreckleaf represent our departed. My mother stands alongside Kendra, behind the last one in the row, and nods her head. The grieving mothers of Cecelia, Rena, and Cassidy take their places behind the shells representing their daughters.

"Maids, may the lives of our loved ones not be forgotten," my mother begins, her voice shaky. "We release them back to the ocean, of which they are a part. May they find peace, as we find peace as well."

She stops and clears her throat.

"The lives of our sisters, our daughters, our mother, Matriarch, and best friend"—she's barely holding on—"will not have been in vain." Her jaw clenches. "The crimes of the men responsible will not go unpunished."

"They've been punished, Mother." My voice escapes me without my consent. "They have been... the labs were destroyed. Their plans are ruined. They can no longer grow Wreckleaf... at least, not for a long time. Leyla Banks got off the island with Alakier. She's going to expose all of Officer Banks' corruption and—"

"Stop!" my mother commands.

I halt mid-sentence. Fire burns in my cheeks as I realize everyone is gawking at me. My outburst is inappropriately timed. I bow my head and gaze at the ground. But just as I begin to shrink away, a flame lights in my belly as well.

"No. I will not stop. I'm sorry, Mother, but I won't stop until everyone knows what happened, what we all did to destroy William Banks. And everyone needs to know that I vow to do whatever I can to ensure—"

"Nerissa!" Kendra shouts. "You've already done enough. You've done too much, again. Now shut up and let us mourn our dead." Her voice bends and halts before the last word comes out.

I am silenced, and stunned, and hurting as though I have just been stung by a poisonous insect. But she's right. This time, as my gaze falls, my heart sinks into the ground with it. I am emptied at once, of breath and hope ... of all feeling. I am instantly numb, and deservingly so. That's right. Shut up, Nerissa.

After my mother places Giovanni's crown atop her nautilus shell, the remainder of the ceremony is a blur. I'm vaguely aware of words spoken by each of the mothers and watching as the vessels are released, one by one, into the current at the water's edge. I regain only a small sense of the moment as my mother hands Kendra Giovanni's vessel. There is a muffled mix of sobs and words as Kendra places the nested shell into the water. I can't bear to watch any longer, and I walk away, back toward the protection of the covered arena.

I walk slowly, not by choice but out of necessity; I'm wobbly and unbalanced. When I reach the arena, I stand with my back to the ongoing ceremony, steadying myself on a rough-hewn wall. I can barely hear them, can barely feel anything. I close my eyes and fight the approaching dizziness.

My ears are suddenly filled with an unfamiliar whooshing sound, and I'm sure it's another residual effect of my head injury. The noise grows louder, bigger somehow, and it makes me feel like I might pass out. Great, like anybody is going to want to come to my aid right now. Maybe I'll just pass out and never wake up. That may be preferable.

Someone screams, which confuses me.

A second scream rises, then another. I spin around and realize at once that the strange sound was not inside my head but came from above. Descending upon the rocky alcove, some kind of hybrid chopper appears out of nowhere. It resembles a dark, iridescent dragonfly, but with four rotating propellers on each 'wing'.

Devin told me they didn't use choppers. I guess secrets are kept from everyone.

Inside the bizarre craft sit three men—one at the controls and two strapped in the open sides, manned with large weapons. The whooshing morphs back and forth into a buzz as the aircraft effortlessly darts and hovers above.

As the fuzz inside my head keeps its grip on me, nothing seems real. But this is as real as it gets. The two men with weapons aim into the funeral ceremony and open fire. Five maids drop immediately. My feet feel stuck in mud, and all I can do is watch in horror.

"Nerissa John, this is a gift from Officer William Banks," a voice booms from inside the chopper. Everyone scrambles—some jump in the water, others dart behind rocks. But it's useless for many.

More weapon fire. More screaming. Blood. Death ... more death.

"Water Dolls," continues the omniscient voice from above, "you can thank your own Nerissa John for this visit. She is responsible for this retaliation."

Another round of fire. I shut my eyes tight and shake my head back and forth, forcing myself to clear the fuzz and regain sharper focus. But when I open my eyes, I wish my efforts had failed. Fifteen yards ahead, clear and undeniable, a foot lies motionless just behind a dark, jagged boulder. I recognize it instantly. My mother always insisted on wearing nothing but brilliant gold nail polish on her two perfect toes.

My heart is in my throat.

I will my feet to propel me forward, and they do, without haste, without thought or concern for my safety. The gunfire just misses me twice as I land behind the boulder next to my mother. There is no sound but the chopper above, and I frantically examine her.

"I'm not dead yet." She grunts.

Hot tears spill over my cheeks into her blood-soaked hair. "Mom... I'm so sorry." I lay my head upon her chest and weep, smelling her familiar scent, which only makes me cry harder. She reaches up with her left hand and strokes my head. "Please don't die," I beg.

"I'm not going anywhere. We've got too much to do." She forces a tiny smile, then winces in pain.

"Nerissa John, you can end this all right now," the voice from the chopper announces. My head bolts upright, and my mother grabs my hand. "Come out, or the consequence will be total elimination."

"No, you're not going anywhere," she pleads.

How did things come to this? How did we get here? Because of me, that's how. I've caused enough pain, enough misery ... It ends here.

I rise from my position, turning away from my mother as she fruitlessly grips at me. "I will come out if you stop shooting and let the rest of us go!" I yell as loud as I can.

"That is the deal."

"How do I know you'll keep your word?"

He actually laughs. "You don't."

I look back at my mother, her face wracked in physical and emotional pain. She shakes her head, barely able to move.

"But... Ms. John," the speaker continues in his metallic, robotic voice, "what you can be assured of is this. If you do not come out, every last member of your family will die here today, and you will watch."

My mind twirls. I look around, searching for survivors.

"Kendra?" I yell.

Nothing.

"Kendra? Are you alive?"

"I'm alive." From some unseen hiding place, her weak voice rises above the chopper's buzz.

"Are you injured?"

"Nothing serious."

"Is the baby okay?"

"Yes."

"Lillian? Are you okay?"

Nothing.

"Lillian! Answer me!"

"Ms. John, your time is running out. Come out now, or we will finish this job."

"Okay! I'm coming out... You keep your word. No more shooting!" I turn toward my mother, her eyes a mix of fear and sadness.

"Please don't, my baby. Don't go."

"It's your only chance."

"What will I do without you?" She chokes on her sob.

"You will live." I bend over and kiss her lightly on the forehead. "I love you, Mom."

"*No.* No, you will not do this..." She fights to get the words out, then closes her eyes, unable to watch me leave toward what is most certainly my death.

I step out into the open, fully expecting to be taken down immediately and surprised when I keep walking forward. "Kendra!" I call. "My mother is alive but injured. Please take care of her." I proceed slowly, waiting for the pain to come. "Kendra... I love you. You are going to be an excellent mother."

"Nerissa! Don't do this. You don't have to do this."

I stop just below the hovering dragonfly. Tears pour freely down my face. "I do. I do have to do this." It's the only thing I *can* do.

"Ms. John, fall to your knees and put your hands behind your head!"

I comply and fall, my left knee instantly torn by the sharp, rocky ground. I lift my hands up to lace my fingers behind my head and against my shorn copper hair; suddenly, I am filled with an uncanny, nostalgic love for the unkempt nest that once adorned me. In fact, I'm filled with a love so deep, so intense, and so complete—for this crazy, unconventional life of mine, for my family, for my experiences, and for my stubborn refusal to conform. My mistakes, my indiscretions, my flaws. For my compassion, my unyielding love, and my loyalty. All I've ever wanted was for those I love to be happy, to be free, to have a better life, to fulfil their dreams. Maybe now, they can.

A smile so bold, so pure, so unleashed from the shackles of fear and doubt spreads across my face. I gaze out at the raw and rugged beauty of the ocean in front of me and emblazon its power within my soul. I close my eyes. This will be the last thing I see.

A shadow drops in front of me. I don't look. I won't look. The ocean, the beautiful ocean ... my silent blue ... my freedom...

Someone grabs my wrist, and a tight band locks around it, then onto the other. A hand moves under my armpit, lifting me to my feet.

"Walk. Now step up."

He never leaves my side as we step onto some platform, which then lifts into the air. When will the pain come? When will I feel the white-hot beam rip through my flesh?

Hands at my shoulders guide me to sit. "It'll just be a short flight, Ms. John," he says as he straps me in, which strikes me as ironic.

Against my own damn will, my eyes flutter open. As the chopper bends and turns, I get one last look at what remains of my breed. There don't appear to be many survivors; dozens are gone. Just before they're out of sight, I see Kendra run to my mother's side, then look up, searching. Waving goodbye.

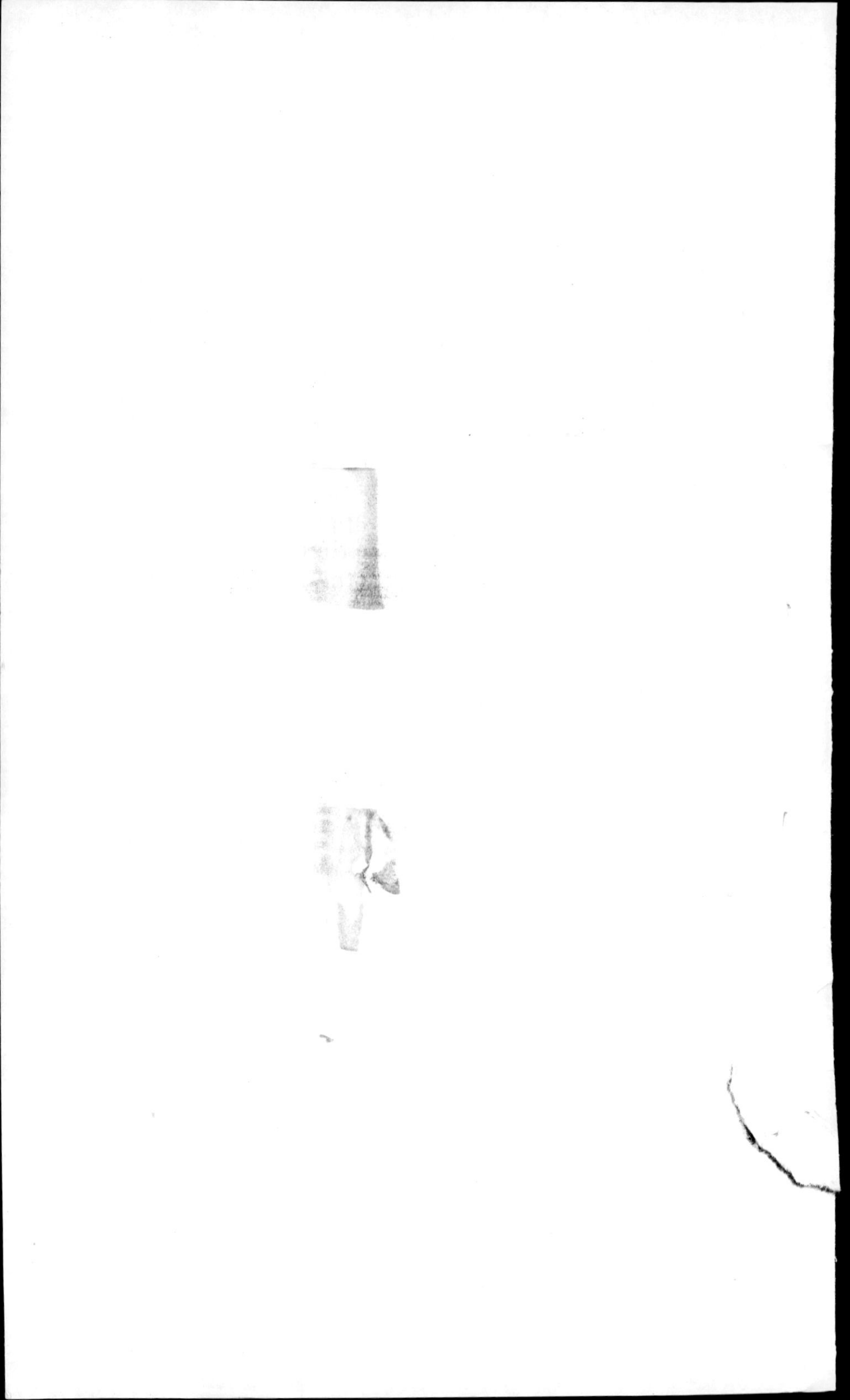

About the Author

JD Steiner credits her studies at the acclaimed Chicago Writer's Loft for her drive to create new worlds, and for her propensity to pile conflict onto her characters, while crafting her stories into rich, dramatic, and relatable YA fiction. A member of OCWW—the oldest writer's group of its kind in America—JD draws inspiration from the entrepreneurial spirit and stories of real people. An advocate for young writers, and artists of all kinds, JD lives and works north of Chicago, Illinois, nurturing and promoting the aspirations and dreams of youth.

www.Wreckleaf.com

www.JDSteiner.com

on Instagram @authorJDSteiner

my MC is on Instagram @NerissaJohn2000

on Twitter @authorJDSteiner

On Facebook: www.facebook.com/AuthorJDSteiner/